P9-DJA-641

ASSASSIN'S
C R E E D ®
UNDERWORLD

OLIVER BOWDEN

ACE BOOKS, NEW YORK

An imprint of Penguin Random House LLC
375 Hudson Street, New York, New York 10014

ASSASSIN'S CREED® UNDERWORLD

An Ace Book / published by arrangement with Penguin Books, Ltd.

ISBN: 978-0-425-27974-8

PUBLISHING HISTORY
Ace premium edition / December 2015

PRINTED IN THE UNITED STATES OF AMERICA

10 9 8 7 6 5 4 3 2

Cover art: Hugo Puzzuoli & Grant Hillier.
Interior text design by Kristin del Rosario.

Penguin
Random
House

ASSASSIN'S
CREED®

UNDERWORLD

PART I

GHOST TOWN

ONE

The Assassin Ethan Frye was leaning on a crate in the shadows of Covent Garden market, almost hidden by the tradesmen's carts. His arms were folded across his chest, chin supported in one hand, the soft, voluminous cowl of his robes covering his head. And as the afternoon dwindled into evening he stood, silent and still. Watching. And waiting.

It was rare for an Assassin to rest his chin on his leading hand like that. Especially if he was wearing his hidden blade, which Ethan was, the point of it less than an inch from the exposed flesh of his throat. Closer to his elbow was a light but very powerful spring mechanism designed to deploy the razor-sharp steel; the correct flick of his wrist and it would activate. In a very real sense, Ethan was holding himself at knifepoint.

And why would he do this? After all, even Assassins were not immune to accidents or equipment failure. For safety's sake the men and women of the Brotherhood tended to keep their blade hands clear of the face. Better that than risk ignominy or worse.

Ethan, however, was different. Not only was he practiced in the art of spying—and resting his chin on his strongest arm was an act of deception designed to fool a potential enemy—but he also took a dark delight in courting danger.

And so he sat, with his chin in his hand, watching and waiting.

Ah, he thought, what was this? He straightened and shook the rest from his muscles as he peered through the crates into the market. Traders were packing up. And something else was happening, too. The game was afoot.

TWO

In an alleyway not far from Ethan lurked a fellow by the name of Boot. He wore a tattered shooting jacket and a broken hat, and he was studying a pocket watch lifted from a gentleman not moments ago.

What Boot didn't know about his new acquisition was that its erstwhile owner had intended to take it to the menders that very day, for reasons that were shortly to have a profound effect on the lives of Ethan Frye, Boot, a young man who called himself The Ghost and others involved in the eternal struggle between the Templar Order and the Assassin Brotherhood. What Boot didn't know was that the pocket watch was almost exactly an hour slow.

Oblivious of that fact, Boot snapped it shut, thinking himself quite the dandy. Next, he eased himself out of the alleyway, looked left and right, then made his way out into the dying day of the market. As he walked, his shoulders hunched and his hands in his pockets, he glanced over his shoulder to check he wasn't being followed and, satisfied, continued forward, leaving Covent Garden behind and entering the St. Giles Rookery—the slum they called Old Nichol. The change in the air was almost immediate. Where before his bootheels had rung on the cobbles, now they sank into the ordure of the street, disturbing a stink of rotting vegetable and human waste. The pavements were thick with it, the air reeking of it. Boot pulled his scarf over his mouth and nose to keep the worst of it out.

A wolfish-looking dog trotted at his heel for a few paces, ribs visible at its shrunken belly. It appealed to him with hungry, red-rimmed eyes but he kicked it away and it skittered then shrank off. Not far away, a woman sat in a doorway wearing the remnants of clothes tied together with string, a baby held to her breast as she watched him with glazed, dead eyes, rookery eyes. She might be the mother of a prostitute, waiting for her daughter to come home with the proceeds and woe betide the girl if she returned empty-handed. Or she might command a team of thieves and cadgers, soon to appear with the day's takings. Or perhaps she ran night lodgings. Here in the rookery the once-grand houses had been converted to flats and tenements, and by night they provided refuge for those in need of shelter: fugitives and families, prostitutes, traders and laborers—anyone who paid their footing in return for space on a floor, who got a bed if they were lucky, and had the money, but most likely had to make do with straw or wood shavings for a mattress. Not that they were likely to sleep very soundly anyway: every inch of floor space was taken, and the cries of babies tore through the night.

While many of these people were unfit or unwilling to work, many more had occupations. They were dog-breakers and bird dealers. They sold watercress, onions, sprat or herring. They were costermongers, street sweepers, coffee dealers, bill stickers and placard carriers. Their wares came into the lodgings with them, adding to the overcrowding, to the stench. At night the houses would be closed, broken windows stuffed with rags or newspaper, sealed against the noxious atmosphere of the night, when the city coughed smoke into the air. The night air had been known to suffocate entire families. Or so was the rumor. And one thing that spread about the slums more quickly than disease was rumor. So as far as the slum dwellers were concerned, Florence Nightingale could preach as much as she liked. They were going to sleep with the windows sealed.

You could hardly blame them, thought Boot. If you lived in the slum, your chances of dying were great. Disease and violence were rife here. Children risked being suffocated when adults rolled over in their sleep. Cause of death: overlaying. It was more common at weekends when the last of the gin had been drunk and the public houses emptied, and mother and father felt their way home in the soupy fog, up the slick stone steps, through the door and into the warm, stinking room where they at last laid down their heads to rest . . .

In the morning, with the sun up but the smog yet to clear, the rookery would ring to the screams of the bereaved.

Deeper into the slum went Boot, where tall buildings crowded out even the meager light of the moon and fogbound lanterns glowed malevolently in the dark. He could hear raucous singing from a public house a few streets along. Every now and then the singing would grow louder as the door was thrown open to eject drunkards onto the street.

There were no pubs on this street, though. Just doors and windows wadded with newspaper, washing hanging from lines overhead, sheets of it like the sails of a ship, and apart from the distant singing just the sound of running water and his own breathing. Just him . . . alone.

Or so he thought.

And now even the distant singing stopped. The only sound was dripping water.

A scuttling sound made him jump. "Who's that?" he demanded, but knew immediately it was a rat, and it was a pretty thing when you were so scared you were jumping at the sound of a rat. A pretty thing indeed.

But then it came again. He whirled and thick air danced and eddied around him, and it seemed to part like curtains and for a moment he thought he saw something. A suggestion of something. A figure in the mist.

Next he thought he heard breathing. His own was short and shallow, gasping almost, but this was loud and steady and coming from—where? One second it seemed to be ahead of him, the next from behind. The scuttling came again. A bang startled him, but it came from one of the tenements above. A couple began arguing—he had come home drunk again. No, *she* had come home drunk again. Boot allowed himself a little smile, found himself relaxing a bit. Here he was, jumping at ghosts, scared of a few rats and a pair of old birds quarreling. Whatever next?

He turned to go. In the same moment the mist ahead

of him billowed and striding out of it came a figure in robes who, before Boot could react, had grabbed him and pulled his fist back as though to punch him. Only instead of striking out, his assailant flicked his wrist and with a soft snick a blade shot from within his sleeve.

Boot had squeezed his eyes shut. When he opened them it was to see the man in robes behind the blade that was held steady a millimeter from his eyeball.

Boot wet himself.

THREE

Ethan Frye awarded himself a small moment of satisfaction at the accuracy of his blade—then swept Boot's legs from beneath him and slammed him to the filthy cobbles. The Assassin sank to his haunches, pinning Boot with his knees as he pressed his blade to his throat.

"Now, my friend"—he grinned—"why don't we start with you telling me your name?"

"It's Boot, sir," squirmed Boot, the point of the knife digging painfully into his flesh.

"Good man," said Ethan. "Good policy, the truth. Now, let's you and me have a talk, shall we?"

Beneath him the fellow trembled. Ethan took it as a yes. "You're due to take delivery of a photographic plate, am I right, Mr. Boot?" Boot trembled. Ethan took it as another yes. So far so good. His information was solid; this Boot was a connection in a pipeline that ended with erotic prints being sold in certain pubs in London. "And you are due at the Jack Simmons to collect this photographic plate, am I right?"

Again Boot nodded.

"And what's the name of the fellow you're supposed to meet, Mr. Boot?"

"I . . . I don't know, sir . . ."

Ethan smiled and leaned even closer to Boot. "My dear boy, you're a worse liar than you are a courier." He exerted a little more pressure with the blade. "You feel where that knife is now?" he asked.

Boot blinked his eyes yes.

"That's an artery. Your carotid artery. If I open that, you'll be painting the town red, my friend. Well, the street at least. But neither of us want me to do that. Why ruin such a lovely evening? Instead how about you tell me who it is you planned to meet?"

Boot blinked. "He'll kill me if I do."

"That's as may be, but I'll kill you if you don't, and only one of us is here holding a knife at your throat, and it's not him, is it?" Ethan increased the pressure. "Make your choice, my friend. Die now, or later."

Just then Ethan heard a noise to his left. Half a second later his Colt sidearm was in his hand, the blade still at Boot's throat as he drew aim on a new target.

It was a little girl on her way back from the well. Wide-eyed she stood, a bucket brimming full of dirty water in one hand.

"I'm sorry, miss, I didn't mean to startle you." Ethan smiled. His revolver went back into his robes and his empty hand reappeared to assure the girl he wasn't a threat. "I mean harm only to ruffians and thieves such as this man here. Perhaps you might like to return to your lodgings." He was gesturing to her but she wasn't going anywhere and just stared at them both, eyes white in a grubby face, rooted to the spot with fear.

Inwardly Ethan cursed. The last thing he wanted was an audience. Especially when it was a little girl watching him hold a blade to a man's throat.

"All right, Mr. Boot," he said, more quietly than before, "the situation has changed so I'm going to have to *insist* you tell me exactly who you intended to meet . . ."

Boot opened his mouth. Maybe he was about to give Ethan the information he required, or perhaps he was going to tell Ethan where he could stick his threats, or more likely it was to simply whine that he didn't know.

Ethan never found out because just as Boot went to reply, his face disintegrated.

It happened a twinkling before Ethan heard the shot, and he rolled off the body and drew his revolver just as a second crack rang out. He remembered the girl, his head whipping round just in time to see her spin away, blood blooming at her chest and her bucket dropping at the same time, dead before she hit the cobbles from a bullet meant for him.

Ethan dared not return fire for fear of hitting another unseen innocent in the fog. He pulled himself into a crouch, steeling himself for another shot, a third attack from the dark.

It never came. Instead there was the sound of running feet, so Ethan wiped the shards of bone and bits of brain from his face, holstered the Colt and flicked his hidden blade back into its housing, then leapt for a wall. Boots only just finding purchase on the wet brick, he shinned a drainpipe to the roof of a tenement, finding the light of the night sky and able to follow the running footsteps as the shooter tried to make his escape. This was how Ethan had entered the rookery and it looked like this was how he was going to leave, making short leaps from one roof to the next, traversing the slum as he tracked his quarry silently and remorselessly, the image of the little girl seared onto his mind's eye and the metallic smell of Boot's brain matter still in his nostrils.

Only one thing mattered now. The killer would feel his blade before the night was out.

From below he heard the boots of the shooter clopping and splashing on the cobbles and Ethan shadowed quietly, unable to see the man but knowing he'd overtaken him. Coming to the edge of a building and feeling he had a sufficient lead, he let himself over the side, using the sills to descend quickly until he reached the street, where he hugged the wall, waiting.

Seconds later came the sound of running boots. A moment after that the mist seemed to shift and bloom as though to announce this new presence, and a second after that the curtains parted and a man in a suit, with a bushy moustache and thick side-whiskers, came pelting into view.

He held a pistol. It wasn't smoking. But it might as well have been.

Though Ethan would later tell George Westhouse that he struck in self-defense, it wasn't strictly true. Ethan had the element of surprise; he could—and should—have disarmed the man and questioned him before killing him. Instead he engaged his blade and slammed it into the killer's heart with a vengeful grunt and watched with no lack of satisfaction as the light died in the man's eyes.

And by doing that the Assassin Ethan Frye was making a mistake. He was being careless.

"My intention had been to press Boot for the information I needed before taking his place," Ethan told the Assassin George Westhouse the following day, having finished his tale, "but what I didn't realize was that Boot was late for his appointment. His stolen pocket watch was slow."

They sat in the drawing room of George's Croydon home. "I see," said George. "At what point did you realize?"

"Um, let me see. That would be the point at which it was too late."

George nodded. "What was the firearm?"

"A Pall Mall Colt, similar to my own."

"And you killed him?"

The fire crackled and spat into the pause that followed. Since reconciling with his children, Jacob and Evie, Ethan was pensive. "I did, George, and it was nothing less than he deserved."

George pulled a face. "Deserve has nothing to do with it. You know that."

"Oh, but the little girl, George. You should have seen her. She was just a tiny wee thing. Half Evie's age."

"Even so . . ."

"I had no choice. His pistol was drawn."

George looked at his old friend with concern and affection. "Which is it, Ethan? Did you kill him because he deserved it or because you had no choice?"

A dozen times or more Ethan had washed his face and blown his nose, but he still felt as though he could smell

Boot's brains on himself. "Must the two be mutually exclusive? I'm thirty-seven years of age, and I've seen more than my fair share of kills, and I know that notions of justice, equity and retribution play a distant second to skill, and skill is subordinate to luck. When fortune turns her face to you. When the killer's bullet goes elsewhere, when he drops his guard, you take your chance, before she turns away again."

Westhouse wondered who his friend was trying to fool, but decided to move on. "A shame, then, that you had to spill his blood. Presumably you needed to know more about him?"

Ethan smiled and mock wiped his brow. "I was rewarded with a little luck. The photographic plate he carried bore an inscription identifying the photographer, so I was able to ascertain that the dead man and the photographer were one and the same, a fellow by the name of Robert Waugh. He has Templar associations. His erotic prints were going one way, to them, but also another way, to the rookeries and alehouses, via Boot."

George whistled softly. "What a dangerous game Mr. Waugh was playing . . ."

"Yes and no . . ."

"Well, he was bound to meet a sticky end sooner or later."

"Quite."

"And you were able to divulge all of this postmortem?"

"Don't look at me like that, George. I'm fully aware I was lucky, and that on any other day my impetuous killing of Waugh might have had unfortunate consequences. On this day it did not."

George leaned to poke the fire. "Before, when you said 'yes and no' that Waugh was playing a dangerous game, what did you mean?"

"I meant that in many ways his gamble of the two worlds staying separate paid off. I saw the slums afresh today, George. I was reminded of how the poor are living. This is a world so completely separate from that of the Templars that it's scarcely believable the two share the same country, let alone the same city. If you ask me, our friend Mr. Waugh was perfectly justified in believing the paths of his disparate business enterprises might never cross. The two worlds in which he operated were such poles apart. The Templars know nothing of the rookeries. They live upriver of the factory filth that pollutes the water of the poor and upwind of the smog and smoke that pollutes their air."

"As do we, Ethan," said George sadly. "Whether we like it or not, ours is a world of gentlemen's clubs and drawing rooms, of temples and council chambers."

Ethan stared into the fire. "Not all of us."

Westhouse smiled and nodded. "You're thinking of your man, The Ghost? Don't suppose you have any thoughts about telling me who The Ghost is or what he is doing?"

"That must remain my secret."

"Then what of him?"

"Aha, well, I have formulated a plan, involving the recently deceased Mr. Waugh and The Ghost. If all goes well, and The Ghost can do his job, then we may even be able to lay our hands on the very artifact the Templars seek."

FOUR

John Fowler was tired. And cold. And by the look of the gathering clouds he was soon to be wet.

Sure enough, he felt the first drops of rain tap-tapping on his hat, and the engineer clutched his leather-bound tube of drawings more tightly to his chest, cursing the weather, the noise, everything. Beside him stood the Solicitor of London, Charles Pearson, as well as Charles's wife, Mary, both flinching as the rain began to fall, and all three stood marooned by mud, gazing with a mixture of forlornness and awe at the great scar in the earth that was the new Metropolitan Line.

Some fifty yards in front of the trio the ground gave way to a sunken shaft that opened into a vast cutting—"the trench"—twenty-eight feet in width and some two hundred yards long, at which point it stopped being a cutting or trench and became a tunnel, its brickwork arch providing a gateway to what was the world's very first stretch of underground-railway line.

What's more, the world's first *operational* stretch of underground-railway line: trains ran on the newly laid rails night and day, pushing wagons heaped with gravel, clay and sand from unfinished sections farther up the line. They chugged back and forth, smoke and steam nearly suffocating the gangs of unskilled laborers working at the mouth of the tunnel, who shoveled earth into the leather buckets of a conveyor that in turn brought the spoil to ground level.

The operation was Charles Pearson's baby. For almost two decades the Solicitor of London had campaigned for a new line to help ease the growing congestion in London and its suburbs. Its construction, meanwhile, was John Fowler's brainchild. He was, quite apart from being the owner of remarkably luxuriant whiskers, the most experienced railway engineer in the world, and thus had been the obvious candidate for chief engineer of the Metropolitan Railway. However, as he'd told Charles Pearson on the occasion of his employment, his experience might count for naught. This was, after all, something that had never been done before: a railway line beneath the ground. A huge—no, a *gargantuan*—undertaking. Indeed, there were those who said that it was the most ambitious building project since the construction of the pyramids. A grand claim, for sure, but there were days that Fowler agreed with them.

Fowler had decided that the majority of the line, being of shallow depth, could be dug using a method known as "cut and cover." It involved sinking a trench into the earth, twenty-eight feet in width, fifteen feet deep. Brick retaining walls were built into it, three bricks thick. In some sections iron girders were laid across the top of the side walls. Others were made using brickwork arches.

Then the cutting was covered and the surface reinstated, a new tunnel created.

It meant destroying roads and houses, and in some cases building temporary roadways, only to have to rebuild them. It meant moving thousands of tons of spoil and negotiating gas and water mains and sewers. It meant forging a never-ending nightmare of noise and destruction, as though a bomb had detonated in London's Fleet Valley. No. As though a bomb was detonating in the Fleet Valley every day and had for two years.

Work continued overnight, when flares and braziers would be lit. The workers labored in two major shifts—the change signaled by three tolls of a bell at midday and midnight—and smaller duty shifts when men would move between tasks, swapping one backbreaking and monotonous job for another but working, always working.

Much of the noise came from the seven conveyors used on the project, one of which was erected here: a tall wooden scaffold built into the shaft, towering twenty-five feet above them, an agent of dirt and ringing noise, like hammerblows on an anvil. It brought spoil from farther along the excavation, and men worked it now, gangs of them. Some were in the shaft, some on the ground, some dangling like lemurs off the frame, their job to ensure the passage of the conveyor as giant buckets full of clay were hoisted swinging from the trench.

On the ground, men with spades toiled at a mountain of excavated earth, shoveling it onto horse-drawn wagons, four of which waited, each with a cloud of gulls hanging over it, the birds swirling and dipping to pick food from the earth, unconcerned by the rain that had begun to fall.

Fowler turned to look at Charles, who appeared ill—he held a handkerchief to his lips—but otherwise in good humor. There was something indomitable about Charles Pearson, reflected Fowler. He wasn't sure if it was resolve or lunacy. This was a man who had been laughed at for the best part of two decades, indeed, from when he'd first suggested an underground line. "Trains in drains," so the scoffing went at the time. They'd laughed when he unveiled his plans for an atmospheric railway, carriages pushed through a tube by compressed air. *Through a tube*. Little wonder that for over a decade Pearson was a fixture of *Punch* magazine. What fun was had at his expense.

Then, with everybody still chortling at that, there came a scheme, Pearson's brainchild—a plan to build an underground railway between Paddington and Farringdon. The slums of the Fleet Valley would be cleared, their inhabitants moved to homes outside the city—to the suburbs—and people would use this new railway to "commute."

A sudden injection of money from the Great Western Railway, the Great Northern Railway and the City of London Corporation, and the scheme became a reality. He, the noted John Fowler, was employed as chief engineer for the Metropolitan Railway Company and work began on the first shaft at Euston—almost two years ago to the day.

And were people still laughing?

Yes, they were. Only now it was a jagged, mirthless laugh, because to say that Pearson's vision of the slum clearance had gone badly was to put it mildly. There were no homes in the suburbs and as it turned out, nobody especially willing to build any. And there's no such thing as an undercrowded slum. All of those people had to go somewhere, so they went to other slums.

Then of course there was the disruption caused by the work itself: streets made impassable, roads dug up, businesses closing and traders demanding compensation. Those who lived along the route existed in an eternal chaos of mud, of engines, of the conveyor's iron chime, of hacking picks and shovels and workers bellowing at one another, and in perpetual fear of their foundations collapsing.

There was no respite; at night fires were lit and the night shift took over, leaving the day shift to do what men on day shifts do: drink and brawl their way through to morning. London had been invaded by unskilled laborers, it seemed; everywhere they went they made their own; only the prostitutes and publicans were glad of them.

Then there were the accidents. First a drunken train driver had left the rails at King's Cross and plummeted into the works below. Nobody hurt. *Punch* had a field day. Then almost a year later the earthworks at Euston Road had collapsed, taking with them gardens, pavements and telegraph wires, destroying gas and water mains, punching a hole in the city. Incredibly, nobody was hurt. Mr. Punch enjoyed that episode, too.

"I'd hoped to hear good news today, John," shouted Pearson, raising his handkerchief—a finicky thing, like a doily—to his mouth. He was sixty-eight to Fowler's forty-four but he looked twice that; his efforts over the last two decades had aged him. Despite his ready smile there was permanent tiredness around the eyes, and the flesh at his jowls was like melted wax on a candle.

"What can I tell you, Mr. Pearson?" shouted Fowler. "What would you like to hear other than . . . ?" He gestured over the site.

Pearson laughed. "The roar of the engines is encouraging, that's true enough, but perhaps also that we're back on schedule, or that every compensation lawyer in London has been struck dead by lightning. That Her Majesty the Queen herself has declared her confidence in the underground and plans to use it at the first opportunity."

Fowler regarded his friend, again marveling at his spirit. "Then I'm afraid, Mr. Pearson, I can give you nothing but bad news. We are still behind schedule and weather like this simply delays work further. The rain will likely douse the engine and the men on the conveyor will enjoy an unscheduled break."

"Then there is some good news," chortled Charles.

"And what's that?" shouted Fowler.

"We will have . . ."

The engine spluttered and died . . .

". . . silence."

. . . and for a moment there was indeed a shocked still as the world adjusted to the absence of the noise. Just the sound of rain slapping on the mud.

Then came a cry from the shaft: "*Slippage!*" and they looked up to see the crane scaffold lurch a little, one of the men suddenly dangling even more precariously than before.

"It'll hold," said Fowler, seeing Mr. Pearson's alarm. "It looks worse than it is."

A superstitious man would have crossed his fingers. The workers were taking no chances either, and the gangs on the crane scrambled to ground level, swarming the wooden struts like pirates on rigging, hundreds of them it seemed, so that Fowler was holding his breath and willing the structure to hold the sudden extra weight. It should, it must. It did. The men emerged shouting and coughing, carrying shovels and pickaxes, which were as precious to them as their limbs.

Fowler and Charles watched them congregate in the expected groups—London, Irish, Scottish, rural, other—hands shoved into their pockets or wrapped around them for warmth, shoulders hunched and caps pulled tight against the rain, every single one of them caked in mud.

Just then there came a shout and Fowler turned to see a commotion by the trench. As one the laborers had moved over to look and now surrounded the lip of the shaft, staring at something inside the cutting.

"*Sir!*" The site manager Marchant was waving at him, beckoning him over. He cupped his hands to shout. "Sir. You should come and see this."

Moments later, Fowler and Charles had made their way across the mud, the men parting to let them through, and they stood at the top of the trench looking down—past the struts and buckets of the silent conveyor to the lake of muddy water that had formed at the bottom and was already rising.

Bobbing in it was a body.

FIVE

The rain had eased off, thank God, and the water level in the trench had fallen, but the machines remained silent. With a hand on his hat, Marchant had rushed away to inform his immediate boss, Cavanagh, a director of the Metropolitan Railway, while another man had been sent to find a bobby. It was the peeler who arrived first, a young constable with bushy side-whiskers who introduced himself as Police Constable Abberline then cleared his throat and removed his custodian helmet in order to get down to the business of seeing the body.

"Has anybody been down to it, sir?" he asked Pearson, indicating the trench.

"The area was cleared as soon as it was discovered, Constable. You can imagine, it caused quite a stir."

"Nobody likes to see a dead body before their elevenses, sir."

Those assembled watched as the peeler leaned tentatively to stare into the trench and signaled to a man nearby. "Do you mind, mate?" he said, and handed the worker his helmet, then unbuckled and removed his belt, truncheon and handcuffs before descending the ladder to inspect the corpse at close quarters.

They crowded to stare down into the cutting and watch as he stepped around the body, lifting one arm and then the other. Presently, the peeler crouched and the watchers held their breath in expectation as he turned over the body.

In the trench, Abberline swallowed, unaccustomed to being on show and wishing he'd left instructions that the men be asked to move back. They lined both sides of the trench and even the figures of Fowler and Mr. and Mrs. Pearson were there, all of them gazing down at him, fifteen feet below.

Right. He turned his attention back to the corpse, putting aside all self-conscious thoughts to concentrate on the job at hand.

The body, which wore a tweed suit, was facedown in the mud, with one arm raised as though trying to hail a carriage. His brown boots were well shod, and though covered in mud were otherwise in good condition. Not the attire of a derelict, thought Abberline. Crouching, heedless of the mud that soaked his clothes, he took a deep breath and reached to the man's shoulders, grunting with the effort as he rolled him over.

From above came a ripple of reaction but Abberline had his eyes closed, wanting to delay the moment he saw the man's face. With trepidation he opened them and stared into the dead gaze of the corpse. He was in his late thirties and had a bushy white-flecked Prince Albert moustache that looked cared for, as well as thick side-whiskers. By the looks of him he wasn't a rich man but neither was he a worker like Abberline, one of the new middle classes.

Either way, this was a man with a life whose next of kin, when they were informed, would want an explanation as to how he ended his life in a trench at New Road.

This was, without doubt—and Abberline couldn't help but feel a small, slightly shameful thrill at the thought of it—an investigation.

He tore his gaze away from the man's sightless open eyes and looked downward at his jacket and shirt. Visible despite the mud was a bloodstain with a neat hole at the center. If Abberline wasn't very much mistaken, a puncture wound.

Abberline had seen victims of stab wounds before, of course, and he knew that people armed with knives stabbed and slashed the same way they punched: in quick, haphazard multiples, *bomf, bomf, bomf.*

But this was a single wound, direct into the heart. What you might call a clean kill.

By now, Abberline was vibrating with excitement. He'd feel guilty about that later, remembering that there was, after all, a dead man involved, and you shouldn't really feel anything but sorrow for him and his family in that situation, and certainly not excitement. But even so . . .

He began a quick search of the body and found it immediately: a revolver. Christ, he thought, this was a geezer armed with a gun who'd lost a fight with a knifeman. He pushed the gun back into a jacket pocket.

"We'll need to lift this body out of here," he called up in the general direction of the boss men. "Sir, could you ask men to help me cover him and put him in a cart for taking to the police morgue?"

With that he started to ascend the ladder, just as orders were called out and a team of men began to descend the other ladders with varying degrees of eagerness and trepidation. At the top, Abberline stood wiping his mucky hands on the seat of his trousers. At the same time he scanned the lines of assembled men, wondering if the killer was in there somewhere, admiring his handiwork. All he saw was row upon row of dirty faces, all watching him intently. Others still crowded around the mouth of the cutting, watching as the body was brought up then laid on the flat bed of a cart. The tarpaulin flapped as it was shaken out then draped over him, a shroud, the face of the dead man hidden again.

By now it had started to rain in earnest, but Abberline's attention had been arrested by the sight of a smartly dressed man making his way over the boards that crossed the expanse of mud, toward them. Not far behind lolloped a lackey carrying a large, leather bound journal, its laces dancing and jerking as the lackey tried unsuccessfully to keep up with his master.

"Mr. Fowler! Mr. Pearson!" called the man, gesturing with his cane and instantly commanding their attention. The entire site quietened but in a new way. There was much shuffling of feet. Men were suddenly studying their boots intently.

Oh yes? thought Abberline. *What have we here?*

Like Fowler and Pearson the new arrival wore a smart suit though he wore it with more style—in a way that suggested he was used to catching the eye of a passing lady. He had no paunch and his shoulders were squared, not stooped with stress and worry like his two colleagues. Abberline could see that when he doffed his hat it would be to reveal a full head of almost shoulder-length hair. But though his greeting was warm, his smile, which was a mechanical thing that was as quickly off as it was on, never reached his eyes. Those ladies impressed by his mode of dress and general demeanor might well have thought twice upon seeing the look in those cold and piercing eyes.

As the man and his lackey drew close to them Abberline looked first at Pearson and Fowler, noting the discomfort in their eyes, the hesitation in Charles Pearson as he introduced the man. "This is our associate, Mr. Cavanagh, a director of the Metropolitan company. He oversees the day-to-day running of the dig."

Abberline touched his brow, thinking to himself, *What's your story, then?*

"I hear a body has been discovered," said Cavanagh. He had a large scar on the right side of his face, as though somebody had once used a knife to underline his eye.

"Indeed, sir, it has." Pearson sighed.

"Let's see it, then," demanded Cavanagh, and in the next moment, Abberline drew back the tarpaulin only for Cavanagh to shake his head in nonrecognition. "Nobody I know, thank God, and not one of ours by the looks of him. A soak. A drunk like the poor soul serenading us over there, no doubt." He turned his back on the cart. "Marchant! Get these men back to work. We've lost enough time as it is."

"No," came a lone voice, and it was the voice of Mrs.

Pearson. She took a step in front of her husband. "A man has died here, and as a mark of respect we should suspend the dig for the morning."

Cavanagh's automatic smile was switched on. Instantly oleaginous he swiped his tall hat from his head and bowed low. "Mrs. Pearson, please forgive me, how remiss it is of me to forget that there are more delicate sensibilities present. However, as your husband will attest, we are often the site of misadventures and I'm afraid that the mere presence of a dead body is not enough to prevent the tunnel work's continuing."

Mrs. Pearson turned. "Charles." In return, her husband lowered his eyes. His gloved hands fretted at the handle of his stick.

"Mr. Cavanagh is correct, my dear. The poor soul has been removed, work must continue."

She looked searchingly at her husband, who avoided her eyes, then Mrs. Pearson picked up her skirts and left.

Abberline watched her go, noting the look of sly triumph in the eyes of Cavanagh as he went about the business of mustering Marchant and the men, and the sadness in the face of Charles Pearson, a man torn, as he too turned to leave in the wake of his wife.

Meanwhile, Abberline had to get this corpse to Belle Isle. His heart sank to think of it. There was scarcely a worse place on the whole of God's green earth than the Belle Isle slum.

Among the men who were at that very moment being urged, cajoled, bullied and threatened back to work by the site manager, Marchant, was a young Indian worker who, though he appeared on the worksheet as Bharat, and if any of the men working beside were curious enough to ask, that was the name he would give them, thought of himself by another name.

He thought of himself as The Ghost.

To all outward appearances The Ghost was unremarkable. He wore similar clothes to the other workers: shirt, neck scarf, railwayman's cap, waistcoat and work coat—though no boots, he went barefoot—and he was a competent, conscientious worker, no better or worse than the next man, and he was perfectly personable should you engage him in conversation, not especially loquacious and certainly not the sort to initiate a conversation, but then again not particularly retiring either.

But The Ghost was always watching. Always watching. He'd caught sight of the body and by good fortune had been close enough to look before the order was given to evacuate the trench. He'd also seen the drunkard by the trench and in the ensuing commotion had been able to catch his eye, then, as if responding to an itch, he had rubbed his own chest, a tiny insignificant gesture practically invisible to anybody else.

Then he'd watched as Abberline arrived. He watched Cavanagh come bustling onto the site, and he watched very carefully indeed as the tarpaulin was drawn back and Cavanagh gazed down upon the face of the dead man and hid his look of recognition.

Oh, he was good. The Ghost had to give him that. Cavanagh's powers of concealment were almost on a par with his own, but his eyes had flickered briefly as he looked down upon the face. He knew the man.

Now The Ghost watched as Abberline left on the cart, taking the body to Belle Isle, no doubt.

He watched as, shortly after Abberline had left, the drunk departed also.

Six

Prince Albert had been dead a year, and though his taste in facial hair lived on, his adherence to decency and good manners had evidently failed to percolate through to the general public. Quite the reverse it seemed; there was a pall that hung over London, dark and malignant. Some blamed it on the Queen's absence; she mourned Albert still and had taken to the Highlands to do so. Others said the overcrowding was to blame; the terrible stink, the poverty and crime; among them those madmen who thought the best way to solve that problem was by building an underground railway. Still others said that actually it was not the overcrowding that was to blame; rather it was the construction of the underground railway that had thrown the city into disarray. This last group was apt to point out that the underground railway had thus far exacerbated overcrowding by evicting thousands of tenants from their homes on the Fleet Valley, the city's biggest slum. Which was true, it had.

Ah, but at least we've got rid of the city's biggest slum, said the first group.

Not really, scoffed the second group. You've just moved another slum into first place.

Have patience, pleaded the first group.

No, said the second, we won't.

Sitting on the board of his cart, reins held loosely in hand, Abberline thought over how the higher-ups made decisions in the clubs and boardrooms that affected them all. And to what end? For the greater good? Or their own personal benefit? A line from Lord Tennyson's poem about the Charge of the Light Brigade sprang to mind: *"Theirs is not to reason why, theirs is but to do or die."*

His cart clattered over the rails toward where the tall, spired buildings of Belle Isle appeared like a smudge of dirt on the horizon. Already he could smell the foul stench of the horse slaughterers, the bone boilers, fat-melters, chemical works, firework makers, lucifer-match factories.

To his left some poor deluded idiot had made a valiant attempt to grow a kitchen garden but it was overrun with sickly weeds that climbed the iron fences sprouting on either side of him. Dirty, barely clothed children were running in the wasteland on either side, lobbing old tin cans at one another, scurrying in the street outside the cottages. Inside each home were rooms and washhouses, and at night the householders and their tenants would cram inside, just as they would at the Old Nichol.

His cart came past the horse slaughterers. Under the arch went living horses, whose sense of smell and instinct must surely have warned them what lay ahead, and in the factory they would be put to death, then the flesh boiled in copper vats for cat food.

Outside in the yards men stripped to the waist used

sledgehammers to break up bones, watched by ever-present groups of children clad in filthy rags tinged yellow from the sulfur in the air.

Abberline saw a group of children who had obviously tired of watching men break bones with sledgehammers—after all, it wasn't an activity with an awful lot of variety—and set up a game of cricket instead. Without the usual equipment they improvised with part of an old bedstead for a bat, while the ball was . . . Abberline winced. Oh God. The ball they were using was the decapitated head of a kitten.

He was about to shout across to them, to urge them to for pity's sake use something else for a ball, when he became aware of a child who had wandered in front of the cart, forcing him to pull up.

"Oi," he called, waving an irate hand at the young ruffian, "police business. Get out of the bleedin' way."

But the scruffy urchin didn't move. "Where are you off to, sir?" he asked, taking the head of the horse in both hands, stroking it. The sight softened Abberline's heart a little, and he forgot his irritation as the boy rubbed his fingertips over the animal's ears, enjoying the rare intimacy of the moment, boy and horse.

"Where are you off to, sir?" the boy repeated, tearing his eyes off the horse and turning his urchin gaze on Abberline. "Not to the knackers yard with this one, I hope, say it ain't so."

In his peripheral vision, Abberline sensed a movement and turned to see three other young scallywags climb beneath the fence and come onto the road behind him.

Let them, he thought. Nothing of value back there. Not unless you counted a soggy corpse and the tarpaulin.

"No, don't worry yourself, son, I'm off to the mortuary with a body on the back."

"A body, is it?" This came from the rear, one of the new arrivals.

A couple more children had arrived by now, a little crowd of them milling around.

"Oi you, get out of it," warned Abberline. "Nothing back there to interest you."

"Can we have a look, sir?"

"No, you bloody well can't," he called over his shoulder. "Now get out of it before you feel the business end of my truncheon."

The first boy stood petting the horse still, raising his face to speak to Abberline again. "Why is the police involved, sir? Did this one meet a sticky end?"

"You might say that," replied Abberline, impatient now. "Now stand aside, son, and let me past."

The cart bounced and jerked and he was about to turn to admonish the kids who were obviously trying to peek beneath the tarpaulin, ghoulish little sods. Then it bounced again and this time Abberline, irritated and wanting to get the hell out of Belle Isle, shook the reins decisively.

"Walk on," he commanded, and if the kid stood in the way, well, that was his lookout.

He drew forward and the child was forced to step aside. As he passed, Abberline looked down to see the young urchin smiling inscrutably up at him. "Good luck with your body, sir," he said, touching his knuckle to his fore-lock in a derisive way that Abberline didn't care for. In return he merely grunted and shook the reins again, setting his face forward. He went past the rest of the houses to the mortuary gate, where he coughed loudly to rouse a worker who'd been dozing on a wooden chair, who tipped his hat and let him through into the yard.

"What have we got here?" asked a mortuary worker as he emerged from a side door.

Abberline had clambered down from the cart. At the entrance, the sleepyhead closed the gates again, behind him the Belle Isle slum like a sooty thumbprint on a window. "Body I need keeping cold for the coroner," replied Abberline, securing the reins as the attendant went to the rear of the wagon, lifted the tarp, peered beneath then dropped it again.

"You want the knacker's yard," he said simply.

"Come again?" said Abberline.

The attendant sighed and wiped his hands on his apron. "Unless this is your idea of a joke, you want the bleedin' knackers yard is what I said."

Abberline paled, already thinking of his encounter with the slum children, the way his cart had shaken; remembering how his attention had been arrested, cleverly perhaps, by the kid nuzzling the neck of his horse.

And sure enough, when he skidded to the back of the cart and swept back the tarpaulin, it was to see that the body from the trench had gone, in its place a dead pony.

SEVEN

Every night The Ghost made the same journey home, one that took him along the New Road and past Marylebone Church. In the churchyard, among the ramshackle and raggle-taggle groupings of headstones was one in particular that he would look at as he went by.

If the stone was upright, as it was most evenings, that meant no message. If the stone leaned to the right, it meant danger. Just that: "danger." It was up to The Ghost to work out what manner of danger.

However, if it leaned to the left, then it meant his handler wanted to see him, usual time, usual place.

Then, having performed that check, The Ghost began his five-mile walk home to Wapping and his living quarters at the Thames Tunnel.

It had once been called one of the great wonders of the world, and even at ground level it cut an imposing figure among the surrounding buildings: a spired, octagonal marble building acting as an entrance hall. Entering through doors that were never shut, he crossed the mosaic flooring to reach a side building, the watch house. During the daytime, pedestrians had to pay a penny to pass through to reach the steps down into the tunnel but not at night. A brass turnstile was closed but The Ghost climbed over, just as everybody did. All of the other ghosts, who haunted the tunnel by night.

Ice had formed on the marble steps that spiraled around the inside of the shaft so he trod more than usually carefully as he descended to the first platform, then to the next, and finally to the bottom of the shaft, the vast grand rotunda, eighty meters underground. Once it had been vast and opulent, now it was merely vast. The walls were dirty, the statues scruffy. The years had had their say.

Even so, it was still a sight to see: alcoves set into grubby stucco walls. Inside the nooks, curled beneath sacks, slept the people of the rotunda: the necromancers, fortune-tellers and jugglers who in the daytime plied their trade to those visiting the tunnel, the famous Thames Tunnel. Eighth wonder of the world.

The first of its kind anywhere ever, the Thames Tunnel stretched from here, Wapping, below the river to Rotherhithe and had taken fifteen years to build, almost defeating Mr. Marc Brunel and almost claiming the life of his son Isambard, who had nearly drowned in one of the floods that had plagued its construction. Both had hoped to see their tunnel used by horse-drawn carriages, but had been undone by the cost, and instead it became a tourist attraction, visitors paying a penny to walk its four-hundred-meter length, an entire subterranean industry springing forth to serve them. One that needed policing.

The Ghost moved from the entrance hall to the black mouth of the tunnel itself, its two arches pointing at him like the barrels of pistols. It was wide and its ceiling high, but the brickwork pressed in and each footfall became an echo, while the sudden change in atmosphere made him more aware of the gloom. In daytime, hundreds of gas lamps banished the darkness but at night the only illumination belonged to the flickering candles of those who made the tunnel their home: traders, mystics, dancers and animal handlers, singers, clowns and street dealers. It was said that two million people a year take a walk down the tunnel, and had since it opened some seventeen years ago. Once you had a place at the tunnel opening you didn't leave it, for fear that some other hawker might steal it with you absent.

The Ghost looked over the slumbering bodies of the tradesmen and entertainers as he passed by, his footsteps ringing on the stone floor. He peered into alcoves and passed his lantern over those sleeping under the arches of the partition that ran the length of the tunnel.

A strict hierarchy operated inside the tunnel. The tradesmen took their places at the mouth. Farther along, the derelicts, the homeless, the vagrants, the wretched, then even farther along the thieves, criminals and fugitives.

Come morning time, the traders, who had a vested interest in making sure the tunnel was free of vagrants and as sanitary as possible, were enthusiastic in helping the peelers clear out the tunnel. The blaggers and fugitives would have departed under cover of darkness. The rest of them, the vagabonds, beggars, prostitutes would come grumbling and blinking into the light, clutching their belongings, ready for another day of surviving on nothing.

The Ghost's lantern played over a sleeping figure in the gloom of an alcove. The next alcove was empty. He swung the torch to illuminate the arches of the tunnel partition and they too were vacant. He sensed the miserly light receding behind him, the glow given off by his lantern so very meager all of a sudden, dancing eerily on the brick.

From within the darkness had come a scuttling sound and he raised his light to see a figure crouched in a nook ahead of him.

"Hello, Mr. Bharat," said the boy in a whisper.

The Ghost went to him, reaching into his coats for a thick crust of bread he'd put there earlier. "Hello, Charlie," he said, handing it over. The boy flinched a little, far too accustomed to the slaps and punches of grown-ups, then took the bread, staring at The Ghost with grateful eyes as he bit into it, cautiously at first.

They did it every night. The same flinch. The same caution. And every night The Ghost, who knew nothing of his background, just that it involved violence and abuse, smiled at him, said, "See you tomorrow night, Charlie, take care of yourself," and left the boy in his alcove, his heart breaking as he made his way farther into the tunnel.

Again, he stopped. Here in another alcove lay a man with a leg broken from a fall on the icy steps of the rotunda. The Ghost had set the leg and he held his breath against the stench of piss and shit to check that his splint was still in place and that the leg was on the mend.

"You're a fine lad, Bharat," said his patient, in a growl.

"Have you eaten?" asked The Ghost, attending to the leg. He was not a man of delicate sensibilities but even so—Jake was ripe.

"Maggie brought me some bread and fruit," said Jake.

"What would we do without Maggie?" wondered The Ghost aloud.

"We'd die, son, is what we'd do."

The Ghost straightened, pretending to look back up the tunnel in order to take a lungful of uncontaminated air—relatively speaking. "Leg is looking good, Jake," he said. "Another couple of days and you might be able to risk a bath."

Jake chuckled. "That bad, eh?"

"Yes, Jake," said The Ghost, patting his shoulder, "I'm afraid it's that bad."

The Ghost left, pressing farther on into the tunnel, until he came to the last of the alcoves used for sleeping. Here was where he and Maggie stayed. Maggie, at sixty-two, was old enough to be his grandmother, but they looked after one another. The Ghost brought food and money, and every night he taught Maggie to read by the light of a candle.

Maggie, for her part, was the tunnel mother, a rabble-rousing mouthpiece for The Ghost when he needed one, an intimidating, redoubtable figure. Not to be trifled with.

Beyond this point few people dared to tread. Beyond this point was the darkness, and it was no coincidence that this was where The Ghost had made his home. He stayed here as a kind of border guard, protecting those who slept in the tunnel from the miscreants and malfeasants, the lawbreakers and fugitives who sought shelter in its darker regions.

Before he arrived the outlaws would prey upon those who lived in the tunnel. It had taken a while. Blood had been spilled. But The Ghost had put a stop to that.

EIGHT

On the night that The Ghost had first met Maggie, he had been taking his route back home—if you could call it "home," his lodging, his resting place—at the tunnel.

Occasionally, as he walked he let his mind drift back to his real home, Amritsar in India, where he had grown up.

He remembered spending his childhood and adolescence roaming the grounds of his parents' house then the "katras"—the different areas of the city itself. The memory can play tricks on you—it makes things seem better or worse than they really were, and The Ghost was fully aware of that. He knew he was in danger of idealizing his childhood. After all, how easy it would be to forget that Amritsar, unlike London, had not yet acquired a drainage system and thus rarely smelled of the jasmine and herbs that he recalled so vividly. He might forget that the walled streets that loomed so large in his recollections had played host to characters as unsavory as anywhere else in India. Possibly the sun didn't really bathe the entire city in warm golden light all day and all night, warming the stone, making the fountains glimmer, painting smiles on the faces of those who made the city their home.

Possibly not. But that was how he remembered it anyway, and if he was honest that was how he preferred to remember it. Those memories kept him warm in the tunnel at nights.

He was born Jayadeep Mir. Like all boys, he idolized his father, Arbaaz Mir. His mother used to say that his father smelled of the desert and that was how The Ghost remembered him too. From an early age Arbaaz told Jayadeep that greatness lay ahead of him, and that he would one day be a venerated Assassin, and he had made this future sound as thrilling as it was inevitable. In the comfortable confines of his loving parents' home, Jayadeep had grown up knowing great certainty.

Arbaaz liked to tell stories just as much as Jayadeep loved to hear them, and of all the stories Arbaaz would tell, Jayadeep had liked the tale of how he met his mother best of all. In this one, Arbaaz and his young mute servant, Raza Soora, had been trying to find the Koh-i-Noor diamond, the Mountain of Light. It was during his attempts to retrieve the diamond from the Imperial Palace that Arbaaz became involved with Pyara Kaur, granddaughter of Ranjit Singh, the founder of the Sikh Empire.

The Koh-i-Noor diamond was what they called a Piece of Eden, those artifacts distributed around the globe, which were the sole remnants of a civilization that preceded our own.

Jayadeep knew of their power because his parents had seen it for themselves. Arbaaz, Pyara and Raza had all been there the night the diamond was activated. They had all seen the celestial light show, and talking of what they'd witnessed, his parents were candid about the effect it had upon them. What they'd seen made them more devout and more fervent in their belief that such great power should never be wielded by their enemies, the Templars. They instilled that in the boy.

Back then, growing up in an Amritsar painted gold by the sun and being mentored by a father who was like a god to him, Jayadeep could not have conceived of a day when he might be named The Ghost, huddled in a freezing dark tunnel, alone in the world, venerated by nobody.

Training had begun when he was four or five years old, but although it was physically demanding work, it had never seemed like a chore to the boy; he never complained or played truant, and there was one very simple reason for this: he was good at it.

No. More than that. He was great. A natural from the day he was handed his first wooden training blade, a kukri. Jayadeep had a gift for combat such as had rarely been witnessed in the Indian brotherhood. He was extraordinarily, almost supernaturally fast in attack, and more than usually responsive in defense; he could boast tremendous powers of observation and anticipation. He was so good, in fact, that his father Arbaaz felt impelled to call upon another tutor.

Into the boy's life came Ethan Frye.

Meeting Ethan Frye was among The Ghost's earliest memories, this tired-looking, melancholy man, whose Western robes seemed to hang heavier on him than those of his father.

Just a tiny child, the boy had neither the inclination

nor the initiative to ask about Ethan Frye. As far as he was concerned, the elder Assassin might as well have fallen from the skies, tumbled to earth like a downhearted angel come to sully his otherwise idyllic existence.

"This is the boy, then?" Ethan had asked.

They had been sitting in the shaded courtyard at the time, the clamor of the streets outside drifting over the wall and joining the birdsong and the soft tinkle of a fountain.

"This is indeed the boy," said Arbaaz proudly. "This is Jayadeep."

"A great warrior you say."

"A great warrior in the making—or at least I think so. I've been training him myself and I've been astonished, Ethan, *astonished* by his natural aptitude." Arbaaz stood and walked. In the house behind him Jayadeep glimpsed his mother and for the first time, perhaps due to the presence of this gruff stranger, he was aware of their beauty and grace. He saw them as people rather than just his parents.

Without taking his eyes from the boy, Ethan Frye clasped his hands over his belly and spoke over his shoulder to Arbaaz. "Supernatural in his abilities, you say?"

"It is like that, Ethan, yes."

Eyes still on Jayadeep. "Supernatural, eh?"

"Always thinking two or three moves ahead," answered Arbaaz.

"As one should."

"At six years old?"

Ethan turned his gaze on Jayadeep once again. "It's precocious, I'll admit, but . . ."

"I know what you're going to say. That so far he has

been sparring with me and as father and son we naturally share a bond and that maybe, just maybe, I'm exhibiting certain tells that give him the edge, yes?"

"It had crossed my mind."

"Well, that's why you're here. I'd like you to take charge of training Jayadeep."

Intrigued by the boy, Ethan Frye agreed to Arbaaz's request and from that day he took up residence at the house, drilling the boy in swordcraft.

The boy, knowing little of what drove Ethan, was confused at first by his new tutor's gruff manner and rough tone. Jayadeep was not one to respond to the touch of a disciplinarian, and it had taken some months for the two of them to form a tutor-pupil relationship that wasn't characterized by sour asides (Ethan), harsh words (Ethan) and tears (Jayadeep).

For some time, in fact, Jayadeep believed that Ethan Frye simply did not like him, which came as something of a culture shock. The boy was pretty and charismatic. He knew next to nothing of the adult world and although he remained oblivious to concepts such as charm and persuasion, he was instinctively adept at being both charming and persuasive, able to twist his family and household around his little finger seemingly at will. He was the sort of little boy that grown-ups loved to touch. Never was a boy's hair so constantly ruffled by the men, his cheek rarely lasting longer than half an hour without one of the household women praising his smile and planting a kiss on him, inhaling his fresh, little-boy smell at the same time, silently luxuriating in the softness of his skin.

It was as though Jayadeep were a drug to which all who met him became addicted.

All, that was, except Ethan, who wore a permanently pensive and preoccupied expression. It was true that occasionally the light would come to him, and when it did, Jayadeep fancied he saw something of the "old" or maybe the "real" Ethan, as though there were a different Ethan struggling to peer out from beneath the gloom. Otherwise it seemed that whatever Jayadeep had that intoxicated other grown-ups simply failed to work on his tutor.

These were the rather shaky foundations on which their tutorials were built: Ethan, in a gray study; Jayadeep, confused by this new type of grown-up, who didn't lavish him with affection and praise. Oh, of course, Ethan was forced to offer grudging praise for Jayadeep's skills in combat. How could he not? Jayadeep excelled at every aspect of Assassin craft, and in the end it was this more than anything that cracked open their relationship, because if there's one thing a skilled Assassin can admire and appreciate, even grow to like, it's an initiate with promise. And Jayadeep was most certainly that.

So as the years passed, and master and pupil sparred in the shade of the courtyard trees, discussed theory by the fountains, and put their teachings into practice in the streets of the city, it was as though Ethan began to thaw toward his young charge, and when he spoke of taking the boy from wood to steel there was an unmistakable note of pride in his voice.

For his part, Jayadeep began to learn a little about his reflective mentor. Enough, in fact, for him to realize that "glum" was the wrong adjective, and that "troubled" was more accurate. Even at that age he was remarkably intuitive.

What's more, there came a day when he overheard women in the kitchen talking. He and Ethan were practicing a stealth exercise on the grounds of the house, and Ethan had commanded him to return with information obtained using covert means.

When The Ghost thought about this years later, it occurred to him that sending a small child to gather covert information was a plan fraught with possible pitfalls, not least that the child might learn something unsuitable for young ears.

Which, as it turned out, was exactly what happened.

As he later learned, Ethan was—despite outward appearances—prone to making the odd rash and hasty decision as well as being possessed of what you might call a sense of mischief. Thinking back, Ethan's instructions for the exercise were perhaps the first time Jayadeep saw an outward manifestation of this in his tutor.

So Jayadeep went on his exercise and two hours later joined Ethan at the fountain. He took a seat on the stone beside where his master sat looking pensive as usual, and did not acknowledge Jayadeep, as was his custom. Like everything else about Ethan, this had taken Jayadeep time to get used to and getting used to it was a process that involved moving first from being offended to then being confused and lastly accepting that his lack of warmth was in its own way a measure of the familiarity the two of them shared, these two men so far apart in age and culture, one of them an experienced killer, the other training to be one.

"Tell me, my dear boy, what did you learn?" asked Ethan.

Ethan's calling Jayadeep "my dear boy" was a relatively new development. One that pleased Jayadeep, as it happened.

"I learned something about you, Master."

Maybe then Ethan regretted sending his young charge on this particular assignment. It's difficult to imagine that he planned it, but then who can say what was in Ethan Frye's mind. Who can ever say? The boy had no way of knowing, but as an eager pupil and as one who had been schooled in observation he naturally watched his tutor closely for signs that he might have caused offense or stepped over a line.

"This was tittle-tattle you overheard was it, son?"

"Tittle-tattle, Master?"

"Tittle-tattle means gossip—and as I've always told you, gossip can be a very powerful information tool. You did well to glean what you could from what you overheard."

"You're not angry?"

A certain placid look had crossed Ethan's features. As though some feeling of internal turmoil were being laid to rest. "No, Jayadeep," he said, "I'm not angry with you. Pray tell me what it was that you heard."

"You might not like it."

"I don't doubt it. Go ahead anyway."

"The women were saying that you had a wife in England but that she died giving birth to your two children."

It was as though the courtyard stilled as the boy awaited his master's response. "That's true, Jayadeep," said Ethan after a while, exhaling through a sigh, "and when I tried to look at my children, Evie and Jacob, I found I could not. Invited back to India, I suppose you would have to say that I fled, Jayadeep. I fled my home in Crawley and my children to come here and swelter in the sun with you."

Jayadeep thought of his own mother and father. He thought of the love and affection they lavished upon him, and his heart went out to these two children. He had no doubt they were looked after, but even so they lacked a father's love.

"But not for much longer," said Ethan, as though reading Jayadeep's mind. He stood. "I'm to return to England, to Crawley, to Jacob and Evie. I shall see to it that you move on to steel; I shall satisfy myself you will be ready in combat, then I will return home and there, Jayadeep, I shall do what I feel I should have done in the first place: I shall be a father to my two children."

Ethan's words rang with a significance that Jayadeep, for all his preternatural intuition, failed to pick up on. In his own way, Ethan was confessing to Jayadeep that his friendship with the boy had awakened a parental instinct unseen since his wife had died. In his own way, Ethan was thanking the boy.

Jayadeep, though, had heard the word "combat."

It was some time after that—in fact, once the boy had made the transition from wood to steel—that Ethan discovered Jayadeep had a weakness. A serious weakness.

NINE

On the night he first met Maggie, The Ghost had been returning home to his place in the tunnel. He had passed Marylebone churchyard and glanced to check the angle of the stone—as he always did—but found his attention arrested by events taking place in the graveyard.

It was dark, of course—this was almost exactly a year ago, when the days were as short as they were now—and it was cold, too, the kind of night where you didn't hang around in darkened churchyards unless you had a very good reason to be hanging around in a darkened churchyard.

Nobody had business to be in a darkened churchyard on a night like this, though. Not any kind of business that wasn't wicked business.

Sure enough, what The Ghost heard was very wicked business indeed.

He stopped on the pathway by the low church wall. Listened. And he decided that on a scale of wickedness, with not-very-wicked at one end (some fornication, perhaps, a consensual business proposition conducted between a prostitute and her client), he was hearing something from the other end. He heard the sound of several men—The Ghost knew instantly, five men—some of whom were laughing and urging others on, as well as the sound of violence, of boots being used in a way their innocent maker never intended, and above all that the sound of a woman— The Ghost knew instantly, one woman—in very great pain.

There were others who passed by, of course, who would have heard the commotion in the churchyard, the unmistakable sound of a woman screaming and calling for mercy as the blows rained down, but it was only The Ghost who stopped. He shouldn't have done so as his job was to blend in at all times. But he stopped because he was an Assassin—he was still an Assassin—trained by Arbaaz Mir and Ethan Frye, instilled in the values of the Brotherhood.

And he was damned if he was going to walk on by while five men got their jollies beating up a woman.

He vaulted the low stone wall that acted as the churchyard boundary and moved farther into the gloom. The drunken, boisterous sound of men at play continued. From their accents The Ghost was able to tell that two of them were gentlemen, the other three of indeterminate class.

Now he saw the glow of lanterns, and what he made out in a clearing in the shadow of the great church were two well-dressed men and a figure on the floor.

"What do you call that?" one of them was saying as he stood astride her, slapping her face, the second man laughing and swigging from a flask.

In the foreground were three bigger men, all of whom

wore bowler hats. They stood with their backs to the two gents and their victim. Bodyguards, they stiffened as The Ghost navigated the graves toward them. Arbaaz and Ethan would have advised a stealthy intrusion; The Ghost could have killed two of the men before they even had a chance to react, but what he saw had awakened in him a primal anger, a sense of righteous justice, and he wanted a confrontation. He wanted for justice to be done and for justice to be seen to be done.

"Move along, mate," said one of the bodyguards. He had his arms folded. "Nothing for you to see here, lad."

The other two bodyguards had shifted. One of them had his hands pushed deep into the pockets of his coat. The other clasped his hands behind his back.

"Let the woman go," said The Ghost.

The two men had stopped their game, and they stood from the prone and bleeding body of the woman. Released, she groaned with a mixture of pain and relief and rolled over to one side, her skirts in disarray at her legs, face bloodied behind a tangle of matted hair. A poor, pitiable creature, she looked to be in her sixties.

"Move away from her," commanded The Ghost.

One of the toffs sniggered and passed the flask to the second man, whose eyes twinkled with delight as he put it to his lips and drank greedily. Both looked as if they were anticipating the beginning of an entertaining show. Standing there, a lone man against five, The Ghost hoped he wouldn't disappoint.

He hoped that with all his fine thoughts of seeing justice done, he hadn't bitten off more than he could chew.

The first bodyguard tilted his chin and spoke again,

his words like stones dropping in the newly still church-yard. "Move along, my lad, before we do it for you."

The Ghost regarded him. He regarded them all. "I'll move on when I'm satisfied the woman will be harmed no longer . . ."

"Well, that . . ."

"And when I'm satisfied that the two men who did this to her have been sufficiently punished."

The other two bodyguards burst out laughing but the leader stilled them with a hand. "Well, now, look, that ain't going to happen because you see these two gen'men here? They pay handsomely for the services of myself and my two colleagues, specifically to ensure that no harm comes to them as they tour the less salubrious sides of this nation's great capital, if you catch my meaning. To get to them you have to come through us, and you know, don't you, that ain't gonna 'appen."

Behind him the two pleasure-seeking toffs tittered some more, passing the flask back and forth, enjoying the show, an aperitif prior to the main course. They were weak and drunk and The Ghost knew he could take them both with one hand tied behind his back, but . . .

First the bodyguards. Number three's coat was unbuttoned, his hands still clasped behind his back. Either he was carrying a revolver or a cutlass hanging at his flank. He looked dangerous but also a little too relaxed, too confident.

The same went for number two. He wore a coat that was buttoned up, ankle length, and though his left hand flexed in the pocket of his coat, his right hand was still, which meant he'd be holding a cosh or knife in there.

Good. He was wearing a coat that was not conducive to close-quarter combat and secondly, though unwittingly, he'd shown The Ghost from where his weapon would appear. For these two reasons, The Ghost would target him first. He would be easiest to overcome, and The Ghost needed a weapon. He hoped it was a knife that the man had in his pocket.

Number one was cleverer. He didn't think a lone attacker would face up to five without good reason. His arms had remained folded across his chest—he carried a shoulder holster, perhaps?—but his eyes had roamed the area behind The Ghost, seeking out whatever reinforcements might be lurking there.

When he saw nothing he regarded The Ghost with even greater interest, suspicion and apprehension, guessing what his colleagues did not even suspect: that this Indian lad was playing some kind of angle. That he was more than he seemed to be. Number one was sharper. He would be the hard one.

The Ghost had finished sizing them up. He wished he held a kukri in one hand and had his hidden blade strapped to his other wrist. Were that the case, the battle's outcome would be in no doubt. What's more, it would have ended some moments ago. But even so, he was confident he could prevail. He had certain factors on his side: that his foes were largely underestimating him; that he was disgusted and supremely motivated; that he was highly trained and very adept and very fast and had assessed his distance, his surroundings, his opponents.

And now came one more thing in his favor. For as number one began to speak, saying the words, "I'll give you one last chance, lad . . ." The Ghost awarded himself the advantage of surprise.

And he struck.

Number two was still trying to pull his hands free of his coat pockets when The Ghost's forehead smashed into his nose. This blow—a "dirty trick" that Arbaaz had never fully endorsed but of which Ethan was most fond—had the advantage of causing massive pain, instant, traumatic blood loss and temporary blindness and disorientation. For the first crucial moments of the battle, number two was incapacitated. He was out of the game, unable to resist as The Ghost spun and jabbed an elbow back to knock the wind out of him as his other hand delved into the coat pocket and found . . . a cosh, *damn*.

But it had some weight at least, and he pulled it out of the coat then swung back in the other direction, the black-leather cosh in his hand connecting with the temple of number three. The Ghost swung hard, with all his might—which was a lot of might indeed—and the blow almost took the top of his target's head off.

The third man had been reaching inside his coat at the time, but his hand never withdrew so The Ghost never got to find out what he had inside. Instead the man's hand was still inside his coat as he staggered to one side with his mouth gaping like a fish on dry land. The ball bearings in the cosh had opened a gash in the side of his head and blood was already pouring from it. He would probably live, but would be brain-damaged, likely to spend the rest of his days in a bathchair drooling, being fed mushed-up food on a spoon and lacking the faculties to wonder how a mere boy had so easily bested him in a fight. The Ghost stepped forward, punched him twice in the throat and his body was still folding to the floor as The Ghost spun back around.

The whole move was over in the time it took to draw a sword, which was exactly what number one had done. Between them both was number two, reeling from the headbutt yet still on his feet and about to gain control of his senses when The Ghost, keen not to relinquish his forward momentum, struck once more, swinging with the cosh and not making full contact but doing enough to break the man's jaw. He kicked out at the same time, this one a clean connect, snapping the bodyguard's leg, which folded beneath him and sent him sprawling to the dirt of the churchyard. This one would never walk again and the broken jaw meant that very few people would understand him when he spoke.

In the same movement The Ghost lashed out with his other foot, kicking a lantern into the face of number one, who was hoping to use the opening to his advantage. The bodyguard knocked the lantern away with a cry of surprise and frustration that his move had met failure, and it gave The Ghost a moment to gather himself.

He checked his balance, moved away from the possible obstacle of a nearby headstone and shifted the cosh from one hand to the other, then back again.

The guardian gathered himself. He raised his cutlass, moved into position between The Ghost and the two men he was paid to protect; and then he called to them over his shoulder, saying, "Sirs, run."

The two toffs needed no further invitation, stumbling over one another and crashing into the stones as they took their leave, disappearing noisily into the night. Behind them on the floor lay the flask of booze.

The Ghost clenched his teeth. He couldn't let them get away.

"You don't have to die for the likes of them," he told the bodyguard, who gave a short chuckle.

"You're wrong, my friend," he replied. "Dying for the likes of them is *exactly* what the likes of me do. We do it all over the world."

Young though he was, The Ghost knew how it worked. The rich purchased commissions so they could rise quickly through the ranks of the British Army, ensuring that for the most part they stayed out of the bloodiest fighting and enjoyed the best comforts. "It doesn't need to be that way," he said.

"It does, lad. When you're as wise in the ways of the world as you are in combat—and by Christ you're wise in that—then you'll know."

The Ghost shook his head. Time was wasting. "It doesn't matter, sir. Either way, it's not you I want, it's whom you serve."

"Still can't do it, son," said the bodyguard sadly. "I can't let you do it." The cutlass was raised, he kept his opponent on point and his stance remained firm, but there was something in his eyes The Ghost recognized. A look of impending defeat. The look of a man who knows he's beaten, whose death or downfall is not a matter of *if*, but *when*.

"You have no choice," The Ghost replied, and was already in motion.

To the bodyguard he was a mere blur, as though the

night had rippled, the darkness shifting to accommodate the young Assassin's sheer speed as he sprang forward.

The Ghost had not made the mistake of underestimating his foe, of course. He had anticipated how his opponent might defend as well as factoring in the fact that his opponent would expect him to attack a certain way. And so he feinted first one way then the other, feeling the flow of his own body as he manipulated it in two different directions at once as he leapt, using a gravestone as a springboard to come at the bodyguard from an unexpected height and angle.

Too good, too fast, and much too combat-intelligent for the bodyguard. This man, trained no doubt by the English military, tough as old boots to begin with and toughened even more by countless overseas campaigns, even he was no match for The Ghost. No match at all. The cosh, sticky with blood from its last victim, crashed into the back of his head and his jaw slacked and his eyes rolled as he fell, unconscious, to the ground.

An hour or so later he would awaken, with a sore head but otherwise unharmed, when he would need to answer searching questions as to how he and his two equally battle-hardened companions could possibly be bested by a mere squit of a lad.

For now, though, he was out cold.

Meanwhile, The Ghost vaulted a gravestone, coming to the woman who had pulled herself up on her hands and now stared at him with a mixture of fear and awe and gratitude.

"Bloody hell, lad, what the bloody hell are you, some kind of demon or summat?"

"Go," he told her, "leave this place before our friend gets his wits back about him," and with that he took off after the two pleasure-seeking gentlemen, the sight of the woman's bruised, bloody and swollen face spurring him on, kindling his anger as he snatched up the cutlass and ran.

Catching them was easy. They were drunk, noisy and slow. Though they were frightened, they were probably confident that their champions could best this young upstart because men like this had never needed to worry about anything. They employed people to do their dirty work; they had servants and lackeys to do their worrying for them.

So, yes, The Ghost caught them easily, and he reached the one who lagged behind, barreling into him so that the besuited toff fell and The Ghost was on him in an instant, rolling him over and pinning him down with his knees on either side of the man's chest, raising the cutlass and channeling his fury, remembering that it was this man—*this very man*—who just moments ago he'd seen laughing as he kicked a defenseless woman, as he went to deliver the killing blow.

TEN

The time had come for Ethan to leave Amritsar, but there was something troubling him and he had called a meeting of the family, the outcome of which was to send shock waves through the Mir family.

At this meeting Arbaaz had been expecting Ethan to announce that his promise had been fulfilled, which was to nurture his son's obvious talents and hone them into an Assassin-ready whole, so that he might go on to embark upon the next phase of his education, one for which there was no set or predetermined end, the chapter of his career that would determine his legacy, his work in the field.

However . . .

"I don't think he's ready," said Ethan bluntly, without ceremony or warning.

Arbaaz broke bread and smiled. "Then you cannot leave, Ethan. That was our agreement."

The two men had shared great adventures together. Jayadeep had lain awake in bed, hearing them talking in the courtyard outside. They talked of the Koh-i-Noor diamond. How Arbaaz had retrieved it. Sometimes Jayadeep's mother would be present and all three would reminisce. Names like Alexander Burnes and William Sleeman meant nothing to Jayadeep, but to his parents they were like a doorway into another world of exciting memories.

"I've already sent word. They expect me home and I intend to honor the commitment I've made to them. I will return, Arbaaz, of that you can be sure."

"Then I fail to understand. Our agreement was that you should train Jayadeep until he was ready for the field."

The boy had sat beside his mother feeling invisible as they discussed him without acknowledging his presence. It wasn't exactly an unknown occurrence; the more important the issue the less likely he was to have a say. He had never been consulted on his future, nor would he expect to be; it was simply a matter of fact that until further notice he had no say in matters involving his own destiny.

"You're going to have to enlighten me, my old friend," said Arbaaz. "Throughout your years here you have assured me that Jayadeep is one of the most talented young Assassins you have ever encountered, which we all know means you think Jayadeep is *the* most talented Assassin you have ever encountered. And why not! He was tutored first by me then by your good self. I've seen for myself that he has no lack of skill, and unless you've been honey-coating my ears all this time, you think so, too, and yet now, on the eve of your departure, comes this news the boy isn't ready. You must excuse my confusion. In what way is this highly trained, consummately skilled boy whose mentor is about to embark for home *not ready*? And more to the point, *why*?"

A note of angry irritation was evident in his father's voice, which had risen as he delivered his speech. Even a bread crumb clinging obstinately to his bottom lip did nothing to diminish his formidable look. Jayadeep shrank back. Even his mother appeared concerned.

Only Ethan was unperturbed, returning Arbaaz's daunting stare with an unfathomable gaze of his own.

"It's true that the boy has astonishing natural skill. It's true that I have been able to mold that natural talent into Assassinship of a greater-than-usual standard. For my own part, I have learned much from the boy, which is partly the reason I intend to leave for home and have no intention of deviating from that path, no matter how many bread crumbs you spit at me, old friend."

Arbaaz, abashed, wiped his mouth and when his hand came away it revealed the very beginnings of a smile. "So why, then?" he asked. No, *demanded*. "Why leave us at this crucial time, when there is still so much to teach the boy?"

Ethan's smile wasn't so much a smile as a look of kindness and concern that reached his lips as well as his eyes. A look that he passed first to the parents then to the boy.

"He lacks the killer instinct. The boy can kill and no doubt will, but he lacks something we have, you and I, or perhaps he has something we lack."

Arbaaz tilted his chin, color rising. "Are you saying my boy's a coward?"

"Oh for God's sake, Arbaaz," huffed an exasperated Ethan, "no, of course I'm bloody not. It's a matter of disposition. If you put this boy in the field, he will either fail or . . ."

"I won't," said Jayadeep suddenly, surprising even himself, anticipating a scolding, maybe even a more painful punishment for this sudden, unwarranted and uninvited outburst.

Instead his father looked proud of him, reaching over to squeeze his shoulder in a gesture that made Jayadeep's heart swell with pride.

Ethan ignored him. He had turned his attention to Pyara. "There is no shame in this," he told her, and he could see the softness in her eyes, the secret hope that maybe just maybe her family might at long last be free of bloodshed. "He can serve the Brotherhood in other ways. What a mentor he will be. A master tactician. A policymaker. A great leader. And somebody has to be these things. Jayadeep can be these things. Just not . . . *never* . . . a warrior."

Arbaaz could contain himself no longer. Pyara, calm and resolute, accustomed to the sight of her husband in full flight, remained implacable as he exploded with rage. "Jayadeep, my son, *will* be a great warrior, Frye. He will be a master Assassin, a mentor of the Indian Brotherhood . . ."

"He can still . . ."

"Not unless he has proven himself in combat. As a warrior. As an Assassin."

Ethan shook his head. "He is not ready and, Arbaaz, I'm sorry if it breaks your heart but in my opinion he never will be."

"Ah," said Arbaaz, rising, and shepherding Jayadeep too. Pyara surreptitiously wiped a tear from her eye as she, too, stood, loyal despite her torn emotions. "There we have it, Ethan. It is just your opinion. What do you think, Jay, shall we prove our English friend wrong?"

And Jayadeep, the boy who would one day be The Ghost, who was not even ten years old but so desperately wanted to please his father because his father was his king, said, "Yes, Father."

ELEVEN

Letter from Ethan Frye to Arbaaz Mir, decoded
from the original.

Dear Arbaaz,

*Six years have passed since I left India in order to
return home here to England. Six years since we last
spoke, my old friend. And far, far too long.*

*In the meantime, I have learned to mourn the loss
of my beloved wife, Cecily, and do so in a manner of
which she would have approved, which is to say that I
have set aside my former resentment in order to build
a relationship with our two children, Evie and Jacob.
I regret that I ever considered them responsible for my
loss; I have done my best to make reparations for the
lost years of their childhood.*

*It was the years spent with your extraordinary son,
Jayadeep, that galvanized me, and for that I am
eternally grateful to you both. Jayadeep set me on a
path of enlightenment that made me reevaluate my*

thinking. I'm sorry to say, Arbaaz, that it has only strengthened my resolve regarding the matter that drove a wedge between us all those years ago, and now prompts me to make contact once again.

I should explain. As Assassins we are instilled with a certain philosophy. Unlike the Templars, who divide the world's inhabitants into shepherds and sheep, we see millions of bright spots: intelligent, feeling beings, each with their own potential and capable of working within a greater whole.

Or so we like to think. These days I wonder. Do we always put this philosophy into practice? When we train our young Assassins, we put swords into their hands when they have only just learned to walk. We instill in them philosophies and values that are not their own but passed down the generations, sculpting the child into a creature of preconception and discrimination and above all, in our particular case, a killer.

What we are doing is right. Please don't read into this an expression of ideological doubt on my behalf, for I have never been more firm in my beliefs that the Brotherhood stands for what is right in this world. My doubt, dear Arbaaz, lies in the application of that ideology, and this doubt is what keeps me awake at night, wondering if we fail our children by molding them into our image, when in fact we should be teaching them to follow a path of their own. I wonder, are we merely paying lip service to the very principles we espouse?

With my own children, Jacob and Evie, I have attempted to take an alternative path to the one I

*have always followed in the past, and different from
the one I tried to follow with Jayadeep. Rather than
indoctrinating them, I have instead strived to give
them the tools with which to teach themselves.*

*It pleases me that their trajectory follows my own.
As you know, in London, the Assassin presence is long
since depleted. Our Brotherhood is weak here, while
the Templars, under the command of their Grand
Master, Crawford Starrick, continue to thrive;
indeed, news has reached us that our enemy's infiltration into the city's elite is even more pronounced than
we feared. They have plans afoot, of that there is no
doubt. Big plans. And one day, when they are ready,
Jacob and Evie will join the struggle against them.*

*When they are ready. Note that well, Arbaaz. I
allowed them to find their own path, and I have
abided by the principle that they should only call themselves fully fledged Assassins when I know them to be
as mentally capable of fulfilling the task as they are
physically. I do this in the knowledge that we are all
individuals, some of us suited to one direction, some
suited to another. Assassins we may be in name, yet
not all of us can be "assassins" in nature.*

*And so it is with Jayadeep. I understand how heart-
breaking it must be for you. He is, after all, your son.
You yourself are a great Assassin and he has the potential to be one. However, what I know for sure is that
though he may be skilled and talented in the means of
dealing death, Jayadeep lacks the heart to do so.*

*He will kill. Yes, he will kill, if needs be. In a heart-
beat if it were in defense of himself or of those he loves.*

But I wonder. Will he do so in the name of an ideology? Will he do so for the Creed?

Will he do so in cold blood?

Which brings me to the timing of my letter. The troubling news has reached me that Jayadeep is to embark upon his first real-world assignment. An assassination.

Firstly, I must say how much I appreciate that you took my concerns of six years ago seriously enough to delay his blooding until after the time of his fifteenth birthday. For this I am grateful, and commend you for your wisdom and restraint. However, it is my view that Jayadeep lacks the core resolve needed for such an act—and nor will he ever attain it.

Simply put, he is different from you and me. Perhaps different from Jacob and Evie. Further, it is my belief—and a belief that is entirely consistent with the core values of the Brotherhood—that we should embrace what is different about him. We should celebrate that individuality and turn it to good use for the Brotherhood, rather than try to deny it and mold it into rough and awkward shapes.

To put it another way, by sending Jayadeep into action, you are inviting something far worse than your (imagined, if I may say so) disgrace that your son cannot follow in your own esteemed footsteps, in favor of a much, much more profound disgrace: abject failure.

I beg of you, please, retire him from this assignation, take a fresh view of him, utilize the best of your

*extraordinary son's abilities for the good of the Broth-
erhood rather than depending on the worst.*

*I hope to hear your decision by return, and I pray
that you show the same wisdom and restraint for
which I have already commended you. You have
trusted me in the past; please, Arbaaz, trust me
again.*

*Yours, as ever,
Ethan Frye
London*

TWELVE

Letter to Ethan Frye from Arbaaz Mir, decoded from the original.

Ethan, I thank you for your correspondence. However, I regret that you chose to build bridges over such turbulent waters. There is no debate to be had regarding Jayadeep's abilities as an Assassin. You gave him the skills, I in the interim have provided him with the moral fiber necessary to put them into practice. You're fond of putting things simply, Ethan, so I shall do so now: it is six long years since you last saw Jayadeep and you are no longer in a position to make judgments concerning his suitability as an Assassin. He has changed, Ethan. He has developed and grown. I am confident he is ready for his blooding, and he will indeed carry out the assassination as planned. His target is a low-ranking Templar whose termination is a necessity in order to warn our enemies that their increased presence in India shall not be tolerated. I apologize if these next words appear to be a gibe against you and George Westhouse in London, Ethan, but we are keen that the Templars should not gain a foothold here as they did in London, for we know where that leads.

I thank you for your correspondence, Ethan. I hope and trust that the foundations of our relationship are secure enough that this need not be the end of a great friendship for you and me. However, I have made my decision, and just as you abide by your own principles, I must abide by mine.

Yours, as ever,
Arbaaz Mir
Amritsar

THIRTEEN

Internal dispatch sent to George Westhouse of London, decoded from the original.

Please relay immediately to Ethan Frye: Jayadeep Mir in The Darkness.

FOURTEEN

The door closed behind them. Torches bolted to the walls
lit stone steps down to a second door, the dungeon portal.

Ahead of Ethan was the meeting-room custodian, Ajay.
Like Ethan, his cowl covered his head as though to
acknowledge the grim nature of their business here in
this dark, cold and unforgiving place. In addition, Ajay
wore a curved sword at his belt and Ethan had caught a
glimpse of his hidden blade as he opened the door. Yes,
Ajay would do his duty if needs be. With regret, for sure,
but he would do it.

They called this place The Darkness. A series of small
chambers beneath Amritsar's main Brotherhood meeting
room. Nominally the rooms were designated for document storage or as an armory, but their crepuscular atmosphere and cell-like design ensured rumors constantly
swirled around what might have taken place there in the
past: plots hatched, enemies interrogated. It was said that
even a baby had been born in The Darkness though few
gave the story much credibility.

Today, however, The Darkness would earn its reputation. Today The Darkness had a guest.

Ajay led Ethan through a second fortified door and into a dimly lit stone corridor beyond, doors lining either side. At the passage end, he unlocked a door inset with nothing but a tiny viewing hole then stood to one side, bowing slightly to allow his visitor inside. Ethan stepped over the threshold into a tiny chamber which, whatever its previous function, had been repurposed as a cell, complete with a wooden cot.

Out of respect for Ethan, Ajay laid his lantern at the Assassin's feet before withdrawing and closing the door behind him. And then, as light glowed on the forbidding dark stone of the room, Ethan gazed upon his former pupil for the first time in over six years, and his heart broke afresh to see him laid so low.

Jayadeep sat cross-legged in a corner among the dirty straw that covered the floor. He'd been here for weeks, while Ethan made the lengthy crossing from England to India. As a result, his new living quarters were none too fresh and he'd no doubt been in better health, too, but even so, Ethan was struck by the boy's looks. In the intervening years he had matured into a handsome young man, with intense, piercing eyes, dark hair that he would reach to brush from his eyes, and flawless chestnut-colored skin. *He'll break some hearts,* thought Ethan, gazing at him from the doorway.

First things first, though.

The Assassin put a fist to his nose and mouth, as much to replace the stink of the cell with the familiar scent of his own skin as to register his dismay at his former pupil's predicament. The possibility that he himself could have done more to prevent the situation sharpened his regret; the look in Jayadeep's eyes as he turned his gaze from contemplating his lap to find his old tutor in the doorway, a penetrating, heartwrenching stare of gratitude, relief, sorrow and shame, only sharpened it further.

"Hello, Master," said Jayadeep simply.

It wasn't particularly pleasant, but Ethan took a seat beside Jayadeep, the two men together again, circumstances so different this time, the smell of jasmine a memory of an ancient and now-unattainable past.

Ethan reached a hand to pull at the rags Jayadeep wore. "They stripped you of your robes, then?"

Jayadeep gave a rueful look. "There's a little more to it than that."

"In that case, how about we start with your telling me what happened?"

The boy gave a short, sad snort. "You mean you don't already know?"

Ethan had arrived in Amritsar to find the Brotherhood in mild disarray, a more-than-usually-visible presence as they worked to nullify the repercussions of what had taken place. So, yes, of course he knew the story. But even so . . .

"I'd like to hear it from the horse's mouth, as it were."

"It's difficult for me to talk about."

"Please try."

Jayadeep sighed. "Your training had shaped my mind and body into a series of responses and reactions, into combinations of attack and defense, calculations, forecast and prognostication. I was ready to go into action in all but one respect. You were right, Master, I lacked the heart. Tell me, how did you know?"

Ethan said, "If I were to say to you that it all came down to the difference between a wooden training kukri and the real thing, would you believe me?"

"I would think it was part of the story. But just part."

"You would be right, Jayadeep. For the truth is that I saw in your eyes something I have seen in the eyes of men I killed; men whose very own lack of heart in combat was a weakness I recognized and exploited in order to plunge my blade into them."

"And you thought you saw it in me?"

"I did. And I was right, wasn't I?"

"We thought you were wrong. Father believed I could be instilled with the mettle needed to be a killer. He set about showing me the way. We practiced and rehearsed with live subjects."

"Putting an animal to the sword is very different from—"

"I know that now." The words came out sharply. A little of the old master-pupil interaction returned and Jayadeep lowered fearful eyes in apology. "I know that now, Master, and believe me I regret it."

"But you and Arbaaz felt that you were ready to take the life of one of your own species, to take from a man everything he ever was and everything he ever will be; to leave his family grieving, to begin a wave of sadness and sorrow and possible revenge and recrimination that might ripple throughout the ages? You and your father felt you were ready for that?"

"Please, Master, don't make this more difficult for me. Yes, you are right, in the face of what you say, our preparations might seem dreadfully feeble, but then again what

Assassin can claim differently? Everything is theory until it is put into practice. And my turn came to put theory into practice. For my blooding I was to kill an Indian Templar by the name of Tjinder Dani. A man we believed was making plans to establish a Templar outpost in the city."

"And what was to be the method of his execution?"

"The garrotte."

Inwardly, Ethan cursed. A garrotte. Of all things. You didn't need a huge amount of skill to use a garrotte, but you needed resolve, and what Jayadeep had was plenty of skill but not so much resolve. What the hell was Arbaaz thinking?

Jayadeep continued. "Under cover of darkness, Father and I rode out to the street where Dani kept his lodgings. One of our agents had bribed a night watchman for the key, and in the street we took possession of it, thanked and paid the man and sent him on his way."

A witness, thought Ethan. It gets better.

"I know what you're thinking. I could have picked the lock."

"You are an excellent picklock."

"The information given to us by the agent was that the Templar Dani was expecting an attack and thus was accompanied by bodyguards during the day. Our enemies were relying on the fact that a daytime attempt on his life would have resulted in a public confrontation. A street skirmish involving multiple Assassins and Templars was to be avoided at all costs. For that reason it was decided to make a nighttime incursion and so we assembled as much information as possible regarding the target's nocturnal activities."

"And you did this, didn't you?"

"I did, Master, yes, and I learned that Dani barred his door and laid traps at night; that an invasion either by the door or the window would result in alarms being activated."

"And so?"

"And so, you see, the key given to us was not to the door of Dani's room, not even to his lodgings, but to the warehouse next door, where I was able to make an unobtrusive entrance. There were three men stationed in the street, looking for all the world as though they were providing security for the warehouse, but I knew them to be Templar guards, and their job was to see to it that no Assassin scaled the walls of either the lodging house or the warehouse. It was clever. They had the outside of the buildings covered while inside Dani had his room secure. It would take a measure of stealth and guile to get inside. I have both.

"And so, I waited in the shadows, taking strength and reassurance from the knowledge that not far away my father waited with our horses, ready for our escape. At the same time I measured the movements of the guards as they carried out their patrol.

"I had been there on previous nights, of course, timing just as I was on this occasion, and what I'd learned was that the guards coordinated their movements to prevent anyone's having the opportunity to scale the walls. Under their robes they carried crossbows and throwing knives; they kept a safe distance from one another so as to prevent a quick double kill, so taking out one of them would alert the others. I had no reason to suspect that they were anything but supremely competent. That is why I had the key, Ethan."

"The key was to the warehouse?"

"As I've already said, the key was to the warehouse. I had greased the keyhole myself that very morning, and now I counted, I timed, and I made my move when the moment was right. I streaked across the apron behind the warehouse and to the rear door, where I thrust the key into the lock. The sound was muffled, a well-oiled click that, even though it sounded to my ears like a gunshot, was in reality just another indistinguishable night noise, and I was inside. I locked the warehouse door behind me but took the key. This was to be my escape route also.

"Or so I thought at the time. But of course I was wrong about that."

The boy's head dropped once more to his lap and he wrung his hands, tortured by the pain of the wretched memory.

"The warehouse was empty. All I saw on the stone floor was a long, slatted table and some chairs. Possibly it was to have been used by the Templars for some reason. In either case the idea of its needing an exterior guard was laughable. Of course, they hadn't bothered to post a guard inside, but even so I stayed silent as I made my way up steps and then ladders and to the roof of the building. Once outside, I stayed in the shadows and took my neckerchief from around my neck. You ask about my Assassin's robes, but in fact I never wore them. I was wearing then what I'm wearing now. If by some chance I'd been discovered by the warehouse guards, they would have taken me for a street boy of no consequence, given me a slap and sent me on my way.

Had they investigated more thoroughly they would have known that I differed from a street urchin in only one respect—that I had in my pocket a coin."

Ethan was nodding sagely. He knew the weapon. The coin is wrapped in the neckerchief, the neckerchief used as a *lumal*, a kind of garrotte. The coin chokes the victim's windpipe, crushing his larynx, hastening death and preventing him crying out. It is one of the most basic but effective of the Assassin's tools. Ethan began to understand why Arbaaz had selected it. He even began to understand why Arbaaz had chosen Jayadeep for the job. "Continue," he said.

"I made the jump easily. And then, staying in the shadows of the lodging-house roof and wary of the guards who still patrolled below, I crept toward the hatch I knew to be in the ceiling of Dani's room. I had brought grease with me, a dab of it behind my ear, and I used it on the hatch, which I opened as carefully as possible, before letting myself down into the dark space below.

"My breath was held and my heart hammered. But as you had always taught me, the presence of a little fear is to be welcomed. Fear makes us careful. Fear keeps us alive. There was nothing so far about my mission to give me cause for worry. Everything was going to plan.

"Now I was in Dani's room. I could see the traps he had placed at his door and at the window. A pulley system attached to a ceiling bell that hung not far from the hatch I had just used to make my grand entrance.

"And there in bed was my target. Dani, a man about whom I had learned a great deal in the weeks leading up to the assignment. My breathing became heavy. My temple seemed to throb as though the vein there was beating in time to my increased heart rate. This was my nerves worsening."

Ethan stopped him. "While you were learning about Dani he was also becoming a human being in your eyes, wasn't he? You had begun to think of him as a person rather than as a target, hadn't you?"

"In retrospect, you're right, I had."

"Who could have seen that coming?" said Ethan, regretting his inappropriate sarcasm immediately.

"Perhaps it would have been too late, even if I had. Too late for second thoughts, I mean. There was no going back. I was an Assassin in the room of a slumbering man. My target. I had to act. I had no choice but to go through with the job. The issue of whether or not I was ready had ceased to be relevant. It was not a question of being ready, it was a question of action. Of kill or fail."

"And looking around, I think we all know what happened there." Again, Ethan regretted his flippancy, remembering that when this conversation was over he would pull himself to his feet, brush the straw from his backside, call for the custodian and leave the boy alone in this dark and damp place. No, this was no time for smart remarks. Instead, he tried to imagine the scene in the room: the darkened lodging house, a man asleep—did a man ever look so innocent as when he was asleep?—and Jayadeep, his breath held, wringing his neckerchief in his hand as he gathered his nerves ready to strike, the coin rolled into the neckerchief, and . . .

The coin falling from the neckerchief. Striking the floorboards.

"Your garrotte," he said to Jayadeep. "Did the coin fall from it?"

"How did you know? I didn't tell anybody that."

"Visualization, my dear boy, haven't I always taught you about it?"

Across the boy's face came the first hint of a smile since Ethan had entered the room. "You did. Of course you did. It's a technique I use constantly."

"But not on this occasion?"

A cloud of sadness stole the smile's slight beginnings. "No, not on this occasion. On this occasion all I heard was the blood rushing in my head. All I could hear was my father's voice urging me on to do what had to be done. When the coin dropped, the noise surprised me and it woke Dani and he was quicker to react than I was."

"You should have struck the moment you were in the room," said Ethan, and an anger that didn't really belong with the boy was directed at him anyway. "You should have struck the second you had the chance. Your hesitation was your undoing. What did I always tell you? What did your father always advise? You hesitate, you die—it's as simple as that. An assassination is not a cerebral act. It requires great thought, but all of that thought goes into the planning and preparation, the contemplation and visualization prior to the act itself—*that* is the time for second, third, fourth thoughts, as many thoughts as you need until you are sure—absolutely certain—that you are ready to do what needs to be done. Because when you are in the moment, when you stand before your target, there is no time for hesitation."

Jayadeep's eyes swam with tears as he looked up at his old friend. "I know that now."

Ethan laid a comforting hand on his. "I know. I'm sorry. Tell me what happened next."

"He was quick, I'll give him that, and I should credit him with a lot more besides, because he was quick and he was strong, and he sprang from the bed with a speed that surprised me in a man of his age and size and he caught me, by now practically unarmed, and thrust me backward to the window.

"We went straight through it, Dani and I. We went straight through the shutters and plummeted to the cobbles below, a fall that was thankfully broken by the canopy beneath. Looking back, perhaps I hoped that my training might return to me, a kind of instinct, if you like. But it failed me. Even as I rolled away from Dani, hurt and stunned and desperately trying to get ahold of my senses, I saw faces appear at the windows on the other side of the street and heard the sound of the running feet as the guards hastened toward us.

"I rolled away from Dani, feeling a blinding pain in my head and another in my hip. The next moment he was upon me, his teeth bared, his eyes bright and wide with hatred, his hands fixed around my neck.

"He never heard the horse. Neither did I. Earlier we had used strips of blanket to muffle the hooves, Father and I, and he came riding over the stone toward us, silent as a wraith, and the first I saw of him was a robed figure on horseback looming behind Dani, one hand on the reins of the horse, the other held out, crooked at the elbow and flexing, his hidden blade ejecting, moonlight running along the steel. Father wrapped the reins in his hand and wrenched back, forcing his horse to rear up on its hind legs, and for a second I saw him as the fearsome Assassin-warrior of legend. I saw the death-dealing glint in his eye, his intent to kill as strong and true as the weapon he wielded. I saw a man I could never hope to be. Perhaps I knew then that I was lost.

"And perhaps, also, Dani, my intended victim knew that death had come from behind. But it was too late, and my father's blade punched through the top of his skull and into his brain, killing him instantly—an instant in which his eyes widened then rolled back and his mouth dropped open in surprise and a half second of excruciating agony before his life was extinguished—an instant during which I saw the blood-streaked steel inside his mouth.

"Father withdrew his blade and droplets of blood flew from it as he swept it back, this time to slice the throat of the first oncoming guard, who fell in a mist of arterial spray, his sword not even drawn. Father's arm swept back the other way, this time across his chest and there was a ring of steel, as sharp and loud in the night as Dani's warning bell as his blade met the sword of the second guard. His parry sent the attacker staggering back, and in a blink Father was off his horse to claim his advantage, drawing his sword with his other hand and attacking at the same time.

"It was over in a heartbeat. In a blur of robes and steel, Father attacked with both weapons. Instinctively the guard had straightened his forearm to defend against the sword attack but it left him exposed to a strike from the other side and that's exactly what Father did, slamming his hidden blade into the guard's armpit.

"The man fell. His tunic already crimson, the cobbles gleaming with it. He would bleed out in moments. Either that or choke on his own blood if . . ."

"If the blade punctured his lungs. Yes, I taught you that myself."

"Whether more guards were simply slow in arriving or had witnessed my father in action and decided that discretion was the better part of valor, I don't know. Without a word he regained his horse, reached for me and swept me up to ride behind him, and we were gone, leaving the street in pandemonium behind us."

There was a long pause. Ethan said nothing, feeling the boy's trauma almost as if it were his own. So that was it, he thought. Jayadeep's action had broken the tenets of the Creed: he had been forced to surrender hiding in plain sight; worse, he had been forced to compromise the Brotherhood.

"I know what you're thinking," said Jayadeep at last. "You're thinking I'm a coward."

"Well, then you don't know what I'm thinking because that's not what I'm thinking. There's a world of difference between thought and action and one thing I know of you, Jayadeep, is that you're not a coward."

"Then why was I unable to deliver the killing blow?"

Ethan rolled his eyes. Had nobody listened to a bloody word he'd said? "Because you're not a killer."

Again came silence. Sorrow bloomed from the boy and Ethan thought, *What a world we live in, when we mourn an inability to kill.*

"What did your father say to you, on the journey home?"

"Nothing, Master. He said nothing, not a word. But of course his silence spoke volumes, and has continued to do so. He has not been to see me. Nor Mother."

Ethan fumed. The bloody tyrant, leaving his own son in this hole. "The Assassins will have forbidden your mother from coming to see you."

"Yes."

And Ethan could well imagine how Arbaaz had been feeling. He could picture it as he and his son rode home, dropping off Jayadeep, packed off to his quarters in silent disgrace, then riding off to see the mentor, Hamid. The boy went on to tell him that he had been asleep in bed when he was awoken by a black hood over his head, bundled away to end up in The Darkness. Ethan wondered whether Arbaaz was one of the men who had taken Jayadeep into custody. Had his own father led the arrest party?

He stood. "I will be doing my best to get you out of here, Jayadeep, of that you may be certain."

But as he called for Ajay, in English and in Hindi, what stayed with Ethan was the look in the boy's eyes as he shook his head in sad denial of hope.

Ethan and Ajay made the short journey along the passage and up the stone steps to the meeting room above. There stood a second guard, a striking-looking woman who stood with her feet planted slightly apart and her hands on the hilt of a large sword, its point on the flagstone at her feet. She regarded Ethan implacably from beneath her cowl.

"This is Kulpreet," said Ajay by way of introduction. He tilted a stubbled jaw in her direction. "She is the best swordsman in the Brotherhood."

And yet the sword she minded was longer, had a flatter blade . . .

"When?" Ethan asked her.

"Tomorrow morning," she replied.

And Ethan could see from her eyes that he was talking to Jayadeep's executioner.

FIFTEEN

"I thank you for seeing me."

Ethan had every reason to fear that Arbaaz might simply refuse his request for an audience. What had happened wasn't Ethan's fault—far from it—but in Arbaaz's eyes he must have been held at least partly responsible. Then, of course, there was the small matter of the exchange of letters.

Not that he would have taken no for an answer. He was here to save the life of Jayadeep Mir, and he wasn't leaving until the job was done.

Sure enough, his old friend regarded him warily, with eyes that were tired from worry and sleeplessness, face pinched and drawn. What must he have been going through? What agonies of torn loyalty, parental love and duty to the Brotherhood?

His worries had evidently relieved him of his obligations as a host. There was no offer of bread or olives or wine for Ethan, and certainly no warm greeting. The Assassin had been led through the cool marble corridors of the Mir household, disappointed not to catch sight of

Pyara—he might have had an ally there—and then deposited in one of the back offices, a room he himself had once used for tutoring Jayadeep. Back then he'd chosen the room because of its spartan furniture and decoration. No distractions. Today, there wasn't even hot tea. Just a simple woven wall covering, two straight-backed chairs where they sat, an unpolished table between them, and an unmistakable atmosphere.

"Don't mistake my reasons for agreeing to see you, Ethan. I have something I need to ask you."

Wary, hoping he might have had a chance to state his case, Ethan spread his hands. "Go on."

"I want to know, Ethan, how you intend to do it?"

"How do I intend to do what?"

"Free Jayadeep, of course. Do you plan to break him out of The Darkness or perhaps rescue him from the execution itself? How many Assassin's lives did you plan to take in the process?"

The gaze of Arbaaz was flat and terrible.

"I had rather hoped to talk to you about it first, Arbaaz, as one of my oldest and dearest friends."

Arbaaz shook his head. "No. There is to be no discussion. What's more, I must tell you that you will be under surveillance for the duration of what I hope is a short stay in Amritsar. The reason you are under surveillance is to ensure you don't try to free Jayadeep."

"Why might I want to free Jayadeep, Arbaaz?" asked Ethan softly, a reasonable tone in his voice.

The other man picked at a knot in the wood with his fingernail, regarding it as though he expected it to do something. "Because your life in the West has made you soft,

Ethan. It's why the Brotherhood in London is practically wiped out, and why you and George are mere insurgents compared to the Templar stranglehold.

"You're weak, Ethan, you have allowed your Brotherhood over the water to deteriorate to the point of irrelevancy and now you want to bring your progressive policies over here and you think I'll let you."

Ethan leaned forward. "Arbaaz, this is not about Templar versus Assassin. This is about Jayadeep."

His eyes slid away, clouding for just a moment. "Even more reason that he should pay the ultimate price for his . . ."

"What?"

"Misconduct." Arbaaz's voice rose. "His misconduct, his incompetence, his negligence."

"He needn't be executed."

"You see? You have come to plead for his life."

Ethan shrugged. "I make no bones about it. I do come to plead for his life, but you misjudge me if you think me weak, or that I disapprove of the hard line you take. Quite the opposite, I admire your inner strength and resolve. This is, after all, your son we're talking about. I know of no Assassin forced into such a difficult position as the one you find yourself in now, forced to put duty before family."

Arbaaz gave him a sharp, sideways look, as though unsure what to read into Ethan's words. Seeing his old friend was genuine, his face folded. "I lose a son and wife, too," he said in a voice that drowned in misery. "Pyara will never look at me again. She has made that perfectly clear."

"You need not make that sacrifice."

"How so?"

"Banish him—banish him into my custody, where I have an important job for him, one that, if it is successful, may help to restore the Brotherhood in London. An operation, Arbaaz, a covert operation for which Jayadeep, with his particular talents, is ideally suited. He need not die. Do you see? He can return to England with me and your honor will be satisfied. Suitable judgment will have been passed upon him, but he will live, Arbaaz. Not in the comfort to which he is accustomed, I grant you. What I have in mind involves extraordinarily reduced circumstances. But perhaps you will consider that part of his punishment. And after all, you needn't tell that to Pyara. Simply that he is with me. I will be his handler."

Praying for the right outcome, Ethan watched the indecision flit across the other's face.

"I would need to talk to Hamid," said Arbaaz thoughtfully.

"You would," said Ethan, and suppressed a burst of relief. Arbaaz had no desire to see Jayadeep put to the sword; Ethan was offering him a way out of a situation that would have torn his family apart, and all with no loss of face. What's more, "I think you will find that conversation an easier one than you might imagine," continued Ethan. "I saw Ajay and Kulpreet today, and if their mood is representative of the Brotherhood as a whole, then they no more wish to see Jayadeep executed than you or I. Let the punishment be exile. There are many who consider it even worse than death."

"No," said Arbaaz.

Ethan started. "I beg your pardon."

"The punishment must be death."

"I don't understand . . ."

"If this assignation is as undercover as you suggest, then wouldn't it be advantageous if the agent did not exist? Who can link him to Jayadeep Mir if Jayadeep Mir is dead?"

Ethan clapped his hands. "A ghost?" he said happily. "That's a stroke of genius, Arbaaz, worthy of the great Assassin I know."

Arbaaz stood then, came round the table and finally took his old friend in an embrace. "Thank you, Ethan," he said, as the Assassin stumbled clumsily to his feet, "thank you for what you are doing."

And Ethan left, thinking that, all in all, it had been a good afternoon's work. He had not had to use the letter in his pocket, the one in which Arbaaz explicitly rejected Ethan's advice, a letter that proved that any charges of incompetence or negligence lay not with Jayadeep but with his father. What's more, he had saved the life of a boy who was as close to his heart as his own two children, and quite possibly saved the marriage of Arbaaz and Pyara into the bargain.

Also, he had an agent, and not just any agent. The most promising Assassin it had ever been his fortune to train.

Sixteen

Two years later Jayadeep, now The Ghost in name and deed, knelt astride the upper-class pleasure seeker in the churchyard at Marylebone and raised the short sword, ready to deliver the death blow.

And then, just as he had on the night of his blooding, he froze.

Froze. In the face of the moment. His mind went back to the open mouth of Dani, the blood-streaked dull gleam of his father's blade inside the dying man's mouth and he saw again the light blink out in Dani's eyes and knew he had watched death: fast and brutal and delivered remorselessly. He could not bring himself to do it.

The toff saw his chance. The man had never fought a fair fight in his life. Any military service would have been spent toasting his good fortune in the officer's mess while the lower orders went out to die in the name of his Queen. But like any other living being, he had an instinct for living, and it told him that his attacker's moment of hesitation had given him his best chance to survive.

He bucked and writhed. He thrust his hips with such

sudden, desperate strength that it reminded The Ghost briefly of being back at home, taming wild ponies as a child. Then he found himself thrown to the side, still dazed, but with his mind sent in a turmoil by this latest failure of nerve. The short sword tumbled from his fingers and the toff made a dive for it, a cry of triumph escaping his lips at the same time. "Aha!" And then the toff swung about, ready to use the blade on The Ghost, and as amazed by the sudden favorable turn of events as he was enthusiastic to take advantage of them. "You little bastard," he spat as he lunged forward, arms straight, the point of the sword aimed for The Ghost's throat.

It never got there. From their left came a cry and the night tore open to reveal the woman, her long gray hair flying as she came shrieking from the darkness and barreled into the toff with all her might.

As attacks went, it wasn't pretty. It wasn't even decisive. But it was devastatingly effective and with a shout of surprise and pain and anger, the high-class lout was sent tumbling into gravestones. He tried to raise the cutlass again but the woman was there first, jumping on his sword arm and breaking it with an audible snap then using her other foot to stamp on his face so that for a second it looked as though she were dancing on a carpet of toff.

The man pulled away, snarling, his face a mask of fresh blood as he grabbed for the blade with his good arm and rose at the same time. Off balance the woman fell, and the tables were suddenly turned again, the sword about to have its say, but The Ghost had gathered his senses and he wasn't about to let the high-class yokel finish what he had started, and he struck, ramming the flat of his hand into the shoulder of the man's wounded arm, causing him to spin and scream in pain at the same time.

The scream was abruptly cut off as The Ghost delivered his second blow—the death strike—again with the heel of the hand but this time even harder and into the spot just below the toff's nose, breaking it and sending fragments of bone into the brain, killing him instantly.

There was a thump as the unlucky aristocrat hit his head on a gravestone on the way down and came to rest on the untended grass. Dark runnels of blood and brain fluid trickled from his nostrils. His eyelids flickered as he died.

The Ghost stood, shoulders rising and falling to catch his breath. Sprawled by a nearby headstone, the old woman watched him, and for a long moment the two of them regarded each other cautiously: this strange gray-haired old lady, thin-faced and weathered and bloody from the beating, and this strange young Indian man, filthy from his day's work at the dig. Both were clad in torn and dirty clothes. Both exhausted and bruised from battle.

"You saved my life," he said, presently. His words seemed to evaporate in the silence and gloom of the graveyard, and the woman, feeling reassured that he wasn't a man on a killing spree and about to do her in with a final flourish of nocturnal bloodlust, pulled herself painfully up to rest on one arm.

"I was only able to save your life because you saved mine," she said through broken teeth and raw and bloody lips.

He could tell she was badly injured. The way she held

a hand to her side, she probably had a broken rib or two. The wrong movement and it might easily puncture a lung.

"Can you breathe all right?" He scrambled over the body of the toff to the grave marker where she lay and put gentle hands to her flank.

"Hey," she protested, suddenly flustered again, thinking maybe she might have been a bit premature in relaxing, "what the bloody hell do you think you're doing?"

"I'm trying to help you," he said distractedly, feeling for broken bones, then adding, "You need to come with me."

"Now look here, you. Don't you be going and getting any ideas . . ."

"What else do you suggest? We have a dead man here and three injured men back there, and somewhere is yet another man who's either going to be looking for the constables or reinforcements or maybe both. And you're injured. Stay here by all means, but I'd prefer it if you didn't."

She looked at him warily. "Well, where are you going to take me? Have you got a boardinghouse somewhere? You don't look too prosperous."

"No," he said, "it's not quite a boardinghouse."

At this he gave a wry smile, and to the woman, whose name was Maggie, it was quite a sight to see, like the sun peeking through the clouds on an overcast day. She was in her sixties but perhaps because he had saved her life and perhaps because of that sun-and-moonlight smile, Maggie fell just a little bit under his spell, and she accompanied him to the tunnel that very night. From him she learned his name was Bharat and he worked as a laborer at the railway works up near Regents Park.

She rather took to life at the tunnel. At night she and The Ghost slept in an alcove back-to-back for warmth: together, but alone with their thoughts, and she never gave much consideration to the other men who were there that night. Two of the men were too busy being fed by uncaring sanatorium staff to care, but two men were still out there. The last bodyguard and the surviving toff had also seen The Ghost in action. They, too, knew he was a most unusual young man.

Seventeen

When Abberline made a return trip to Belle Isle, it was with the ridicule of his fellow bobbies still ringing in his ears.

Not so long ago they'd been calling him "Fresh-faced Freddie" because of his enthusiasm and tireless pursuit of justice, and on that score they were right: he had no wife or family; he was devoted to his job, and it was true that he did regard his colleagues as men who could always be depended upon to take the path of least resistance.

But what was it they were calling him now? "The no-body bobby." "The cadaverless copper." Or, slight alteration, "the copper without a corpse." None were witty or funny. In fact, as far as Abberline could tell, they consisted solely of an alliterative connection between one word for a dead body and another word for a law-enforcement officer. But even knowing that didn't help. It failed to alleviate the considerable pain of his colleagues' taunts, not to mention the fact that when all was said and done, they had a point. He had, after all, *lost* a body. And without a body there might as well have been no murder. Which meant . . .

He really wanted to find that body.

He found himself traipsing back into Belle Isle, without the benefit of a horse and cart this time, but a little wiser and more wary of any surprises the slum might have to offer. Over his shoulder was slung a sack. In there was his secret weapon.

He came deeper into Belle Isle, where the stench from the factory and the slaughterhouse was almost overwhelming. Today the denizens of the rookery were hidden by a dense fog. Proper slum fog, it billowed and boomed threateningly, and within it danced flakes of soot as well as thicker, eddying clouds of lung-choking smoke. Devil's breath.

Every now and then Abberline would see shapes in the fog, and he began to get a sense of figures gathering, tracking his progress as he came deeper and deeper into this godforsaken land.

Good. That was just how he wanted it. He required an audience for what came next.

By now he was at the spot where the children had halted his cart and where, presumably, they had made the switch: his dead body for an equally lifeless pony.

He stopped. "Ahoy there," he called, catching himself by surprise, unsure what had compelled him to talk like a sailor. "You'll remember me, no doubt. I'm the plum whose cadaver you stole."

It was possible he imagined it, but even so—was that a *titter* he heard from within the veil of darkness?

"I need to speak to the young lad who petted my horse the other day. See, it occurs to me that someone put you up to that caper. And I would dearly like to know who."

The fog stayed silent. Its secrets safe.

"Did he pay you?" pressed Abberline. "Well, then I'll pay you again . . ." He jingled coins in his palm, the noise a soft, tinkling bell in the suffocating stillnesss.

There was a pause, and Abberline was about to unveil his secret weapon when at last came a reply, and a young, disembodied voice said, "We're scared of what he'll do."

"I understand that," replied Abberline, peering into the murk in what he thought was the right direction. "He threatened you, no doubt. But I'm afraid you find your-selves in a location known as between a rock and a hard place, because if I leave here without the information I need, then I'll be coming back, and I won't be alone. I'll be returning with one of them covered carts you see, the ones passing in and out of the workhouse gates . . ." He paused, for dramatic effect. "On the other hand, if I'm given the information I want, then I'll forget about the workhouse carts, I'll leave this money behind, and what's more . . ."

He hoisted the sack from over his shoulder, placed it on the ground and took a cricket bat and ball that he held up. "These as well. No more playing cricket with a kitten's head, not when you get your hands on these little beau-ties. Cost a pretty penny, I can tell you—you won't find a better set."

The response came again, causing Abberline to jerk his head this way and that, feeling at a distinct disadvan-tage as he tried to pinpoint the source of the sound.

"We're frightened of what he'll do," said the young voice. "He's like a demon."

Abberline felt his pulse quicken, knowing for sure he'd been right to suspect something out of the ordinary about this murder.

"I've made my offer," he called back to his unseen intermediary. "On the one hand I have gifts. On the other I have dire consequences. And I can tell you this: as well as returning with the workhouse carts, I'll put it about that I was given the information I needed anyway. The wrath of this demon—and he's not a demon, you know, he's just a man, just like me—may well fall upon you anyway."

He waited for the fog to make its decision.

At last it billowed and parted, and from it stepped the same boy who had stopped him the other day. Dirty face. Rags. A hollowed out, hungry expression. This was a child whose appointment with the grave was surely imminent. Abberline felt bad for the way the boy and others like him were used and abused by him and men like him. He felt bad for threatening them with the workhouse when threats and cold and hunger were all they knew.

"I mean you no harm, you have my word," he said. He laid down the bat and ball on the ground between them.

The boy looked down at the cricket gear then back at the policeman. Abberline sensed the expectancy of figures cloaked by the fog. "You'll be angry we took your body," the boy said, with the reticence and caution of painful experience.

"I'm not best pleased you took my body, no, you're right about that," conceded Abberline. "But listen, I understand why you did it. Let me tell you this, if I were in your shoes right now, I would have done the exact same thing. I'm not here to judge you. I just want the truth."

The boy took a step forward, more to acknowledge a growing trust of Abberline than for any other reason. "There's not much more to say, sir. You was right. We was paid to distract you in your duties and trade the corpse for the pony. We wasn't told why, and nor did we ask. A handful of chink was what we got for delivering the body."

"And the gun?"

"I didn't see no gun, sir."

"It was in the dead man's pocket."

"Then it stayed with him, sir."

"And where did you deliver this body?"

The boy hung his head. Instead of answering he raised a hand to indicate where the horse slaughterers would have been, if not for the smog. "Some of us saw the man go in there with it, then not long after come out without it."

"And what did he look like, this man?" asked Abberline, trying to keep the eagerness out of his voice and failing miserably.

Not long after, the constable breathed a deep, grateful sigh of relief as he left the choking fog of Belle Isle behind and made his way back to the relatively clean air of his district. He was light some coins, a cricket bat and ball, but his conscience was thankfully clean, and he had a description of this "demon" whose motives were so much a mystery. It was a description that rang bells. He'd heard talk of a man dressed this way, this very particular—you might even say "idiosyncratic" way—who had been involved in some ructions at the Old Nichol a week or so ago.

Abberline found his pace increasing as it all came back to him. There was a bobby in another district he could speak to, who might know something about this strange figure who should be easy to spot—a strange figure who wore robes and a cowl over his head.

Eighteen

Ethan never told The Ghost anything of his home life. The Ghost knew names of course—Cecily, Jacob, Evie— but nothing distinct, apart from the fact that the twins were close to him in age. "One day I hope to introduce you," Ethan had said with a strange, unreadable expression. "But that won't be until I'm certain they're ready to join the fight."

That was as much as The Ghost knew. On the other hand, he didn't pry, and besides, he hadn't told Ethan anything of his own life away from the excavation. Ethan knew nothing of Maggie or the denizens of the tunnel, and The Ghost hadn't told his handler that he often lay awake shivering with the cold, his eyes damp with memories of Mother and Father and jasmine-scented Amritsar. Or that the dying face of Dani continued to haunt his nightmares. Lips drawn back. Bloodied teeth. A mouth full of steel and crimson.

He just continued to exist, working shifts at the dig, burying his spade in its special hiding place before going home to the tunnel, looking after the people there.

Then, four nights ago—four nights before the body was discovered at the dig, this was—The Ghost had been making his way home, when as usual he'd glanced into the churchyard—but this time saw the gravestone leaning to the left.

Instead of going back to the tunnel he turned and went in the opposite direction, heading for Paddington. It would be a long walk but he was used to it. It was all part of the daily penance he paid for his . . .

Cowardice, he sometimes thought, in those moments of great darkness before the dawn, freezing in the tunnel.

But he hadn't been a coward the night he saved Maggie, had he? He had fought for what was right.

So maybe not cowardice. At least not that. Failure to act instead. Hesitancy or unwillingness—whatever it was that had stayed his hand the night of his blooding and heaped such great shame on himself and his family name.

By rights he should have paid with his life, and would have done—were it not for the intervention of Ethan Frye. Sometimes The Ghost wondered if his ultimate act of cowardice was in accepting the older Assassin's offer.

The sounds of the street—a cacophony of hooves, of traders and a busker's sawing fiddle—all fell away as he walked, lost in thought, his mind going back to The Darkness. When the door had opened that morning it was to admit his executioner. Or so he had thought. Instead, Ethan Frye had reappeared, grinning broadly from ear to ear.

Ethan had checked himself at the sight of Jayadeep, whose expectation of death was written all over his face, and he took a seat on the straw, just as he had the previous day. Here, Ethan had explained to Jayadeep that he was required in London for an important mission; that Arbaaz had given his blessing for it.

It would involve him going undercover. "Deep cover" was how Ethan put it. Before Jayadeep went thinking this was some kind of pity mission—that Ethan was doing anything he could just to save the youngster from the Assassin's blade—Ethan told him he wanted Jayadeep because Jayadeep had been his star pupil.

"You'll remember I advised against sending you on Assassin assignment?" Ethan had said that afternoon, and Jayadeep nodded sadly. "Well, that's because I saw in you a humanity that I think can be helpful to the Brotherhood. The job I have in mind is by no means pleasant. You will become a different person, Jayadeep, all vestiges of your former self buried within the folds of a new disguise. You will no longer be Jayadeep Mir, do you understand?"

Jayadeep had nodded, and Ethan had left. Only this time the door remained open.

It took Jayadeep some moments of contemplation before he, too, rose to his feet and left the cell—stepping out of The Darkness at last.

"The mission begins now," Ethan Frye told him the next morning at dusk. The warmth Jayadeep was used to seeing in his tutor's eyes was absent. Ethan's relief at having freed Jayadeep was short-lived. Now was time to attend to the next phase of the operation.

They stood alone on a harbor wall. The hulls of boats clunked together in the gentle swell; gulls swooped and

called and preened. "I'm about to leave you," said Ethan,
looking the boy up and down, noting the pauper's clothes
he wore, just as directed. "You need to make your own
way to London. Find somewhere to live, somewhere befit-
ting a man of very limited means indeed. Here . . ." He
handed Jayadeep a small pouch of coins. "This is for your
subsistence. It won't go very far so spend it wisely. And
remember that from this moment forth you are no longer
Jayadeep Mir, son of Arbaaz and Pyara Kaur of Amritsar,
accustomed to comfort and wealth and the attendant
respect of others. When you arrive in London you arrive
as the scum of the earth, a brown-skinned outsider without a penny to your name, which, incidentally, will be
Bharat Singh. However, your alias—the name that I will
know you by—is The Ghost."

Jayadeep had thought then that he hated the name
Bharat Singh. The Ghost suited him better.

"When you have lodgings I need you to find work,"
continued Ethan, "but at a very specific place, the significance of which will become clear in some months' time.
I need you to find work at the Metropolitan Railway dig
in the northwest of the city."

Jayadeep had shaken his head in confusion. Already
there was so much to take in. A new life? A new job? All
of it in a strange, foreign land, without the benefit of his
family name, without his father's tutelage and Ethan's
guidance. It seemed impossible, what was being asked of
him, and now this. A railway?

"Don't worry about that just at the moment," said
Ethan, reading his thoughts. "All will become clear when
you're in London." He ticked things off his fingers. "First

find lodgings of some kind. Lodgings suited to a man on the very lowest rung of the social ladder; then become acquainted with your surroundings, then secure employment at the Metropolitan Railway dig. Is that clear?"

"I think so." The young man could only nod and hope these mysteries would somehow solve themselves in due course.

"Good. You have three months from today to do it. In the meantime I need you to study this . . ."

A leather-bound folder tied with a thong was duly produced from within the older Assassin's robes.

Jayadeep took it, turning it over, wondering what lay within.

"I suggest you read the papers during your passage then toss the lot in the ocean. Just make sure you have committed its contents to memory. In the meantime, we shall meet on this day three months' hence, in the gardens of the Foundling Hospital on Gray's Inn Lane Road at midnight. Now, and this is the most important aspect of what I'm telling you. Under no circumstances are you to demonstrate that you have any abilities beyond those expected of a dirt-poor seventeen-year-old Indian boy. Walk small, not tall. You're not an Assassin and you are not to behave like one. If you find yourself under threat, then be cowed. If you appear to be a more competent and able worker than your fellow men, then try less hard. The important thing for you now is to blend in every single way. You understand?"

The Ghost nodded, and water lapped at the harbor wall as the sun poked its way into a new day.

NINETEEN

Lost in his memory of his last morning at home in India, The Ghost had almost walked past the house that acted as his meeting place with his handler.

Number Twenty-three and Twenty-four Leinster Gardens, Paddington, looked just like any other houses on the street, but what only a handful of people knew—the neighbors, the builders, and, more pertinently, The Ghost and Ethan Frye—was that the two houses were in fact false fronts built to hide a hole in the ground.

It had been Charles Pearson's idea. Constructing his railway, he had come across an immediate problem, which was finding an engine suitable for use underground. An ordinary steam engine, with its usual emission, would have suffocated passengers and crew straightaway. It is unacceptable for railway operators to kill their passengers, so Mr. Pearson cast about for a solution. First he had the idea of dragging carriages through the tunnels using cables, then, when that proved impractical, came up with a plan to use atmospheric pressure. That proved impractical, too—though it was of course great fodder for the city's many satirists.

It was John Fowler who came to Mr. Pearson's rescue, in this as in so many aspects of the line. He had overseen the construction of an engine where smoke and steam would be diverted into a tank behind the engine. The only trouble was that the smoke and steam would need to be released at some point, and that was why Number 23 and 24 Leinster Gardens, W2, were set aside, so that the engines from below could, quite literally, "let off steam."

The opening of the Metropolitan Line was still over a year away, and it was here that The Ghost and Ethan Frye would meet.

"How are you?" said Ethan that night. He had been sitting on the edge of the void, staring down to where timbers crisscrossed just below his dangling boots.

The Ghost nodded but said nothing, a closed book. He took a seat next to Ethan. His bare feet dangled next to the boots of his mentor, a great darkness below them.

"You will be pleased to know we are moving to the next phase of the operation," said Ethan. "Matters are going to come to a head. You will find yourself under scrutiny. I have no doubt whatsoever that you will be followed and your credentials checked by our Templar friends. Are you confident your cover remains absolutely secure?"

The Ghost pondered whether this was the time to tell Ethan about Maggie and his unofficial guardian role at the tunnel. It was a conversation he'd carried out in his head many times, imaginary explanations where he'd tell Ethan that he hadn't intended to set himself apart, just that he had been unable to stand by and allow injustice to prevail, and one thing had led to another. Surely Ethan would . . . well, even if he didn't approve, then he would certainly understand. After all, it wasn't as though The Ghost were a recognizable public hero, news on the front page of the *Illustrated London News*.

But no. He kept his mouth shut. He said nothing and walked willingly into the next phase of the plan.

"Which is what?" he asked.

Mischief lit his master's eyes. It was a look that The Ghost had come to love when he was a child in the security of Amritsar. Now, staring down into the void in noisy, dirty London with only uncertainty ahead of him, he wasn't so sure.

"You will need to write a letter to our friend Mr. Cavanagh. You can use your knowledge of Cavanagh to establish your credentials. I'll leave the details up to you. The important thing is that you tell Mr. Cavanagh that he has a traitor in his ranks and that you hope to curry favor with him by unveiling this traitor."

Ethan nodded, his gaze fixed on the darkness below. "I see," he said, when Ethan had finished. "And what then?"

"Wait for a body to be discovered at the dig."

"When?"

"Difficult to say. In the next few days, I'd imagine, depending on the rainfall."

"I see. Am I allowed to know whose body will be discovered?"

"You remember our Templar friend, Mr. Robert Waugh."

The Ghost did indeed remember him. "The pornographer?"

"The very same. Only Mr. Waugh hasn't been altogether straight with his associates. He's been using his erotic prints to make a little extra money, a sideline I uncovered last night."

"When you killed him?"

"Oh no, I didn't kill him." Ethan slapped The Ghost heartily on the shoulder. "You did."

TWENTY

As he returned from his meeting with Ethan, The Ghost reflected on the first time he became aware of the man he now saw every day at the dig. The man known primarily as Cavanagh. It was on the passage from Amritsar to England, when he had done as he was told and opened the folder given to him by Ethan on the harbor wall.

Inside was an introductory note from Ethan, explaining that the contents were dispatches copied and decoded from a Templar haul. The papers had been replaced; as far as the Assassins knew the Templars had no idea they were in possession of the information.

The dispatches had been compiled from firsthand accounts assembled by Templar documentarians, and they began innocuously enough, with a factual account of the English retreat from Kabul in 1842.

The Ghost knew all about the march from Kabul, of course. Everybody did. It was one of the most disastrous events of English military history, and the turning point of the godforsaken war in Afghanistan. Sixteen thousand soldiers, families and camp followers had embarked on a ninety-mile retreat from Kabul to Jalalabad in January 1842. Only a handful made it.

Not only did they have food for just five days, but their leader, Major-General William Elphinstone—otherwise known as Elphy Bey—had a head as soft as his body was frail. Not only was he idiotic, but he was gullible and believed every lie that the Afghan leader, Akbar Khan, told him.

Akbar Khan told Elphy Bey a lot of lies. In return for the British Army's handing over the majority of their muskets, Khan guaranteed safe passage, as well as offering an escort through the passes. He also gave assurances that the sick and wounded left in Kabul would be unharmed.

It took Khan roughly an hour to go back on his word. The march had only just left the cantonment when his men moved in to loot, burn tents, and put the wounded to the sword. Meanwhile, the rear guard was attacked. Porters, camp followers and Indian soldiers were butchered, and with little or no resistance from the column, the Afghans began mounting increasingly brazen sorties, swiftly devastating the baggage train. They were barely out of Kabul and the march left behind a trail of trunks and corpses.

Very few tents were taken on the march, and they were reserved for women, children and officers. That night most lay down to sleep in the snow and by next morning the ground was littered with the corpses of those who had frozen to death in the night. Frostbitten and starving, the march pressed on, hoping to beat the worst of the weather and withstand the constant Afghan attacks.

For reasons known only to himself, Elphy Bey ordered

a rest at just two o'clock in the afternoon, when what he should have done was heed the advice of his officers and press on through the dangerous Khord-Kabul Pass. Perhaps the old boy had simply lost his mind completely, for his decision meant handing the pass to the Afghans whose snipers took up position on the ledges, while their cavalry readied themselves for more sport.

Sure enough, shots began to ring out as the column entered the pass the following morning, and the march stopped as negotiations were carried out. Akbar Khan agreed to let the column through in exchange for hostages, but his deceit knew no bounds, for after the hostages were handed over, the firing began again, while mounted tribesmen rode into the column, scattering followers, hacking down civilians and soldiers and even carrying off children.

Three thousand lost their lives in the pass, and all supplies were lost. That night the remnants of the march camped with just four small tents and no fuel or food. Hundreds died of exposure.

The killing continued over the next few days. To escape the massacre some killed themselves while others deserted, though they were not allowed to escape by the Afghans, who only spared those they might ransom later—the officers, wives and children. Soldiers, servants and followers were butchered.

By the fifth day the column numbered just three thousand—five hundred of them soldiers. Elphy Bey gave himself up, later to die in captivity, while the wives and families surrendered also. Still the march struggled on, numbers dwindling, and was attacked at the Jugdulluk

Crest, suffering appalling casualties. Running battles took place overnight, in feet of snow, until the survivors got to Gandamak, by which time they numbered fewer than four hundred.

They took up position on a hill, but found themselves surrounded by Afghans, who commanded them to surrender. "Not bloody likely!" scoffed a sergeant, and his retort would become something of an English national catchphrase. He was as good as his word, though, so the Afghan snipers went to work before a final attack.

Jugdulluk Crest was no battle; it was a massacre. Six officers escaped, five of whom were cut down on the road to Jalalabad. Just one, William Brydon, made it. Part of his skull had been sheared off by an Afghan sword stroke but he'd survived the blow thanks to a copy of *Blackwoods Magazine* stuffed into his hat. "Never knew this old bit of Lolland drivel could come in so handy," he'd apparently remarked.

Of the sixteen thousand who had set off from Kabul six days previously, he was the only one to reach his destination.

Except . . . not quite. The story of good old William Brydon making it alone to Jalalabad was a good one—such a good one that it loomed large in the public consciousness for some time. Sadly, however, it was not quite the truth, because there were other survivors. Just that the methods and means of their survival were not quite as noble as the stoicism of Dr. William Brydon. A man will do anything to survive, to live to see another sunrise, feel the lips of his wife and children, laugh along with a drink in his hand. So, yes, there were others who lived through that disastrous march, but their exploits were not to be applauded, celebrated, sung about nor later immortalized by artists. They were not even "exploits" at all, in the sense that the word suggests adventure and derring-do. They were acts of survival, pure and simple. Dirty and mean and ruthless and executed at a dreadful cost to others.

And so it was that on the march there was a certain commander who went by the name of Colonel Walter Lavelle. This man Lavelle belonged to the Order of the Knights Templar. He was not an especially high-ranking Templar, not a person of interest to the Assassin Brotherhood but known to them nevertheless.

Shortly before the march was due to leave Kabul, a corporal by the name of Cavanagh inveigled himself with Walter Lavelle.

"I wonder if I could have a word, sir," said this Cavanagh on the morning of the march.

Seeing a certain seriousness and, if he was honest with himself, a little danger in this man's eyes, Lavelle had nodded, despite the fact that the man was a mere corporal, and the two men moved to the shelter of a cypress tree, away from where servants and followers were loading carts, and horses struggled beneath the weight of panniers and saddlebags. Indeed, the courtyard was a hive of industry. Above the sound of men cursing and struggling and orders being issued and women wringing their hands and crying, came the constant exhortations of Lady Florentia Sale, the wife of Major General Robert Henry Sale, a woman in whose honor the word "redoubtable" might well have been minted. Lady Sale left nobody in doubt that she considered this march a mere afternoon excursion, a matter of little import for the might of the English army and that to think otherwise was treacherously un-English. "Oh, do cease your bawling, Florence, and make yourself useful," she would exhort. "You there, have a care. That is my very best Madeira wine. And you, watch that china or my Jalalabad soirées will be somewhat lacking in finesse. I'm planning my first one for two days' hence. What a hoot it will be to meet the good ladies of Jalalabad."

Away by the cypress tree, Corporal Cavanagh turned to Lavelle and in a dead-eyed way said, "She's a fool."

They were well out of earshot but even so, the colonel spluttered indignantly, as colonels were in the habit of doing. "Have you gone mad, sah? Have you taken leave of every single one of all your senses at bloody once? Do you know who you're talking to, man? Do you know who you're talking *about*? That is . . ."

"I know full well who I'm talking to and who I'm talking about, sir," replied Cavanagh evenly (by gad the man was a cool fish and no mistake), "and it's precisely because I know who I'm talking to that I feel I can talk openly. Forgive me if I misjudged the situation and I shall retire to continue preparing the men of my section."

He made as though to walk away from the cypress tree, but Lavelle stopped him, curious to hear what was on the impertinent corporal's mind. "I'll hear you out, man. Just mind your tongue is all."

But Cavanagh did nothing of the sort. He planned to speak his mind and speak it he did. "Do you know how far it is to Jalalabad? It's ninety miles. We have an army of fourteen thousand, but hardly a quarter of them are soldiers, the rest of them a great rabble: porters, servants, women and children. Hardly a fighter among them. Do you know what the conditions are like, sir? We'll be marching through a foot of snow on the worst ground on earth and the temperature freezing. And what of Akbar Khan? He's been in the hills, going from this chief to that, gathering support for further hostilities. Khan will not stand by his word. As soon as we step outside those gates he will begin taking us apart. Lady Sale thinks she'll be having her first Jalalabad soirée in two days' time. I say we'll be lucky to make that march in two weeks. We don't have arms, ammunition, or enough food or supplies. The march is doomed, sir, and we are doomed with it unless we join forces to take action."

He went on to tell Lavelle that he had a reasonable command of Pushtu, and suggested that he take a position as Lavelle's batman. But Lavelle hadn't finished spluttering, and he did a bit of blustering as well, and when that was over he dismissed Cavanagh with a flea in his ear, telling him not to be so impertinent and to keep his treacherous thoughts of desertion to himself.

"You must have hoped to curry favor with me, y'wretched lickspittle," he roared. "For whatever reason I cannot imagine, but I'm telling you, I remain General Elphinstone's faithful servant to the very last."

By the first night of the march it was clear that Akbar Khan had indeed gone back on his word and that Elphy Bey was a fool. And as the column rang to the screams of wounded men and the Afghan sorties continued, and poor unfortunates froze where they lay, a terrified and craven Lavelle crept into Cavanagh's tent to ask if the corporal would agree to be his batman.

"Me, a mere wretched lickspittle?" said Cavanagh, his face betraying nothing of the dark satisfaction he felt at the look of panic on the colonel's face. He demurred and refused, acting offended, until he elicited an apology from the quaking colonel.

The next morning, as British Lancers rode against the Afghans in a futile attempt to deter further attacks, Cavanagh, Lavelle and a faithful sepoy whose name is not recorded left the company for good.

Their path through the hills and passes was treacherous. They didn't dare get too near the column for fear of being seen by either the British soldiers or their Afghan attackers, but neither did they want to stray too far from established routes. The Afghanistan countryside was well-known for being one of the most hostile on the face of the known world, never more so than in the unforgiving frost of January, and what's more, the men feared falling into the hands of far-flung tribes.

They had feed for their mounts, but as they made their way through the cliffs and peaks of the pass, it became clear that they had seriously miscalculated when it came to food for themselves. So when, in the late afternoon of the third day, the chill breeze brought to them the smell of cooking meat, their stomachs were as alert as their senses.

Sure enough they soon came upon five Afghan hillmen on the track. They were tending to a fire in a clearing, over which they were roasting a goat, with a sheer rockface on one side of them and a vertiginous drop on the other.

The three deserters took cover immediately. Like all English soldiers they maintained a healthy respect for the fighters of Afghanistan—theirs was a warrior nation: the men were skilled and fearsome and the women notorious for their ghastly methods of execution, with flaying and "the death of a thousand cuts" among the least sadistic of them.

So the trio stayed hidden behind a large boulder: the sepoy, implacable, a picture of steely resolve despite knowing how the Afghans treated their Sikh prisoners; Lavelle wordlessly ceding authority to Cavanagh, who thanked God the tribesmen had not thought to post a lookout and, in a series of quick glances, took stock of the situation.

There was no making a detour around the position, that was for sure. In order to continue along the path, Cavanagh, Lavelle and the sepoy would have to engage them in combat—either that or return to the column and explain their absence and most likely be shot for desertion.

Combat it was, then.

There were five of them, wearing skullcaps or turbans, and long coats. Tethered nearby were horses loaded with supplies, including the carcass of a second goat. The Afghan rifles, called jezzails, were arranged in a tepee shape not far from the campfire.

Cavanagh knew the jezzail well. Homemade weapons, their long barrels gave them a considerable range advantage over the British Brown Bess musket used by Elphinstone's men. These Afghan warriors would use their jezzails to great effect against the column, with expert snipers firing a deadly barrage of bullets, nails and even pebbles down upon the beleaguered retreat some 250 meters below. They were intricately decorated, as was the Afghan custom; one of them was even adorned with human teeth.

However, noted Cavanagh with relief, the jezzail was a muzzle-loaded weapon, and by the looks of things those stacked in front of them were not primed. Either way, the tribesmen would reach for the curved Khyber knives at their waists. Excellent close-quarter weapons.

Cavanagh looked at his two companions. The sepoy, as he knew, was a decent shot. He wasn't sure about Lavelle, but he himself had trained at the Domenico Angelo Tremamondo fencing-master academy and was an expert swordsman.

(Here, The Ghost came across a note, presumably left by whichever Assassin curator had assembled the dossier. The correspondent wondered how a mere corporal had studied at the great Angelo School of Arms in Carlisle House, Soho in London, where the aristocracy were tutored in swordsmanship. Or, perhaps, to turn the question around, how a graduate of that particular academy had ended up a mere corporal? The note was appended with an inscription from Ethan, a single word The Ghost knew well from the dreaded Latin lessons Ethan had insisted upon as part of his tutelage. *"Cave"* it said, meaning beware.)

Cavanagh knew this was his chance to impress upon Lavelle that he was more than a mere deserter. The day before, when Lavelle had asked him why he might wish to curry favor, the question had gone unanswered. But the truth of it was that Cavanagh was well aware of Lavelle's position within the Order and wished to take advantage of it. So Cavanagh drew his saber silently, gave his own service pistol to the sepoy and indicated for Lavelle to ready his.

When the two men were in place he indicated for them to take the two tribesmen on the left.

Next he rose slightly on his haunches, stretching out his calves. The last thing he needed was his legs seizing up when he made his move.

Which he did. Trusting Lavelle and the sepoy to be accurate and putting his faith in the element of surprise and his own not-inconsiderable swordsmanship, Cavanagh sprang from behind the boulder to do battle.

He saw the soldier on the left spin and scream at the same time as he heard the pistol shot from behind, then came a second shot, this one not so accurate but enough to lift the next man off his feet and take him down clutching at his stomach. As the second tribesman turned and snatched for the Khyber knife at his waist, Cavanagh reached him and attacked with the saber, a single chopping blow to the neck that opened the carotid artery, then he stepped nimbly away to avoid a rhythmic pumping fountain of blood.

The Englishman had chosen his first strike deliberately. Afghan warriors were as tough and unflappable as they come, but even they could not fail to be disturbed by the sudden appearance of bright arterial spray arcing and splattering in the dying light of the afternoon. It sent the other two into a state of disarray, one of them wiping his comrade's blood from his face with one hand even as he reached for his curved knife with the other.

His knife cleared the belt, but that was all. Cavanagh spun his own blade in midair as he swung backhand, slicing open the luckless hillman's throat. The man's skull-cap tumbled from his head as he folded to the dirt with blood sheeting down his front and a final wet death rattle but there was no time for Cavanagh to bring his saber to bear and take the last man. He heard a shot from behind and felt the air part, but the shot went wild. Too late he saw the Khyber knife streak from outside of his peripheral vision and though there was no immediate pain he felt the hot wash of blood coursing down his face.

(A note from the dossier curator: "N.b. Cavanagh bears this scar to this day.")

Had the Afghan pressed home his advantage he might have made it out of the clearing alive, and maybe even with the blood of a British corporal to show for his pains. Instead he chose to make a break for the horses. Possibly he hoped to escape and warn his friends; maybe he knew of a loaded pistol secreted within the saddlebags. Unfortunately for him the sight of a terrified man running toward them was too much for the normally imperturbable Afghan steeds and they reared up, pulled their tethers free and scattered.

Hell's teeth, cursed Cavanagh, as he watched the horses, the supplies, not to mention the second goat carcass, go scarpering out of sight along the frosty track.

Meanwhile, the Afghan wheeled, his teeth bared and

his Khyber knife slashing. But Cavanagh went on guard saber style, his right hand raised, the point of the sword tipping downward and it was with some satisfaction that he saw the tribesman's eyeballs swivel up and to the left a second before he buried the tip of his blade into the man's face.

In the aftermath of the battle was silence. The gutshot Afghan writhed and moaned, and Cavanagh delivered the *coup de grace*, wiping his saber clean on the man's robes, which were already so bloodstained as to be useless.

"Quick, grab whatever clothes you can before the blood ruins them," he told Lavelle and the sepoy, who had emerged from behind the rock. The sepoy had acquitted himself well, just as Cavanagh always thought he would, and Cavanagh congratulated him. Lavelle congratulated Cavanagh. Nobody congratulated Lavelle.

The three men ate heartily of goat, which, having been left unattended during the conflict, was slightly overdone. Not that it mattered to the ravenous British. They ate until their bellies were full of overcooked goat, and after that they donned the robes and turbans of the dead, cobbling together outfits that didn't show obvious bloodstains. When that was done, they hid the bodies as best they could, rounded up what horses they could find and continued on their way.

For a day they rode, staying ahead of the retreating column, a mile or so as the crow flies. Despite the distance they heard the constant crack of shot, even the occasional shriek of pain that was carried to them on the chill wind. Cavanagh began to grow in confidence. They drew farther away from prescribed routes, finding a new track higher up the rock pass. And then, on the afternoon of the fifth day, they came upon the outskirts of another, much larger traveling encampment. And they faced their most difficult test yet.

TWENTY-ONE

Thinking about it later, Cavanagh would come to the conclusion that they had happened upon a roaming settlement belonging to one of Akbar's warlords. From such a base the chieftain could dispatch snipers to take up position on the passes above the column where they would use their jezzails to rain devastation on the poor marchers below. He could also send riders to make their way down near-hidden paths to the floor of the pass below where they could make terrifying, damaging charges into the rear, less-well-guarded sections of the column, mercilessly cutting down servants, women and children and plundering what few supplies were left.

It was here that Cavanagh's knowledge of Pushtu came in handy. Indeed, it saved their lives. Coming over the brow of a hill, with their horses slipping and sliding on a frosty, flinty path, they were hailed by a lookout.

Thank God. The man had taken one look at their garb and from a distance taken them to be Afghans. When he called hello, Cavanagh's quick thinking once again saved the day, for instead of showing surprise and taking flight, he kept his composure and replied in kind.

At his signal, the three men came to a halt. Some two hundred yards in front of them the lookout had risen from behind a rocky outcrop, his jezzail slung across his back. His features were indistinct as he cupped his hands to his mouth and called again in Pushtu, "Hello!"

Cavanagh's mind raced: there was no way they could get too close; they would be recognized as imposters. But the Afghans would mount a pursuit if they turned tail and fled, and being the superior horsemen it would in all likelihood be a short pursuit indeed.

Sitting beside him, Lavelle flicked nervous eyes. "What the hell are we going to do, man?"

"Shut up," hissed Cavanagh, oblivious to Lavelle's outrage. "I'm thinking. Just whatever happens, don't say another word and follow my lead."

Meanwhile, the lookout, again with his hands cupped to his mouth was calling to unseen others behind him, and other faces appeared from the landscape. Six or seven men. Christ, they'd almost ridden slap-bang into the middle of the camp. They now stood staring across the space between the two groups, one or two of them shielding their eyes against the dying winter sun, all no doubt wondering why their three visitors had stopped on the perimeter of the camp.

Still Cavanagh's mind reached for answers. Couldn't run. Couldn't advance. His attempts to answer any further interrogation would surely expose his shaky grasp of Pushtu.

One of the men unslung his rifle, but Cavanagh

preempted what might happen next and called out to him before he could bring the weapon to bear. "My good friend, we come from hounding the British cowards. With us is a captured Sikh scum. A man trying to adopt our dress and escape as a deserter."

From over the way came Afghan laughter. Unschooled in Pushtu, the sepoy sat, oblivious to what awaited him. Loyal, faithful.

"What are you saying, man?" demanded Lavelle.

"Quiet," snapped Cavanagh back.

His voice rose again. "Here. We'll leave our prize with you as a gift for your women and take our leave if we may."

With that he drew his stolen Khyber knife and then in one quick movement pretended to cut binding at the sepoy's hands. Confused, the sepoy turned in his saddle to face Cavanagh, face clouding with confusion. "Sir?" But Cavanagh reached down, snatched the man's foot and dragged it upward, unseating him at the same time as with one almighty and merciless slice of the Khyber knife blade, he slashed open the desperate man's Achilles tendon.

As the Afghans over the way jeered and laughed, Cavanagh waved to say good-bye, and he and Lavelle pulled their horses around. At the same time the sepoy tried to pull himself up, but his torn-open heel folded beneath him, gushing blood, and he was sent back to the ground, mewling and pleading, "Sir? Sir?"

But they left him there, to his fate at the hands of the Afghan women. Flaying alive or death of a thousand cuts. They left the nameless sepoy there, to die an unspeakable death, so that they might save themselves.

"Christ, man, that was cold," said Lavelle later, when they had made camp in the rocks above the pass.

"It was him or us," said Cavanagh.

That night the sound of gunfire came to them, and both men fancied that they could also hear the screams of the sepoy in the far distance as the Afghan women began their work.

TWENTY-TWO

The Ghost had seethed with hatred for Cavanagh, a man
for whom he had, up until that precise moment, developed something approaching a respect.

A month or so later, when he faced the men in the
churchyard, he understood the strength of the impulse
to survive. That he understood. But what he could not
understand (and maybe this was why he was never truly
cut out for a life of bloodshed) was the ability to sacrifice
another man's life, to let another man die in your stead.
Not only that, but a man who'd shown you nothing but
loyalty.

He wondered, did the face of that sepoy haunt Cava
nagh in his dreams? Did he feel anything at all?

The dossier had gone on. Cavanagh and Lavelle had
turned up at Jalalabad a day after William Brydon made
his historic appearance. Their survival went unheralded,
shrouded as it was in rumor and suspicion.

Despite their insistence, and the fact that they steadfastly
stuck to a prepared and detailed story about becoming
detached from a cavalry section and losing their way, the

gossip at the Jalalabad Cantonment was that the two men had deserted. Nothing about Lavelle suggested any other explanation but when, on April 17, 1842, the Jalalabad garrison attacked Akbar Khan's lines, Cavanagh acquitted himself well, proving indomitable in combat.

His movements were next noted sometime after his return to England, by which time he had gained a position for himself within the Templar Order. It was shortly after this that Colonel Walter Lavelle met with a fatal accident. According to the dossier the Assassins believed it was Cavanagh who had not only recommended but carried out the execution.

Up until this point, The Ghost had been wondering where he came in. Why was he reading about this man Cavanagh?

Then it became clear. The next time Cavanagh appeared as a person of interest to the Assassins was when, quite out of the blue, he had secured an appointment to the company building the world's first underground-railway line. He became a director at the Metropolitan Railway, directly involved with the excavation. The company's "man on the ground," as it were.

Now The Ghost was beginning to understand.

When he arrived in England he did as he'd been told by Ethan. He found lodgings at the tunnel and he, too, gained an appointment to the Metropolitan dig though in a rather less exalted position than his quarry. And so it was that he had been there at New Road to see the shaft sunk. He had seen wooden houses on wheels come into view, then wagons piled high with timbers and planks, men armed with pickaxes and shovels marching by their side like an oncoming army.

He had bought a spade from a drunken man in a pub, etched the name of "Bharat Singh" into it and joined them. He had helped to enclose hundreds of yards of roadway, when New Road had been transformed from a part of London's history to a significant part of its future. Horses, carpenters and troops of laborers had arrived; the sound of pickaxes, spades and hammers and the passing of steam began, a clamor that was rarely to cease, day or night.

Huge timber structures sprung up at intervals along the center of the road, spots for opening shaft holes were marked out, iron buckets had been brought on the roadway, buckets that were dragged up, peeled reluctantly away from the surface of the earth and carted off to be tilted down a gaping pit, the noise of it like a storm, another distant rumble to add to the din that was to reign from then on.

The Ghost had been there for all of the problems encountered by the line. On paper it had been a simple— well, a relatively simple—operation: Paddington to Euston Road and the Fleet Valley to the city. But gas pipes, water mains and sewers had all stood in its way, and along Euston Road they had discovered that the land was made up of sand and gravel that had to be drained, while at Mount Pleasant the usual policy of cut-and-cover had been abandoned and a tunnel dug.

Meanwhile, The Ghost had watched the world around him change. He had seen the squalid streets of the Fleet Valley destroyed. A thousand homes were demolished and the twelve thousand people who lived there (a damning statistic by itself) displaced to other slums.

Some of them, of course, had come to the Thames Tunnel. Perhaps some of them had enjoyed the benefit of the benign form of protection that The Ghost provided there. There was a circularity to the process that he could appreciate.

At the site his bare feet were often the subject of a remark, and of course his skin tone marked him apart, but otherwise he never did anything to stand out. He never attempted a jump he knew he could make. He never carried loads he knew he was capable of bearing. If a joke was cracked, he laughed. Not too loudly, and not distinctively. This was how he maintained his cover, by ensuring that it remained solid at all times. So that when in the future he was called upon to penetrate the organization further it would withstand any amount of examination. He must be Bharat, the dirt-poor but conscientious Indian worker, below contempt and thus above suspicion. He must maintain that cover at all times.

Maintaining his cover was essential to staying alive.

The first day he clapped eyes on Cavanagh, he had been manning one of the buckets, dragging it from the mouth of the trench to deposit its contents into a cart. Over the way he'd seen the door to the mobile office on wheels open and a familiar face emerge. Not Cavanagh, but Marchant, who managed the roster, ticked off names and passed the worksheets to the wages clerks who appeared every Friday, setting up at a desk and handing out coins with pained expressions, as though it was their very own money. Oh yes, The Ghost knew Marchant. A weasel of a man with a wheedling, nasal voice.

And then came Cavanagh himself.

Just as The Ghost had been led to believe, Cavanagh had a horizontal scar below his right eye, almost two inches long. The eyes themselves were hard. The chin set. In all the times that The Ghost ever saw Cavanagh, it was impossible to know what he was thinking.

Which was?

"I want to find out what they're up to," Ethan had said.

They had met on the grounds of the Foundling Hospital, just as arranged on the harbor wall at home in India. Ethan had led The Ghost to a folly in the hospital grounds, where they were obscured from view by foliage. There the master had taken a good look at his former pupil, eyeing up the boy's rags, his general demeanor.

"Very good," said Ethan, when he'd finished giving the boy the once-over. "Very good. You look the part, that much is certain."

"I have a position at the dig," said The Ghost, "just as instructed."

"I know," said Ethan. "I've been keeping tabs on you."

"Is that wise?"

"Why wouldn't it be?"

In response, The Ghost shrugged and spread his hands. "Anything that increases the chance of my deception being uncovered is to be discouraged."

"I see I taught you well." Ethan smiled.

"You need to practice what you preach."

"You'll excuse me if I don't accept advice from a young pup like your good self." Ethan smiled in pretense of a little friendly badinage, but his eyes were flinty.

"You know," said The Ghost, "you shouldn't sit with your chin on your leading hand."

"Oh?" Ethan's eyebrows raised in surprise. "Pupil has turned teacher, has he? You have another lesson in Assassincraft for me?"

"You risk an accident with the blade."

"I deceive any potential opponent."

"There are no opponents here."

"Now who's being careless?"

"I didn't say you were being careless, Master. Just that mistakes can happen. They can happen to the best of us."

He hadn't meant that last statement to sound as significant as it did, and for a second he allowed himself to hope that Ethan might not pick up on it, but of course, what Ethan lacked in focus he more than made up for in intuition and perception. "You think me careless?"

"I didn't say that."

"You didn't need to."

The Ghost glanced away. He had been looking forward to this meeting. Part of him anticipated his master's praise. Somewhere along the line—and he wasn't even sure how—the conversation had taken a wrong turn.

When he turned back to look at his old friend and tutor, it was to find Ethan regarding him with hard, baleful eyes, but he decided to ask a favor anyway. "May I try on your hidden blade, Master?" he asked.

Ethan softened. "And why would you want to do that? Check it for maintenance, perhaps?"

"I'd like the feel of it once again, to remind myself of what I am."

"To remind yourself you are an Assassin? Or to remind yourself of home?"

The Ghost smiled, unsure of the answer. "Maybe a little of both."

Then Ethan frowned. "Well, I'd rather not, it's perfectly calibrated."

The boy nodded understandingly though sadly.

"Oh, get the stick out of your arse," exploded Ethan. "Of course you can have a go." And he yanked up the sleeve of his robes and reached for the buckles . . .

Sometime later the two men, having resolved their unspoken differences, sat in silence. The Ghost could see the bronze glowing lights of the Foundling Hospital from his seat inside the folly and thought how peaceful it seemed and how difficult it was to believe that just a few hundred yards away lay the turbulence of the Metropolitan Line dig. The new underground line was like a bent arm, and right now they sat somewhere near the elbow: Grays Inn Lane Road, New Road—a world of turmoil.

Beside him, Ethan finished recalibrating his blade. That familiar snicking sound it made when he ejected it. Ethan was right—wearing it hadn't made The Ghost yearn for his life as an Assassin. It had made him yearn for home.

The older Assassin flexed his hand to check for unintended discharge. He slapped his hands on his thighs, satisfied all was in order.

"I wonder if now is the time to tell me the purpose of my mission," said The Ghost.

"You've guessed it has something to do with our friend Cavanagh, of course."

The Ghost nodded. "The dossier on him made interesting reading."

"His position at the Metropolitan is an example of the level of power the Templars currently hold in London. They are very much in the ascendancy. They have the advantage of knowing how weak we are, though I rather doubt they realize just how weak. 'We' in this context being myself, another member of the Brotherhood based not far away . . . and now you."

"That's it?"

"That's it, my dear boy. The best we can do to challenge their supremacy is take little potshots in the hope of diminishing some of their fringe activities. Well, we can do that and we can do this. This being, we can try to find out what their game is here."

"Here?"

"Yes, here. This area of land in the northwest of London is, we think, of interest to the Templars. We think that they are digging for something. Perhaps an artifact."

"An artifact? Like the Koh-i-Noor diamond?"

"Something like that, perhaps. Who knows? Something related to the First Civilization, Those Who Came Before. The point is, we don't know and nor do we have the resources to interrogate the issue at any higher level.

"There is an advantage to that, of course. Without our involvement the Templars have no need to suspect that we harbor any suspicions about their activities. As a result, they may get careless. Nevertheless, it's a sad state of affairs. The fact is we have no idea how deep the Order has penetrated into London society beyond a handful of names."

The Ghost nodded as though satisfied but nevertheless harboring doubts. Meanwhile, Ethan opened his robes to reveal the brown-leather strap of a documents case. He lifted the flap and pulled from it a dossier—bound in the livery of the Assassins, just as the Cavanagh file had been— and handed it to The Ghost, watching wordlessly as the younger man began to leaf through pages of information gathered on active Templars in London.

Leading the pack, of course, was Crawford Starrick, the Templar Grand Master. Owner of Starrick Industries, Starrick Telegraph Company and the Millner Company, he was once called "a great rail baron" by none other than Charles Dickens. Then there was Benjamin Raffles, the Templar Kingpin and Starrick's "head of security," as well as another kingpin, Hattie Cadwallader, the keeper of the National Gallery, who maintained Starrick's extensive art collection.

Another kingpin: Chester Swinebourne, who had apparently infiltrated the police. Philip "Plutus" Two- penny, the Governor of the Bank of England, no less; Francis Osbourne, the Bank of England manager.

Second-in-command was Lucy Thorne. She specialized in the occult. The Ghost had seen her at the dig. Starrick, too. Then there was Rupert Ferris of Ferris Ironworks.

He'd been spotted at the works as well. As had Maxwell Roth. He wasn't a Templar but had helped them set up the London gangs.

Dr. John Elliotson. Ethan knew him personally. He was the inventor of the panacea "Starrick's Soothing Syrup."

Then there was Pearl Attaway, the proprietor of Attaway Transport and a cousin to Starrick. A gang boss called Rexford Kaylock. A sleazy photographer by the name of Robert Waugh (and now, of course, The Ghost knew all about him).

Still others: Sir David Brewster, Johnnie Boiler, Malcom Millner, Edward Hodson Bayley. James Thomas Brudenell, otherwise known as "Lord Cardigan," a soldier called Lieutenant Pearce, a scientist called Reynolds . . .

The list was seemingly endless.

"This is a rather large dossier," said The Ghost at last.

Ethan smiled ruefully. "Indeed it is, and these are just the ones we know about. In opposition? Just the three of us. But we have *you*, my dear boy. One day you will be recruiting spies of your own. One of them may very well be in this motley crew we have here."

TWENTY-THREE

The night after the body was discovered, The Ghost glanced into the graveyard as he always did on his way home from the dig, and as usual his eyes sought out the gravestone through which Ethan communicated, and as usual it was . . .

Ah, no it wasn't. Not tonight. It was leaning to the right. *Danger*. Which to The Ghost meant something significant. Not that he was being followed by Cavanagh's men. He already knew that. But that Ethan was around, keeping tabs on him still.

But to more pressing matters. There were indeed men following him. One of them had left the dig a few minutes before him. As the shift-change bell rang, The Ghost had seen Marchant nod discreetly to one of the three hired hands who were constantly to be found hanging around the office or on the dig. Their names were Hardy, Smith and Other Hardy—Cavanagh's own predilection for using his surname had either rubbed off on his men or been imposed upon them—and they were passed off as payroll security. The other men called them "punishers," a certain breed of men who were expert at giving out a good hiding if you greased their palm with silver. But while The Ghost didn't doubt they were punishers of a sort, he also knew them for what they really were: Templar fighters. They were professionals, too. Big men, they were fit and alert; they didn't spend their time cracking jokes or whistling at the prostitutes who hung around by the perimeter fence touting for business. They kept their minds on the job.

But they weren't *that* good, as the commencement of their covert pursuit of The Ghost proved; they weren't good enough to hide from him. The man who left at Marchant's signal—Other Mr. Hardy—was next to be seen leaning on a barrow wearing a look of studied disinterest, like he wasn't really scanning the crowds of departing workers who thronged the street for his quarry. When he caught sight of The Ghost, Other Mr. Hardy pushed himself off his barrow and moved on with a walk that could only be described as an "amble," like he wasn't really set on staying just the right distance ahead of The Ghost.

Meanwhile, there would be another man behind him. Probably two: Smith and Hardy. And that was good, thought The Ghost, because that was just where he wanted them.

I hope you like a nice long walk, my friends, he said to himself, then spent the rest of the journey speeding up and slowing down, setting himself the challenge of making life as difficult as possible for his pursuers without actually tipping them off that he knew they were there.

Until, at last, he reached the tunnel. He'd long since left the crowds behind, of course. Ahead of him Other

Mr. Hardy was an almost lone figure now, as The Ghost approached the shaft. Some way away, the man stopped, making a pretense of needing to tie his bootlace, as The Ghost took the steps down into the tunnel rotunda. He had spent his day underground, and now he would spend his night there too.

Reaching the bottom, The Ghost stood among the neglected statues and careworn features—once so swanky and plush, now rotting—and gazed upward, making a show of enjoying the view. Sure enough, he sensed figures on the steps above him pushing themselves into the shadows. He smiled. Good. This was good. He wanted them to see where he lived.

"Some men may come in the next few days," he told Maggie later. By then he had checked on Charlie and given him bread, and he'd attended to Jake, pleased to see the old lag's leg was on the mend. And with those two tasks complete, he had continued farther along, deeper into the sepulchral darkness of the tunnel, picking his way past alcoves crammed with rag-swaddled bodies.

Some of them slept; some stared at him with wide white eyes from inside their unwelcoming hidey-holes, silently watching him pass; and some greeted him, "Hello, Bharat," "Hello, lad," with a wave, or perhaps a simple blinked salute.

Some he knew by name, others from their jobs: Olly, for example, who was a "pure-finder," which meant he collected dog shit to sell on Bermondsey Market, but who had a tendency to bring his work home with him. The Ghost held his nose as he passed Olly, but raised a short wave anyhow. Many of them had candles, and he was grateful for the light; many did not, and lay shivering in the dark, alone with their pain, weeping as they awaited the crispy dawn and the beginning of another day of soul-destroying survival in London—the world's most advanced city. The shining jewel of Her Majesty's great empire.

He reached Maggie, who tended a small fire. She would have been doing so most of the evening, ladling broth into the bowls of any tunnel inhabitant who came asking. They all received their food, or "scran," as it was known, with a mixture of gratitude and devotion, and left thanking Maggie and singing her praises. Mostly they all looked fearfully beyond her, too, to where the light finally lost its battle with the dark shadows, and darkness reigned literally and metaphorically, and they thanked God for the young Indian man whom some of them knew as Bharat and some of them knew as Maggie's lad, who had brought order to the tunnel and made it so that they could sleep more easy in their alcoves at night.

There they sat, side by side, Maggie and The Ghost with their backs against the damp tunnel wall and the dying fire at their feet. Maggie's knees were pulled up and she hugged herself for warmth. Her long gray hair—"my witchy hair," she called it—lay over the fabric of a filthy gray skirt, and though her boots had no laces, she said she preferred them that way. She hated feeling "trussed up" she always said. Once upon a time, long ago—"before you were even a glint in your daddy's nutsack"—she'd seen pictures of Oriental ladies with bound feet, and after that she'd never worn laces in her boots again. She felt things keenly for her fellow man, did Maggie.

Now her features rearranged themselves into a picture of apprehension and concern. "And why," she asked, "will men be coming for you?"

"They'll be asking questions about me," The Ghost told her, "and they might well be pointed in your direction."

She gave an indignant harrumph. "Well, I bloody well hope so. They bloody well *ought* to be."

As well as helping others, Maggie liked people to know about it. She liked her efforts to be recognized.

"I'm sure they will," said The Ghost with a smile. "And I would like to ask you to be careful about what you say."

She looked sharply at him. "What do you mean?"

"I mean that there will be others who live in the tunnel who will say that I protect you from the thieves and vagabonds who live farther along, and that is acceptable; they will paint a picture of me as a man who is no stranger to violence and I have no problem with that. What I don't want is for these men to be furnished with an exaggerated account of my abilities as a fighter."

She dropped her voice. "I've seen you in action, don't forget. There ain't no exaggerating your abilities as a fighter."

"That's exactly what I mean, Maggie. That's exactly the sort of thing I don't want you to say. A man of violence but not necessarily a man of great skill, do I make myself understood?"

"I'm getting there."

"They are likely to ask you exactly how we met, but . . . Tell them what you like. Tell them you found me drunk in a gutter. Just don't tell them about what happened at the churchyard."

She reached for his hand. Her weathered hand was almost the color of his own. "You're not in any trouble, are you, Bharat?"

"I'm touched you should worry."

She chuckled. "Oh, like I say, I've seen you in action, it's the others who should worry, but . . ."

His head dropped. "But . . . ?"

"But I also saw you hesitate when you had that murderous little toff bang to rights, and I saw the fight drain out of you, just as surely as you'd been uncorked. I saw someone who's very good at dealing death but ain't got no heart for doing it. Now, I've met lots of evil bastards with a sadistic streak long as your arm, who would go knocking your teeth out of your mouth just because they had too many ales and fancied swinging their arm. Evil bastards who loved dishing out pain but only to those weaker and more vulnerable than themselves. Christ only knows, I've been married to two of them. And what's more, I've seen men who was good at fighting and could handle themselves if a brawl broke out, and who would do what they had to do given the circumstances, and maybe take a grim pride in their work, and maybe not.

"But what I ain't *never* seen is a man so good at fighting as you, who had so little stomach for it."

The Ghost watched as she shook her head in disbelief, her gray hair sweeping her skirts. "I wondered about that an awful lot, young man, believe you me. I've wondered if maybe you was a deserter from the army but not out of cowardice, oh no, I've never seen a man so brave, but because you're one of them, what you call it? *Conscientious objectors.* Well, the truth of it is, that I don't know, and from the sounds of what you're saying now, it's probably best I don't know, but what I do know is that you've got a big heart and there's no room in this world for people with a heart like yours. This world eats up people with hearts like yours. Eats them up and spits them out. You ask if I worry? Yes, my boy, I worry. You ask why? That's why."

TWENTY-FOUR

As he waited with the other men for their shift to begin, The Ghost wondered if the Templars had found what they were looking for, this artifact left by a civilization before our own, a buried record awaiting discovery. What tremendous power might it have?

His mind went back to Amritsar as it so often did—his memories were all he had now and he would revisit them with all the reverence of a devout man before a religious shrine—and he thought of the Koh-i-Noor diamond and the spectacular, all-powerful light show it had revealed, as though providing a portal to other worlds, deeper knowledge, more profound understanding—a map for mankind to find a better world.

But if it fell into the wrong hands?

He dreaded to think on it, but into his mind came unbidden images of enslavement. He saw every man and woman ground down like those at the tunnel, virtual slaves to be spat at and looked down upon, treated as something less than human by grinning masters who ruled from plushly appointed buildings. Men who took symbols and twisted their meaning to meet their own ideology. He saw agony and anguish. He saw a world without hope.

The bell rang, and the new shift barely acknowledged the departing men as they met like two opposing armies who couldn't be bothered to fight, passing one another on the mud, clutching their precious tools. Next The Ghost descended a series of ladders into the shaft, walking along the line until he came to the face, where the digging and scooping and carrying continued—it never really stopped—and soon he was filthy. Soon they all were. There were no divisions of color in the underground; there was just whether you could work and how fast, and a cheerful or encouraging word for the man next door.

Bells were supposed to denote the passing of time, tolling on the hour. But either Marchant didn't enforce their ringing or The Ghost didn't hear them, because time simply trudged on without demarcation. Dig, dig, dig. The noise was the incessant scrape and clang of spades and pickaxes and the chatter of men along the line, certain voices louder than the others, the comedians who, they say, kept the other's spirits up.

Most men preferred working on the cranes. They saw more sunlight. The metronomic to and fro of the crane served as a clock, denoting the passing of time that was absent in the trench. But not The Ghost. Down here seemed like a respite from all that. *Dig, dig, dig,* like an automaton. Mind wandering to home, to where he was Jayadeep again.

Besides, he was used to being underground.

TWENTY-FIVE

"Well, if it isn't Police Constable 72 Aubrey Shaw of Covent Garden's F Division," said Abberline, "all the way out here in Regent Street."

A red-faced, rotund and rather glum-looking peeler looked up from his mug and peered balefully at Abberline, a moustache of ale froth gleaming on his top lip.

"Well," he sneered back, "if it isn't Police Constable 58 Frederick Abberline of Marylebone's D Division, also some way out of his jurisdiction, who can take his insinuations and stick them where the sun don't shine."

"Who's insinuating?" said Abberline. "I'm coming straight out and saying that you're playing truant, mate, and I've caught you bang to rights."

It was true. Both constables were a long way out of their respective patches, being as they were in The Green Man pub on Regent Street. Abberline had thought he might find Aubrey here, seeing as how he wasn't to be found on his patch and had a name as something of a regular. Aubrey was fond of cricket, and The Green Man was a haunt of players and enthusiasts. In the window were bats and stumps and other cricket paraphernalia, which no doubt suited Aubrey fine, as he could savor his ale without members of the public peering through the glass and seeing a peeler apparently enjoying a boozy break.

"Anyway, I'm not."

"Well, what do you call it, then? Shirking, sloping off, showing a clean pair of heels to The Green Man to sink a brace of ales—it's all much the same thing, ain't it?"

Aubrey's shoulders sank. "It ain't shirking, and it ain't sloping off. It's more like skulking. No, wait a minute, it's *sulking*. That's what it is."

"And why would you feel the need to sulk, Aubs, eh?" Abberline took a seat at the bar beside him. A barman wearing a clean white apron approached, but Abberline waved him away, because Fresh-faced Freddie didn't drink on duty.

Beside him, Aubrey had unbuttoned the top pocket of his tunic to take out a folded piece of paper that he handed to Abberline. A crude imitation of a newspaper screamer was handwritten across the top of the page. "Have You Seen This Man?" it said, while below it was a charcoal drawing of a man in robes carrying an improbably long knife.

"The blokes at the station house are having a lot of laughs at my expense, I can tell you," said Aubrey ruefully.

"Why would that be?"

"A double murder in the Old Nichol. I expect you've heard about it. I have a witness that saw . . ."

"A man in robes, yes, I did hear."

Aubrey threw up his hands in exasperation. "See? This is exactly what I mean. The whole of bloody London knows all about my strange robed man with the very long knife. The whole of bloody London knows I'm *looking* for a man in fancy robes with a long knife, but no bugger apart from some old crone in the rookery has actually seen him. Mind you"—he looked sideways at Abberline—"they all know about your missing body too, Freddie. Matter of fact, and you'll have to forgive me for thinking this, but since I heard about Freddie Abberline's incredible disappearing corpse, I did rather hope it might take the heat off me."

Abberline gave a dry laugh. "And no such luck?"

"No such luck. That's why you're here, is it? You're sulking, too?"

"No. And as a matter of fact your robed man has cropped up in my missing-body case, would you believe?"

Aubrey's look of open incredulity was instantly replaced by another of derision. "Oh yes, I know your game." He looked over Abberline's shoulder as though expecting to see pranksters come chortling from the shadows of the pub. "Who put you up to this?"

"Oh, do pipe down, Aubs. I'm telling you that I believe in your robed man. That's something, isn't it?"

"Well, you'd be the first. You'd be practically the only one. Like I say, apart from the crone, nobody else has seen a robed man. I've asked every trader in Covent Garden market. I must have asked half of the Old Nichol, and you would think that a robed man with an enormously long knife would stand out, wouldn't you? Eye-catching, like. But no. Nobody's seen him. Nobody apart from that one witness. It's like he just appeared—and then disappeared."

Abberline thought. For some reason that chimed with how he felt about the stranger at Belle Isle—a mysterious figure within the mist, his motives just as much a mystery. "So who are your marks?" he asked.

"One of them was a lowlife went by the name of Boot. Petty thief. Runner for various East End gangs."

"No stranger to the blade, no doubt."

"Yeah, but, no . . . Actually, he was shot."

"He was shot? What about the other one?"

"Ah, here's where it gets sad, Freddie. It was a little girl. Got in the way, looks like."

"And was she shot, too?"

Aubrey threw him a look. "Most people take a second to reflect on the tragedy of a little girl being gunned down, Freddie."

"Ah, so she *was* shot?"

"Yeah, she was shot."

"Right, so a witness saw a man in robes, carrying what looked like a wickedly long blade?"

"Thin as well, this blade. More like one of them fencing swords. Like a rapier blade."

"Not a blade for cutting. For combat. For stabbing. Yet this man Boot and the little girl were both shot?"

"That's right."

"So you're looking for a mysterious robed figure who shot two people with a knife?"

"Ooh me sides, I think you've split 'em."

Abberline sighed. "Was the gun ever found?"

"No."

Now the younger peeler was thinking about the gun and the puncture wound he'd found on the body.

"You only had the one witness?"

"Another one, who only saw a bloke running away."

"Was he wearing funny robes?"

"The witness or the guy running away?"

"The guy running away."

"No."

"So he could be the shooter?"

Aubrey looked at him, a little shame-faced. "Well, he could be, I suppose. Never really thought about it. I had the knife-carrying figure in the robes to occupy me, didn't I?"

Abberline threw up his hands. "Bloody hell, Aubs. Come on, sup up. You and me are going back to the Old Nichol."

An hour later and poor old Aubrey Shaw was even more despondent. His first witness, the crone who saw the man in robes, was nowhere to be found. "She's disappeared, just like the mythical knifeman," Aubrey was bemoaning, although both men knew that such was the itinerant life of the slums, she'd probably just packed up and moved on.

Thank God for small mercies, then, that they were able to find the second witness. Abberline thought he might have had a broken man on his hands otherwise.

"Here she is," said Aubrey through the side of his mouth as they approached Number Thirty-two. There on the steps of a tall, smoke-discolored and flat-fronted tenement sat a defeated woman. She gazed at them with eyes shorn of all emotion. She held a baby to one bare breast.

Aubrey coughed and looked down. Abberline desperately wanted to be worldly but failed, and he, too, felt himself coloring as he found something of great interest in a line of washing nearby. Both men did what a gentleman should do in such circumstances. They took off their hats.

"Excuse me, madam," said Abberline. "I believe you talked to my colleague here, Police Constable Aubrey Shaw, upon the matter of something you might have seen on the night of an horrific double murder right here in The Old Nichol. Would I be correct in making such an assumption?"

"Saint preserves us." She smiled through teeth like timeworn gravestones. "Don't you talk pretty?"

Abberline wasn't sure if she was taking the piss or genuinely being nice, but her face had lit a little, and her eyes softened, so he pressed home the advantage. "Madam, did you see some fellow running down this very street on the night of the murder?"

She seemed to think, looking down at the baby's head. She adjusted the infant on her nipple then returned her attention to the two peelers on the steps below. "That I did."

"And he was just running, was he?"

"That he was."

"Can you describe him?"

She sniffed haughtily. "Like I told your friend there, I don't think I could describe him, no. Not without a couple of pennies like."

Frowning, Abberline turned to Aubrey. "You mean to tell me you could have got a description but for a few pennies?"

"It was all about the bloke with the robes, wasn't it?" Aubrey raised his hands defensively, coloring even more than usual.

"All about you being a tight-arse, more like."

"How was I to know you'd suddenly get all interested in some bloke running in the street. Matter of fact, why *are* you so bleedin' interested? He probably just saw the blood, or better still the bloke with the knife, and thought he'd do well to make himself scarce. Wouldn't you?"

Abberline had stopped listening. He was already climbing the steps to press coins into the woman's palm, gallantly averting his face from her naked breast as he did so. "Now, can you tell me what he looked like?"

She looked down at her hand as though wondering whether to quibble but then decided against. "He were a bloke in a suit with a big puffy moustache like what Prince Albert used to wear before he up and died, God rest his soul. And he had big thick side-whiskers down here."

"And tell me, madam, was he carrying anything?"

She looked shifty. Afraid.

Abberline leaned forward, still keeping his eyes primly averted but able to speak into the woman's ear. "Was he carrying a revolver, by any chance?"

With her eyes she said yes. Abberline thanked her with his, then withdrew.

As he and Aubrey made their way out of the slum, Abberline was ebullient. "You see what this means, Aubs? It means that more than likely your running man and my corpse are the same bloke. And your man in robes is the same man who turned up at Belle Isle. This, my friend, could crack the case wide open."

"Thank God for that." Aubrey sighed. "Just maybe I'll be able to restore my reputation."

Abberline sighed. "There's also the small matter of truth and justice, Aubrey. Let's not forget that, eh?"

In return the older man gave him a look that told him, *You may be keen but you have an awful lot to learn*, and said, "Truth and justice ain't gonna bring that little girl back, Freddie."

Back at the station house Abberline badgered Aubrey into asking the desk sergeant for the logbook, and as Aubrey went to make what he described as a "well-earned brew," Abberline sat it on a lectern, hoisted himself up to a tall chair, and began leafing through the heavy pages in search of persons reported missing on the night of . . .

Ah. There it was. Bloody hell. Just one person reported in this area, a man whose wife had made the report the evening after the night in question. He'd gone out to—oh, this was good—the Old Nichol, telling her he had a bit of business to attend to, and that he'd be back soon. Only, he hadn't turned up.

His name was Robert Waugh and he lived not far from here.

"Aubs," said Abberline, as the other PC returned to the front desk, two steaming mugs of tea in his fists, "no time for that, we've got a house to visit. We're going to the home of Robert Waugh."

TWENTY-SIX

"Bharat Singh!"

It was late afternoon when his name came down, bouncing like a ball dropped into the shaft as it was passed from one man to another: "Bharat Singh . . . Bharat Singh . . . Bharat Singh . . ."

Though he was conditioned to respond to the name he'd been given, he was too lost in thought to respond until the man next to him, barely pausing in his work, tapped him with the head of his pickaxe. "Hey, Indian, you're wanted up top."

He took the ladders to find Marchant waiting for him at ground level. With him were the three punishers and together they led The Ghost across the planks, traversing a reservoir of filth to the mobile office on wheels. Inside was Cavanagh—no Mr. Pearson or Mr. Fowler today—just Cavanagh, and he sat behind a wide, polished-oak desk that was empty save for a document that The Ghost recognized at once.

Afternoon was becoming extinct, and in the dim light

of the office, Cavanagh's scar shone dully as he picked up the letter for The Ghost to see. "Your name is Bharat Singh," he said without emotion, "originally from Bombay, author of this correspondence?"

The Metropolitan director spoke in a more confidential register than The Ghost was used to hearing from the commands he barked to Marchant and the foremen of the trench.

"Yes, I did, sir," The Ghost acknowledged with a bow of the head.

Marchant had taken a place just behind his master, wearing the same oily smile he always wore. He stood close, as though he wished to reach out and touch Cavanagh just to draw on some of his master's greatness. Meanwhile, behind him, the three fighters had stepped in and fanned out.

This was it. This was that moment that, if Cavanagh had his suspicions, he would act. The Ghost weighed up possibilities. He already knew which of the men were strongest and which were weakest. Marchant had the honor of propping up that particular list. At the top, however, was the man behind the desk, a man The Ghost knew from his dossier to be as ruthless as he was quick in combat.

"And your father was a sepoy at Jalalabad in 1842, you say?" continued Cavanagh, allowing the letter to flutter to the tabletop.

The Ghost nodded.

"Very brave, the sepoys," continued Cavanagh. "I knew an especially courageous one once."

The Ghost looked at him, hardly able to believe his ears as he thought of the poor, nameless sepoy, but Cavanagh had already moved on. "And your father knew me?"

"Knew *of* you, sir, though he would have liked the opportunity to become acquainted, I'm sure. I feel certain he would be envious of me now."

Cavanagh raised a faintly bemused eyebrow. "Oh yes? And why would that be, exactly?"

"He spoke very highly of you, sir. He talked of you as a hero, as the great soldier who survived the march from Kabul; that I should look out for your name as you were surely destined for greatness."

"He thought I was 'destined for greatness'? Why, because I can bear the cold and I'm handy with a saber? Go out there and you'll find a hundred men who fought as fiercely as I did, served their country just as I did, and did what they could to survive, just as I did. None of them have achieved greatness. Not unless you consider it a great achievement to have Marchant shout at you day and night. None have reached my rank. What on earth made your father think I would be the one to thrive?"

"He was right, though, sir, wasn't he?"

Cavanagh acknowledged the point with a tilt of the chin, but . . . "The question remains."

The Ghost swallowed. *Here comes the moment of truth.* "He mentioned an organization, sir," he said, "an organization that had taken an interest in you because of your talents. A very powerful organization, sir, and that having this organization's seal of approval was certainly enough to ensure your rise."

"I see. And does it have a name, this organization?"

"The Knights Templar, sir."

Marchant's oily smile remained fixed but his eyes narrowed as the words "Knights Templar" dropped like a stone into the still pool of the room. Behind him, The Ghost sensed the three fighters tense. Were they readying themselves for something The Ghost might do? Or for something Cavanagh might do?

"That's right. Your father was correct." A brief smile flickered on the otherwise impassive face. His scar twisted. "How gratifying to know such recognition existed within the lower orders."

The moment hung as Cavanagh sat back in his chair, fixing The Ghost with an assessing look, as if trying to decode signals the younger man refused to send. Whatever decision the director reached must be his alone, a product of trust in his own instinct. Nothing else mattered now apart from gaining Cavanagh's trust.

And then the man behind the desk seemed to relax, indicating the letter. "The second interesting aspect of your missive is this information you have on an employee of mine you are going to expose as a traitor. I wonder if that would have anything to do with my employee Robert Waugh, who was found dead at the dig two days ago?"

The Ghost nodded.

"Tell me, how did you make the connection between him and me?"

"I saw him visiting your office, sir." At this Cavanagh looked up to Marchant with a meaningful stare. "And then when I saw him in a public house I knew it was him."

"And that's how you knew that he was indulging in, as you say, *treacherous activities*?"

"That's when I suspected, sir, yes."

"And what made you decide to report it to me?"

It was another moment of truth for The Ghost, another point in his favor or a nail in his coffin, depending on what Cavanagh decided to believe.

"After what my father had told me, sir, I couldn't believe my luck in seeing you. Seeing your name and seeing the scar and knowing it was the same scar with which you had returned from the doomed retreat, I decided that fate had brought me into your wider circle but that it was up to me to enter the immediate one. The Knights Templar once looked upon you as a man of talent, who might be of use to them. I hope, now, that is how you look upon me."

"That's all very well, and maybe even commendable, but at the moment, all I have is your word and a dead body, and I'm really not sure that either is all that much use to me."

"It was I who killed Robert Waugh, in the hope that you would have given me the job eventually."

Cavanagh snorted. "Well, that was rather presumptuous of you, wasn't it? Because to return to my first point, I only have your word that he was a traitor."

"He was selling your goods in the public houses, using a man named Boot to do the dirty work."

Cavanagh shrugged. "It sounds plausible, but it's still lacking in concrete evidence."

"I killed him in the Old Nichol, sir. I took from him the evidence, a photographic plate that I have at my home."

"At the tunnel?"

The Ghost switched on a look of surprise. "You know where I live, sir?"

"Oh yes. You like your tunnels, don't you? We've been there and we've asked around, and you are a little bit more than just an *occupant* of the tunnel, aren't you? By all accounts you're the closest they have to a leader."

"I can read and write, sir. I was taught on my passage from India. I gained some medical knowledge also. For this reason, and the fact that I have on occasion stood up against the scum who also make the tunnel their home, some of the people who live there consider me their friend."

Cavanagh smiled tightly. "Yes, well, in the land of the blind the one-eyed man is king, I suppose. Even so, it's a very resourceful picture of you that is being painted."

Judging this to be the right moment, The Ghost let a little eagerness creep into his voice. "A man who can be of use to you, sir. I do not nominate myself to your services lightly, sir. I hope that in me you see something of yourself."

"Yes, well, that remains to be seen." Cavanagh gave a tilt of his chin, suggesting he'd reached a decision in The Ghost's favor. He addressed one of the fighters. "Smith, go to the tunnel, retrieve this photographic plate he's talking about. Oh, and, Smith, be nice to the old lady, won't you? From what I can gather, she and our friend here are close."

He looked significantly at The Ghost, who suppressed a dread thought before continuing. "In the meantime you, Mr. Bharat Singh, are going to accompany Marchant and Mr. Hardy to visit the home of the recently widowed Mrs. Waugh. And Mr. Hardy? Given that I'm certain we're going to learn that our new associate is telling the truth, you don't need to worry about being nice to Mrs. Waugh. You can be as unfriendly to that old baggage as you like."

Mr. Hardy grinned, revealing a gold tooth. He spoke with a voice like the scrape of spades at the tunnel face. "It would be my pleasure, sir."

TWENTY-SEVEN

"I don't suppose you can drive a carriage can you, lad?" rasped Hardy when the three men stepped outside the gates of the dig to where their transport was tethered.

The Ghost, who was an excellent horseman, and who had driven many a carriage back home, and who recognized an excellently sprung beautifully upholstered Clarence when he saw one, took pains to look like the clueless bumpkin Hardy clearly thought him to be, and shrugged his shoulders and looked lost.

"Good," said Hardy with flinty eyes. He scratched at his stubble, then corrected the set of his hat. "Because nobody gets to drive Mr. Cavanagh's carriage apart from me, Mr. Smith or Other Mr. Hardy. Is that clear?"

"I have no problem with that, sir," replied The Ghost. "Should I just join Mr. Marchant inside, sir, where it's warm?"

Hardy shot him a look, as though to say, *Don't push your luck*, and in the next moment occupied himself with pulling on a scarf, topcoat and mittens, ready for the short journey to Bedford Square.

The Ghost, meanwhile, stood to the side of the Clarence, awaiting Marchant, then opening the door for the clerk when he appeared. Without a word of thanks Marchant stepped inside before fussily arranging a blanket over himself and leaving none for The Ghost, who took a seat opposite. When he was settled, Marchant yanked a cord and made a point of ignoring The Ghost to stare out of the carriage window. Up top Hardy shook the reins and their carriage set off for the home of Mrs. Waugh.

They arrived and The Ghost watched with implacable interest as Hardy stepped down from the seat of the carriage, removed his mittens and pulled on a pair of leather gloves instead, flexing his fingers with a grim and businesslike air and fixing The Ghost with a malevolent stare at the same time. *Watch your step, I've got my eye on you.*

Next, Hardy reached to the storage box on the carriage. From it he took a pair of brass knuckles that he fitted over one leather-gloved hand. Out came something else: a thick wooden truncheon with a leather loop that he slid over his wrist before slipping the baton into his sleeve. Lastly, he produced a knife from somewhere within the folds of his topcoat. He twirled it in his fingers, light dashing down the blade, and all the time never took his eyes off The Ghost.

Watch your step, I've got my eye on you.

Now the three men considered the house across the road. The shutters were closed, just a dim light burning somewhere within. Otherwise there was no sign of life, except . . .

The Ghost saw it, a slight disruption of ceiling shadow glimpsed through the window of the front door. With a hand held out—*Wait there*—to the other two, he darted quickly across the road, having to satisfy himself with merely imagining the outraged looks on the men's faces at being given an order by this new recruit. A boy. An *Indian* boy, no less. An outsider.

Stealthily mounting the front steps, he crouched to listen at the front door. From inside he heard voices retreating up an interior passage. He tried the front door but found it locked then scuttled back to the Clarence. "There's somebody in there with her," he told Marchant and Hardy. "Sounds like the peelers."

"Been a long time since I bagged myself a blue bottle," Hardy said through a wicked smile. Gold glinted malevolently in the dark.

"I would guess that whoever's there is in one of the back rooms," said The Ghost. "In the kitchen, perhaps. I say we assess how many before we go rushing in."

"*Assess*, now, is it?" sneered Hardy. "How about we do it another way? How about we knock on the door and take them by surprise." His brass knuckles shone as he performed a quick boxer's one-two, just in case they were in any doubt exactly what he meant by taking them by surprise.

"We may be outnumbered," warned The Ghost, turning his attention to Marchant instead. "There are only three of us, after all."

At last the clerk was spurred into a decision. "Right. Hardy, put those bloody things away before anybody sees them. This is a respectable square. You, Indian, go to the back. I and Mr. Hardy here will await your signal that it is safe to proceed. Assuming it is, we'll enter by the front, Hardy and you can make sure nobody tries to leave from the back, is that a plan?" The others agreed. The Ghost demonstrated his owl call, then made off, finding an alleyway that ran through the terrace and darting along it until he came to a door into the grounds of the Waugh's home. The door would be bolted but The Ghost didn't even bother trying it. Instead, with a quick look left and right, he leapt, grabbed an overhang on the wall and nimbly pulled himself to the top.

He crouched there for a moment or so, a dark silhouette against the gunmetal night, enjoying a brief moment of pride in a life that was otherwise shorn of it. He wished he was wearing his robes and could feel the weight of his hidden blade along his forearm but, for the time being, just crouching here would do.

Moment over, he dropped silently to the other side, where he waited in the shrubs and shadows for his vision to adapt to the new, less malevolent darkness. Stretching away from him was a garden, well maintained—evidently there was money to be made in selling these "erotic prints"—while looming to his left was the rear of the house. He made his way there now, guessing from the glow of interior lamps which was the kitchen window, and there he squatted, allowing the night to claim him.

And then—very, very carefully—he peered inside.

Standing in the kitchen with their hats in their hands were two peelers. One was a red-faced, plump fellow he didn't recognize, and the other was Abberline, the constable who'd come to the dig. The Ghost remembered that he'd paid close attention to Waugh's chest wound. It sounded like a contradiction in terms, but such a clean kill had been careless of Ethan. Abberline's suspicions had been raised.

Which was probably the reason he was standing in the Waughs' kitchen right now.

He and his mate were talking to a flustered-looking old maid complete with bonnet and apron, who held a rolling pin like she might be tempted to use it in anger. This was Mrs. Waugh, no doubt. The Ghost couldn't see her lips to lip-read, but she spoke so loudly he could hear her through the glass anyway.

"I always said he was getting in too deep there. I always knew he was playing with fire."

Something caught his eye. There in the kitchen doorway, hidden in the shadows, was a figure The Ghost recognized as Mr. Hardy. The Ghost had no idea how he'd got into the house, but the reason why was clear from the wicked glint of the knife he held.

The two constables had their backs to Hardy; they wouldn't stand a chance. The woman was too busy gesticulating with the rolling pin to see him.

None of them stood a chance.

The Ghost had a second to decide: save the peelers and endanger his mission or let them die for the greater good.

TWENTY-EIGHT

They rubbed along without too much strife, but even so, Abberline and Aubrey weren't exactly crazy about one another. For a start, Abberline thought rather poorly of Aubrey's qualities as a police constable, while for his part, Aubrey reckoned Abberline might learn a thing or two about basic human compassion.

Aubrey had returned to the point earlier, as the two of them made their way to the address of Mr. and Mrs. Waugh on Bedford Square.

"The job's about people, too, you know, Freddie," he told his companion as they threaded through the hustle and bustle of Tottenham Court Road. "Serving truth and justice is all very well. But what about serving the people?"

"That's what the rules is there for, Aubrey," Abberline reminded him. "Rules is for the good of everybody."

They skirted rival pure-finders who were about to brawl over a particularly sizable pile of dog shit but stopped when they saw the peelers approaching and made a showy pretense of looking like old pals. Aubrey frowned at them as they passed. *I've got my eye on you.*

"That's as may be," he said, when they were past and it was safe to exhale. "Just as long as you don't start putting the rules first and the good of everybody second, is what I'm saying. Besides which, it's not always so cut-and-dried, is it? After all, if our theory's right, then your man with the gun shot down a little girl in cold blood. Where's the justice in apprehending the man who killed her killer?"

"Well, let's get to the truth of the matter first, shall we? And then we'll question the justice of it all."

They had reached their destination, a deceptively handsome bay-fronted building in an appealing Bedford Square of other deceptively handsome bay-fronted buildings. It was just close enough to Tottenham Court Road for the square's no-doubt-smartly-attired residents to reach their offices each day, but far enough away so that the noise of the thoroughfare was just a distant hubbub rather than the never-ending clamor that might send people mad if they had to live on top of it.

The two bobbies stood with their thumbs in their belts, regarding the house in question. Shutters at the bay window were closed. A light at the window above the front door was the only sign of life. As they trod the steps to knock, Abberline wondered if Mrs. Waugh was inside now, weeping as she pined for her husband . . .

"Where is he, that bastard?"

Abberline had been correct in one regard. Mrs. Waugh was indeed inside the house. When she opened the door it was clear from her flour-covered face that she was mid-baking. But as for weeping and pining?

"Come on," she demanded of the two peelers on her doorstep. She had the appearance of a well-fed butcher's wife, complete with ruddy complexion and a white apron bearing stains of unknown provenance. "Where the bloody hell is he?"

"We don't know . . ." started Abberline, sent off guard by her ferocity.

It wasn't the best way to begin, and sure enough, Mrs. Waugh—at least, they assumed it was Mrs. Waugh, unless Mr. Waugh had an exceptionally bad-tempered and insolent housekeeper—was sent into a spin.

"What do you mean, you don't know where he is? Why are you coming here, then? You should be out there, looking for him." She threw up her hands in frustration and dismay, turned away from the door and stomped off up the hall, muttering to herself as she went, leaving little flour footprints on the terra-cotta tiles.

Abberline and Aubrey looked at one another, Abberline giving Aubrey a look up and down. "Just your type." He smiled.

"Oh, give over," said Aubrey. "Are we going in or what?"

They closed the door behind them, throwing the bolt before following the sound of feminine distress to the kitchen. There they found her already using a rolling pin to take out her frustration on a vast mound of dough, pounding at it furiously and almost obscured by clouds of flour.

Hanging nearby was a photograph of Mrs. Waugh with the man whose body Abberline had lost. *They were in the right place*. Abberline nudged Aubrey in the ribs and gave him the nod.

"Madam," he began, trying again, with what he hoped was a little more composure this time. "A man matching your husband's description was seen in the vicinity of the Old Nichol at the scene of a . . ."

"Well, he was on his way to the Old Nichol the night he went missing, so that's about right," she said, continuing to work at the dough with the rolling pin.

This was the new middle class, mused Abberline. They ate just as well as the highborns but did it all themselves. Something occurred to him.

"What trade was your husband in?" he asked.

"He was a photographer," she replied, in a tone of voice that left them in no doubt what she thought of *that* particular profession.

"A photographer, eh?" said Abberline. "And what business does a photographer have in the Old Nichol, then?"

Still pounding, she fixed Abberline with a contemptuous look. "Are you having me on? How am I supposed to bleeding know what business he has in the Old Nichol at any sort of hour? He don't tell me what he's doing, and to be quite frank with you, I don't bother asking."

There was something about her protestations that were a little too theatrical for Abberline's liking, but he put that to one side for a second.

"Aren't you worried about your husband, Mrs. Waugh?"

She shrugged. "Not especially. How would you feel if your wife went and made herself scarce, you'd probably throw a party, wouldn't you?"

"I'm not married."

"Well, come back to me when you are and we'll have this talk again."

"All right, then. If you're not worried about him, then how come you reported him missing?"

Indignation made Mrs. Waugh's voice rise, and she was already fairly indignant. "Because who's going to pay for all this if he's bleedin' missing?"

"My point being, Mrs. Waugh, that the Old Nichol is a dangerous place at the best of times and perhaps not somewhere that a respectable photographer like your husband might want to visit."

"Well," she snapped back, "perhaps that's why he took his pistol."

Abberline and Aubrey shared a look, barely able to believe their ears.

"He took his gun, did he?"

"That's what I said."

"Yes, except, Mrs. Waugh, the man matching your husband's description who was seen in the vicinity of the Old Nichol may or may not have been involved in a shooting."

Now at last she set down the rolling pin. "I see," she said gravely.

"It would be a great help to us if you could tell us what your husband might have been doing in the Old Nichol. What was the purpose of his visit? Was he there to meet somebody for example. Apart from his pistol did he take anything with him? Did he tell you what time to expect him back?"

She had ignored all the questions. Pinning Abberline

with her gaze, she said, "This shooting that occurred. Was anybody hurt?"

"There were two confirmed fatalities, Mrs. Waugh. A little girl . . ." He watched as the woman winced, closing her eyes, absorbing the pain. ". . . and a street thug who went by the name of Boot."

She opened her eyes again. "Boot? Robert was on his way to meet Boot. As far as I know, Boot was a business associate."

"I'm sorry, I thought you just said he never told you about his business and you never asked?"

"Well, I picked up the odd thing, didn't I? Any road up, he was on his way there for some kind of deal . . ."

"A deal?"

Her eyes darted. She had already said too much. "Yes, well, he's a photographer, he . . ."

". . . takes pictures. That's what photographers do. Photographers take pictures of men and their wives and the children of men and their wives. Big bustles, buffed-up boots, buttoned-up jackets and uncomfortably starched collars, grim and forbidding looks into the camera, all that kind of thing. That's what photographers do. They don't do deals in slums with street thugs after dark."

"Wait a second, you haven't said yet—if there were two confirmed deaths, does that mean Robert's still alive?"

Again, Abberline and Aubrey shared a look. "I'm afraid our most likely theory at the moment is that your husband might have been killed by a second assailant. In fact, I was wondering if you have a photograph of him, so that I can confirm if his body was found at the Metropolitan Line dig in the north."

His asking was a formality so he could break the news, but it was at the mention of the Metropolitan Line that a dark look passed across her face. "Oh, lummy," she said, shaking her head with the terrible inevitability of it all, "I always said he was getting in too deep there. I always knew he was playing with fire."

Trying to contain his excitement, and as far as police constable Aubrey Shaw was concerned, not succeeding in the slightest, Abberline leapt on her words. "What do you mean 'too deep'? Tell me exactly what you know, Mrs. Waugh . . ."

The Waughs' kitchen window was tall and as black as night, like a stained-glass window without the stained glass. As Mrs. Waugh looked at him, about to speak, something there caught Abberline's eye.

A second later, the window exploded.

TWENTY-NINE

A split second of indecision before The Ghost decided he couldn't have the blood of two innocent peelers on his hands, and he made his move.

In the end he gambled on two things: his own marksmanship, and that Mrs. Waugh would make enough noise to wake the dead.

He was not disappointed in either respect.

Two objectives: to save the peelers and to prevent them from seeing either him, Marchant or Hardy. He cast around for a stone, found a large pebble fringing a flowerbed nearby and slipped it into his palm, then, as he saw Hardy tense and the silver blade rise in the doorway, he made his move.

The Ghost wore only rags and had nothing to protect him from the glass, so when he hit the window full force he felt what seemed like a thousand knife cuts as he crashed through glass and splintered wood and to a crockery table on the other side.

A single lamp hung from the ceiling as the only light source in the room, and The Ghost let fly with his pebble at the same time as he crashed through the window. His aim was true and the light blinked out and night fell like swift death in the room at exactly the same time as a shout went up and Mrs. Waugh started screaming.

Dislodged crockery fell and smashed and added to the din but The Ghost was already on the move, and he propelled himself to a draining board, going round Mrs. Waugh to the peelers by traversing the room without touching the floor, like the games children play—like a game he himself had played at home in Amritsar. Another jump from the draining board took him to the peelers, neither of whom saw or heard him or had time to react, as he landed on the tiles just in front of them, and delivered two quick throat punches, felling first Abberline, then his companion, all done in a matter of a half a second, and all done to the accompaniment of screams from Mrs. Waugh.

It was over in a trice. Nobody but The Ghost knew what was happening and that suited the young man fine. Confusion was his friend.

"Grab her," he commanded. Hardy and Marchant had come barging into the room and The Ghost saw the fury of denial on Hardy's face. "Grab her before her screams bring other bobbies running."

Then Marchant was barking orders like he was a man in charge and not a man who was hopelessly confused about a situation that had spun irretrievably out of his control. "You heard him. Grab her! Blooming well shut her up!" And perhaps grateful for the chance to carry out a little violence, Hardy strode across the room to where Mrs. Waugh stood screaming, and The Ghost saw the flash of brass knuckles and he turned his head away as Mrs. Waugh's screams abruptly stopped.

It took all three of them to carry her out of the house and bundle her in the Clarence. The Ghost made sure he was last to leave and closed the front door behind him.

In the house an icy wind blew through the smashed window of the kitchen. On the floor the two peelers lay out cold.

THIRTY

It was a day of recrimination.

The name Bharat Singh came bouncing down the shaft and into the tunnel, and The Ghost once again scaled the ladders and made his way across the planks to the office. There sat Cavanagh, just as he had the day before, and there stood Marchant, Hardy, Smith and Other Hardy, just as they had the day before.

Only things were different now. Where yesterday Hardy had looked at The Ghost with curiosity at best, now he gazed at him with unmasked hatred; Marchant, too, saw him with new interest.

"I have some important news for you, young Bharat," said Cavanagh with hooded eyes. "You are to be promoted. No more working in the tunnel. No more laboring in the trench. From now on you will work under Marchant here, putting your reading and writing skills to good use. Congratulations, you have achieved everything your father would have wanted."

It was a fictional father's admiration that Cavanagh

mocked, but that didn't stop The Ghost's feeling a twinge of something approaching pure hatred for him.

"You may ask why," continued Cavanagh. "Why have you been promoted? It appears from talking to Mrs. Waugh that everything you told us was correct. As I'm sure you are already aware, Mr. Smith here recovered a photographic plate from your hole at the Thames Tunnel. Therefore your first task is to carry out the sentence of death on the treacherous Mr. Waugh. Only, of course that sentence has been carried out, and you have proven yourself in my eyes."

The Ghost nodded. "Thank you, sir. What of my victim's widow?"

"She's been taken care of."

The Ghost kept his face blank but chalked up one more innocent.

Meanwhile, from behind him, Hardy cleared his throat.

Cavanagh acknowledged him, turning his attention to The Ghost. "Mr. Hardy here feels aggrieved about your actions last night. Neither seem quite sure what happened"—at this he looked hard at Marchant then at Hardy—"but both are agreed that you acted impulsively and put them at risk."

The Ghost opened his mouth about to defend himself.

"But . . ." Cavanagh held out a hand to stop him. "I happen to disagree with Mr. Marchant and Mr. Hardy. We had a body discovered at the dig, which raises questions. The last thing we need is two dead constables as well. There are only a certain number of questions we can withstand. You, Mr. Hardy, should know better."

"That's as may be," growled Hardy, "but the lad went rogue. It was agreed that Mr. Marchant and me would take the kitchen and he would stop somebody leaving from the rear. He smashed through a bloody window, guv. It wasn't exactly stealthy, know what I mean?"

Cavanagh gave a thin smile. "Something tells me our newest employee knew exactly what he was doing."

THIRTY-ONE

Abberline and Aubrey had pulled themselves from the floor of the Waughs' kitchen, made their way back to the station house with pounding heads and their tails tucked firmly between their legs then bedded down for the night.

Bedraggled, pained and still exhausted, they found themselves at the front desk not long after dawn, when the alarm was raised. A woman had rushed in screaming about a suicide.

"Where?" Abberline asked.

"House on Bedford Square . . ." the woman gasped.

They'd looked at one another, a mirror image of slack-jawed shock, then both bolted for the door.

Less than half an hour later, they were back in the very same kitchen they'd left in the early hours. When they left it was dark, with a wind gusting through the smashed window, the terra-cotta tiles crunchy with broken glass, and a dropped rolling pin on the floor.

Now, though, it was light, and everything was just as

it had been the previous night with the exception of one thing: Mrs. Waugh had returned. She was hanging from the ceiling lamp, a noose fashioned from linen tight around her neck, head lolling, tongue protruding from blue lips and a puddle of urine on the tiles beneath her dangling boots.

Nobody likes to see a dead body before their elevenses, thought Abberline, and he turned on his heel and marched out.

"They piss themselves, you know!"

Cavanagh, Marchant, the punishers and The Ghost were still in the office when Abberline and Aubrey announced their presence with a loud, not-to-be-denied, we-are-the-peelers knock, clomped inside and started talking about people pissing themselves.

Aubrey was as red-faced as ever, but anger had given Abberline an expression to match, and he glowered from man to man, his eyes alighting finally on The Ghost. "You," he snapped, "where did you get those cuts?"

"Mr. Singh is a laborer, Constable," broke in Cavanagh, before The Ghost could answer, "and I'm afraid his English isn't very good, but he suffered an accident in the trench last night."

Cavanagh made no effort to be charming or ingratiating with Abberline. He simply stated facts. At the same time he indicated to Other Mr. Hardy, who turned to leave.

"Where do you think you're going?" Abberline barked, wheeling on Other Mr. Hardy.

"He's going where I say he goes, or where he likes, or maybe even your own station house, should he so desire to speak to a sergeant there . . . Unless of course you plan to place him under arrest, in which case, I'm sure we're all interested to hear on what charge, and what compelling evidence you have to support it?"

Abberline spluttered, lost for words. He hadn't been sure how this would go, but one thing was for sure, he didn't picture its going like this.

"Now, you were saying, about people pissing themselves?" said Cavanagh drily. "Which people would this be, exactly?"

"Those who find themselves at the end of a noose," spat Abberline.

"Suicides?"

"Not just toppers, no, but murders too. Anywhere you find a poor soul at the end of a noose you find some effluent not far away. The bowels open, you see." He paused for effect. "Lucky for Mrs. Waugh that she didn't need number twos."

His gaze went around the room: unreadable Cavanagh, sly Marchant, the three punishers seemingly having the time of their lives, and . . . the Indian.

Abberline's gaze lingered on the Indian the longest, and he could swear he saw something there, a flicker of emotion, and not an emotion out of the gutter, either, but a proper one. The kind that Aubrey was always saying he himself could do with learning.

Abberline removed his eyes slowly from the Indian, taking them instead to the big guy, the punisher with the gold tooth.

"You," he said, "it was you, wasn't it? You was at the house."

The guy, "Mr. Hardy" if Abberline remembered correctly, displayed his golden dentistry as well as some other splendid specimens. "No, I was here all night, Mr. Blue Bottle, as Mr. Cavanagh will confirm."

"You just blooming watch yer sauce-box, you . . ." said Abberline, pointing at Hardy

"Yes, Mr. Hardy"—Cavanagh sighed—"perhaps it might be wise *not* to excite our visitor here any more than he is already excited. And as for you, Constable, may I reiterate that Mr. Singh, Mr. Hardy, Marchant, Smith and Other Mr. Hardy were all with me last night and, ah . . . Abberline, it appears you have a visitor."

"Abberline," the constable heard from behind him, and cringed at the distinctive sound of his sergeant's voice. "Just what the bloody hell do you think you're playing at?"

THIRTY-TWO

Furious, Abberline stepped out into the noise and drive of the tunnel works, with Aubrey at his heels, struggling to keep up.

"Hold up, hold up, where are you bleedin' going?" yelled his red-faced companion over the never-ending din of machinery.

"Back to City Road is where I'm bleeding going," Abberline roared back over his shoulder. He reached the wooden gate at the perimeter of the site, yanked it open and brushed past a sleepy worker whose job it was to keep the riffraff out. "This lot are into it right up to their eyeballs. They stink of it, I'm telling you."

Outside in the street they weaved their way through the human detritus that were either attracted by commercial possibilities of the dig—traders, hawkers, prostitutes, pickpockets—or genuinely had business in that part of town, and began the short hike back to the home of the unfortunate Mr. and Mrs. Waugh.

"What do you think it is they're up to their necks

in?" Aubrey held on to his hat as he tried to keep up with Abberline.

"I don't know that, do I? If I knew that, then life would be a lot bloody simpler, wouldn't it?" He stopped, turned and raised a finger like an admonishing schoolmaster. "But I tell you this, Aubrey Shaw. They're up to something." He shook the selfsame finger in the direction of the fenced-off rail works. "And whatever it is they're up to, it's no good. You hear me?" He returned to his marching. "I mean, did you see them all, stood there, guilty as you like? That young fella, the Indian bloke, had blood all over him. Accident in the tunnel my fat arse. He got all cut up when he came through Mrs. Waugh's window."

"You think that was him?"

"*Of course* I think it was him," exploded Abberline. "I know it was him. *I* know it was him. *They* know it was him. Even *you* know it was him. Proving it is the bloody problem, but it was him all right. He came through the window, knocked out the light then knocked us out."

By now Aubrey had drawn level, speaking through gulps as he tried to catch his breath. "Do you realize what you've just said, Freddie? I mean, isn't that where this theory of yours falls down? Because there ain't no way he could have done all that. He'd have to be some kind of acrobat or something."

By now they were back at City Road, like they had never left, and Abberline strode inside while Aubrey stood in the doorway, one hand on the door frame, almost doubled over as he tried to get his breath.

From the kitchen came the sounds of Abberline muttering then an exclamation. "What is it?" said Aubrey, holding his side as he joined the other peeler in the kitchen.

Abberline stood at the far end of the room beneath the comprehensively broken window. Triumphantly he indicated the disturbed crockery table.

"Here," he said, "what do you see here?"

Whatever it was he was pointing out looked very much to Aubrey like a smudge of blood, and he said so.

"Right, a bloodstain left by whoever it was who dived through the window, right? You'd expect that, wouldn't you?"

"Well, yes."

"Blood from that Indian geezer we've just seen standing in Cavanagh's office like butter wouldn't melt, I would wager," said Abberline.

"That's an assumption, Freddie. Haven't we always been taught—look for evidence never assume, look for evidence."

"How about if you formulate theories then find the evidence to back it up?" asked Abberline with a glint in his eye. You had to give it to him, thought Aubrey. When he was on a roll . . .

"Go on . . ." said Aubrey.

"See the Indian geezer? He had bare feet, didn't he?"

"I know. Bloody hell, must save a few bob on boot leather . . ."

"Bear that fact in mind, and now take another look at your smudge of blood."

Aubrey did as he was told and Abberline watched as the light slowly dawned on his companion's face.

"Christ Almighty, you're right, it's a footprint."

"That's right. That's bloody right, Aubrey. A footprint. Now, look, you and I was standing over here." He pulled the other man over to where they were the previous evening, when they'd been remonstrating with the permanently indignant Mrs. Waugh. "Now, you have to imagine the window is intact. That makes it like a mirror, right? Like a black mirror. Well, I'm telling you, about half a second before that black mirror smashed and seven years of bad luck came in at us all at once, I saw a movement in it."

"You saw the assailant before he came smashing through?"

"Except now we think the Indian geezer was the assailant, don't we? But it wasn't the Indian geezer I saw. Who I saw was much bigger than that. So now I'm wondering . . . now I'm wondering if what I saw was a reflection." He pressed a hand to his forehead as though to try and massage a solution out of his brain. "Okay, what about this, Aubrey? What if one or maybe even two of those security geezers from the rail works were standing behind us? What would you say to that?"

"I'd say we bolted the door so how did they get in?"

"Here." Abberline dragged Aubrey out of the kitchen and toward the coal-cellar door. It was ajar. There was nothing suspicious about that, but inside was the coal with a distinct man-sized groove running through its middle, from the stone floor of the coal hole, right up to the hatch at street level.

"Gotcha!" exclaimed Abberline. "Now . . ." He returned Aubrey to the kitchen, where they resumed their positions. "We're standing here, right? Now say if we're right and I saw the reflection of a bugger who stood right behind us, just waiting to knock us out or worse. I saw how close he was. And we had our backs to him, don't forget. What I'm saying is that he had us, Aubrey. He had us, Aubrey, like a pair of sitting ducks, fattened up and ready for the slaughter. Could have knocked our block off with a truncheon. Could have slit our throats with a knife . . .

"And yet, for some reason, even though his mate was in position, the Indian fellow comes crashing through the window."

Abberline looked at Aubrey.

"Now why would that be, Aubrey? What the bloody hell was he doing coming in through the window?"

PART II

LOST CITY

THIRTY-THREE

Fifteen-year-old Evie Frye, the daughter of Ethan and the late Cecily, had developed a new habit. She wasn't especially proud of it, but still, it had developed anyway, as habits have a way of doing. She had taken to listening at her father's door during his meetings with George Westhouse.

Well, why not? After all, wasn't her father always saying she'd soon be joining "the fight," as he called it? Wasn't another of his favored expressions that there's no time like the present?

For years now Evie and her twin brother, Jacob, had been learning Assassincraft, and the two of them were enthusiastic students. Jacob, the more athletic of the pair, had taken to combat like a fish to water; he loved it, despite lacking the natural gift that his sister possessed. At nights, sharing a bedroom, the siblings would talk excitedly of the day that they would be introduced to the fabled hidden blade.

Nevertheless, Evie found her interest wandering. What came naturally to her didn't quite engross her the way it did her brother. While Jacob would spend his days in the yard of their home in Crawley, whirling like a dervish to practice moves taught by Father that morning, Evie would often creep away, declaring herself bored with the constant repetition of sword practice, and make her way to her father's study, where he kept his books.

Learning was what fired the imagination of Evie Frye. The writings of Assassin elders, chronicles of legendary Assassins: Altaïr Ibn-La'Ahad, whose name meant "the flying eagle," the handsome and dashing Ezio Auditore da Firenze, Edward Kenway, Arno Dorian, Adewale, Aveline de Grandpré and, of course, Arbaaz Mir, with whom her father had spent so much time when they were younger men.

All of them had joined the fight to hold the Templar scourge at bay, fighting for freedom in whatever time and territory they plied their trade; most had at one time or another become involved in helping to locate what were known as artifacts. No museum pieces, these. The artifacts that preoccupied Assassins and Templars were materials left by Those Who Came Before. Of them all, the most important were the Pieces of Eden. The power they harnessed was said to be biblical and the knowledge supposedly coded into them was said to be the learning of all ages, past, present and future. There were others, Altaïr Ibn-La'Ahad, for example—Evie had pored over a transcription of his codex—who had expressed doubt about them, wondering if they were mere trinkets. Evie wasn't sure, and perhaps that formed part of the appeal. She wanted to see these artifacts for herself. She wanted to hold them and feel a connection with a society that existed before her own. She wanted to know the unknowable powers that helped shape mankind.

Thus, when she overheard the word "artifacts" from inside her father's study one night, she had lingered to listen further. And listened again the next time George Westhouse visited and the time after that.

Sometimes she asked herself if Father knew there were eavesdroppers present. It would be just like him to say nothing. What mitigated her guilt was the feeling that he wouldn't *necessarily* disapprove. After all, she was merely harvesting early the information she'd be gathering later anyway.

"He's a brave one, this man of yours," George Westhouse was saying now.

"Indeed he is, and essential to any chance we have of one day taking back our city. The Templars believe us to be reduced to just you and me, George. Let them think that. Having an agent in their midst gives us a crucial advantage."

"Only if he learns something of use to us. Has he?"

Evie's father sighed. "Sadly not. We know that Cavanagh is regularly visited by Crawford, and in particular we know that Lucy Thorne spends a great deal of time at the dig . . ."

"Lucy Thorne, probably the Templars' greatest expert on the occult. Her very presence at the site indicates we're on the right track."

"Indeed. I never doubted it."

"But there's nothing to suggest when the Templars hope to find what they're looking for?"

"Not yet, but when they do, The Ghost is in place to snatch it for us."

"And if they already have?"

"Then at some point, as he continues to gain their trust, he will learn that and, again, be in the right place to retrieve the artifact and put it into our hands."

From behind Evie came a whisper. "What are you doing there?"

Startled and straightening with a slight cracking of her legs, Evie turned to find Jacob behind her, grinning as usual. She put a finger to her lips then ushered him away from the door and to the stairs so they should retire for bed.

Evie would tell Jacob what she had learned, knowing full well that for all he would insist on every little detail, he wouldn't really bother listening. Assassin history, tactics, policy, the artifacts—these were all aspects of the Assassin life that Jacob was happy to leave for a later date, when their father was good and ready to teach them.

Not for Evie, though. Evie was thirsty to learn.

THIRTY-FOUR

Months had passed since the events at the Waughs' home, and during those months, Abberline had brooded. Occasionally he brooded alone. Occasionally he had help, in the form of Aubrey who, while not quite as broody as Abberline, did a little out of sympathy, as well as being glad of an ale or two in The Green Man.

During these occasions, despondently hunched over a table in the pub and trying not to stand out like two truant-playing bobbies, Aubrey would attempt to lighten the mood with one of the best new music-hall jokes.

"I say, I say, I say, Freddie, when is a boat smaller than a bonnet?"

"I don't know, when is a boat smaller than a bonnet?"

"When it's capsized."

And sometimes he would try to lighten the mood with one of the worst.

"I say, I say, I say, Freddie. Why do tailors always please their customers?"

"I don't know, why?"

"Because it is their business to suit people."

And other times he would try to engage Abberline in more profound and philosophical discussion.

"It's just one of those things," he said one day.

"But it's not, though, is it?" Abberline, who had long since forgone his no-drinking-on-duty rule, drained the rest of his pint. "If it was just one of those things, I wouldn't be so bothered. Because you know what really irks me, Aubrey? It's the not knowing. It's the fact that liars and murderers are walking around out there, thinking they got one over on the peelers. No, what am I talking about? Not the peelers, because no bugger else apart from you and me could give two hoots about robed men and missing bodies. Thinking they got one over on you and me is what it is."

Aubrey shook his head sadly. "You know what your problem is, Freddie? You want everything to be black-and-white. You want answers all the time. And sometimes, you know, there just ain't no answers, and there ain't no black-and-white, there's just different shades of gray, which is to say that things are as murky as the bottom of the Thames and just as rotten-smelling, but there ain't nothing you can do about the Thames and there ain't nothing you can do about that either."

"No, you're wrong." Abberline stopped himself and reconsidered. "Well, all right, maybe you're only half-right. There are shades of gray when it comes to right and wrong. I'll give you that and stand you a pint for your insights"—he held up two fingers and was rewarded with a response from across the room—"but you're wrong about answers. There *are* answers. And I want to know those answers."

Aubrey nodded, tried to dredge up another joke, but the only one he could think of was one whose last line was, "No noose is good noose," and he didn't think that was appropriate in the circumstances. So instead they drank their next pint in silence and did some more brooding.

Outside they went their separate ways along Regent Street, and Abberline wondered if a man from the pub who had seemed to be taking an inordinate interest in them would follow either him or Aubrey.

Glancing in the reflection of the shop window, he saw that he was the lucky one.

THIRTY-FIVE

"So, how about you tell me why you've been following me these past few days?"

It was an especially vexed Abberline who had led his shadow up an alleyway on the New Road in order to confront him. Especially vexed because that very morning he had been called into the division sergeant's office and given a telling-off. No, not just a telling-off, but a severe reprimand. And why? Because apparently a certain Mr. Cavanagh of the Metropolitan Railway—that dead-eyed bastard—had made a complaint about him. According to him, Constable Abberline was spending a disproportionate amount of time at the site. Making something of a nuisance of himself, he was, what with his insinuations that Cavanagh and five of his employees were involved with a murder.

And he was to stop that at once.

So, yes, an especially vexed Abberline, given strength by his vexation, was watching the man's face turn purple above the blue serge of his forearm. The man wore a dark suit, and a bowler hat, a little tatty, but was otherwise fairly respectable-looking. In fact, thought Abberline, he was dressed not unlike one of the detectives from the division.

Except, Abberline knew all the detectives from the division. He knew all the detectives for miles around, and this bloke wasn't one of them, which had made him wonder if it was a different kind of detective altogether. With his other hand he frisked the man and came up with a small leather truncheon that he slipped into his own tunic pocket.

"Private dick, are we?" said Abberline.

In response the man nodded furiously. "Gak, gak, gak," he tried.

Abberline relaxed his grip.

"Yes, Constable Abberline, a private detective is what I am, and one who might be of benefit to you if you were to let me speak," gasped the man against the wall.

Cautious but curious, Abberline let him go. "What's your name?" he demanded.

"Leonard. Leonard Hazlewood."

"Right, now state your case, Mr. Hazlewood, and make it a good one."

Hazlewood straightened himself up first, adjusting his hat and his suit and his collar before he went on. "You're right, I'm a private detective in the employ of a member of the aristocracy, a viscount, if you please, who pays well and doesn't mind who he pays it to, if you know what I mean."

"Yes, I know exactly what you mean. How about I take you in for attempting to bribe a member of Her Majesty's constabulary?"

"Who's bribing anyone, Constable? I know my business, and I know that the other men at the division call you Fresh-faced Freddie, and that you like to do things by the book, and that you don't even take a drink on duty . . ."

Abberline cleared his throat guiltily. *Yeah, mate, if only you knew.* "What of it?"

"So I reckon you'd be just as interested in solving a crime as you would be in lining your own pocket. Maybe even more so. And that if I can help you do one, while maybe also doing the other, then maybe that isn't a bribe so much as a gift in recognition of your sterling police work, such as a benefactor might bestow."

"Just say what you have to say and say it outright."

"This viscount of mine. Him and his mate were set upon not far from here, in the Marylebone Churchyard. His mate was so viciously attacked that he lost his life there in the graveyard."

"He didn't have far to travel for his burial, then, did he?"

"A somewhat off-color joke, if you don't mind my saying so, Constable."

"It's an off-color joke because I know a load of drivel when I hear it, and I'm hearing it now. If two members of the aristocracy had been set upon in a graveyard and one of them killed right here in the division, I think I'd have known about it, don't you?"

"Both my employer and the family of the murdered man preferred not to report the matter, in a bid to keep out of the public spotlight."

Abberline curled a lip. "Oh yes? Up to no good, were they?"

"I didn't ask. I've simply been appointed to find and detain their attacker."

"Detain, is it? And then what? Deliver him into the hands of the police? Don't make me laugh. Do him down or top him completely is what you've got in mind."

Hazlewood pulled a face. "Does it matter? The fact is that justice will be served."

"Justice is served by the courts," said Abberline— although these days he wondered if he still believed it.

"Not always."

"You're right. Not always. Not on young nobles who get drunk, take a trollop or two into a graveyard then find themselves being rolled over by the ladies' pimps, am I right? I mean, unless you're trying to tell me they was in there putting poppies on a grave? One thing you can always depend on the aristocracy to do is get their jollies at the expense of the lower orders. Maybe the tables got turned for once."

The detective shrugged. "It wasn't a pimp. No simple cash carrier attacked my employer and killed his friend and disabled two of his bodyguards . . ."

Abberline's eyebrows shot up. "They had *bodyguards*, eh? Bloody hell, you really know how to play on a man's sympathies, you do, don't you?"

Hazlewood frowned and tugged at his collar again. His neck had reddened. This wasn't going well. "This was a dangerous man, Constable. Hardly even a man, they say, and it would be in all of our best interests if he were to be off the streets for good."

Abberline was thinking of Aubrey's different shades of gray. He was thinking about justice and how that fitted into the picture when two aristocrats took bodyguards for drunken jaunts into the less salubrious parts of town. Why should he care if a lone man taught the little bastards a lesson by giving them a good hiding—in other words, a really nasty thrashing. Abberline knew what Aubrey would say. Good luck to the fella. More power to his bloody elbow.

For maybe the first time ever, Abberline found not that he didn't care, but that him caring was in abnormally short supply. He chuckled. "And tell me, what did he look like, this man who was not even a man? I'll keep an eye out for . . . what? A monster, perhaps, six feet tall and armed to his jagged pointy teeth, with talons for hands and a roar to split the night?"

The private detective rolled his eyes. "If I didn't know better, I'd say you'd been drinking, Constable. No, when I say not quite a man, I don't mean *more* than one, I mean a young lad."

"A young lad?"

"That's right. An Indian boy, with bare feet. And they say he fought like the devil. Quite the acrobat, he was."

Abberline looked at him, suddenly serious as everything else fell away, and all other considerations were sidelined.

"An acrobat, you say?"

THIRTY-SIX

The next day, The Ghost stood by the shaft, overseeing the work. He clutched laced-up files full of dockets, manifests, schedules and work rotas to his chest—Marchant had off-loaded almost every aspect of his clerk's work onto The Ghost—and tending to them all was proving more taxing than anything he could remember doing ever, and that included learning the finer points of the kukri with Ethan Frye.

One of the foremen approached, wiping his nose on his sleeve. "Shall I toll for the shift change, Mr. Singh?"

The Ghost looked at him without seeing, trying to focus on words he wasn't used to hearing, specifically the words "Mr. Singh."

"Oh, yes," he said at last, "thank you." He watched as the foreman touched a hand to his forelock and stepped away, still not quite accustomed to this sudden change of events. "Indian" was what they had called him, the men, up until he started at his new post. But now . . . Mr. Singh. It had *respect*—power, even—because, yes, what was respect, if not a kind of power? For the first time in his life, The Ghost could understand its allure and the constant pursuit of it. For with power came money and influence and perhaps most importantly, it meant being heard, and these things were as seductive as love, friendship and family, probably more so because they spoke to selfish ego rather than the gentle heart.

Yes, he'd allowed himself to think, *I could, in another world, get used to being called Mr. Singh. I could come to truly enjoy that.*

Indeed, he had no choice, what with his new, exalted position at the dig.

Through Marchant, Cavanagh had insisted The Ghost smarten up. Hardy had handed him a brown-paper-wrapped bundle. "Here you go, mate, some new trousers and boots, shirt and a jacket for you. Hat in there, too, if you want it," and that night at the tunnel, The Ghost had tried on his new ensemble for Maggie's approval.

"Well, what a swell; you look quite the man about town," she told him when he was all tarted up. "You'll have all the ladies after you—if they're not already."

The Ghost smiled and Maggie felt her heart open at the sight of that smile, just as it had on the night they met, and now, just as she had then, she thought to herself, *If only I were forty years younger . . .*

In the event, The Ghost had done away with the hat. He never much liked his railwayman's cap and he'd give it to someone farther up the tunnel. The trousers were way too short, and The Ghost thought this was probably Hardy's evil trick. But the punisher would have been disappointed to know that the shorter trousers, flapping just above the ankle, suited The Ghost just fine. He gave the boots to Maggie. She gleefully tore out the laces before putting them on. Her old ones she'd pass to another tunnel dweller.

The next day he went back to the site, literally a changed man.

The work was demanding. Kukri-training hard. All his time was spent scratching out names and numbers on the various schedules Marchant presented to him, as well as keeping up with the constantly changing shifts or liaising with the many foremen, some of whom had taken "Indian's appointment" better than others. Interestingly, he'd found that a sharp but soft word accompanied by a glance to the office was enough to set any recalcitrant foreman straight. It wasn't respect that ruled, he knew. It was fear.

Nevertheless, his primary purpose for being here was not to ruminate on ideology or learn new workplace skills. It was to spy on behalf of the Brotherhood, to ascertain exactly what the Templars were up to, and in that regard he'd been slightly less successful. For a start, his new work kept him busy; secondly, he rarely had an excuse to visit the office, where the plans were kept.

One day he had looked up from his vantage point by the cranes to see Crawford Starrick and Lucy Thorne arrive, the two of them picking their way across the mud-flats before disappearing inside.

Now's the time, he had thought, and trod across the mud to the office on the pretext of delivering some dockets—only to be stopped by Mr. Smith and Other Mr. Hardy, the two punishers guarding the portal to the inner sanctum. They'd taken the documents from him and sent him away. The Ghost's introduction to Cavanagh's immediate circle was only theoretical, it seemed. Perhaps they were still testing him; indeed, not long after that day was an incident that The Ghost was still puzzling over.

It came one late afternoon when The Ghost approached Marchant on the mudflats. Shouting to make himself heard over the racket of a steam engine laden with spoil, he had tried to hand the site manager the rota, just as he did at the end of every shift.

"All in order, sir," he said, indicating the hive of industry behind him: men were swarming on the cranes, buckets of earth swinging black against the dwindling gray light of the day, filthy-faced laborers with spades and pickaxes slung over their shoulders, leaving the trench like defeated men on a retreat. The conveyor was rattling, always rattling.

On this occasion, instead of taking the rota as he would have done normally, Marchant shrugged and indicated the wooden site office behind them.

"In there," he said. "Leave it on the side near the plans table. I'll look at it later."

His eyes betraying nothing, The Ghost nodded assent and made his way across. There was no Cavanagh. No Mr. Hardy, Mr. Smith, or Other Mr. Hardy. There was just The Ghost, stepping into the office, the heart of the operation, alone.

He stopped himself. This was a test. This was surely a test. Conscious that Marchant might be timing him, he lit a lamp, then moved over to the plans table.

Marchant had been very specific about that. The plans table.

Sure enough, there, rolled up on the plans table, were the plans.

Placing the lamp to the tabletop, The Ghost bent to inspect the rolled-up document. If it was a trap as he suspected, then this was how it would be laid, and . . . *there*, he saw it. A single black hair had been left rolled into the plans, just the tip of it protruding. His heart hammering, The Ghost reached and plucked the hair out of the plans between his fingernails, and then, praying it would be the only trap they set, unrolled them.

There, laid out in front of him, were the designs for the excavation and the building of the railway, but not the official designs. Those he had seen, craning over the heads of fellow workmen as Charles Pearson and John Fowler gave presentations on their baby. Those plans looked exactly like these but for one vital difference. They had the crest of the Metropolitan Railway in the top right-hand corner. This set sported the crest of the Knights Templar.

Marchant would be wondering where he was. Quickly he scanned the drawings in front of him, eyes immediately going to a section of the dig; in fact, the section they were currently digging. Here was a shaded circle. Inside that shaded circle was another, smaller, Templar cross.

The Ghost rolled up the plans, replaced the hair, extinguished the lamp, and left the office. As he left the office with the image of the plans fresh in his mind, his thoughts went back to the events of a few days ago, when boxes had been brought and a makeshift stage built. Cavanagh had taken to it, with Marchant and the punishers standing at the hem of his coat, and through a speaking trumpet went

on to regretfully announce that there had been some
instances of theft from the site—that men's tools had been
stolen.

This had elicited a gasp. The men cared about their tools
as much as they did their families. More so, in many cases.
The Ghost had long since been in the habit of burying his
own spade at a spot on the perimeter of the dig, but for
many men their spades and pickaxes weren't just the means
of their livelihood, they were symbolic of it. When they
walked through the streets with the tools of their trade
over their shoulders, they walked tall, with their heads held
high, and passersby knew they were in the presence of a
hardworking man rather than just a dirty one. Thus, the
idea that some wretch was stealing the men's tools, well,
this fellow might as well have been stealing the food from
out of their mouths. Cavanagh had the men wrapped
around his little finger, and his proposal that men would
be searched as they left the site from now on, was therefore
met with fewer than expected grumbles. Shift changes now
took three times longer but at least the men could be reassured that the Metropolitan Railway had their best interests
at heart.

The Ghost hadn't been fooled, but now he knew
exactly what lay behind the decisions. It was because the
excavation had finally reached the shaded circle. The end
was in sight and though the men were under strict orders
to report any unusual finds—with the promise of a reward
to match the value of anything precious—there was still
a possibility that one of the men might simply purloin what
he found. Chances were the Templars were as clueless

about this artifact as the Assassins were. They were taking no chances.

Then there was the other issue, the small matter of the persistent police constable Abberline, who had been turning up at the works and, according to Marchant, making accusations against him. "Don't you worry," the clerk had said, "we've got you covered." The implication was that their "having him covered" came with a price.

He would see to it that he repaid them. Yes, he would repay them.

Now Abberline had returned with a consortium, two of whom he recognized—the other peeler, Aubrey, and the division sergeant—and two of whom he didn't—a smartly dressed man who had a habit of tugging at his collar, and a fourth man, who . . .

There was something about this fourth man The Ghost recognized. He looked closer now, feeling as though his brain was moving too slowly as he tried to place the man . . .

Marchant was walking toward him, coming closer, hailing him with a weasel grin "Oi, you're needed over here . . ."

Still The Ghost was staring at the new arrival, who had stood slightly apart from the group and was looking right back at him. As their eyes met, they recognized one another.

He was the bodyguard from the graveyard.

THIRTY-SEVEN

Abberline watched him come.

That morning he had stormed into the sergeant's office, with his new friend Hazlewood the private detective in tow, and told the sergeant that he had something new on the Indian at the dig.

"Tell him what you told me," he insisted to Hazlewood, who wore an expression that seemed to indicate things were quickly moving away from him, like this wasn't the way he had planned it: one minute, trading confidences with a contact who might be of use finding this Indian fellow; the next being hauled before the division sergeant by an excited Abberline.

Sure enough, the sergeant looked him up and down before returning his attention to Abberline. "And who the bloody hell is this, Freddie?"

"He's a private detective, is what he is. He's a private detective who happens to have information regarding our friends at the rail works."

"Oh, not the bloody rail works." The sergeant sighed. "Please not the bloody rail works, *again*."

"Now, hold on, hold on a minute." Hazlewood had his hands held out to Abberline and the sergeant like a man trying to control a small crowd. "I've been asked to locate a young thug involved in a brutal attack on a member of the aristocracy who wishes to see justice served. I don't know anything about any goings-on at the rail works."

"One and the same, mate, one and the same," Abberline reassured him. "Now just tell him what you told me before I do it, and believe you me, I ain't leaving anything out and I may even add a few bits and pieces that won't reflect at all well on either you or your employers."

The detective shot him a furious look and directed himself to the sergeant. "As I was telling the"— he paused, for extra contempt—"*constable* here, I have been employed by some very high-ranking gentlemen in order to help apprehend a very dangerous man."

"*A very dangerous man,*" spoofed Abberline. "That's a matter of opinion. You say that there was another body-guard there, apart from the two in the sanatorium?"

"There was."

"Then he could identify the boy. We could take him to the rail works and get him to identify the man who attacked him and your employer."

"We could do that, I suppose . . ." said Hazlewood cautiously.

"And why *would* we do that?" roared the sergeant from behind his desk. "I've already had Mr. bloody Cavanagh of the Metropolitan Railway giving me the reaming out to end all reamings out on account of your behavior, Abberline, and if you think I intend to risk another one— or worse still have him talk to John Fowler or Charles

Pearson and the next minute have the superintendent breathing down my neck—you've got another think coming."

Abberline winked. "Our friend here can make it worth your while, Sergeant."

The sergeant narrowed his eyes. "Is this true?" he demanded of Hazlewood.

The detective admitted it was true. He could indeed make it worth the sergeant's while, and the sergeant did a little weighing up. True, there was the risk of another reprimand, but then again he had a scapegoat in Abberline.

What's more, a little extra would come in handy, what with Mrs. Sergeant's birthday coming up.

So he'd agreed that if they could produce this bodyguard, then they had enough of a reason to confront the Indian lad at the dig, and now the Indian was coming over the mud toward them. Bloody hell, thought Abberline, he'd gone up in the world. Wearing a new pair of trousers, he was, as well as braces and a collarless shirt open at the neck. Still barefoot, mind, his new trousers flapping about his calves as he came closer toward them, the whole of the group, it seemed, fixed by his dark, impenetrable gaze.

"Bharat Singh?" said Abberline to the group. "I'm pleased to see all those cuts and bruises have healed since the last time I saw you."

Barely acknowledging them, The Ghost stood before the group, holding files to his chest and looking quizzically from man to man. Abberline watched as the lad's gaze swept past the bodyguard, and he reminded himself that if even half of what they said about this young man was true, then he might be a very slippery, not to mention dangerous, customer indeed. He readied himself. For what, he wasn't sure. But he did it anyway.

"Now," he addressed The Ghost, "if you don't mind, we have a matter to attend to." Surreptitiously, he felt for the handle of his truncheon and directed his next question to the bodyguard. "Is this the man who set upon you and your two employers in the churchyard? Have a good long look now, it's been a while, and he's spruced up a bit in the meantime. But if you ask me, that's not the kind of face you forget in a hurry, is it? So, come on, is it him or not?"

The Ghost turned his attention to the bodyguard, meeting his eye. The man was tall, like the three punishers, but not cocky and arrogant like they were. A reduced man; the encounter in the graveyard had left him changed but here was his opportunity to recover some of that lost pride and dignity.

Abberline's fingers flexed on the butt of his truncheon; Aubrey was ready, too, and the punishers stood with their eyes narrowed, hands loose by their sides, ready to reach for whatever concealed weapons they carried as they awaited their next set of orders and anticipated bloodshed to come.

Every single man there expected the bodyguard to give the answer yes.

So it came as something of a surprise when he shook his head, and said, "No, this ain't the man."

THIRTY-EIGHT

"So, what is the truth of it, then?" asked Abberline.

"I don't think I know what you mean."

The impromptu meeting at the rail works had broken up and Abberline had left with his tail between his legs, then, back at the station house, the sergeant had given him a flea in his ear, and, with his tail between his legs and his flea in his ear, Abberline had gone searching for the bodyguard.

Why? Because he'd seen the look on the geezer's face and he'd seen the look on Mr. Bharat Singh's face into the bargain and there was something there. Nonrecognition my arse, those two knew each other. They had a . . . well, strange as it may sound, but Abberline would have said he'd witnessed a kind of grudging, mutual respect pass between them.

So the next order of business was to find the bodyguard, which wasn't difficult; he'd done it with Hazlewood, the previous day, and this afternoon he found the bodyguard in the same place, The Ten Bells on Commercial Street in Whitechapel, a favorite haunt of prostitutes and con men, the occasional police constable and disgraced former bodyguards attempting to drown their sorrows.

"You're protecting him is what I think," said Abberline.

Without a word, the bodyguard picked up his drink and moved to a table in the bar parlor. Abberline followed and sat opposite. "Someone paying you to protect him—is that it? Not a man in robes by any chance."

No answer.

"Or perhaps you're protecting him out of the goodness of your own heart?" said Abberline, only now the man looked up at him with sorrowful eyes and Abberline knew he was on the right track. He pressed the point home. "What if I were to tell you that I had my own suspicions about this young Indian man? What if I were to tell you that I think he might well have saved my life a while back, and that in fact, far from trying to put this guy in the clink, I'm actually beginning to wonder if he might be on the side of the angels?"

Another pause then the bodyguard began to speak in a voice that rumbled from between his hunched shoulders. "Well, then you would be right, Constable, because if you ask me, he is indeed on the side of the angels. He's a good man. A better man than either you or I will ever be."

"Speak for yourself. So he was in the churchyard that night, then?"

"He was indeed and there wasn't no 'setting upon' anyone being done. There was a wrong—a wrong with which I was involved, to my shame—a wrong that he put right. My employers at the time, two nobs, were doing down a slattern, just for kicks, because they could. And me and my mates were looking out for them. Ours not to reason why and all that."

Abberline gave a thin smile of recognition.

"And this young man turns up, the only passerby who did anything more than react to her screams with mild puzzlement. And when the two nobs wouldn't stop their game, he stopped it for them.

"I've never seen anything move so fast, I'm telling you, boy, man or animal. He bested all of us, including yours truly, he did it in the blink of an eye, and we deserved it, every last one of us, we had it coming.

"So if you're asking why I didn't identify him at the rail works, and if you're sincere when you say you believe he fights for good, and as long as you're asking me in the parlor of The Ten Bells, knowing I'll deny it at the site, at the station or if I'm up before a judge, then yes, it was the same man. And bloody good luck to him."

"Of course it was the same man."

Marchant and Cavanagh had met Hazlewood at The Traveler's Club on the Strand, where they took him to the smoking room overlooking Carlton Gardens.

Cavanagh was a member at the Traveler's, nominated by Colonel Walter Lavelle, shortly before Cavanagh killed him; Marchant, as Cavanagh's right-hand man, was also familiar with the club; Hazlewood, on the other hand, was agog or, as he'd later say to his wife, "as excited as a dog with two cocks." Men like him weren't accustomed to being entertained in The Traveler's Club on the Strand, and he smelled money, as well as maybe the chance to solve this bloody case into the bargain. Maybe, if he played his cards right, the chance to solve the case *and* make a bit of extra chink on the side.

Not forgetting, of course, the fact that it was a swanky old place, and no mistake.

Around them was the laughter and raised voices of drunken lords and gentlemen getting even drunker, but it was hard to imagine Cavanagh participating. He sat in a voluminous leather armchair with his hands on the armrests, wearing a smart black suit with flashes of white shirt at the collar and cuffs. But even though he fitted in among the toffs and swells, Cavanagh radiated a certain danger, and it was telling that when the occasional passing gentleman greeted him with a wave, the gentleman's smile dipped momentarily, more as though he was paying his respects than saying hello.

"You think the man who attacked your client and my employee Bharat Singh are one and the same?" he asked of Hazlewood now.

"I'm sure of it, sir."

"What makes you so sure?"

"Because when I hear hooves I look for horses, not zebras."

Marchant looked confused but Cavanagh nodded. "In other words you think logic dictates it must be the same man."

"That I do—that and the fact that I spoke to our friend the bodyguard afterward and it was pretty obvious that for reasons best known to his own self, he was keeping quiet."

"Then perhaps we need to persuade the bodyguard," said Cavanagh, and Hazlewood thought "money," and wondered if some of it might be coming his way.

"Tell me," said Cavanagh, "if this young Indian man set upon the bodyguard, and—what? Four other men?—in an unprovoked and vicious attack, then why would the bodyguard want to protect him?"

Hazlewood looked shifty. At a nod from Cavanagh, Marchant took folding money from his pocket and laid it on the table between them.

Here we go, thought Hazlewood, palming it. "Well," he said, "I only know what I've been told, but it seems the Indian lad took it upon himself to rescue a damsel in distress who was being used as a bit of a plaything by the two toffs.

Cavanagh nodded, eyes flitting around the wood-paneled room. He knew the type. "Getting their jollies, were they?"

"By the sounds of things. Your man, this Indian boy, was quite the dervish, it seems. He took on the lot of them and won, and by all accounts carried the poor tail they was doing down off into the night."

"I see," said Cavanagh. He paused for nearby laughter to die down. "Well, Mr. Hazlewood, I thank you for your honesty, and for bringing this matter to our attention. If you leave this matter with us, we should like to conduct our own investigations. Perhaps, when this process is complete, and assuming that our findings are in accordance with your own suspicions, we can join forces, so that we can root out the bad apple, and you can get your man."

When Hazlewood had left, a happy man, Cavanagh turned to his companion. "We shall be true to our word, Marchant. We shall look very closely into our interesting Indian colleague."

THIRTY-NINE

Early the next morning, as was quickly becoming his custom, Abberline was staring at a dead body. Beside him stood Aubrey, and the two constables took off their helmets as a mark of respect. They knew the man who lay sprawled on the street, his face barely recognizable beneath eyes that had swelled shut, a face that was a mixture of purple bruises and open cuts, and a broken jaw that hung at an obscene angle.

It was the bodyguard.

"Someone who wanted to shut him up, obviously," said Aubrey.

"No," replied Abberline thoughtfully, staring at the corpse and wondering how many more had to die. "I don't think they were trying to shut him up. I think they were trying to make him talk."

Across the city, Cavanagh sat behind his desk at the rail-works office, Marchant on one side, Hardy on the other.

In front of the desk, sitting on forbidding straight-backed chairs and wearing expressions to match, were the Templar Grand Master Crawford Starrick and Lucy Thorne. As usual, they wanted a report from Cavanagh, the man who had promised to deliver them the artifact but had so far conspicuously failed to do so, and as usual, they wanted that report to include encouraging news.

"We're close," Cavanagh told them.

Lucy sighed and frowned and rearranged her skirts. Starrick looked distinctly unimpressed. "This is what you said last time and the time before that."

"We're closer," added Cavanagh, unperturbed by his Grand Master's irritation. "We have to be. We're in the immediate vicinity of the artifact's location."

There came a knock at the door and Other Mr. Hardy showed his face. "Sir, sorry to disturb you, but Mr. and Mrs. Pearson have arrived."

Starrick rolled his eyes but Cavanagh held out a hand to show it was a matter of no concern. "Ill as he is, Pearson prefers the company of the workers to the hospitality of the office. He'll have his usual royal tour, don't worry."

Other Mr. Hardy glanced back out of the door. "Seems all right, sir. Like you say, he's making his way over to the trench."

"Even so," said Starrick, "I believe that concludes our business. Miss Thorne and I shall take our leave. See to it that the next time we visit, you have some more encouraging news for me."

When they had gone, Cavanagh looked at Marchant with hooded eyes. "He's a fool; he knows his time is short."

"He is the Templar Grand Master, sir," said Marchant,

and added, with an obsequious smile, "for the time being."

"Exactly," said Cavanagh. "For the moment. Until such time as I have the artifact."

And he allowed himself a smile. The ghost of a smile.

Meanwhile, as Cavanagh, Marchant and company were occupied with Starrick and Thorne—and with The Ghost yet to begin his shift—Pearson was doing just as Cavanagh said he would and conducting a small tour of the works, his wife Mary on his arm.

The men loved Pearson, and on this particular occasion, had cooked up a plan to show him just how much. At the office steps, with Starrick and Thorne making their way to the gates, Marchant watched the men gather around Mr. and Mrs. Pearson, frowning that work seemed to have been abandoned for no good reason he could think of. There was definitely something going on, though. He leaned on the rail to speak to Other Mr. Hardy. "Get over there, would you? See what's going on . . ."

FORTY

It was a rare afternoon off for Police Constable Aubrey Shaw.

No, that wasn't strictly speaking true; firstly, because Aubrey's afternoons off were comparatively frequent, and secondly because it wasn't really an "afternoon off." Not in the officially sanctioned sense anyway. A more accurate way of putting it would be to say that Police Constable Aubrey Shaw had donned plain clothes and was playing truant again.

As usual, Aubrey's behavior incorporated a cricketing element. Most of the time this meant hoisting ale in The Green Man but today was a special day. He had taken his business to Lord's cricket ground in order to watch the annual Eton versus Harrow match. It was a nice sunny day to spend with a spot in the stands (albeit crowded, the event was attended by tens of thousands) a pie and maybe an ale or three, with plenty of bustles and bonnets to catch a man's eye and the cricket whites blinding in the sun.

Truth be known, Aubrey didn't much care for cricket,

but the gentleman's sport was a pastime his wife approved of, and what's more it involved pies and beer—and meeting those two requirements was central to Aubrey's journey through life.

He thought of Abberline. Unmarried Abberline, constantly preoccupied Abberline—the two undeniably connected as far as Aubrey could see.

"A wife is what you need," was what he'd told Abberline one afternoon in where else but The Green Man.

"A fellow bobby who cares more about police work and less about how to get out of doing it, is what I need," was what Abberline had replied.

Which was rather hurtful; after all, he, Aubrey, had become almost as involved in their ongoing case as Freddie, and . . .

Oh no, he thought, as he took his place on the stands, *I'm not thinking about Freddie today. Freddie begone.* To signal an end to work-related thoughts he began lustily joining in with the cheers, happy to submit himself to the tides of the game and the rhythm of the day. Just another face in the crowd. Worries ebbing away.

Still, though. He couldn't help it. His thoughts returned to Abberline and his ongoing obsession with what he called "the goings-on at the rail works." The two bobbies had asked themselves who beat the bodyguard to death. "One of them fighters from the rail works," said Freddie predictably, but on this occasion Aubrey had to agree with him. It was plain as the nose on your face that Cavanagh and company were up to no good. After all, weren't they all? Aristocrats and industrialists and politicians all feathered their own nests and breaking a few laws was a small inconvenience if you had enough influence to ride roughshod over them anyway.

Bloody hell, thought Aubrey. Hark at him. He was starting to think like Freddie himself. It was catching, that was what it was.

But they might know—this was what Abberline said. If they'd got it out of the bodyguard, then Cavanagh and company might be aware that Bharat Singh was the boy at the graveyard.

"What would it matter to them if he was?" Aubrey had asked.

"Maybe nothing, Aubrey, maybe nothing. Who knows?"

It was a puzzle, no doubt about it. Like those carved wooden shapes that fitted together. You turned it over in your hands to try to figure out how it worked.

A combination of cogitation, ale intake, the sheer volume of other spectators and the fact that he was here at Lord's on an unofficial day off and probably wouldn't have noticed anyway, meant that Aubrey wasn't aware of three men who had barged through the crowds to take places at the rear of the stand. They stood with their backs to the fence of the stand, with their arms folded and the brims of their bowler hats pulled down in the universal pose of the man trying to look unobtrusive.

The three men weren't watching the game from beneath the brims of their hats. Their gaze was fixed firmly on Aubrey Shaw.

Forty-one

The last occupant of The Darkness had been Jayadeep Mir, some three years ago. Nevertheless, the rooms had to be maintained and so, as regular as clockwork, Ajay and Kulpreet would take the steps down from the meeting house to sweep out the chambers and allow fresh air from outside to temporarily banish the dank air of gloom that otherwise hung about the place.

And as regular as clockwork, Ajay would think it a great joke to lock Kulpreet in one of the rooms.

Clang.

He'd crept up on her and before she could stop him, done it again, only this time, instead of standing outside snickering and mocking her as usual, he was making off down the passageway.

Her shoulders sank with the sheer boring inevitability of it all. Would he ever grow bored of it? Possibly not, because Ajay was nothing if not juvenile and, despite the fact that she had a husband and a little boy at home, was probably a little bit in love with her, too. And in her experience that was a very tiresome combination in a man.

Exasperated, she called through the viewing aperture, "Ajay, not again," cursing that he'd been able to sneak up on her like that, the rat.

There was silence from outside. Ajay had gone. Damn his eyes. She hoped it wasn't one of those days when he decided to string out the joke. He'd left her in there for half an hour once. Thank heavens she'd long since learned to bring a candle into the chamber with her.

"Ajay," she called again, the word falling flat on the dank stone. She rattled the door, the sound bouncing away into the darkness. "Ajay, this stopped being funny months ago. Open up, will you?"

Still there came no sound from outside and, come to think of it, she hadn't heard him for a while. Ajay wasn't one for keeping quiet. Even with him upstairs and her downstairs, he would have been calling to her, making bad jokes and puns, teasing her. In fact, when *was* the last time she'd heard any voice other than her own? You could lose all sense of time down here.

From outside the door came a sound that made her jump. "Ajay," she said sharply, but brought her leading arm to bear, tensing her wrist in readiness.

Then he was there, face at the window, grinning at her.

"I got you that time, Kulpreet. You thought they'd come to get us, didn't you?"

Right, she thought, and she arched one eyebrow and engaged her blade, precision-controlling its length so that it shot through the aperture and into the tip of Ajay's nostril.

Not just one of the Indian Brotherhood's best swordsmen, Kulpreet was also one of the best with a blade, and it was a perfectly judged, expertly balanced deployment.

"Impressive," said Ajay, with a newly acquired nasal twang. He was pinned in place by the blade, knowing that with the slightest movement he could effectively slice open his own nostril, and thinking that by God, she kept that thing sharp. Constantly greasing and recalibrating it, she was. "It'll never jam, Ajay," she'd tell him, sliding the blade into its housing, and then follow it with her best disapproving stare. "Not like some others I could mention."

Kulpreet kept her blade where it was. "Toss me the keys," she said, and then when he'd done as he was told, she was free again, barging angrily past him on her way to the dungeon portal.

Upstairs they locked up and prepared to leave for the night. Kulpreet studiously ignored Ajay which, she knew, was a far worse punishment than a hidden blade up the nose.

As she did every night she placed her flat-bladed sword into the wall rack, kissed her fingers and touched them to the fine Indian steel, before joining Ajay at the meeting-house door. The two Assassins said their parting words then slipped outside and locked the door behind them.

Neither noticed faces in the crowded street that watched them leave with interest—and then moved to follow.

FORTY-TWO

What a great day, thought Aubrey as he joined the thousands of spectators leaving Lord's. He was a little merry if he was honest with himself. Merry enough to decide to coax a flower girl to give him a deal for a bunch, take the flowers home to Marjorie, and tell his wife he loved her; merry enough to have forgotten all about acrobatic Indian boys and mysterious disappearing men in robes; and way too merry to notice the three men who were following him, their heads bowed and their hands in their pockets, in the classic manner of men trying to look inconspicuous.

He was even merry enough to consider hailing one of the four-wheeled cabs constantly popping to and fro, but then decided against. Best to sober up a bit. Just a bit. So he kept on walking, turning off the main drag into quieter side streets, leaving the crowds and clopping hooves behind as he weaved his way through darker streets where the constant sound of running water reminded him that he needed a piss, and ducking into an alleyway to relieve himself.

Because in the end it's the small things that matter as

much as the big ones: a stolen pocket watch that is slow, a man in need of a piss.

Aubrey sensed the light in the alleyway change before he saw anything, and still putting himself back into his trousers, he glanced to one end and saw that in the mouth of the alleyway stood a figure. Then back at the other end, another figure.

Aubrey felt a shiver. Any other day and this would be a pair of mutchers, the street ruffians who preyed on the poor souls who were too drunk to offer much resistance— and of course Aubrey could deal with them all right, drunk or sober.

But this wasn't any other day. And besides, he fancied he recognized the two men who blocked both exits, and that made it worse than a pair of mutchers.

They were moving up the alley toward him. A third figure had appeared at the mouth of the alley. Aubrey desperately wished he had his truncheon but knew it would be no good. He cast his eyes at the streaming wall right in front of him in the hope that a ladder might magically be present, then back at the men, who were upon him now.

He recognized the grinning faces in the second before the light went out. Just as he'd known he would.

Striding through the streets of Amritsar in their robes, Kulpreet and Ajay had been preoccupied with their own thoughts. Perhaps because years of Assassin dominance in the city had made them complacent, or perhaps because even Assassins are not immune to mistakes, but whatever the reason, before they knew it the crowd seemed to dematerialize, and standing in the street before them was a line of seven men in matching brown suits. Something they had always been told to train for and expect was actually happening. They were under attack.

Kulpreet and Ajay wheeled around. The street was emptying. Behind them was another phalanx of men in brown suits, nervous crowds moving away from them like ripples from a dropped stone. A tempo of fear increased as the brown suits began to produce kukris from within their coats. Over a dozen blades versus two.

Ajay and Kulpreet looked at each other. With a reassuring smile she pulled her cowl over her head and he did the same, then he reached to give her three quick taps and a squeeze on her upper arm, and she responded to the code with a nod. They knew what to do.

Mentally they both counted—one, two, three—and then, in one coordinated movement, went back-to-back, deploying their blades at the same time, and it was a measure of how quiet everything had become that the noise was even audible, and a measure of how confident the brown suits felt that they didn't even flinch, didn't even look nervous.

The one in the middle was the leader. He gave a whistle and rotated a finger. As one, the brown suits began to advance, the end of each line edging forward, closing the circle in the hope of trapping Ajay and Kulpreet at its center.

"*Now*," said Kulpreet, and they made their move. She dashed to a canopy on her left and he went in the opposite direction, and both reached their respective targets before the brown suits could get to them.

Ajay's blade was back in its housing as he hit the wall running, his bare feet clinging to the stone as he reached for a sill and heaved himself up. Two more grunting efforts and he was on the roof traversing the building, jumping down to the street on the other side and sprinting into a passageway. At the end was one of Amritsar's street walls separating one thoroughfare from the next, and Ajay went for it now, knowing he'd be home free if he could scale the wall and get over.

He never made it. The brown suits had anticipated his move, and as Ajay reached the end of the alleyway they appeared, taking him by surprise. He stumbled and saw a kukri flashing toward him, and acting on instinct brought his hidden blade arm into defense, engaging the steel . . .

Only, the blade didn't engage.

It jammed.

FORTY-THREE

Aubrey had no idea where he was but sensed that was the least of his concerns.

What mattered was that he was bound to a chair in a room that was dark apart from a flickering orange glow given off by lamps bolted to the walls, while in front of him stood the three punishers, gazing at him with smiling dispassion, preparing to do their work.

Hardy stepped forward. He pulled on black leather gloves then from his jacket pocket took a pair of brass knuckles that he slipped over his fingers. The two other men shared a look and stepped back into the shadows as Hardy came to Aubrey and put his gloved hand to the peeler's face, like a sculptor testing the consistency of his unmolded clay.

Then he stepped back and placed his feet with the expertise of a boxer, and Aubrey thought that closing his eyes might be a good idea right now, so he did. It was funny because he'd always found it difficult to picture his family when he was away from them; it was something he always wished he could do—just to have them with him.

But they came to him now. A perfect image of them that he clung to as the blows began raining in. There was that to be said for being beaten up, at least.

Thank God for small mercies.

Kulpreet awoke with a sore head and found herself squinting in the gray dark of a warehouse: an empty, cavernous space, with just the slapping sound of rain pouring through the roof and birds nesting in the rafters. Rusting stairways led to ancient, dilapidated gantries overhead.

She was restrained in an unusual manner. Seated at one end of a long slatted table, it was to all intents and purposes as though she were an honored guest for dinner—apart from the fact that you tended not to tie up honored guests. Her chair was pushed neatly beneath the table. She couldn't see her feet but they were bound to chair legs. Meanwhile, her hands were laid out in front of her, tied tightly around a slat with a leather thong, palms flat to the tabletop. They were placed almost as though she were about to receive a manicure.

In a sense, she was. A few inches from her fingers, laid very deliberately so that she could see them, was a pair of pliers, the sort of rusting pliers one might use to extract a fingernail.

She knew of this torture, of course. The cumulative pain. Apparently there was an Assassin who had managed five before he broke.

As far as she could tell, there were three brown suits in the warehouse with her. With clenched jaw she watched as one of them inspected her hidden blade, and if there was one thing that made her angry—beyond being captured, beyond having it taken from her and beyond being told by sniggering brown suits that Ajay had been cut down like a dog in the street, it was that. They had Ajay's blade as well. Another Templar thug stood at the end of the table, turning it over in his hands.

"This one jammed," he told his friends, and they laughed.

But that's not why you can't deploy it, you idiot, thought Kulpreet. *Not unless you can slip it over your wrist and arrange your muscles and tendons in such a way as to precisely emulate Ajay, or can activate the failure-avoidance switch, and to be honest, you could spend the rest of your life looking for the switch and still not find it.*

The lead brown suit turned his attention from his colleagues to Kulpreet. "It's calibrated to each individual Assassin," he called back over his shoulder as he came forward to Kulpreet. Behind him the two thugs had grown bored of inspecting the blades and dropped them to the table, and she wanted to look over at them, to check their position, but didn't dare.

She was thinking about that switch.

"Well, well, she's awake," said the grinning inquisitor. "Looks like it's time to begin."

He picked up the pliers but then made a show of pretending to reconsider and dropped them back to the table with a clunk. "Maybe I won't be needing those," he said, almost to himself. "I mean, it's not as if it's a difficult question, the one I have to ask. Did you put Jayadeep Mir to death three years ago, or was he banished to London instead? It's quite straightforward really."

He looked at her, but if he was hoping for a response, she didn't give him the satisfaction. He continued, "You see, pretty one, we have a colleague in London who was a British army officer who spent some time in India, and he heard all about the extraordinary Jayadeep Mir, and now he's met a rather extraordinary Indian boy in London and what with one thing and another, he wonders if the two might be one and the same. What do you have to say about that?"

She said nothing but when he stepped to one side and retrieved the pliers she was able to see past him and check the position of the hidden blades. Now she needed to check the stability of the table, and she feigned a helpless fury, shaking herself as though trying to wrench free. The men shared an amused glance but she'd learned what she needed to know: the table was not secured to the floor, but it was heavy, too heavy for her to tip by herself. She'd need help to do that.

But if she could tip it, then maybe she could reach one of the hidden blades.

"Water," she said, softly.

"I beg your pardon," said the inquisitor. He'd been turning the pliers over in his hand, staring at them fondly. "What was that?"

She made as though she were too parched to form words. "Water . . ."

He leaned a little closer. "What did you say?"

Was he close enough to grab with her teeth? She had two chances to do this, and this was one of them. But if she messed it up . . .

No. Best to wait. Best to try and lull him into a false sense of security.

And so, as though making a Herculean effort, she managed to say the word "water" audibly enough for her inquisitor to hear, and he stepped away, beaming.

"Ah, I thought that's what you said." He indicated to one of the men, who disappeared then reappeared a few moments later with an earthenware mug that he placed on the table in front of her.

She made an attempt to reach for it with her teeth before fixing him with a look of appeal, and with a smile he picked up the mug and lifted it to her lips, excited and titillated at having this beautiful woman so much in his control that she needed help even having a sip of water. Oh, how he was going to enjoy what came next. The inquisitor was a man who enjoyed his work. He was good at it; he was an expert when it came to inflicting . . .

Pain.

It shot up his arm. With her teeth she had clamped onto his hand and she wasn't just biting him, she was eating him. Oh my God, she was eating him alive.

He yelled in agony. The mug dropped but didn't smash. Kulpreet kept her teeth clenched on the inquisitor's hand, tasting sweat and dirt and wrenching her neck at the same time, maximizing his pain and using every ounce of her strength to bring him closer. At the same time she tipped the legs of the chair out to one side, resting all her weight on her forearms as she used them to slam into the inquisitor's shins, sending him off balance and increasing the speed of his downward journey so that at last he sprawled to the table, face breaking the earthenware mug as he made contact, and if that added to his pain, then great, thought Kulpreet, but that wasn't her main objective, because what she needed to do now was . . .

With all her might and using the weight of them both, she bore down on the table, which tilted so the hidden blades came skidding down the surface toward her waiting fingertips. The inquisitor was in the way so she couldn't even see them come but she felt one reach her fingertips just as he managed to yank his hand free of her mouth, and she gasped with her own pain as one of her teeth went with it. Blood and torn flesh were around her mouth but she didn't care about that now, all she cared about was the blade she was turning over in her hands, feeling for the switch. Over the body of the inquisitor she could see the other two men exchanging an amused glance before reaching for their kukris and of course they were in no hurry, because after all, what could she do? The odds were not in her favor. Even with a blade she was still tied to a chair, and there were three of them and a locked door. Skilled and clever and lucky as she was, there wasn't enough luck in the world to save her now. They knew it, she knew it. They all knew how this would end: she would tell them what they wanted to know then she would die.

Kulpreet realized this, of course. But the object of getting the hidden blade was not to use it on her captors.

It was to use it on herself.

But still, thank God for small mercies, because she had the opportunity to take one with her, and so as her thumb went to the switch, she did what looked like an odd thing: she brought her face close to the throat of the inquisitor, and because of the position of her arms it looked as if she were taking him in a lover's embrace, pressing her flesh to his.

One of her captors realized her true intention but it was too late. She had already rammed the blade housing against the inquisitor's neck and then with her eye still at his throat, released the blade, which shot through him and into her.

As Kulpreet died she thought of all she had done. She thought of her husband and little boy at home, who would be wondering where she was. She even thought of poor old Ajay—"well, I'll be joining you soon, old friend"—and she thought of the Brotherhood and wished it well, and it was with a heavy heart that she knew the struggle for a better and fairer world would have to continue without her.

As the point of the blade drove through her attacker's neck and into her own eye and into her brain, Kulpreet knew this was a better death than the one they had planned for her, but she wondered if it was a noble death. She had told them nothing, and she hoped that would count for something. She hoped the Council would decree that she died with honor.

FORTY-FOUR

Two days later on the harbor at Amritsar, three men in brown suits intercepted an Assassin messenger.

The three men killed the Assassin, made sure to retrieve the message he'd been due to deliver to London then bundled his body into a wagon for pig feed.

As instructed the message was handed to Templar code breakers, who set about decoding it, a process that took them a week or so.

"Urgent," it said, when translated. "Mission possibly compromised. Ajay and Kulpreet dead, maybe tortured for information. Suggest abort mission at once."

And then, at the bottom: "Ethan, look after my son."

FORTY-FIVE

Abberline was in The Green Man. But not drinking today. Not brooding nor drowning his sorrows. He was there on altogether more pressing business.

"Hey, Sam, you seen Aubrey today?"

"Not seen him for a while, Freddie," replied the barman. "No, tell a lie, he popped his head round the door earlier, on his way to School's Day at Lord's."

Freddie shot the barman a confused look and Sam was disgusted in return. "What the bloody hell are you doing in here if you don't even know about the Eton-Harrow match?"

"All right, keep your hair on, what's left of it. Aubrey was on his way there, was he?"

Sam suddenly pulled a face, as though he'd said too much. "Well, um . . . no. He was on duty, wasn't he?"

Now it was Abberline's turn to be exasperated. "Look, you can't tell me anything about Aubrey I don't already know. He was playing truant right?"

Sam slapped a bar towel over his shoulder and gave

Abberline the kind of reluctant nod that wouldn't stand up in a court of law.

"Right," said Abberline. "Now we're getting somewhere. He came in here to . . . Oh, I know. He came in here to change his clothes, did he?"

Another reluctant nod.

"All right," said Abberline, sliding off his stool about to make for the door. "When he comes back for his uniform, tell him I'm looking for him, would you?"

"Bloody hell, everyone wants old Aubs at the moment, don't they?"

Abberline stopped and turned. "Come again?"

"Like I say, seems like everyone wants to talk to Aubrey." Again Sam was wearing a queasy look, as though he might have said too much.

"Put a bit more meat on those bones for me, mate. Who exactly is looking for Aubrey, apart from me?"

"Three geezers who came in not long after he'd left for the match."

"And what did they look like?" asked Abberline and felt his heart sink as Sam gave him a description of the three punishers.

Not knowing what else to do, he headed for Lord's cricket ground but immediately regretted it when he found himself swimming against a tide of humanity leaving the ground. Cabs were stopping and turning tail. Nearby, a horse snorted and stamped its feet. The weight of people became too much for an aunt-sally owner and he began packing quickly away. Same for the stallholder who called for the shoving, ebbing crowds to pay attention—*Mind the bloody barrow*—as little hands reached to grab produce from his stall. Another was pushing a cart away from the crowds through a shoving sea of bonnets and caps and children carried on shoulders. Abberline felt something drag his clothes and looked to see a dog weaving through a forest of legs.

Despite the crowds the mood was genial. A good time was being had by all. The masses certainly enjoyed cheering on the sons of the nobility as they played their annual game, that was for sure, thought Abberline. One day the highborn progeny would be doing what all the upper classes did: lining their pockets at the expense of the lower orders, taking their fun where they found it and who cares if we ruin a few lives in the process.

And no, he didn't find Aubrey. He found lots of drunks passed out in the road. Found lots of women trying to sell him matches and posies. Found lots of swells and ladies in posh frocks looking down their noses at the drunks and match-sellers. But no Aubrey.

He went back to The Green Man.

No, Sam shook his head, there had been no further sign of Aubrey, and no, not the three men either.

The punishers, that's who it was, them at the line. He'd be paying those rail works a visit unless Aubrey turned up pretty soon. One more place to try, though, and he took himself to Aubrey's rooms in Stepney, where he lived with his wife and two children.

They were rooms much like his own, as it turned out. He, too, had the first floor of a bay-fronted building in a terrace of other bay-fronted buildings, similar to the Waughs' place, only this one had been split into apartments for renting out. It was all he could afford on a constable's wage. Police work wasn't as lucrative as pornography.

Mrs. Shaw opened the door and relaxed when she saw his uniform. "Don't tell me," she said. "You're Freddie Abberline?" When he nodded, she burst out with, "Well, haven't we heard a lot about you! Children, come and meet the famous Fresh-faced Freddie."

She had ruddy cheeks but was otherwise different from Aubrey in every way, being slight where he was well built, and while he wore a permanently nervous and bewildered expression, she was an entirely different kettle of fish, beaming with welcome and fussing about her hair as she invited her guest inside.

Two children, a boy and a girl, both around five or six, came running, only to skid to a halt, cling to her skirts and gaze at him with the kind of naked curiosity that only children can get away with.

Abberline's heart, already heavy with worry for Aubrey, sank a little more at the scene. It would have been easier to keep a safe distance between him and the things Aubrey loved. Seeing them like this would only make things harder if what Abberline feared was true. Most of the time he envied men like Aubs, who went home to wives and families, but not at times like this. Not when you saw what you left behind.

"I can't stay, Mrs. Shaw, I'm afraid," he said, reluctantly having to dampen the warm welcome he was being given. "I was just wondering if you knew of Aubrey's whereabouts at all?"

Her smile slid off her face, replaced by a look of immediate worry. The two children, sensing their mother's sudden distress, clung to her skirts more tightly, eyes widening into frightened saucers.

"No, not since he went out this morning," she said.

"On his way to Lord's?"

She chewed her lip. "I can't rightly say."

"I know he was on his way to Lord's, Mrs. Shaw, but the match is over, and I was wondering if he'd returned."

"Maybe he went for an ale in The Green Man?"

"Of course," he said. "That's it. I'll take my leave for there, if I may, and wish you all the best, and if you'd let Aubrey know that I'm looking for him, then I'd be much obliged."

And Abberline did just that. He took his leave. He went back to The Green Man, just in case, and Sam shook his head and said no, and Abberline went to the station house, just in case, and the desk sergeant shook his head no, with a suspicious expression, as though he knew Aubrey had been playing truant. And then, lastly, Abberline went to the rail works, where he stood by the fence and looked over the site. The work continued: fires had been built as they were every night and braziers glowed on the mudflats. As Abberline watched, a steam train pulled in from farther up the line and the activities on the wooden cranes grew even more frenetic as laborers began to unload the spoil.

But Abberline wasn't watching that. He was keeping his eye on the office. He watched as the door opened and out came the Indian lad, clutching his files.

Good, thought Abberline, finding it a reassuring sight. For some reason he doubted any harm would come to Aubrey if the Indian lad was around.

*"He is indeed on the side of the angels. He's a good man.
A better man than either you or I will ever be."*

What Abberline saw next was an even more reassuring
sight. Coming out of the office were the punishers, all
three of them, as casual as you like. And if they were here,
well, then they weren't out there somewhere, hurting
Aubrey. Abberline wondered if maybe their paths had
been similar to his own. Perhaps they had reached The
Green Man and been sent to Lord's, where they were
deterred by the crowds.

Yes, he thought, turning away from the fence and putting the site to his back. Yes that was it. Hopefully by now,
Aubrey was safely back in the bosom of his smiling
family . . .

His landlady lived on the ground floor and she appeared
the minute he showed his face. "Busy day, Constable?"
she said.

"You might say that, ma'am," said Abberline, removing
his helmet.

"Too busy to tell me you were expecting a delivery?"

He looked at her sharply. "A delivery?"

"Three gentlemen delivering a large rug, so they said.
Must have been a bloody heavy rug, too, because it took
all three of them to get it up there . . ."

Abberline was already mounting the stairs.

The bastards had left the body sitting up in one of Abberline's chairs, as though awaiting Abberline's return.

They'd left it there as a warning: *This is what lies in store for you.*

They'd beaten him to death. He was barely recognizable beneath puffed-up livid flesh, bulging bruises, closed-up eyes, blood that oozed from cuts made by brass knuckles.

"Oh, Aubrey," said Abberline.

It's not like they'd been friends, but . . . wait a minute, yes, they *had* been friends, because friends supported one another. You could turn to them for advice. They helped you think about things a different way. And Aubrey had done all that and more for Abberline.

Before he knew it, his shoulders were shaking and tears dropped to the boards of his room. "Oh, Aubrey," he repeated, through a wet mouth, wanting to reach and embrace the man, his friend, but at the same time repulsed by what they had done to him, his features pummeled away like so much tenderized meat.

Instead he tried to imagine Aubrey as he was, telling him music-hall jokes in The Green Man. Mourning the death of a slum girl. He had too much compassion, that was Aubrey's problem. He had too much heart for this world.

He wondered what it would have been like for Aubrey in his dying moments. They would have demanded information, of course. They would already have known about the Indian from the bodyguard, so what might Aubrey have told them? About the man in the robes, perhaps. As if it mattered now. The other day Abberline had told himself the killing had to stop, but the whole business had claimed yet another life, a precious one.

Maybe Aubrey was right. Maybe there were no answers. Maybe he just had to accept that once in a while.

For the time being, he simply stood with his friend, Aubrey Shaw, shoulders shaking, tears flowing more freely now.

"I'm sorry, mate," he said, over and over again. "I'm so bloody sorry."

And then Aubrey's eyes opened.

FORTY-SIX

Months passed. In May, the Chancellor of the Exchequer Gladstone declared himself delighted after taking the first full journey on the new underground railway. He and various other Metropolitan dignitaries, including John Fowler, Charles Pearson and Cavanagh, had traveled the entire length of the line, all four miles of it, from the Bishop's Lane Station in Paddington, through tunnels and other half-built stations—Edgware Road, Baker Street, Portland Road, Gower Street, King's Cross—and lastly to Farringdon Street in the city. A journey of some eighteen minutes or so.

Gladstone's seal of approval was important to the Metropolitan, especially as the prime minister, Palmerston, had always been rather sniffy about the project, declaring that at his age he wanted to spend as much time as possible aboveground, thank you. But Gladstone's approval gave a boost to a project that was otherwise greeted with at best mild suspicion and apathy by the general public and at worst outright hatred and hostility. The railway's reputation was dented further when, the following month, the Fleet Sewer burst. The brick pipes through which London's "foul black river" flowed had been weakened and eventually broke, water and filth flooding the tunnel to a depth of ten feet, putting the project back by months while remedial work was carried out.

Then, early one morning in late July, the Clarence belonging to Mr. Cavanagh of the Metropolitan Railway left the site, bearing its owner to St. Katherine Docks.

There the carriage waited for a ship to discharge its cargo, which in this case was three Indian men in brown suits, two of whom were escorting a third man, who they delivered to the Clarence, taking their leave with a bow and returning to their ship.

The new arrival took a seat across from Cavanagh, who had loosened his jacket but otherwise made no concession to the July heat.

"Hello, Ajay," said Cavanagh.

Ajay looked at him flatly. "I was promised money. Lodgings. A new life here in London."

"And we were promised the full benefit of your knowledge with regard to Jayadeep Mir," said Cavanagh, then pulled the cord and sat back as Hardy shook the reins and they made their return to the site. "Let's see if we can both abide by the terms of the agreement, shall we?"

A short while later the carriage came to a halt outside the rail works and Ajay was directed to look out of the window. As arranged, Marchant brought the unsuspecting Bharat Singh to a designated spot some one hundred yards away on the other side of the fence, close enough for Ajay to see.

"That's our man," said Cavanagh.

"And what does he call himself?" asked Ajay.

"He goes by the name Bharat Singh."

"Then that must have been something of a comedown for him," said Ajay, who pulled down the blind and settled back into his seat, "because that man is Jayadeep Mir."

"Excellent," said Cavanagh. "Now, how about you tell me everything you know about him?"

There was a trick the gangs used when they wanted information. "Two birds" they called it. Gang members would take two unlucky souls to the roof, throw one of them off and make the other one watch.

Two birds. One of them flies, one of them sings.

Ajay had been outside the door when Kulpreet died her honorable death. He had seen what lay in store for him: either the world's most painful manicure or death.

Then he made them his offer. They could torture him, and good luck to them if they tried, for he'd do everything to resist, and if their questioning was successful, they'd get what they needed to know but nothing else besides, and they'd never be sure if it was the truth or not.

Or . . . if they met his demands, then he would tell them everything they needed to know and a *lot* more besides.

So the Templars had it put about that Ajay died in the alley, and the Assassin—now an ex-Assassin, a traitor—was given passage to London.

There outside the railway, he upheld his side of the bargain and told Cavanagh everything the director needed to know. He told them the man they knew as

Bharat Singh was in fact Jayadeep Mir. He told them Jayadeep had been imprisoned because of a failure of nerve, and Cavanagh had been most interested in that particular aspect of the story before Ajay went on to tell him that Jayadeep had been delivered into the custody of Ethan Frye for a mission. More than that he did not know.

"A mission?" mused Cavanagh, staring with interest at The Ghost, seeing him anew. "An *undercover* mission, perhaps?"

Cavanagh's mind went to the information relayed by the punishers. The two Hardys and Smith had returned from questioning Constable Aubrey Shaw with news that a man in robes was responsible for killing Robert Waugh, and now, with this latest piece of information, things had finally fallen into place.

How ironic. Their newest recruit, who had curried favor with them by killing a traitor, did so with treachery on his own mind—and was not even responsible for the kill.

All in all, thought Cavanagh, it was a delightful outcome. He had long since decided that when he killed Crawford Starrick and wrested the position of Grand Master from him, when he had the artifact and was the most powerful man not just in London but in the known world of the Knights Templar, that his first order of business would be to smash what remained of the Assassin resistance in his city.

Here, though, was a chance to do both simultaneously, an opportunity to ascend to the rank of Grand Master with a feather in his cap as well as the artifact to prove his suitability for the role. In one fell swoop he would secure

command of the rite as well as the respect of its member-
ship. Oh yes, this was most opportune.

"And now for your side of the bargain," said Ajay.

"Yes, my side of the bargain."

The door to the carriage opened, and there stood
Hardy. "I promised you riches and lodgings in London,
and you shall have them, on one condition."

Guarded and ready for the double cross, with an escape
route in mind, Ajay said, "Yes, and what is that?"

"That you continue to tell us everything you can about
the Brotherhood."

Ajay relaxed. They would keep him alive that long, at
least. Plenty of time to make his escape.

"It's a deal," he said.

FORTY-SEVEN

Months passed, during which Aubrey stayed in Freddie Abberline's rooms and Freddie nursed him back to health. Aubrey had fewer teeth and spoke differently, as though his tongue were too big for his mouth, and there were other injuries besides, but he was alive, and there was a lot to be said for that. He was also a good companion, and Abberline soon found that there was a lot to be said for that, too.

One night, a fortnight or so after the beating, Abberline had brought Aubrey some broth, leaving it on a bedside table, and thinking him asleep was about to depart when he looked at his friend's face and saw it wet with tears.

He cleared his throat and looked down at his stockinged feet. "Um, are you all right there, me old mate? You getting a bit of the old bad-memory gubbins, are you? Thinking back to what happened?"

Aubrey winced with pain as he nodded yes and through broken teeth said, "I told them everything, Freddie. It weren't a lot, but I sang like a bird."

Abberline had shrugged. "Good luck to 'em. Hope it means more to them than it does to either of us."

"But I told them. I told them everything." Aubrey was wracked by a sob, his bruised face crumpling with the shame of it.

"Hey, hey," said Abberline, perching on the edge of the mattress. He reached for Aubrey's hand. "It doesn't matter, mate. Anyway you had no choice. And look, something tells me that our friend in robes can look after himself."

He sat like that for a while, in silence, grateful for the comfort they each provided. And then Abberline had helped Aubrey with his broth before taking his leave, telling his friend that he needed his rest.

Meanwhile, Aubrey was listed as missing. "Missing, presumed bored of police work and retiring to The Green Man for good," was the rumor, but Abberline knew different. He knew that the point of the attack was to send a message, and to all intents and purposes, he heeded the warning. No more site visits for him. By complete coincidence the division sergeant had assigned him a different beat, one that took him nowhere near the rail works. "Just in case you get tempted," was what he'd said as he delivered the news.

You're in it up to your eyeballs, aren't you? was what Abberline had thought, staring with concealed fury across the table at his division sergeant. But he walked his beat, and when his shift was done, he went home to peel off his uniform, check that Aubrey was okay and then ignore the other man's warnings and return to the rail works.

Every night, hidden in the shadows. A lone vigil of what, he didn't know, but a vigil nevertheless.

Aubrey was up and about by now, albeit with limited locomotion, and later the two men would sit before the fire, having a chat. Abberline would talk about the case. He was consumed by it. Aubrey talked of little else but his family and, more to the point, when he would see them again.

"No, Aubs, I'm sorry," Abberline told him, "but those geezers left you for dead, and if you turn up alive, they'll want to finish the job. You're staying here, missing presumed croaked, until this thing is over."

"But when will it be over, Freddie?" said Aubrey. He shifted painfully in his chair. Though his face showed no signs of his ordeal apart from a crisscrossing of scars left on his cheek by the brass knuckle-dusters, his insides had taken a pummeling, and there was a pain in his hip that seemed in no danger of going away. It made it difficult to walk; it even made it difficult to sit still at times, and every time he winced with the pain of it, his mind went back to an anonymous darkened room and the relentless thump of fists ramming into a soft body that belonged to him. Aubrey would never walk the beat again, but thanks to a combination of the punishers' carelessness and Abberline's care he was alive, and he never forgot to be grateful for that. On the other hand, what was life if it was a life spent without his loved ones?

"Just how do you think this whole thing—whatever this 'thing' is—is going to end?" he said.

Abberline reached to the fire and gave his friend a mournful smile. "I don't know, Aubs, is the truth, I don't rightly know. But you mark my words, while I can't lay claim to being on top of the situation, I'm there or thereabouts. I'll know when it's time, and I promise you we won't lose a second getting you back to your family."

They had decided for safety's sake that his wife and children couldn't know he was alive, but it meant all four of them lived in purgatory. One day Abberline and Aubrey took a police growler out to Stepney and sat in the street so Aubrey might catch glimpses of his family through the windows. After two hours or so, it had been too much for him and they had left.

Abberline went to them with money and gifts. He took them Aubrey's uniform. There was no light in Mrs. Shaw's eyes now. The visits were traumatic for her, she said. Every time she saw Abberline standing on the doorstep she thought the worst. "Because I know if he was alive he'd be with you. And when I see you alone, I think he's not."

"He may still be alive. There's always hope."

"You think so? I'm not sure I agree, but you know the worst thing?"

"It's not having a body to bury, I know, Mrs. Shaw, and I'm so, so sorry," said Abberline, and left, happy to escape the weight of grief for a man who was not only alive but enjoying the relative comfort and warmth of Abberline's rooms. Taking with him the guilt of having to lie.

It was for the greater good. It was for the safety of them all that Cavanagh and company thought this particular loose end had been tied. But still. The guilt.

FORTY-EIGHT

"You are to be inducted into the Knights Templar," said Cavanagh. He, Marchant and two of the punishers—Mr. Hardy was missing—had taken The Ghost away from his duties and to a corner of the excavation site, to all intents and purposes conducting an impromptu works meeting.

"Thank you, sir," said The Ghost. He bowed his head low, hating himself at that moment. When his eyes returned to Cavanagh he saw something unreadable in the man's eyes, like a distant, mocking expression.

"But first, I have a job for you."

"Yes, sir," replied The Ghost. He maintained a blank expression but inside his mind raced and he felt his pulse quicken, thinking, *This is it.*

Indicating to his men to remain where they were, Cavanagh took The Ghost's arm and began to lead him away from the group, toward the perimeter fence. There The Ghost could see Cavanagh's Clarence. Tending to the horse was Mr. Hardy, who looked up at them briefly then returned to brushing the nag's mane.

Away from the noise, Cavanagh no longer needed to

raise his voice. "What I'm about to tell you is information known only to members of the Knights Templar. You are yet to be inducted and so, by rights, I shouldn't be revealing this, but you've proven yourself an asset to my operation and your task is what we might call 'time-sensitive.' In other words it needs to happen before the council can meet to ratify your induction. I am a man of instinct and I prefer to act on it. I have faith in you, Bharat. I see much of myself in you."

The Ghost allowed himself a feeling of triumph. Everything he had done, the months of living in the tunnel, of building a life as Bharat Singh, had all been building to this moment.

Cavanagh continued. "This dig you've been involved in, the one to build the world's first underground railway. Perhaps you might have guessed, given my involvement, but there's more to it than meets the eye. The railway will of course be finished, and it will of course be a success, but there is, believe it or not, an ulterior motive behind its construction."

The Ghost nodded.

"The Knights Templar in London are in search of an artifact believed to be buried along the line. Pinpointing its exact location has proven to be a demanding task. Let's just say that, in my opinion at least, Lucy Thorne's exalted position within the Order is not fully deserved. Certainly not on this showing."

"Lucy Thorne, sir?"

Cavanagh shot him a quick look and The Ghost had to suppress a nervous swallow. Was the director trying to catch him off guard?

"All in good time," said Cavanagh. "You have the delights of the ruling council to come. For the time being all you need to know is that Lucy Thorne is among a cadre of high-ranking Templars whose job it is to locate the artifact."

"This . . . artifact, sir, what does it do?"

"Well, you see, this is the trouble with scrolls, isn't it? They're so damnably ambiguous. The details are left to the imagination, I'm afraid; the scrolls simply say that great power will come to whoever has it in his possession. It may not surprise you to know that I intend to be the one in possession of it. Who I have at my side when that day comes will very much depend."

"I hope it will be me, sir," said The Ghost.

He glanced over to where the Clarence was tethered. Mr. Hardy was replacing the horse brush in the carriage stowage box, but as The Ghost watched he took something else from the box and slipped it into his pocket.

"Well, as I say, that will very much depend," said Cavanagh.

The two men walked a few more paces, The Ghost keeping an eye on Mr. Hardy. The punisher seemed to have finished grooming the horse as he had moved to check the harness buckles. And now he was leaving the carriage enclosure and making his way toward the gate, shouldering a match girl out of his way, kicking awake a worker who leaned on the gate post with a railwayman's cap pulled over his eyes.

"On what will it depend, sir?"

"On how well you perform your task."

Hardy was crossing the mudflats some fifty yards away.

"And what task is that, sir?"

"You are to kill Charles Pearson."

Lately they had judged it too risky to meet; The Ghost, in particular, wanted to leave nothing to chance. But this was different. This represented a major escalation of events, he needed Ethan's counsel, and so, after an exchange of gravestone positions in the Marylebone churchyard, the two Assassins convened at Leinster Gardens.

"Why?" asked Ethan. "Why kill Pearson?"

"The rite commands it, so Mr. Cavanagh says."

"Too much of a philanthropist for their taste, eh? Christ, they won't even let him see his beloved railway open."

"Cavanagh has the details worked out, Master. Now that work has resumed after the Fleet Sewer burst, he wants to demonstrate to Mr. Pearson that the line between King's Cross and Farringdon Street is fully operational. What's more, he has a new enclosed carriage to show off, and he plans a train ride to Farringdon Street and back. But at the end of the journey, when Mr. and Mrs. Pearson make their way back to their carriage, I am to kill him."

"But not Mrs. Pearson?"

"No."

There was a long silence, then The Ghost asked his handler, "What do you think?"

Ethan took a deep breath. "Well, it's not a trap, not in the sense that they want to do you down; they could call you into the office for that. What it is is a test."

The Ghost's palms were sweaty. He gulped and

returned to a balmy room in Amritsar, tasting the fear afresh, seeing the blade in Dani's screaming mouth, blood and steel shimmering in the moonlight.

He had to summon all his strength to say the next words, and it hurt to hear himself say them but say them he did. "If it is a test, then I am sure to fail."

Ethan closed his eyes in sad response. "We're *this close*, Jayadeep."

He was almost whispering.

The Ghost nodded. He, too, longed to see the artifact. For years he had dreamed of bearing witness to its unearthly light show. But on the other hand . . .

"This artifact could be nothing more than a trinket. Even the Templars know nothing of its true potential."

"Scrolls are cryptic. That's the point of them. They're passed down through the ages so that our forefathers should think themselves more clever than we."

"Yes. That's what he said, more or less."

"How perceptive of him. Perhaps he also pointed out that, trinket or not, the artifact's actual powers are less important than a perception of their worth. Yes, it's true that what lies beneath the earth may be an ancient bauble fit for nothing more devastating than entrancing old dames and impressionable children. But for centuries Assassins and Templars have fought over artifacts, and we have all heard the tales of their great power: the Koh-i-Noor diamond, the unearthly force unleashed by the Apple of Al Mualim. Is it possible, perhaps, that these tales have become exaggerated in the telling? After all, none of these artifacts have ever been so powerful they proved decisive in the war. And the scrolls are as good at aggrandizement as they are at being abstruse."

"My parents . . ."

"Your parents are a case in point, bouncing you on their knee, filling your head with the tales of their awesome power." He looked across at The Ghost, who returned his gaze, not quite able to believe what he was hearing, and gave a dry chuckle. "Evie's like you. She's fascinated by the idea of artifacts just as you were fascinated by that stupid bloody diamond."

The Ghost bit down on his anger, saying nothing.

"It's the fascination with it, do you see? *The idea of it.* That's where the talismanic power of the artifact lies. Assassin or Templar, we're all in the business of selling ideas to the masses, and we all think our ideas are the ones to save the world, but one thing we have in common is the knowledge that these artifacts contain secrets of the First Civilization. Look around you . . ." He indicated the false house in which they sat, the tunnel through which underground trains—*underground trains*—would soon travel. "We have steam power. Soon we will have electricity. The world is advancing at an almost unimaginable, unthinkable rate. The twentieth century is almost upon us and the twentieth century is the future, Jayadeep. The technology being used to build bridges, tunnels and railways—that same technology will be harnessed to create weapons of war. That's the future. And unless you want to see man enslaved by tyranny and totalitarianism, then we need to win that future for our children and all the generations to come, who will one day sit with storybooks and read of our exploits and thank us for refusing to deliver them into despotism.

"In other words, Jayadeep, we need to win at all costs. And that means you kill Pearson and the mission continues until we have recovered the artifact."

It was quite a speech. The Ghost let it sink in.

"No," he said.

Ethan leapt angrily to his feet. "Damn you, man," he roared, too loudly for the still night. Instead he bit his tongue and turned away from the steam hole to gaze angrily and unseeingly at the false-brick front of the house.

"I cannot kill an innocent man in cold blood," insisted The Ghost. "Surely, after everything that has happened, you know that? Or is your desire for the artifact making you as blind to the truth as my father was?"

Ethan turned and pointed. "He wasn't the only one who was blind, my dear boy. You yourself thought you were ready, I seem to recall."

"I have more self-knowledge now. I know you're asking me to do something I simply cannot do."

There was a catch in his voice, and Ethan softened to see the boy so wrought with despair: a boy brought up to kill for his cause but incapable of doing so. Once again he thought what a sad world, what an obscene state of affairs, when we mourned a man's inability to kill.

"Inform Cavanagh you plan to use a blowpipe. You can tell him you learned its use in Bombay."

"But, Master, I can't kill an innocent man."

"You won't have to."

FORTY-NINE

Breath held, Evie Frye crouched outside her father's study as he sat with George Westhouse, the two men talking in such low voices that she could barely hear through the door. She tucked her hair behind her ear as she strained to listen.

"Tomorrow, then, Ethan," George was saying.

"Yes, tomorrow."

"And if all goes well, then the artifact . . ."

"They're close, they say."

"Well, logic dictates they must be. After all, the tunnel is built."

"There are dozens of service tunnels, rerouted sewer pipes and gas mains still to install. There's plenty of digging to be done yet. Besides, who's to say the burst sewer in the Fleet Valley wasn't their doing?"

"True . . ."

Just then there came a knock on the door that startled Evie, and she stood quickly, slightly disoriented, gathering herself and smoothing down her shirts and skirts before going to answer it. They had no servants. Ethan would not have allowed it, believing the very idea of retaining servants went against the tenets of the Creed. And so it was that young Evie Frye answered her own front door.

There on the step stood a young Indian man wearing a brown suit. He was handsome, she thought, and yet there was something about him that offset his good looks, a wild and hunted expression that he fixed on her, regarding her from the gray lower steps with eyes that didn't really see her. Nevertheless, when he proffered a letter he said her name. "Evie Frye."

She took it, a folded piece of paper. On the flap was written, "For the attention of Ethan Frye."

"Tell him that Ajay came," said the man on the doorstep, already turning to leave. "Tell him Ajay said he is sorry and that he will see him in the next life."

Rattled, Evie was glad to close the door on the strange, haunted man—then rushed to her father's study.

A second later the household was in an uproar.

"*Jacob*," called Ethan, storming out of his study with his forearm extended, buckling his hidden blade at the same time, "arm yourself, you're coming with me. Evie, you too. George, come on, there's no time to waste."

He had unfolded the letter in a burst of panic, only to find a note written in code they had no time to translate. But Ajay—the man with the cryptic apology. Surely not the same Ajay who stood guard at The Darkness, because if that man was in London, then Ethan should have been informed . . . But then again, who else could it be?

All four of them came bursting into the street, Ethan still buckling the blade, holstering his revolver and pulling on his robes at the same time, the two children thrilling to the sight of their father in action.

"Which way did he go, darling?" said Ethan to Evie.

She pointed. "Toward The Broadway."

"Then we're in luck. There are sewer works on The Broadway; he will have to turn onto Oakley Lane. Evie, Jacob, George, get after him. With any luck he'll take George to be me and not suspect I've worked my way in front of him. Go. *Go*."

The two young Assassins and George took off in the direction of The Broadway. Ethan ran for a wall that belonged to an opposite neighbor, and with a leap and a fast tap-tap of his boots, almost as though he were kicking the wall in midair, was on top then over it.

In front of him stretched the garden, and gazing along it, he experienced a brief moment of involuntary garden jealousy. He'd always wondered what size garden the neighbors had and here was his answer. Bigger. Twice the size of his own. Keeping to the shadows, he ran its length and at the bottom, where even the gardeners feared to tread, drew his hidden blade to hack at the undergrowth. Succumbing to the foliage at the back was a wall, but he scaled it easily before dropping to a passageway on the other side.

All was quiet. Just the ever-present drip-drip of water. He strained to hear, picking out sounds from the distant surrounding city, until it came to him, a faraway rhythmic thud of running feet to his right.

Excellent. Ethan set off, darting quietly along the passageway to the end then waiting in the shadows, listening again. The running feet were closer now. Good. This Ajay had seen his pursuers and was taking evasive action. All his attention would be concentrated on what came from behind.

Drainpipe, loose brick, window ledge—and then Ethan was on the roof of the adjacent building, framed against the moonlit sky but knowing his quarry was unlikely to look upward. He was almost directly above the running footsteps in the alleyway below and he sprinted ahead, dashing to the end of the tenement then jumping to the pitched roof of the next.

Flattening himself to the shingles he looked down into the street below and watched as a figure in a brown suit hurried into the alleyway, throwing a look behind him at the same time.

Ethan's robes fluttered as he swung to the lip of the roof then let himself down to the cobbles below, where he took a seat on a crate and rested his chin in his hand as he awaited Ajay's arrival.

FIFTY

Ajay didn't see anything until it was too late and he was brought up short. Ex-Assassin though he was, he still thought like one, and he instantly appraised the situation and drew his kukri on the run, taking note of Ethan Frye's position, posture, his body at rest, his leading hand hanging down by the side and seeing an opponent who was too relaxed and too vulnerable to attack on his weaker side, and it was to that flank that he directed his attack—fast and, if his assessments were correct, then decisively.

But, of course, his assessments were not correct. They were based on assumptions that Ethan had anticipated, and as Ajay's kukri flashed toward him, the older man's hand shot out from beneath his chin, his blade engaging at the same second, and there was a ring of steel as Ajay's sword was blocked in midair, then a scream of pain as Ethan completed his move with a downward slash that sheared off half of Ajay's hand and took the blade away from him.

The kukri dropped to the stone, along with a chunk of Ajay's hand. In pain and disoriented as he was, he acted on instinct, ducking and spinning and kicking his sword back up the alley as he dived away from another attack.

Ethan came to his feet and took a few steps up the alleyway, still reeling from the shock of recognition—*Ajay, it was Ajay, how the hell did he get here?*—just as the other man reached his weapon, stumbled and with one hurt and bleeding hand clutched to his chest, snatched it up from the cobbles with his good one.

"This is a fight you can no longer win," called Ethan. The other three had appeared in the alley behind them and Ajay heard, turning to see his exit barred and swinging back to face Ethan again, knowing, surely, that all was lost.

"Why did you come to my door? Why did you attack me?" Ethan took two steps forward threateningly. "I don't want to hurt you any more, but I will, if I have to."

Again Ajay glanced behind him and back at Ethan, then he stood up straight with his shoulders thrust back, and through a last wretched sob that bubbled up from some place of inner pain, said, "I'm sorry. I'm sorry to you and I'm sorry to Kulpreet, and I'm sorry for everything I have done."

And then drew the blade across his own throat.

FIFTY-ONE

Later, when the children had gone to bed with the image of a choking, gurgling man painting the cobbles scarlet with his own blood still fresh in their heads, George and Ethan had retired to the study. Both were shaken by what had happened and troubled by the questions for which they had no ready answers, and so it was that they drank two glasses of Ethan's best Highland whiskey before either of them even said a word.

(Which, having crept down from upstairs, Evie was there to overhear . . .)

"A new development, then," said George.

"You could say that."

"Damnedest thing."

Ethan stared off into nothing. He was thinking that he needed to send word to Amritsar first thing. Tell them they might be short an Assassin—and what news of Kulpreet?

He said, "I suppose, on the bright side, it prepares the twins for their blooding."

George gave a dry laugh as his friend's eyes came back

to him. "This letter." He held out the document. "Shall we decode it?"

A short while later they sat at the study desk with the document and several Assassin codebooks open in front of them and the translation. Ajay's note had read, "Position compromised, must abort. A friend."

"'A friend' who's lying out there somewhere not far from Oakley Lane." George set down the letter. The body would be discovered soon. At any moment the two Assassins expected to hear the sound of a peeler's rattle.

"The man out there died of shame," said Ethan.

Outside Evie crouched, listening, thinking of Ajay, who had died of shame. She knew from her readings that in the annals of Assassins there was another, Ahmad Sofian, who had taken his life by the same means and for similar reasons.

"Shame. Indeed. It would seem so," George was saying. "A traitor to the Creed. But how much has he told our enemy? What does he even know to tell them? You've always been scrupulous with the information you've given me; I can't imagine what he could have told them."

"Put it this way, George, if you and Ajay had got together then you might have been in possession of most of the facts. But one without the other? No chance."

"Even so, you must inform your Ghost at once."

Ethan chewed the inside of his cheek thoughtfully. "I'm not sure. I know The Ghost. He will err on the side of caution and abort the mission."

"Well, that's what the note says to do." George leaned forward. His face clouding with incomprehension. "I'm not quite sure I can believe what I'm hearing, Ethan. If you inform The Ghost and he decides to continue with the operation, then he is guilty of rank and dangerous optimism at best and a tendency to suicide at worst. If he aborts, he will be doing the right thing—the course of action we would recommend if we were thinking with our heads instead of our desires. Either way, we must tell him so he is able to choose."

Ethan shook his head. His mind was made up. "I trust The Ghost. I trust him to look after himself. Most of all, I trust him to recover the artifact."

"Then you must also trust him to make the right decisions."

"No, George. I'm sorry, I can't do that."

From far away came the familiar clacking of the peeler's alarm.

FIFTY-TWO

And so a day of great excitement came to pass. The Metropolitan Railway had placed an advertisement in the previous evening's newspapers to announce that tonight was a new beginning for the railway: Charles Pearson was to take a journey on the reopened stretch of line between King's Cross and Farringdon Street. Not only that but he would be making the journey in an enclosed carriage. *An enclosed carriage.* Gladstone had traveled in an open one. The new "enclosed carriage" was said to be the last word in underground-railway luxury. Other railway dignitaries would be present, said the notices, and members of the public were also invited to witness this grand occasion—just so long as they stayed on the right side of the picket fence.

The public would come. Despite the excavation turning their lives into a living hell of noise and mud, closing roads and businesses alike; despite the fact that it had made thousands of already poverty-stricken Londoners homeless—twelve thousand in the Fleet Valley *alone*—yet had had no discernible impact on the well-to-do; and

despite the fact that it was over a year behind schedule
and that the cost was now estimated at £1.3 million.

They would come.

A team of carpenters had been employed to build a set
of steps down into the shaft at King's Cross. Unlike Gladstone's inaugural trip from Bishop's Lane two months
before, the underground station at King's Cross had yet
to be built. Next year it would be constructed as an
adjunct to the ten-year-old mainline station, with gables
at either end, as well as pavilion roofs and parapets. What
were currently cuttings acting as makeshift boarding
points would be fashioned into proper platforms with
stairways, ticket offices, kiosks set into the walls and foot-
bridges at each end.

But for now, it was little more than an ugly hole in the
ground, and to accommodate railway top brass and their
wives, the steps were built, and the cuttings were laid with
planks to best approximate a proper platform, and instead
of the flares that the men had used for night work, there
were to be lamps strung along the top of the trench as
well as inside the shaft.

It all added to the celebratory air. When the bell tolled
three times at midday it was to signal the change, but on
this occasion there was no next shift waiting to take over.
The men were welcome to take their leave. They could
stay and watch, of course, just so long as they stayed on
the right side of the fence, but they were also welcome to
spend their free time supping ale in pubs called The Pick-
led Hen or The Curious Orange or The Rising Sun, or
with their families, it was up to them. Either way, for the
first time in three years there would be no clamor of tools

in northwest London, no constant rattle of steam engines, no swinging leather buckets silhouetted against the skyline. No constantly grinding conveyor.

Not that laborers were to be absent from the site. "We want the bigwigs seeing proper workers, not that bloody rabble," Marchant had said, and so a squad of "pretend" workmen had been drafted in. At first glance this new group of thirty or forty workers looked the part as they milled about in time-honored laborer fashion, but a closer look revealed that they were smarter and more serious-looking than their regular counterparts. What's more, as they stood awaiting the arrival of the dignitaries, there were no jokes or laughter, no lolling around or snatching each other's caps and setting up impromptu games of cricket. The Ghost knew that these powerful-looking men were more than mere decoration. They were Templar men.

As he watched day become night he knew one other thing too. He couldn't take the life of an innocent man. He could not allow it to be taken.

FIFTY-THREE

Abberline heard about the run but had gone home to see Aubrey first. "You think you can make it down?" he asked him.

"No, Freddie, but you pop along if you've a mind. Say hello to the old gang for me. You going in uniform, are you?"

Abberline looked down at himself. "I figure our friends will have more on their minds than looking out for me. Plus I can make my way through the crowds more easily as a peeler. There are still some who have respect for the law. Oh, one more thing."

From the drawer of his desk, Abberline took a naval spyglass that he extended, then closed with a satisfying *click click*. "Think I might be needing this," he said, and with that he took his leave into the balmy September evening, feeling a little guilty about leaving Aubrey behind, truth be told; after all, it wasn't so long ago that he, Abberline, had been the one to brood, with Aubrey doing his best to shake him out of it. How was Abberline returning the favor? Exactly. He wasn't. He was off gawping at big nobs taking train rides when he should have been investigating whatever fiddle it was Cavanagh had going. Fraud was his best guess. Some kind of embezzlement scam. It was the not knowing that was the problem—the not knowing how to make it safe for Aubrey to rejoin his family.

Lost in thought, he made his way along a roadway crowded with traffic, where the air seemed to crackle with the constant trundle of horse and carriage. An omnibus passed, packed with men on the upper deck, and to Abberline their top hats were like chimneys. In the distance smokestacks poisoned the East End with ribbons of thick black smog.

Just as predicted, the crowds were thick at King's Cross and he was glad of his bobby's uniform as he elbowed his way through to the fence surrounding the site. *Hypocrite*, he thought. You're not above using your own status when it suits you. Around him was the usual crowd attracted by such events: families, with children on parents' shoulders, sightseers, men in suits and women in bonnets, a general air of expectation. Abberline put them to his back and stood with his hands on the fenceposts feeling like a man imprisoned as he stared out across the site. What a change it was from usual. Where the shaft was, he could see a new wooden structure, with steps leading downward. The whole site had been spruced up. Wagons and carts were lined neatly at the far end of the site, and there were no mountains of spoil awaiting their turn to be taken away. Just an empty apron of mud, a series of lit lanterns providing light and the trench itself, where lamps had been strung up so that it looked almost pretty, like a fairground.

As for the tunnel, it was mostly covered. What had spent so long as a groove in the earth was now a bona fide rail line. All, that was, apart from one short stretch nearest to the newly built steps, which awaited the covering process. Aside from that, Abberline was looking at a real underground railway.

There they were, the men who helped it happen: various Metropolitan Railway Company bigwigs whom he didn't recognize, as well as a few familiar faces: Cavanagh, Marchant, two of the punishers, Mr. Smith and Other Mr. Hardy (and that was a point, where was the third, the charming Mr. Hardy?) *You have to hand it to the murdering scum,* he thought. *Whatever their racket, whatever their fiddle, whatever crime they had perpetrated in the name of the underground railway, they'd done it. They got the bugger built.*

With them was the Indian lad, Bharat Singh. Abberline trained his spyglass on that handsome, implacable face. There was something different about him today, thought the peeler. His eyes seemed to move nervously. Abberline kept his spyglass to his eye as with introductions over, the group began to move across the apron and toward the new steps, the Railway Company men breaking into a polite smattering of applause as they passed.

The group reached the steps, but before descending were due to greet a gang of foremen. Mr. and Mrs. Charles Pearson were ushered forward. There was more shaking of hands as they were introduced to the foremen by Bharat Singh.

When that was over, Cavanagh thanked the foremen and, with doffed caps, they left. Bharat went to move away

as well, to follow the foremen, but Abberline saw Cavanagh's hand shoot out, take Bharat by the upper arm and
usher him toward the steps instead.

Then they were gone. The cap-doffing foremen moved
away, the railway bigwigs stood consulting their watches,
awaiting their turn, and the line of laborers stayed where
it was, a guard of honor, or maybe just a guard—and a
curious silence descended over the site. Until from the
tunnel came the whistle of a steam engine, and great
chuffs of smoke passed through the planks of the uncovered section as the driver stoked his engine.

The train was about to pull off.

Farther along the fence was an enclosure where the
bigwigs' carriages were tethered. There stood drivers
chatting, smoking pipes or tending to their horses.

There was nothing unusual about the scene, but even
so, Abberline's gaze went to it, his eyeglass lingering
there. For some reason he was sure he'd seen something
out of place, as though he'd walked into a familiar room
in which a piece of furniture had been moved but not
knowing what.

Then it hit him. How the devil had he missed it for so
long? Standing there at the fence, bold as brass and with
his eyes on the events at the tunnel, was a man in white
robes.

FIFTY-FOUR

The Ghost had seen the future. It was a future in which he was inducted as a Templar, and the more he was trusted by them, the closer to their inner circle he got, and the more value he became to the Assassins.

Which meant they wouldn't let him leave. Even when this operation was over, they would make him stay, and he would have to do it because the innocent life of Charles Pearson had paid the way to purgatory.

He wasn't prepared to do that, and so he'd decided that when Cavanagh dismissed him he would go to the carriage enclosure as arranged; there he would tell Ethan his decision. That he was out.

Disarm Ethan if necessary. Hurt him if needs be. But end this right now.

Except Cavanagh hadn't dismissed him. Instead, the director had ushered him toward the steps. "You know, I've changed my mind. I really think you should see this." And he had descended with the rest of the party.

He'd flashed his boss a quizzical look. *I should be taking up position*. But Cavanagh dismissed it with a quick don't-worry shake of the head. Why? His mind raced. Would there be time afterward? Was that the game Cavanagh was playing? Was this all part of an ongoing test of The Ghost's mettle?

Or was it something else?

At the makeshift platform stood a locomotive and two carriages. The group proceeded to the front one and Cavanagh led the way inside.

"As you can see our newest carriage is most commodious," said Cavanagh, welcoming the Pearsons into it with a flourish. "Compartments and armrests in first class make overcrowding impossible, while the leather-upholstered chairs mean that even our second-class passengers will enjoy the utmost comfort at all times."

"There are no windows," said Mrs. Pearson with a touch of panic in her voice.

"Ah yes," said Cavanagh, "but windows are not necessary in an underground train, Mrs. Pearson. Besides, first-class passengers shall have the benefit of gas lighting. The gas is carried in long, India-rubber bags in boxes on top of the carriages, and when we pull off you will see that the gas lighting provides easily enough light by which to read a morning newspaper."

They took their seats, with the Pearsons and Cavanagh at the far end, and the rest toward the rear, where a door provided a portal through to the second carriage.

Mr. Pearson thumped the tip of his cane excitedly on the boards. The driver appeared at the open door, gave them a good-to-go signal with a gloved hand, grinned in at the dignitaries, then closed the door and went back to the locomotive. Gas lamps flickered but the darkness was kept at bay, just as Cavanagh had said it would be.

With a clank and a trundle, the train moved off.

The Ghost felt Marchant's gaze on him. Mr. Smith and Other Mr. Hardy were staring at him, too. All had the eyes of men who were hungry for their supper. The absence of Mr. Hardy—so far unexplained—began to gnaw at him. At the other end of the carriage, the Pearsons and Cavanagh kept up a polite conversation but The Ghost wasn't listening. He was wondering what malice lay behind the stares of his companions.

The train pulled in at Farringdon Street and let out a great belch of smoke. Moments later, the driver opened the carriage door and peered inside to check on his passengers, as well as basking in the compliments on the smooth journey from Mr. and Mrs. Pearson. A short while later, and they were on the move for the return journey to King's Cross, Mr. Pearson reaching for his pocket watch to check the journey time.

"My watch?" he said, fumbling for it but not finding it.

The train clanked on.

"What is it, dear?" said Mrs. Pearson. Cavanagh had leaned forward with false concern. The Ghost began to feel a new onset of dread, daring to hope that the Solicitor of London had merely misplaced his pocket watch but knowing somehow that there was more to it than that, knowing that whatever it was involved him.

All eyes in the carriage were on Mr. Pearson now, watching as he patted his belly. "No, no. My watch and chain are definitely gone."

"When did you last have it, dear?" Speaking loudly over the noise of the engine, Mrs. Pearson's voice seemed to shake with the movement of the train.

"I can't remember."

"You had it on the platform, sir," called Other Mr. Hardy from their end of the carriage. He flashed a grin at The Ghost before continuing. "If you don't mind me saying so, sir, because I saw you take it out and consult it."

"Oh well, that's a relief, then it must be around here somewhere . . ." Mr. Pearson planted his cane on the boards and got shakily to his feet, already struggling with the movement of the train.

"Charles, sit down," admonished Mrs. Pearson. "Mr. Cavanagh, if you would be so kind as to ask your men to look for the watch . . ."

"Of course, madam."

As Marchant and the two punishers went through the motions of looking, The Ghost's mind raced, desperately trying to come up with a solution. He surreptitiously checked the pockets of his jacket, just in case the watch had been planted on him, then raising his eyes to the two punishers, caught them smirking at him.

No, they hadn't planted the watch on him. Not yet.

"No, no watch here," said Marchant steadying himself with a hand on the carriage shell.

The Ghost, knowing exactly what was happening, sitting motionless as though watching the whole scene through glass. Cavanagh, sticking to the script, a picture of false concern for poor Mr. Pearson's missing pocket watch.

"Then I must ask that you men turn out your pockets," he said. "No, better still . . . turn out each other's pockets."

They did as they were asked. They went through the charade. The Ghost was near rigid with tension now, knowing where this was going but unable to do anything about it.

He felt a tugging at his coat. "Oh dear, sir," said Mr. Smith or it might have been Other Mr. Hardy, but it didn't matter because the trap was sprung. "I believe I may have found Mr. Pearson's watch. It was in the pocket of young Bharat here."

Mr. Smith took the watch to Mr. Pearson, who identified it and with a rueful look at The Ghost, replaced it in his hip pocket. Meanwhile Cavanagh had stood, the very picture of fury, a man whose trust had been betrayed in the worst possible circumstance. "Is this true?" He glared at The Ghost. "Did you take the watch?"

The Ghost said nothing, stared at him, mute.

Cavanagh turned to Mr. and Mrs. Pearson. "Mr. and Mrs. Pearson, I offer you my sincerest apologies. This is quite unprecedented. We shall place Bharat under arrest. Mrs. Pearson, may I ask that one of my men accompany you to an adjoining carriage, away from this young thief? I fear he could well turn nasty."

"Yes, dear," said Mr. Pearson, concern etched on his face. "You should go."

Marchant wobbled up the carriage toward Mrs. Pearson, giving her an oily grin as he held out his hand in order to accompany her away from the nasty mess that was to come. She left, meek as a lamb, with a fearful, uncomprehending look at The Ghost as she passed.

And then they were alone.

Then, just as the train pulled into King's Cross, Cavanagh drew a pearl-handled knife and plunged it into Mr. Pearson's chest.

FIFTY-FIVE

Cavanagh opened the carriage door in order to call out to the driver, congratulating him on a smooth journey and telling him they would alight presently.

Then he closed the door and turned back to where Mr. Pearson lay with his legs kicking feebly as the life ebbed out of him. Cavanagh had hammered the knife directly into his heart before withdrawing the blade, and Pearson hadn't made a sound; in the next carriage his wife was oblivious to the fact that the Metropolitan Railway director had just stabbed her husband to death.

Anticipating that The Ghost might make a move, the two punishers grabbed him, pinning him to the seat. Cavanagh smiled. "Oh my God," he said, "the young Indian ruffian has killed Charles Pearson." He wiped his blade clean on Pearson's body and sheathed it, then looked at The Ghost. "You would never have done it, would you?"

The Ghost looked at him, saying nothing, trying not to give anything away but sensing it was too late for that anyway.

"'Blowpipe,' that was good," said Cavanagh. "I liked that. You telling me you wanted to use a blowpipe gave me everything I needed to know. It told Mr. Hardy everything he needed to know, too, and he's gone with a squad of men to apprehend or possibly kill, I can't say I am much troubled either way, your friend and my enemy, Ethan Frye."

The train seemed to relax as the locomotive exhaled steam. The Ghost thought of Ethan. The born-warrior Ethan, an expert in multiple combatant situations. But careless Ethan, prone to error.

"He is as good as dead, Jayadeep, as are you. Ah, that surprises you, does it? That I know your name. Knew your name, knew your weakness, knew your protector would be along to take over a job you didn't have the backbone to complete. The jig is up, I'm afraid. You played a good game, but you lost. Mr. Pearson is dead, the Assassins are finished and I have my artifact."

The Ghost couldn't disguise another look of surprise.

"Ah yes, I have the artifact." Cavanagh smiled, enjoying his moment. "Or should I say"—he reached to scoop up Mr. Pearson's cane—"I have it now."

He held the cane up and The Ghost saw that its handle was a bronze-tinged sphere, about three inches in diameter. "There," said Cavanagh, and his eyes were aflame, his lips pulled back over his teeth, a strange and ugly look of love at first sight. "*This* is the artifact. Recovered by laborers some weeks ago and given to Mr. Pearson as a token of their esteem. And Mr. Pearson liked it so much he made it his cane handle. But Mr. Pearson walks with the angels now, and he won't be needing his cane."

* * *

Standing at the carriage enclosure, Ethan Frye had watched the dignitaries descend the steps and wondered why they'd taken The Ghost—and tried to dismiss a queasy sense that maybe something was going wrong.

Next he'd seen the great smoke emissions as the train pulled out of King's Cross, and he'd waited as it went to Farringdon Street then returned, and he'd stood patiently, waiting for the emergence of Mr. and Mrs. Pearson, daring to believe that all would still go to plan. *I'm sorry, Mr. Pearson,* he thought, and reached for the blowpipe beneath his robes.

From within the ranks of carriages, Ethan was being watched. He was being watched by a man who drew a knife that glinted in the moonlight; who, when he smiled, revealed a gold tooth.

Coming closer, Abberline saw that he wasn't the only one making his way toward the enclosure. From among the crowds a group of laborers had materialized and were moving up on it, too. He stopped and lifted out his spyglass, leaning forward over the fence to train it on the man in robes. The man stayed where he was, oblivious to approaching danger, still starkly visible, yet somehow invisible. Abberline saw that he held something by his side and it looked like—good God, was that a blowpipe?

Now he swung his spyglass to peer into the thicket of carriages. The workers were still approaching, and also . . .

Abberline caught his breath. If it wasn't his old friend

Mr. Hardy. The punisher had his back to Abberline but it was unmistakably him. Abberline watched as Mr. Hardy caught sight of one of the laborers and tipped him a wink.

The trap was about to be sprung.

Abberline began to move toward the enclosure more quickly. He no longer cared about robed men and whether they fought for good or bad. What he cared about was giving Mr. Hardy a greeting from Aubrey, and his truncheon was in his hand as he pushed his way through the crowds then vaulted the enclosure fence. He threaded his way through the parked coaches. Once more he was glad of his peeler's threads when one of the oncoming laborers saw him approach and turned smartly on his heel, feigning interest in something behind him. He was a few feet from Hardy now, and the punisher still had his back to him, still watching the man in robes. What he and the man in robes had in common was that both men thought themselves the hunter, not the prey, and that was why Abberline was able to come up behind Hardy undetected.

"Excuse me, sir, but can I ask what business you have in the carriage enclosure?"

"Business," said Hardy, turning. "It's none of your bloody business is what it—"

He never said the word "is."

As it turned out, he would never say the word "is" again, because Abberline swung as hard with the truncheon as he could and it was a vicious attack not worthy of an officer of the law, but Abberline had stopped thinking like an officer of the law now. He was thinking about the weeks of pain and the scars made by a brass knuckle-duster. He was thinking about a man who had been left for dead. He swung that truncheon with all of his might, and in the next moment Mr. Hardy had a mouthful of blood and teeth and an appointment with the dirt at his feet.

To his right Abberline saw a powerful laborer, snarling as he came to him with a cosh in one hand. There were other workers coming, too, but through the carriages, Abberline caught a glimpse of the man in robes, who was aware of the disturbance at his back and was turning, tensing. At the same time, Abberline felt the first laborer's cosh slam against his temple and it felled him, dazed, his eyes watering and head howling in pain, just a few feet away from where Mr. Hardy was already pulling himself to his knees, with his chin hanging at a strange angle and his eyes ablaze with fury —and a knife that streaked out of the darkness toward Abberline.

Abberline rolled but then found himself pinned by the legs and feet of the laborer who had hit him, looking up to see the man towering over him, a knife in his hand.

"*He's mine,*" said Hardy, although because of his injury it sounded more like *hismon,* but the laborer knew what he meant and stayed his hand as Hardy, his lower face a mask of blood, lurched toward Abberline, his elbow pulling back about to strike with the knife.

"*Stop,*" said the man in the robes, and Hardy jerked to a halt midstrike as he felt something, the mechanism of the Assassin's hidden blade, dig into his neck.

"Call off your man," said Ethan.

They heard the running feet of reinforcements.

Hardy spoke, and through his broken jaw and teeth it

sounded like "gufferell" but Ethan Frye knew what he meant and engaged his blade and it tore through Mr. Hardy's throat, emerging blood-streaked and gleaming from beneath his chin. At the same time Ethan drew his revolver with his other hand. A blast tore the night and the laborer pinning Abberline spun away. Ethan wheeled. His revolver spoke again and again, and more bodies fell among the carriages. At the first shot panic had taken over the crowd and their screams spooked the horses. Terrified coachmen flung themselves to the ground.

Ethan was empty but the attack had faded and so he dashed to where Abberline lay. "I'm Ethan Frye," he said, reaching out to help Abberline off the dirt, "and it appears I owe you a favor. I will not forget this, Constable Abberline. The Brotherhood likes to pay its debts. Now, if you will excuse me I have some pressing business to attend to."

And with that, he vaulted the fence and took off over the mud toward the shaft. Men in suits scattered at the sight of this wild figure pounding over the planks toward them. More importantly the squad of laborers at the tunnel edge saw him coming, too, but with just four of them between him and the steps, he wasn't too concerned, and he flipped the blowpipe from beneath his robes. Still on the run he plucked two darts from his belt, clamped them between his teeth, brought the blowpipe up to the first dart, loaded and fired.

The closest man fell with a poison-tipped dart in the neck. Out of deference to Mr. Pearson, Ethan had assembled an expensive poison that was painless and fast-acting. Apart from the prick at his neck, he wouldn't have felt a thing. Had he known he'd be using them on Templars, thought Ethan, he would have dipped them in the cheap stuff.

He reloaded. Spat the second dart. Another man fell. A third drew a cutlass from under his jacket and came forward, cursing Ethan. His mouth shone with saliva and he was slow, and Ethan took no pride in easily deflecting his first blow, anticipating an easy scooping strike and stepping into his body and jabbing back with the blade. He whirled swiftly away to avoid the dying man's final blood-flecked cough and meet the last man at the same time. This one was better, faster, more of a problem. Again, he had a cutlass, and again he began with a chopping strike that Ethan knocked away, trading two more blows then, before driving his blade home.

The other workers were closing in, but he reached the structure first, not bothering with the steps themselves, shinning down the timber uprights until his boots met the planks of the makeshift platform, and there before him stood the stationary train, nothing strange about it at first glance.

Just then he felt the earth move, a rumble. An unmistakable movement, enough to rock him on his feet. The timbers on the unfinished tunnel roof began to tumble.

Inside the carriage The Ghost had watched as Cavanagh bent and smashed the cane on the floor, pulling the orb from the shaft, which he tossed away. Smiling, the triumphant director held up the artifact for inspection. Greedy eyes went from the bronze globe to The Ghost; the two punishers goggled and even The Ghost felt a tremor of something indefinable in the air, as though the artifact had found its worshippers and was showing itself to them. He thought of light shows and depthless knowledge and understanding—and then saw death and destruction, and great explosions on battlefields, and wondered what he had helped unleash on the world. His job had been to recover that artifact. At the very least prevent its falling into the hands of the enemy. He had failed.

"Can you feel it?" Cavanagh was saying. The sphere seemed to glow in his hand and, yes, unless they were all experiencing the same hallucination, they could all feel it.

Like it was humming.

Suddenly the door to the adjoining carriage was flung open and Marchant was back, slamming the connecting door and cutting them off from oblivious Mrs. Pearson, who no doubt wondered when they were due to disembark.

"Ethan Frye's coming," said Marchant breathlessly. At once the waves of energy that seemed to pulse from the orb increased in intensity.

"What?" said Cavanagh.

"Mrs. Pearson wanted to be let out, so I opened the door and saw Ethan Frye at the top of the steps."

"Did he see you?"

"Back to me. He had his back to . . ."

The door to the carriage opened. At the same time, lightning fast, Cavanagh whirled and threw his knife, and there was a short scream from the doorway.

Ethan, thought The Ghost. But it was the train driver's body that fell into the carriage.

They all felt it. The earth seemed to move. There was

a distinct rumble and Cavanagh looked at the object he held, fixing it with a terrible, power-drunk gaze. And was it The Ghost's imagination or did it seem to glow more brightly—almost boastfully? *Look at me. Look at what I can do.*

Then the world caved in.

FIFTY-SIX

The slippage caused the surrounding banks to move. Though the tunnels held, the makeshift roof above the carriage was dislodged and came tumbling, clattering and crashing to the carriage below. The roof cracked and gave, showering those inside with splinters and it gave The Ghost just the chance he needed. He wrenched free of the punishers.

"Ethan," he called, and crashed through the door into the adjoining carriage, where Mrs. Pearson sat screaming and terrified with her hands over her head, and then at the sight of the Indian man screamed even more loudly—and Mrs. Pearson would spend the rest of her life believing that the Indian man had stabbed her husband to death.

The Ghost yanked open the carriage door, leapt out onto the platform—and almost barged into Ethan Frye.

"Kill him," called Cavanagh with a voice that sounded as though it had been dragged from the very pits of hell. "Kill them both."

The two punishers burst out of the carriage door, blocking the way forward, oncoming laborers behind.

Other Mr. Hardy reached into his suit jacket, hand appearing with a revolver aimed at The Ghost.

Unwavering, The Ghost met him, wishing he had a blade but settling for the toughened edge of his bare foot instead, seeming almost to pivot in the air as he leapt, knocking the revolver away with one kick then wrenching the man's head back with a strike to the chin from his trailing foot.

The weapon spun away and the two men both sprawled to the deck, but The Ghost was the first to react, kicking again but this time to the underside of Other Mr. Hardy's chin and hearing a crunch in return that left him either dead or out for the count. The Ghost wasn't too bothered either way.

At the same time Ethan had the pleasure of Mr. Smith's company. The second punisher had drawn a long-bladed dirk and come forward, slashing haphazardly, with not a cat in hell's chance of besting the Assassin. Sure enough, Ethan stepped smartly away, felt the reassuring tickle of the mechanism on his forearm as his blade engaged, and then buried it in the man's neck.

Suddenly the earthquake seemed to increase in intensity and at the same time Cavanagh stepped out of the carriage and onto the platform in front of them. His knife was still buried in the train driver but he had no need of it now. Not now that he had the artifact. It glowed and seemed to pulse in time with the tremors.

Twenty feet away, Ethan and The Ghost exchanged a fearful look as Cavanagh held the artifact before him, as though proffering it to the gods, and there was a great moan of traumatized wood, then a sudden increase in the deluge from above. In the distance were the screams of spectators terrified by the sudden earthquake—an earth-quake that was increasing in intensity now as behind the glowing artifact, Cavanagh's face split into a maniacal grin, his eyes changing, until the man who had spent his life burying his humanity in favor of ambition and cor-ruption had no more humanity left.

He hadn't noticed Marchant edging closer to him.

He didn't see that Marchant had retrieved the pearl-handled knife from the body of the train driver.

"Crawford Starrick sends his regards," shouted the clerk above the crashing of the shaft around them, then buried the knife into Cavanagh's armpit.

The director's eyes widened in pain and shock and incomprehension at the sudden turn of events. Straight-away the artifact's rhythmic pulse faded as he sank to his knees with his suit front already gleaming darkly with blood from his wound. He looked from Marchant to the two Assassins, then sank forward. Perhaps in that final moment a little of him returned, enough to ponder on the evil he had done, and as he left this world with a wet, choking noise as his lungs filled and he drowned in his own blood, The Ghost hoped that the unnamed sepoy was there to greet him in hell.

The laborers swarmed onto the platform behind them as Marchant snatched up the artifact—and Ethan Frye leapt forward to attempt to relieve him of it, all of which happened in the split second before a falling piece of timber ignited the gas supplies on the roof of the carriage, and the Metropolitan Railway's brand-new "enclosed carriage" burst into flames.

FIFTY-SEVEN

Ethan and The Ghost dived for cover, flinging themselves into the tunnel. Behind them was fire and pandemonium and noise, then after a moment during which the after-effects of the explosion died down, they heard Marchant screaming at the laborers, "Get them! Get after them!" and they took to their heels, heading west, back toward Paddington.

"I have something to tell you," said Ethan as they ran. They pounded in between the train tracks in total darkness, sharpened senses leading them along the tunnel as fast as they dared, until they found themselves beneath the steam hole at Leinster Gardens, and there they pulled themselves up to safety. Sure enough the gang of workers ran past right below them. They didn't even look up.

For a moment there was silence as both men tried and failed to make sense of what had just happened.

"What do you have to tell me?" asked The Ghost, his shoulders rising and falling as he caught his breath—dreading what he was about to hear.

Ethan sighed. "This is all my fault," he said. "I was warned."

"What do you mean, *warned*?"

Ethan told The Ghost about Ajay, watched sorrow cripple the man's features.

"How could you?" said The Ghost at last.

Ethan, desolate, said, "I judged it for the best."

"You judged wrong."

Again a silence, broken by Ethan, who said softly, "Was I the only one to make an error of judgment? How were they able to identify you, Jayadeep?"

The Ghost flashed him a furious look. "Anything I did was born of a desire to help my fellow man. Isn't that the right way? Isn't that the Assassin way?"

"It is. But if you excuse yourself on those terms, then you must excuse me because I did what I did for the good of *all* men."

"You were as obsessed with that artifact as he was."

"If so, then I was obsessed with making sure it didn't fall into the wrong hands, and now that we've seen it in action I know I was right to be."

The Ghost had been promised light shows or a pretty talisman from the artifact. Instead he had witnessed something altogether different.

"Well, it's in the wrong hands now," he said.

"Not for long."

From below them came a shout. "Come on, mates. We're to get to the tunnel."

"The coast will be clear soon," said Ethan, drumming his hands on the dirt in frustration, "but the artifact will be halfway to Starrick by now."

The Ghost wasn't listening. Let Ethan fixate on his artifact. The Ghost no longer cared. He was thinking about the order they'd just heard. "The tunnel." The Templars knew about Maggie—they knew that through her was a way to get to him, and through him a way to Ethan, and maybe just having the artifact was not enough. They meant to smash the Assassins as well.

"I have to go to Maggie."

"I have to go after the artifact," said Ethan. "Just as your conscience dictates you must go to the tunnel, so I must go there."

"You should go after your precious artifact," said The Ghost, then took to his feet.

It was a distance of some six miles from Leinster Gardens to the Thames Tunnel, plus the Templar men had a head start and were traveling by carriage, but The Ghost was fast, and he was determined, and he knew the route well, and he made it within the hour.

But he was too late. Wagons were already arranged around the octagonal marble entrance hall of the tunnel shaft. Figures were milling about, some of them holding lit flares and lamps. He saw other figures running, heard screaming and the unmistakable sound of coshes and truncheons being used in anger and the shouts of pain to match. The residents of the tunnel were accustomed to having their refuge invaded but not with such violence, not with so much malice or single-minded purpose.

And the purpose?

To take Maggie.

But he wasn't going to let them do that. At this, he wasn't going to fail.

Pandemonium reigned but through a forest of bodies The Ghost saw Other Mr. Hardy. The last surviving punisher stood at a carriage with his revolver in one hand and the other at his injured face, shouting orders. "Bring the woman, bring the old woman." There was no sign of Marchant and The Ghost guessed Ethan was right: the artifact was on its way to Crawford Starrick. Best of luck, Ethan. You made your choice.

Running past a series of minor skirmishes outside, The Ghost burst into the octagonal hall. Over by the watch house the commotion was at its most heated. He saw the gray hair of Maggie amid a throng of bodies, some of them tunnel dwellers, some of them fighters. She was shouting and cursing loudly as Templar thugs attempted to manhandle her over the turnstile. The tunnel people were trying to save her but they were ill equipped to do so. Templars' clubs and knives rose and fell; shouts of resistance turned to screams of pain that rebounded from the glass of the octagonal hall. The Ghost thought he saw the private detective, Hazlewood, somewhere among the great mass of people but then the face was gone. A second later, he realized that Other Mr. Hardy's urgings seemed to have stopped and then heard a voice from behind him, saying, "Right, you little bastard . . ."

Other Mr. Hardy was right-handed. He was armed with a Webley that pulled to his right.

The Ghost took both factors into consideration as he ducked and wheeled at the same time, going inside Other Mr. Hardy's gun arm and pleased to hear the air part a good six inches away from his head a half second before he heard the blast. There was a scream. One of the Templar thugs fell and that was one less man to deal with, thought The Ghost as he broke Other Mr. Hardy's arm, reached for the dirk that hung sheathed at the punisher's waist and thrust it into his chest.

Other Mr. Hardy reached for The Ghost and their eyes were just millimeters apart as The Ghost watched the light of life die in the other man's eyes—and he experienced a wave of something that was part sickness and part despair, a great hollowing out inside as he took a life.

Maggie had seen him. "Bharat," she screeched from among the brawlers at the turnstile, and Templar thugs turned away from the commotion, saw The Ghost standing over their boss as he slid lifelessly to the mosaic floor, and moved over to attack.

The Ghost tossed the knife from one hand to the other, disorienting the first thug who came forward. Brave man. Stupid man. He died in seconds, and now The Ghost had two blades, the dirk and a cutlass, and used them both to open the throat of a second attacker, then spun, jabbing backhand with the cutlass and opening the stomach of a third. He was an expert swordsman, skilled in the business of death. He took no pleasure in it. Simply, he was good at it.

By now Maggie had been reclaimed by the tunnel people and taken back to the sanctuary of the steps, and perhaps the Templar thugs knew the game was up; perhaps seeing three of their comrades fall so quickly at the hands of the barefoot Indian lad had made them decide that discretion was the better part of valor; or perhaps the death of Other Mr. Hardy took whatever spirit they had left, because a cry went up, "Time to go, mates, time to go," and the beatings stopped as the thugs streamed out of the hall and headed for their carriages.

In a matter of moments the hall had emptied, then the area outside had emptied, too, and the tunnel was no longer under attack.

The Ghost stood with his shoulders rising and falling as he caught his breath. He let the dirk and the cutlass fall to the floor with a dull clang that reverberated around the room, and he walked toward the turnstile, climbing over, heading down toward his berth.

The rotunda was a mass of people and there were cheers for him as he descended. "Maggie?" he asked a woman he knew.

She pointed him to the tunnel. "They took her up there to safety," she said before stealing a kiss and clapping him on the back. The tunnel dwellers kept up the cheering as he passed through the rotunda to the tunnel itself, leaving the press of people and the shock and excitement of the battle behind.

He had already decided that he no longer belonged to the Brotherhood; nor would he ever speak to Ethan Frye again. Let the Assassins and Templars fight it out among themselves. He would stay here, with his people. This was where he belonged.

A thought occurred to him. The woman saying, *They took her up there to safety.*

Who had taken her to safety?

He remembered seeing the face of the private detective in the melee. He broke into a run. "Maggie!" he screamed, dashing up the tunnel toward the berth they shared, where she tended the fire and doled out broth and received her rightful love as tunnel mother.

She lay in the dirt. Whoever killed her had stabbed her multiple times, shredding her smock. Her witchy gray hair was flecked with blood. Her eyes, which had so often blazed with fury and mirth and passion, were dull in death.

They had pinned a note to her chest. "We consider the debt settled."

The Ghost sank to his haunches and held Maggie. He took her head in his lap and the tunnel dwellers heard The Ghost as he wailed his grief and despair.

PART III

METROPOLIS RISING

FIFTY-EIGHT

Cold and damp and gripped by melancholy, the Assassin George Westhouse shivered in the sidings of Croydon Rail Yard. Was it that a tired pall hung over all of England? Or did it hang over him? There was a storm brewing, he thought. Both literally and metaphorically.

It was February, 1868, five years after the wretched events at the Metropolitan Line. After that, he, Ethan Frye and The Ghost had retired in failure: The Ghost to his hidey-hole in the Thames Tunnel, a self-imposed prison of regret and recrimination; George to batten down the hatches in Croydon; and Ethan to busy himself with raising the next generation of Assassin resistance— one unencumbered by the disappointment and failure that tainted their elders. A new generation with fresh ambition and enthusiasm. A new way of doing things.

What a shame, George thought, that Ethan would never see it in action.

Ethan had been just forty-three years old when he died a matter of weeks ago, but he had been ill with the pleurisy for some time before that. During many hours spent at

Ethan's bedside, George had watched his old friend wither, like fruit on a vine.

"Find the artifact, George," Ethan had insisted. "Send Evie and Jacob for it. The future of London lies in their hands now. The twins, you and Henry—you're the only ones left now."

"Hush now, Ethan," George said, and leaned back in his chair to hide the tears that pricked his eyes. "You will be here to lead us. You're indomitable, Ethan. As unbreakable as one of those infernal trains that trundle through Croydon night and day."

"I hope so, George, I truly hope so."

"Besides, the Council has not ratified any operations in this area. They consider us too weak."

"I know when we're ready, better than any Council, and we are ready: Henry will provide. Jacob and Evie will act."

"Well, you had better hurry up, get well and inform the Council yourself, then, hadn't you?" chided George.

"That I had, George, that I had . . ."

But Ethan had dissolved into coughing so hard that the muslin cloth he held to his mouth came away speckled with blood.

"We were so close, George," he said another time. He was even weaker now, becoming more frail by the day. "The artifact was just a few feet away from me, as far away as you are now. I almost had it."

"You did your best."

"Then my best was not enough because the operation did not succeed, George. I ran an unsuccessful operation."

"There were circumstances beyond your control."

"I failed The Ghost."

"He himself made mistakes. Whether he accepts that, I have no idea; whether his mistakes contributed to the failure of the operation, I couldn't say that either. But the fact remains, it failed. Now we must concentrate on regrouping."

Ethan turned his head to look at George and it was all George could do to stop himself recoiling afresh. It was true that Ethan's achievements as an Assassin would never be celebrated along with those of Altaïr, Ezio or Edward Kenway, but for all that he had been a credit to the Brotherhood, and he was a man who even when he was downhearted exuded a thirst for life. With him you got the sense that inside was a personality at war with itself, pushing and pulling this way and that but never at rest, always questing forward.

Now, though, the skin that had once glowed with life was pale and drawn; the eyes that had burned with passion were sunken and dull. Ethan was no longer questing for life; he was taking the long walk toward death.

First he had suffered with the flu; then, when that seemed to have passed, came chest pains and a constant, hacking cough. When he began hacking up blood the physician was called, who diagnosed pleurisy. Benjamin Franklin had died of pleurisy, said the physician phlegmatically. William Wordsworth too.

Even so, the physician assured the family, pleurisy was an infection of the chest. And so long as the patient rested there was every possibility it would clear up by itself. Plenty of patients recovered from pleurisy.

Just not Benjamin Franklin or William Wordsworth, that was all.

And not the Assassin Ethan Frye, it turned out. For each passing day the pleurisy seemed to write its fate upon his skin more emphatically than the last, and to hear him cough, a crunching rattle disgorged from deep within a chest that was no longer functioning as it should, was dreadful to witness. The sound of it tore through the house. Ethan had taken a room in the eaves—"I'm not to be a burden to the twins while I'm ill," he had said—but his cough carried down the stairways to the lower rooms, where the twins shared their concern in bitten lips, downcast eyes, and exchanged glances as they took strength from one another. In many ways, the terrible story of their father's illness could be measured in his children's reactions: rolled eyes when he first got ill, as though he was exaggerating his malady in order to enjoy the benefits of being waited on hand and foot; and then a series of increasingly worried silent exchanges when it became terribly apparent that he was not going to recover in a matter of days or even weeks. After that came a period when the sound of his coughing would make them flinch and their eyes fill with tears; latterly they looked as though they wished for it all to be over, so their father's suffering might be at an end.

He limited their trips to his bedchamber. They would have liked to have been by his bedside night and day, just as he had once sat with his beloved wife Cecily. Perhaps that experience had convinced him the sickbed of a loved one was no place to spend your days.

Sometimes, though, if he was feeling well enough, he would summon them to his room, tell them to wipe the worried looks off their faces (because he wasn't bloody well dead yet), then issue instructions on how they were to lead a new vanguard of resistance against the Templars. He informed them he had written seeking the Council's approval for when it was time to send the twins into action.

Ethan knew that his time was short. He knew he was leaving this world. He was like a chess player maneuvering his pieces, ready for a final attack that he himself would not be around to superintend. But he wanted things in place.

Perhaps it was his way of making amends.

It infuriated him that the Council refused to give him their blessing; indeed, the Council withheld any decision on the London situation until such time as they had news of a situation worth acting upon. Stalemate.

One evening, George visited him. As usual they conversed for some time, then, as usual, George was lulled into sleep in the cozy warmth of the eaves. He awoke with a start, as though some sixth sense were prodding him back into consciousness, to find Ethan lying on his side with both hands across his chest, his eyes closed and mouth open, a thin trail of blood running from his mouth to the sweat-soaked sheets.

With the heaviest heart imaginable George stood and went to the body, arranging it on the bed, pulling a sheet to beneath Ethan's chin, using his handkerchief to wipe the blood from his friend's mouth. "I'm sorry, Ethan," he said, as he worked. "I'm sorry for slumbering when I should have been here to help guide you into the next world."

He had crept quietly downstairs to find the twins in the kitchen. Evie and Jacob had taken to wearing their Assassins' attire, as though to acknowledge that it was they who would carry the torch from now on, and they had both been wearing them that night, their cowls raised as they sat on either side of the bare kitchen table, a candle slowly guttering on the wood between them, the same wordless dialogue of grief that had enveloped them for weeks.

They held hands, he noticed, and regarded one another from under their cowls, and perhaps they already knew; perhaps they had felt the same energy that had prompted George awake. For they had turned their gaze upon him in the kitchen doorway and in their eyes was the terrible knowledge that their father was dead.

No words were said. George simply sat with them and then, as dawn broke, left for home, to attend to the task of notifying the Council that one of the brothers had fallen.

Condolences arrived at the house, but in accordance with Assassin tradition the burial was an unremarkable, quiet occasion, attended by George, Evie and Jacob alone, just three mourners and a priest who consigned Ethan to the grave. Ashes to ashes, dust to dust.

For some time they seemed to exist in a state of limbo until news had reached George that the Metropolitan artifact was close. He had no time to seek the Council's approval for an operation to retrieve it; they probably would have demanded more detailed information anyway. And he knew exactly what Ethan's wishes were; his friend had imparted them on his deathbed.

Jacob and Evie were ready. They would go into action.

FIFTY-NINE

In the Croydon Rail Yard belonging to Ferris Ironworks, a darkened world of smoke-belching locomotives, clanking carriages and complaining brakes, George met the twins for the first time since their father's funeral.

As ever, he was struck by their looks: Jacob had his father's charisma, the same eyes that appeared to dance with a mix of mischief and resolve; Evie, on the other hand, was the mirror image of her mother. If anything, she was even more beautiful. She had a tilted, imperious chin, freckled cheeks, exquisite, questioning eyes and a full mouth that all too rarely split into a wide smile.

Jacob wore a top hat. Evie's cowl lay across her shoulders. Their clothes were free-flowing and customized in the right places: long, three-quarter-length belted coats open over discreetly armored waistcoats and boots with noise-proofed soles and discreet steel toe caps. On their forearms were the gauntlet-blades with which they were both expert (Evie even more so than Jacob, according to Ethan), their fingers snug in hinged steel protectors that doubled as knuckle-dusters.

As the air crackled with the threat of the oncoming storm, George had watched them move through the rail yards to his position crouching behind one of the train cars. Thanks to their looks and garb you could hardly hope to see two more striking figures. Yet their father had taught them well. Just as he himself was a master of hiding in plain sight, so too were his offspring.

They greeted one another, sharing something unspoken of Ethan. George had notified them by letter of the job at hand, warning them what it would entail. Before he died, Ethan had told the twins very little about the Piece of Eden that had been the focus of his failed mission years ago. After all, it was not exactly a glorious episode in the history of the Brotherhood. They knew it was a uniquely powerful object and not to be underestimated. Beyond that there was scarcely much to be said before the job began.

It was to be their blooding.

They hunkered down. Jacob, his top hat perched at its usual rakish angle, was the more brash. His edges were rough, his patience short, and when he talked it was with the growling voice of the streets. Evie, on the other hand, was the more thoughtful and cultured of the two. An outer softness belied a steel within.

"The iron ships from here," said George, indicating the works. "The Templar running things is Rupert Ferris, and our target one. Target two is Sir David Brewster, who's got his hands on the bauble. Think you can handle it?"

The twins were young and keen and fearless and maybe, thought George, turning to find that they had both climbed to the top of the carriage, they would also be cunning.

"Ladies and gentlemen," he said with a smile, "the unstoppable Frye twins. See them nightly at Covent Garden."

Evie gave him a don't-worry look. "George, honestly, I've studied the plans of the laboratory and have every route covered."

"And I've got all I need right here," said Jacob, engaging his blade.

He turned at the sound of a train whistle.

"Jacob . . ." said George.

"I'll extend your regards to Ferris," said Jacob. He and Evie were watching the train as it trundled through the siding toward them. They crouched on the roof of their own rail car, ready to spring forth.

"Evie . . ." said George warningly.

"Chat later, George, we've a train to catch," said Evie and the two of them made their leap, landing with all the grace and stealth of predatory wildcats on the roof of the passing train. A wave to George and the mission had begun.

"May the Creed guide you, you vagrants," George called to them, but didn't think they'd heard. Instead he watched them go with a strange mixture of emotions: envy for their youth, grace and balance. And concern that Ethan was wrong—that the twins were not yet battle-ready. Not for an operation of this magnitude.

But most of all hope—hope the two incredible young Assassins could turn the tide in their favor.

SIXTY

"Poor man, more afraid than ever. The years have not been kind," said Evie to Jacob, shouting above the roar of the locomotive. George was calling to them—"May the Creed guide you, you vagrants"—but his words were mostly lost in the noise.

"Evie Frye," chided Jacob, "where do you get it from?"

"Same place as you, Jacob," she said, and they exchanged a glance, that preternatural meeting of eyes in which they both remembered and honored their mother and father. The knowledge that all they had now was each other.

"Have fun," said Jacob. They were nearing the iron-works on tracks that threaded through dark, industrial buildings and chimney stacks pouring out choking smoke.

Jacob rolled his top hat from his head, collapsed and secreted it within his robes in one well-practiced move as he raised his hood. Evie pulled her own cowl over her head. They were ready.

"Don't die," she told her brother, then watched, heart in mouth despite herself, as he crouched, hands on either side of him on the train roof, fingers splayed. As the train pulled level with the ironworks and the forbidding dark brickwork rushed toward them as the carriage leaned and the train tilted on the rails, Jacob leapt—another perfectly executed jump that took him to a sill on the first floor of the ironworks. A second later and he'd be inside.

She watched him recede. The next time she heard anything of him, it would be via the thump of an explosion as he escaped the ironworks spattered with the blood of Rupert Ferris. For the time being, however, she went to one knee, gloved hands on the roof of the carriage, wind whipping her cowl as the train cut its way through the outskirts of Croydon and to the shipping yard farther along the line. Here, according to the plans sent to them by George, was the laboratory where the artifact was apparently stored; where, providing George's information was correct, Sir David Brewster was working on it. What did she know about it? There was information gleaned from ancient scrolls, of course, but scrolls tended to be a little ambiguous. However, her father had actually seen it in action. He had talked of how it would glow, seeming to feed off some inner energy of the user, transferring something dark and primal into an actual destructive energy.

"Take that look off your face, Evie," he had added, a little crossly. "This is not an object to admire or covet. It is to be treated with the utmost caution, as a weapon of war that cannot be allowed to remain in the hands of the enemy."

"Yes, Father," she said, obediently. But if she was honest with herself, the object's attraction outweighed its possible danger. Yes, it was something to be feared, to be treated with respect. But even so.

The shipping yard to which the train was heading began to loom ever larger on the immediate horizon, so she turned and crabbed along the train roof until she came to a hatch. Fingers prised it open and moments later Evie dropped into the carriage below. She pulled back her cowl, blew hair away from her face and took stock of her surroundings.

She was among crates, all of them marked STARRICK INDUSTRIES.

Crawford Starrick. The mere utterance had sent her father into a painful reverie. He was the Templar Grand Master, the man she and Jacob had pledged to topple. No matter what George said. No matter what the Council was to approve or not, the twins had decided their father's legacy was best observed by removing Crawford Starrick from his position; recovering the artifact, taking out his lieutenants, disrupting his business practices—all were steps on a path that led to the death and dishonor of Crawford Starrick.

Just then the door to the carriage opened, and Evie took cover. A man entered, just a shape in the darkness, framed unsteadily in the open door. A burly man, she thought, and the impression was confirmed when there came the flare of tinder and he lifted a lamp to see in the gloom.

"Where is it?" he said over his shoulder, addressing some unseen comrades. "Where's Brewster's supplies?"

Now there was a name she recognized. Brewster. She crouched in the shadows, waiting. This man would be

her first. Her first live kill, and she flexed her wrist, feeling
the reassuring weight of the gauntlet mechanism along
her forearm, its individual sections moving easily and
silently. She reminded herself that she was trained for this.
At the same time she recalled what her father had always
told her—that no amount of training could prepare you
for taking a man's life. "Taking from him everything he
ever was and everything he ever will be; to leave his family
grieving, to begin a wave of sadness and sorrow and possible revenge and recrimination that might ripple throughout the ages."

Her father knew that there was ready and then there
was *ready*.

And Evie was ready, but was she really *ready*?

She had to be. She had no choice.

The man was cursing his mate for a coward. Crouched
behind a crate Evie used two hands to raise her cowl,
letting the fabric settle over her head, taking strength and
comfort from the symbolism of it, then activated her
blade.

Ready now, she gave a low whistle.

"Who's there?" said the visitor, raising his lantern a
little and moving into the carriage two more steps. He
drew level with Evie's position and she held her breath,
awaiting her moment. Her eyes went from her blade to
the spot just behind the guard's ear where it would penetrate, slicing up into the skull cavity, into the brain,
instant painless death . . .

But death all the same. She was on the balls of her feet
now, the heels of her boots raised off the boards of the
carriage, one hand steadying herself on the floorboards

and her blade hand brought to bear. He was her enemy, she reminded herself, a man who stood alongside those who planned to persecute and tyrannize any who did not share their aims.

And possibly he did not deserve to die. But die he would, in service to a cause that was greater than them both.

With that thought uppermost she struck from her hiding place behind the crate and her blade found its mark and her victim made a tiny, almost imperceptible noise, a final croak, then she was helping him to collapse silently to the dirty floor of the carriage. She held him as he died, this stranger. You were my first, she thought, and silently honored him, closing his eyes.

"It's never personal," was what Father had said. But then he'd stopped himself. "It's *rarely* personal."

She laid him down and left him there. It wasn't personal.

Now, she thought, as the train pulled into the laboratory facility, what she needed was a diversion. If only she could uncouple the carriages . . .

Outside the carriage stood the first fighter's mate. He had been dozing and she took him out easily. Father had always said it became easier and he was right; she barely gave her next target a second thought. She didn't bother closing his eyes and wishing him well; she left him where he fell and moved on up toward the locomotive. In the next carriage she pressed herself into hiding to avoid a pair of gossiping guards.

"How's Sir David and Miss Thorne getting on?" one of them was saying.

"She's turned up like a bad penny, ain't she?" replied

his mate. "I'll put five bob on things not being to her liking."

"Ain't looking too good for old Sir David, then."

Lucy Thorne. Evie had heard the name, of course. Was she with Brewster, then?

She let the guards pass then moved quickly through the final carriage and to the coupling between the locomotive and the carriage. She didn't have long now; they would discover the bodies of the men she had killed, and she was glad of her gloves as she planted her feet apart and reached for the ring of the coupling pin. As the wind rushed and the train tracks passed beneath her feet, she gave a grunt of effort and wrenched it free.

Smartly she stepped onto the locomotive, watching the carriages pull away. From around her came shouts as the men of the yard wondered why the carriages had become detached and came running to investigate. Meanwhile she clambered to the roof of the locomotive, trying to take stock of her surroundings as the train ground to a halt in the yard with a screech of brakes and complaining metal. To one side of her, the water of the Thames inlet glittered darkly; to the other was the tumult of the shipyard, with its cranes and railway sidings and row upon row of office buildings and . . .

Something very interesting indeed.

Flattening herself into almost invisibility, the first thing she saw was two figures she recognized: Sir David Brewster and Lucy Thorne. The two of them had been surveying the sudden chaos around them before turning to continue their progress toward a carriage and coachman stationed close to the entrance gate.

Evie jumped from the locomotive, pleased her diversion had been so diverting, not to mention glad of the smoke that hung like a permanent funeral shroud over the site. Industrialization had its benefits, she thought, as she followed the pair, staying in the shadows of the perimeter, getting a good look at her quarry.

Lucy Thorne wore black. A black hat, long black gloves, and a black crinoline-and-bustle gown buttoned high on the throat. She was young, with attractive looks offset by a scowl that matched her dark ensemble, and as she walked, disturbing layers of smoke that hung like a ship's hammocks in the dimly lit yard, it was with the quality of a shadow. As though she were darkness repelling light.

Scuttling beside her, Sir David Brewster was maybe three times her age, with a fretful face and long side-whiskers. Though considerably older than Lucy Thorne, he nevertheless seemed cowed, subsumed by the darkness of her. This was a man who was recognized as the inventor of the kaleidoscope and something Evie knew only as the "lenticular stereoscope," whatever one of those was. A nervous man, or nervous now at least, overawed by the presence of Lucy Thorne, he struggled to keep up with her, as, speaking in a whining Scottish accent, he said, "I need two more weeks with the device."

Angry, Lucy Thorne retorted, "Your questionable practices are beginning to draw unwanted attention. You have been given more than enough time to achieve results, Sir David."

"I was unaware that you expect me to perform like a cocker spaniel."

"Permit me to remind you of your obligations to the Order."

Brewster made an exasperated noise. "Miss Thorne, you ride me like a racehorse."

As they reached the carriage, the coachman doffed a three-cornered hat, bowed low and opened the door for Lucy Thorne, who acknowledged him with an imperious nod as she took her seat and arranged her skirts before leaning from the open door to address Brewster a final time. "Sir David, I will return tomorrow. If you have not unlocked the device's secret, forget your dogs and your horses. I will leave you to the wolves. Good day."

And with that the Templar cultist indicated to the coachman, who closed the door, tipped Brewster an impertinent wink and resumed his place on the board to drive the horses and remove Lucy Thorne from the chaos of the shipyard.

As it drove off, Evie watched Brewster let out a flabbergasted noise before his attention was drawn to a group of men nearby. Evie's gaze went there, too, and what she saw was several guards escorting a flamboyantly attired man across the yard, the man in custody protesting loudly, "I was merely promised a tour of the premises, m'lords."

"Who sent you?" demanded one of the Templar men.

Another chimed in with, "He's one of Green's spies."

But Brewster was already calling over to them. "Get that man to interrogation. Then I want him brought to the lab."

Evie watched him still. Then her gaze went to the sky overhead. By now the canopy was funeral black with gathering clouds, and the air had a crackle and tension about it that made the storm more of a certainty than ever. She could see that Brewster thought so too; he had spun on his heel and moved over to something she hadn't spotted before. A metal pole fixed into the dirt of the yard. Some kind of lightning conductor, perhaps? With another look up to the gathering clouds, Brewster broke into a sprightly run and disappeared into the door of the building, leaving the uproar of the facility behind him. The first drops of rain were beginning to fall; the men were still attempting to recouple locomotives and carriages while simultaneously conducting an inquest into how the two had become detached.

Evie, the agent of chaos, merely smiled as she slipped through the doorway behind Brewster, and just as she did so came the first crack of thunder and the sky was lit in a flash of blinding white light.

Once inside, she clung to the wall, staying wide of the lamps' illumination and engaging her blade at the same time. Her eyes moved as she had always been taught: section by section around any given space, identifying hostiles, pinpointing areas of vulnerability, thinking like the full-fledged Assassin she was.

However, what greeted her wasn't quite what she expected.

SIXTY-ONE

She had anticipated a laboratory. According to George Westhouse's plans—the selfsame plans that she had pored over at home in Crawley—where she stood now—*at this very point*—should have been the laboratory.

But it wasn't. Instead she was in a roundhouse, some kind of antechamber, and there was no sign of laboratory equipment. There were no hostiles. There were no points of vulnerability.

There was nothing at all.

No, what was that? There came a shout from a door opposite and, with a quick glance back to the yard outside, where rain was falling hard now and the men still shouted and cursed one another, Evie closed the door to the outside and crossed the floor to a second door, this one ajar.

There she stood, controlling her breathing as she peered cautiously through the open door. The scene that greeted her was just what Brewster had ordered: an interrogation. The Templar men had bound their dandily dressed captive to a chair and the questioning had begun.

Perhaps the man had expected to be brought before a

gentleman of high social standing, who would apologize profusely for the rough treatment he had received at the hands of the guards and offer him brandy and cigars in the back office prior to a round of punitive sackings. No such luck. He'd been tossed in a chair and trussed up, for burly security to fire questions at him.

"I ask you, m'lord," he was saying, "can't a gentleman wander the tracks?"

"How did you break into the laboratory? The entrance is hidden," growled one of the men. He had his back to Evie but she could see he was pulling on a pair of black-leather gloves. The prisoner's eyes went from the gloves to the face of his inquisitor, but if he was looking for signs of mercy or compassion, then he was looking in the wrong place.

"What do you wish me to elaborate upon, m'lord?"

There was a wheedling tone to his voice now, an unmistakable note of foreboding.

"Who sent you?" demanded the inquisitor. He flexed his fingers in the gloves. Evie heard another unseen man chortle with anticipation of the great show to come.

"Why, I did, milord. I came on my own two feet."

Now the second thug moved into view, the two of them crowding the man from Evie's view. "Let me put his fingers through the mangle . . ."

"Not yet." The first man stopped his mate. "Not yet." He turned his attention back to the prisoner. "Was it Green?"

"Neither green, nor black nor brown," said the man in the chair.

"Henry Green," said a man Evie couldn't see.

"Ah, Henry Green . . . who's he?"

Threatening now, the unseen man said, "Your very soul hangs in the balance . . . Confess or my sharp friend here will have his way. You shall return empty-handed."

Evie heard the distinctive sound of a knife being drawn from its sheath.

And of course, she couldn't allow it to be used. She flexed the fingers of her gauntlet, engaged her blade and moved into the room to confront the men.

There were three of them. This mission was turning into quite a test of her skills, she thought. This time? Multiple opponents.

She weighed up, she assessed, then struck, dancing in toward a grinning thug on the right but at the last second unexpectedly ducking and swiping her blade up and across the chest of a man in the middle. She rolled and came up with the blade foremost, jamming it through the breast-plate of a Templar goon on the right. The remaining inquisitor, the slowest, had barely drawn his sword when Evie drew back her knee and delivered a high kick with the reinforced edge of her boot.

Damn, she thought, watching as her opponent staggered back. The coat had impeded the height of her strike, and instead of finishing him off, she'd merely unbalanced him. At the same time he'd recovered enough presence of mind to draw his weapon and, even as she steadied herself to meet his attack, was coming forward, demonstrating a little more guile and cunning than she had originally given him credit for.

Stupid. Stupid amateur. Evie turned her head in time to avoid the steel making contact with her face. She checked back quickly and at the same time tapped her left hand on the forearm of her right to retract the blade. Next she turned into his outstretched arm, a movement that was half dance step, half embrace but wholly deadly as she ended it with a jab to the face from her gauntlet then engaged her blade into his eye socket.

Blood, brain and eye fluid sluiced down his cheek as he slumped to the floor. She shook blood from the blade and sheathed it, and then turned to the man in the chair, who was giving her a bemused but otherwise good-humored look.

"Ah, thank you kindly," he said. "I was in ever such a squeaky fix, when—what do you know?—you rescued me."

"Where's the hidden laboratory?" she asked him. The men she'd just fought were taking their time to die. Gurgles, death rattles and the sound of boots scrabbling at the brick in a final, feeble burst of life were the background to their conversation.

"Untie me, and then we can parley, my lady," bargained the trussed-up prisoner.

Evie climbed astride the man and pulled her fist back. His face twisted into a mixture of fear and indecision. He had seen the blade in action. He had seen Evie in action. He had no desire to be on the receiving end of either. This was a man who had been lulled into a full sense of security by a pretty face many times before and wasn't about to let it happen again.

"I'm pressed for time," she said, just in case her intentions weren't already clear. "Tell me now."

"It's underground." He swallowed, inclining his chin toward what looked like a panel of some kind in the wall of the roundhouse. "It requires a key. One of the guards nicked mine, cheeky sod."

"Thank you," she said, and stood, about to leave.

"Now untie me."

"You got yourself in." She shook her head. "I trust you can get yourself out."

He was still calling out after her as she left. "Not to worry, my lady, I can still recall a couple of tricks from my carnival days."

Good luck to you, then, she thought, as she departed by a different door, now looking for another guard who might have the key.

Thank God for the flapping mouths of Templar guards. She pressed herself into the shadows of a passageway, overhearing two of them discussing the very key she sought.

"What are you doing? Keep that key in your pocket or else Miss Thorne will have your guts for garters."

"Let's have a look downstairs, then. I want to see that artifact."

So do I, thought Evie Frye, as she claimed two more victims and recovered the key.

She returned to the roundhouse, deciding to release the prisoner if and when the key worked on the panel, but too late, he was absent, chair overturned and ropes discarded on the floor. She tensed in case he was planning to leap out at her but, no, he was gone. Instead she turned her attention to the panels and was at last able to let herself into the building's inner sanctum.

Inside, the walls were dark and wet. They muffled the sound of the storm and yet somehow, here, it felt as though the elements were at their fiercest.

How could that be? She remembered the lightning rod and thought of power being directed down here. Power needed for an underground laboratory, perhaps?

Then she came upon it and she knew she was right—that she stood at the very epicenter of the storm's channeled energy.

The artifact was close.

SIXTY-TWO

The flagstones stretched away from where she stood at the door, opening out to a large vaulted, underground space where scientific apparatus on tables lay between Tesla coils and upright lightning conductors—all throbbing with a steadily intensifying energy.

Too much? In the roof of the laboratory hung a series of harnesses and platforms. Lightning particles seemed to crack all around them, sparking and flashing, painting the room in a sudden glare of phosphorescent white.

At the other end of the laboratory was what looked like a large inspection tube and in there, she could see, was the artifact. Standing nearby was Sir David Brewster with an assistant, both poring over what lay on the other side of the toughened glass, the orb-like golden Apple. Even from so far away, Evie found herself transfixed by it. Years and years of research into the Pieces of Eden and now here before her was a real one.

Evie stood close by the doorway, but even though she was lit by the sudden lightning flashes, the men were too absorbed in their work to see her. She crept forward, still hypnotized by the sight of the Apple but able to eavesdrop on Brewster and his assistant now.

"By Jove, under blue light it goes completely transparent," exclaimed the scientist.

Brewster was nothing like the man he had been before, weak and small within the dark shadow of Lucy Thorne. Now he was a man in his own domain, in command once again, and feeling confident enough to throw a few gibes Thorne's way. "The cheek of that woman," he shouted, over the buzzing of the lightning conductors, the hissing of the Tesla coils, the rhythmic huffing of automated bellows. "I say, I ought to seize the blasted artifact for Edinburgh."

"If you don't mind my saying, that would be an exceptionally bad idea," retorted his companion.

"Why? It's God's Apple, not hers. I'd display it in public. Darwin would be vanquished. Banished in shame to the blasted Galapagos to roost with his beloved finches."

"Miss Thorne would have your head, and Mr. Starrick the rest," said his colleague.

"You know, Reynolds, it might just be worth the risk," exclaimed Brewster.

"Sir David, you cannot be serious."

"Just a wee joke, Reynolds. Once we unlock the artifact's secret the Templars' grip on London will be fixed. The Assassins will fall, and Darwin will be little more than a bearded memory."

As she drew closer, coming out into the open now where the two men could easily see her, she could see the Apple glowing. Brighter now. Lit by an increasingly heavy shower of sparks.

It was time to make it hers.

She engaged her blade and struck, and had seen the assistant slide off her blood-streaked steel before Brewster was even alerted to her presence. His eyes went to his dead companion then back to Evie Frye, looking at her agog, his brain trying to make sense of this sudden, unexplained appearance.

And then Evie leapt and killed him.

"It is time to lay down your head, Sir David Brewster," she said, letting him slide to the floor.

"But I have so much more to discover."

His eyelids flickered. His breathing ragged now.

"Do not be afraid," she told him

"I am not. God will protect me."

"I will continue your experiments," she said, and saw it clearly, the path that lay before her. She would carry on with the learning that had begun in her father's library at Crawley. She would make it her mission to locate the artifacts, to harness their power and use them for the benefit of mankind. A wind of good fortune, not ill.

"You cannot stop Starrick," said Brewster, his head on her knees as she knelt with him. "Miss Thorne has already found another Piece of Eden, more powerful than the last."

"I will take that one, too," said Evie, never more sure of anything in her whole life.

"We fight to gain what we cannot take with us. It is in our nature."

And then he died. Evie took out her handkerchief and, in a ritual passed down by their father—one he said was an homage to Altaïr's own feather ceremony—touched it to Brewster's wound, soaking it with his blood. She folded the handkerchief and secreted it inside her jacket.

In the same moment everything seemed to happen at once: guards, three of them, came rushing into the laboratory. The bodies had been discovered; they knew an intruder had penetrated the facility, and they wanted blood.

Evie stood, already engaging her blade and ready for battle, just as there came a sudden increase in electrical intensity, and the artifact seemed to bulge with a fresh influx of power—and then exploded.

Evie was immediately below the inspection glass and protected by the plinth on which it stood. The guards, however, were not so lucky. They were peppered with flying fragments and seemed to disappear in a fog of blood mist and debris as beams, harnesses and platforms came tumbling down upon them from above. Evie scrambled to her feet and ran for the door, just as the chain reaction began, lightning conductors bursting into flame, machinery exploding with a flat *whump*.

Then she was outside, grateful to be joining those who were sprinting away from the factory as a series of explosions tore it apart.

SIXTY-THREE

"What was that explosion?"

She had met Jacob back at the rail yard as arranged. He, too, looked as though he had seen plenty of action in the meantime. Both were blooded now.

"The Piece of Eden detonated and took the lab with it," explained Evie, finishing her tale.

Jacob curled a lip. "That magic lump of hyperbolic metal? I'm shocked."

She rolled her eyes. All those nights reading to him. Imparting that knowledge to him. They really, truly had been for absolutely nothing.

"Simply because you have never valued the pieces does not . . ."

An old argument was about to resurface until the appearance of George Westhouse. "All went according to plan?" said the elder Assassin sardonically.

"There was a slight . . . complication," replied Evie, shamefaced.

"The lab exploded," said Jacob with an arched eyebrow at his twin sister. *You want somebody to blame, there she is.*

"You derailed a train," George Westhouse reminded him.

"Oh, he did, did he?" said Evie.

Jacob shrugged. "Well, the train derailed and I happened to be on it. I killed my target."

So. Rupert Ferris, of Ferris Ironworks, an organization that as well as being in Templar hands employed child labor, was dead.

"Brewster is also no more," said Evie.

"Then, all in all, a successful mission, in spite of you two," said George.

"What about London?" said Jacob. Evie glanced at her brother. For her the events of the evening had been an epiphany, a signpost for the way forward. Was the same true of Jacob?

"What about it?" asked George cautiously.

"We are wasting time out here," said Jacob, indicating the rail yard around them, the suburbs. The city of London was close to here—yet so far out of reach.

"You know as well as I do that London has been the domain of the Templars for the last hundred years. They are far too strong yet. Patience."

Ethan had thought differently, remembered George, seeing his friend's belief alive and well and living with the twins.

"But the Templars have found a new Piece of Eden," said Evie.

George shrugged. "Sir David is dead; they do not know how to use it. The Council shall guide us, sound advice that your father would have seconded. I shall see you back in Crawley."

The twins watched George leave with sinking and

somewhat resentful hearts. Fires that burned bright had been comprehensively doused by George and his invocation of the Council. What they both knew, of course, was that their father would certainly not have agreed with the remote Assassin elders. And what they both knew was that they had no intention of abiding by either George Westhouse or the blamed Council.

A train clattered slowly past and blew its whistle.

"What's stopping us?" said Jacob nodding at it. "London is waiting to be liberated. Forget Crawley."

"Father would have wanted us to listen . . ."

"Oh, *Father*. You could continue his legacy in London."

"Freeing future generations from a city ruled by Templars. You know, Jacob Frye, you might just be right."

"Then, shall we?"

"Yes, let's."

With that, the two of them ran and boarded the train, bound for London.

There, they decided, they would meet Henry Green, a man about whom they had no knowledge. "The Assassin watching over London," was what they had been told.

They knew nothing of his true history.

SIXTY-FOUR

After what had happened at the Metropolitan Line, The Ghost had stayed in the Thames Tunnel for over a year.

There he had continued to provide a reassuring presence for the other tunnel dwellers, though in truth he did little but act as a figurehead. Most of the year was spent sitting or lying in his alcove, grieving for Maggie and for the other innocent lives lost in the failure of the operation to retrieve the Piece of Eden. He cursed the age-old hunt for trinkets, scorning Assassins and Templars and their obsessions with baubles.

Ethan had come to him in the tunnel, but The Ghost had dismissed his old mentor. He had no desire to see Ethan Frye.

George came, too, and explained that the Brotherhood needed a man in the city. "Another undercover operation if you like, Jayadeep. Something more suited to your talents."

The Ghost had chuckled at that. Hadn't Ethan Frye said the very same thing to him years ago in Amritsar?

Something suitable for his talents. Look how that had turned out.

"You would be required simply to establish an identity as a cover, full stop," George had said. "There's no infiltration involved. Quite the reverse. We want your cover to be just tight enough to avoid detection but not so tight that you can't begin to assemble a network of spies and informants. You are to be a receptacle, Jayadeep. A gatherer of information, nothing more. You have a way about you." George had indicated along the tunnel. "People trust you. People believe in you."

The Ghost raised his head from where his arms were crossed over his knees. "I am not a leader, Mr. Westhouse."

George hunkered down, grimacing as his old bones complained but wanting to sit with Jayadeep, an unknowing echo of a time when, in The Darkness, Ethan had done the same thing.

"You won't be a leader, not in the traditional sense," said George. "You will be required to inspire people, just as we know you can already do. The Brotherhood needs you, Jayadeep. We needed you before and we need you now."

"I failed the Brotherhood before."

George gave a short, impatient snort. "Oh, do stop wallowing, man. You're no more to blame than Ethan, or I, or a Council that seems intent on allowing the enemy to rise unchecked. Please, do me this one favor. Will you at least think about it?"

The Ghost had shaken his head. "I am needed here in the tunnel more than in any war."

"This tunnel will shortly cease to exist," George told him. "Not like this, anyway. It's been bought by the East London Railway Company. Look around you, there's nobody here. There are no more pedestrians, no more traders to serve them, and none but the most desperate come here to sleep. There's just you and a few drunks sleeping it off until they can go home to their wives and tell lies about being robbed of their wages. They did need you once, you're right. But they don't need you anymore. You want to offer your services to your fellow man, then devote yourself to the Creed."

The Ghost had deferred. He had continued to brood until, as the months wore on, he was visited again.

It was strange, because The Ghost had spent so many nights in this very tunnel dreaming of them and dreaming of home that when his mother and father appeared to him he assumed that this, too, was a dream; that he was having an awake dream, hallucinating the image of Arbaaz and Pyara standing there before him.

It had been a matter of five years or so, and they were just as luminous as he remembered, and around them the dingy darkness of the tunnel seemed to fall away, as if they created their own light, standing in front of him clad in the silken garments of the Indian Brotherhood, the chain that ran from the phul at his mother's nose to her ear glimmering in the soft orange light of a lantern. No wonder he thought he was dreaming at first. Their appearance was ethereal and otherworldly. A memory made flesh.

The Ghost sensed other figures hanging back in the darkness and could make out George and Ethan. No, then—not a dream—and he scrambled to his feet, hands reaching out to the wet tunnel wall to steady himself, the dizziness of suddenly standing, the weakness he felt, having languished so long, the emotion of seeing his mother and father again, making him wobble unsteadily, knees buckling and his father stepped forward to support him. Ethan too, and then the four Assassins led Jayadeep out of the tunnel. Out of the darkness.

SIXTY-FIVE

His mother and father had taken temporary apartments in Berkeley Square. There, The Ghost slept in a bed for the first time in as long as he could remember; he ate well and received his mother's kisses, each one like a blessing.

Meanwhile, between The Ghost and his father hung poisoned air. Was Arbaaz one of those who had arrested Jayadeep and flung him into The Darkness? What had Arbaaz done—or not done—about the death sentence pronounced on his son?

The questions were never asked. No answers offered. Doubt and suspicion remained. So naturally The Ghost gravitated toward his mother, who became a conduit between the elder Assassins and the recalcitrant younger one. It was she who told him he would not be returning to Amritsar. Not now. Maybe not ever. His appearance there would pose too many questions, and anyway the needs of the Brotherhood were best served if he remained in London.

The Ghost had sensed the hand of Ethan Frye and George Westhouse behind these decisions, but he knew his mother agreed that their very presence in London was a risk and taking Jayadeep home an unconscionable magnification of it.

He considered leaving, of course. But he was still an Assassin, and you can't turn your back on a belief. The Ghost had seen the artifact's terrifying potential and knew it should be retrieved. Having previously failed did nothing to change that.

One day, during that honey-coated period at Berkeley Square, his mother had invited The Ghost for a walk, just her and him. They trod streets thronged with Londoners who goggled at his mother as though she were not merely from another country but belonged to a different species altogether. Her robes were silk but otherwise unadorned and in stark contrast to the bustles, whalebone corsetry, unwieldy hats and fussy parasols of the indigenous population. For all that, none could touch his mother for her beauty. He had never been more proud of her than he was at that moment.

"You are aware, I think, of the course of action that Mr. Westhouse and Mr. Frye favor?" she said as they walked. Her arms hung loosely at her sides, shoulders thrust back, chin proud, meeting every stare with the same dignity.

"They want me to be something I'm not, Mother."

"They want you to be something you most definitely *are*," she insisted. "A credit to the Brotherhood."

He forgot his pride for a moment, head hanging in remembrance. "No, I was never that, and fear I never will be."

"Ah, hush," she chided him. "What a load of rubbish.

Did we raise you to welcome defeat with open arms? Do I look into your eyes and see nothing but surrender? I fear you will exhaust my patience if you're to continue being quite so self-pitying."

"Self-pitying? Really? You think me self-pitying?"

She inclined her head with a smile. "Maybe a little, sweetheart, yes. Just a touch."

He thought about that, and said tartly, "I see."

They continued their promenade, heading a little off the beaten track now, toward the less salubrious areas of town.

"I've hurt your feelings," she said.

"Nobody likes to think of himself as a sulky child," he admitted.

"You are never that, and making this journey to see you, I've found my child has grown into a man."

He gave a derisive snort. "Some man. Incapable of completing his blooding."

"There you go again . . ."

"Sorry, Mother."

They had made their way through winding side streets into Whitechapel, until they found themselves in front of a shop, where his mother stopped, turned and reached to take her son's face in her hands. "You're so much taller than me now."

"Yes, Mother."

"You see? You're a man now. A man ready to shed the childish conceits of self-admonishment, guilt, shame, whatever other poisonous emotions crowd that head of yours, and take up the next phase of your destiny."

"Is it what you wish?"

She dropped her hands and half turned away with a laugh. "Ah, now you're asking, Jayadeep. Dear, sweet Jayadeep, grown inside of me, brought into the world nursed by me. What mother dreams of her son growing up a killer?"

"An Assassin, Mother. A great Assassin, not a great killer."

"You can be a great Assassin without being a great killer, Jayadeep. It's what I hope for you now. It's why we are here. For now that you have reconciled yourself to your new life, I welcome you to it."

She was indicating the shop in front of which they stood. His eyes went to it, a window crowded with dusty knickknacks, bric-a-brac and gewgaws.

"A curio shop?" he said to her.

"Just the right thing for an inquiring mind such as yours," she told him.

"I'm to be a shopkeeper," he said, flatly.

"Let's go inside, shall we?"

She produced a key from within her robes and moments later they stepped into the crowded but somehow comforting surroundings of the shop. Inside it seemed to stretch back a long way into spectral and mysterious depths, and when they closed the door they were cut off from the sounds of the street outside. Dust danced in shafts of light that leaked through dirty windows obscured by piled-high trinkets. Shelves heaved and bulged with a variety of goods that were little more than indistinct twilight shapes. He liked it at once.

But even so—a shop.

"I believe it was Napoleon who said that England was a nation of shopkeepers." His mother smiled. She could see he was intrigued, and that he liked the premises too much to simply dismiss them out of hand. "How fitting, then, to become a shopkeeper."

They made their way along a narrow passageway between shelves that groaned with every conceivable ornament and trinket. Here was one crammed with dusty books, another one that seemed in danger of simply collapsing beneath the weight of the china piled onto it. He saw pressed flowers under glass and found he was still able to name them, memories of his mother in Amritsar. She saw him looking; they shared a glance and he wondered how carefully these items had been chosen and placed. After all, his mother had evidently been here before. As they passed along a narrow passageway she indicated more things she thought were of interest to him: a tray of clockwork components that excited him on sight, taking him back to more barely remembered hours as a child, when he had pored over broken clocks and clockwork toys. Not far away a bureau groaned beneath the weight of a multitude of crystal balls, as though the shop had been visited by a gang of hard up fortune-tellers, and he recalled being fascinated by them as a child.

She led him to the back of the shop where she drew open a thick floor-to-ceiling curtain, ushering him into a workroom beyond, picking up an herbarium that she handed to him. "Here. It's something of a British pastime."

He opened it, finding it empty.

"For you to fill," she said.

"I remember gathering flowers with you, Mother, at home."

"They all have symbolic meanings, you know."

"So you often told me."

She chuckled and then, as he laid down the book, indicated their surroundings. "What do you think?" she asked him.

He looked at her, thinking his heart might break with love. "I like it," he told her.

On a table in the workroom were folded-up clothes and a scroll that she picked up and handed to him.

"These are the deeds. It belongs to you now."

"Henry Green," he read from the scroll as he unfurled it. "That is to be my new name now?"

"You always liked the name Henry, and after all, you're wearing a green hat," said Pyara. "And besides, it's an English shopkeeper's name for an English shopkeeper. Welcome to your new life, Henry. From here is where you can oversee the Assassin fightback in the city and control your information matrix. Who knows? Perhaps you might be able to sell the odd curio while you're here too. Now . . ." She reached for the small pile of clothes. "An outfit of which you can at last be proud."

To preserve his modesty she turned around as he changed and then swung back to admire him. He stood there, resplendent in flowing silky robes, edged in gilt, a leather chest strap, soft slippers.

"No more bare feet, Jayadeep, or should I say Henry," his mother said. "And now, one last thing to complete the picture . . ."

She reached to a box that also lay on the table. Henry

had seen its like before, knew exactly what it contained, and he reached for it with a mixture of gratitude and trepidation. Sure enough, his old blade. He strapped it to his wrist, enjoying the feel of it there again, after all this time.

He was no longer The Ghost now. He was Henry Green.

SIXTY-SIX

"Two Assassins," said Henry on a rooftop overlooking the city, "equal in height. One female, one male. Two decades old, and those devilish smiles. You must be the Frye twins."

He assessed them immediately: yes, the smiles were very "Ethan." Otherwise, they seemed to incorporate differing qualities. Jacob: arrogant, impatient, a little rough around the edges; for Henry it was ambivalence at first sight. Evie, on the other hand . . .

"And you are . . ." she said.

His robes flapped in the breeze as he gave a short bow. "Henry Green at your service, miss." He paused. "I was sorry to learn of your father's passing."

"Thank you," she said, and her eyes dipped in sorrow before finding him again and holding him in a gaze in which he swam for a moment or so, reluctant to come to the surface.

"What can you tell us about Crawford Starrick?" said Jacob at last, and it was with some reluctance that Henry turned his attention to the other twin, slightly irritated at having the spell broken and assessing Evie's brother afresh.

"I suppose the Council desires news," he said, remembering himself.

"London must be freed. To provide a better future for all its citizens." The conviction lit Evie's face and danced in her eyes and made her even more beautiful if that was possible.

"Thank goodness the Council saw reason and sent you to aid us."

"Yes, thank goodness," said Jacob in a tone of voice Henry recognized. Young customers who thought him a clueless Indian shopkeeper.

He went on anyway. "I'm afraid I do not have pleasant news. Today, Starrick sits at the helm of the most sophisticated Templar infrastructure ever built in the Western world. His reach extends all across London. Every class, every borough, the industries, the gangs . . ."

Jacob preened. "I've always thought I would make a marvelous gang leader. Firm but fair. Strict dress code. Uniting a mix of disenfranchised outsiders under one name. Evie, that's it. We can rally them to our side."

Evie shot him a well-practiced look of reproach. "Oh? The way you rallied those cardplayers at the Oakbrook Tavern into the river?"

"That's different. They beat me at whist." He stared wistfully off into the distance. "I can see it now. We'll call ourselves The Rooks."

"You were never good at chess, either," she said, casting a sideways look at Henry, apologizing for her brother.

"You have a better plan?" Jacob was saying.

Her eyes were on Henry, a kindred spirit. "Find the Piece of Eden."

Jacob made a disgusted sound.

"Well." Henry cleared his throat. "Now you've quite finished . . ."

SIXTY-SEVEN

Later, Henry took them to his shop. In the years since his mother had unveiled it, nothing had changed. Business in curios wasn't exactly booming but that didn't matter; selling knickknacks wasn't his primary objective and his other business of assembling research into the artifacts, of monitoring Templar activities through a growing coterie of informants, was flourishing. George Westhouse had been right, Henry used the same innate talents that had endeared him to the tunnel dwellers to court the poor and dispossessed of Whitechapel. He had cultivated them almost unknowingly: a little protection, one or two moneylenders taught a lesson, a pimp shown the error of his ways, a violent father who needed reminding of his responsibilities. He had managed it using threat and insinuation. His combat skills falling into disuse suited him fine; he never was a warrior. His gang was unlike others that roamed the East End—like Jacob wished his "Rooks" would be—built on hierarchical principles of power and violence. His ran along far more benign principles. Their leader had earned their respect and also their love.

"Over the years I have established a number of connections across the city," was all he said now.

"Splendid!" replied Evie. "We'll need focused aid . . ."

"Focused aid?" scoffed Jacob. "No, what we need to do is take over Starrick's gangs to cripple his control."

"You're not aiming high enough," said Evie exasperatedly. "Starrick has influence in every branch of society. We need to match him."

"I see what you're saying, Evie. We need The Rooks."

She shook her head, repeating an oft-stated maxim. "You're not starting a gang called The Rooks. We need to locate the Piece of Eden."

"No. We need to reclaim London from Starrick. Just tell me my targets . . ."

"No."

"What?"

"It's not time for that yet."

"I didn't come here to hunt down curios."

"'First understand the dance, only then become the dancer.'"

"Oh? So you're taking over where Father left off?"

"Someone has to."

SIXTY-EIGHT

"Well, Freddie, it's nice to see you."

Abberline sat in the front room of Mr. and Mrs. Aubrey Shaw's Stepney rooms and remembered a time when he was given the warmest of welcomes by Mrs. Shaw and her two children; when he had fervently wished he had better news to impart.

Now was the same. Except this time . . .

"Would you like a cup of tea, Freddie?"

Without waiting for an answer, Mrs. Shaw departed, leaving the two men together.

"Well," repeated Aubrey, "it's good to see you, Freddie. Sergeant Frederick Abberline, as I live and breathe. Fresh-faced Freddie finally came of age, eh? I always knew you'd do it, mate. Of all of us you were always the dead cert to do well in the force."

Aubrey now ran a butcher shop in Stepney Green. Abberline had swiftly discovered it was good to have a butcher friend. Especially when it came to cultivating contacts because it was true, Abberline had done well in the force. A man named Ethan Frye had introduced him to another man, Henry Green, whom Abberline had recognized as the Indian lad from the dig. About that, he was sworn to secrecy but only too happy to maintain the confidence. After all, Ethan Frye had saved his life. He and Henry had gone up against Cavanagh and friends. As far as Abberline was concerned, that put them firmly on his team.

It was funny because Abberline had never got to the bottom of what happened at the Metropolitan dig. The "powerful object" that Ethan had told him about, well, Abberline had imagined some kind of weapon, something that set off an explosion. To what end, he had no idea. But Cavanagh had died, his three lieutenants were dead, too, and as for the other one, the clerk? Well, he had turned out to be working for a third party, and that was when it had got complicated; when it came down to what Ethan described as age-old enemies: men who move among us plotting to wrest control of man's destiny. And that was plenty for Abberline. That had been enough to convince him to stop asking questions because somehow a fervently held belief of his own—that there are forces beyond our control manipulating us from on high—had dovetailed with one of Aubrey's fervently held beliefs: that sometimes there are no answers.

So Frederick Abberline had accepted that there were things he couldn't change but pledged to fight for the things he could change and given thanks for being able to tell the difference between the two. Meanwhile, Henry Green, it emerged, had built up a community of loyal informants in Whitechapel. Abberline joined his gang, sometimes the beneficiary of information, sometimes able to pass information on.

In other words the situation was what you'd call *mutually beneficial*. For the first time since the mess at the Metropolitan, the newly minted Sergeant Abberline had thought he was making progress. Doing a bit of good in this world.

Why, he'd even met a woman, Martha, fallen in love and got married . . . and there, unfortunately, his run of good fortune had come to an end.

"Freddie, is something wrong?" Aubrey was saying. The smile on his lips had died at the sight of his friend's forlorn features. "This is just a social visit, is it? You've not got anything to tell me. You and Martha? You haven't gone your separate ways, have you?"

Freddie wrung his hands between his knees. He had become adept at disguise. His penetration of Whitechapel sometimes depended on his ability to move in the streets unrecognized, unnoticed, unremarked. There were occasions when it had proved invaluable to Henry's gang. He wished for a disguise now, so that he wouldn't feel so very exposed.

"No, Aubs, and I can't tell you how much I wish that we had just gone our separate ways because then my dear Martha would be alive right now."

"Oh, Freddie," said Mrs. Shaw from the door. She hurried in, placed a tray of tea things on the table then came over to Abberline where she knelt and took his hand. "We are so very sorry, aren't we, Aubrey?"

Aubrey had stood, painfully. "Oh my, and the two of you only married a matter of months."

Abberline cleared his throat. "She was claimed by tuberculosis."

"That's a great shame, Freddie. Me and Aubrey always thought you went perfect together."

"We did, Mrs. Shaw, we did."

For some time, they sat; then, not quite knowing what else to do, Mrs. Shaw served the tea and the three of them sat in silence for a little longer, the two Shaws helping Frederick Abberline to grieve.

"What now, Freddie?" said Aubrey.

Abberline placed his cup and saucer on the tabletop. Only the tea leaves knew what the future held in store for him.

"Time will tell, Aubrey," he said. "Time will tell."

SIXTY-NINE

Weeks passed. The twins made their mark in London. Despite Evie's protestations, Jacob had set up his gang, The Rooks, establishing them as a force in the city. Meanwhile, they had liberated the urchins, Jacob had assassinated the gang leader Rexford Kaylock, the twins had found a train hideout and they had secured the trust of Frederick Abberline, who had promised to turn a blind eye to their activities.

And while Jacob's attention was focused on building the reputation of his gang, Evie had thrown herself into investigating the Piece of Eden.

"Ah, another exciting night home for Evie Frye," he had said, spying her with letters, maps and assorted other documents. Perhaps he hadn't spotted the fact that she was also strapping on her gauntlet at the time.

"Just on my way out, actually," she said, with more than a hint of pride in her voice. "I found the Piece of Eden."

As usual, it was lost on Jacob, who rolled his eyes. "What's this one going to do? Heal the sick? Deflect bullets? Control the populace?"

"They are dangerous objects, Jacob. Especially in Templar hands."

"You sound exactly like Father."

"If only."

Now she drew her brother's attention to an image of Lucy Thorne that lay on the table. More and more lately, Evie had found her gaze going to it, remembering the intimidating woman she had seen in the shipping yard. "Lucy Thorne is expecting a shipment tonight. She is Starrick's expert in the occult. I am nearly certain she is receiving the Piece of Eden Sir David Brewster mentioned."

Jacob sniffed action. "Sounds like fun. Mind if I join you?"

"Promise you will stick to the mission?"

"I swear."

A short while later they were at the docks, where they flattened themselves to the roof of a warehouse overlooking the main docking area in order to watch boxes being unloaded below them.

There she is, thought Evie excitedly. Lucy Thorne. The occultist was dressed in her customary black. Evie wondered if she mourned the loss of Brewster's Piece of Eden.

Lucy Thorne's words drifted up to them as she took one of the men to task. "The contents of that box are worth more than your life and those of your entire family," she snapped, one bony finger pointing at a specific crate. "Do you understand?"

The man understood. He doubled the guard then turned back to Lucy Thorne. "Now, Miss Thorne, there's the matter of some papers for Mr. Starrick. If you'd just come this way . . ."

Reluctantly she followed him. From their vantage point, Jacob and Evie assessed the situation.

"Whatever it is she's after, it's in that chest," said Evie. They cast their eyes around the docks, seeing Templar gunmen on the rooftops. Meanwhile, the crate that was suddenly as precious to them as it evidently was to Lucy Thorne had been loaded with others onto a flatbed, horse-drawn wagon. A guard stood holding the reins. Two other guards close by were muttering darkly about the terrifying Lucy Thorne, as well as speculating what might be in the priceless crate.

Jacob slipped off his top hat and raised his cowl, his own little ritual before action, and with a wink at Evie, he left to deal with the guards on the rooftops.

She watched him go before making a move herself, scuttling silently to the edge of the roof then dropping down to crouch by a large water container beneath a dripping downpipe. With one eye on the men guarding the cart, she kept watch on Jacob's activities above. There he was, moving up on an unsuspecting sentry. His blade rose and fell. The man fell silently, a perfect assassination, and Evie hissed a quiet congratulation through her teeth.

It died on her lips. The second gunman had seen his comrade fall and had brought his rifle up to his shoulder. As Jacob dashed across the rooftop toward the gunman, her brother moving faster than the guard could take aim and squeeze the trigger, Evie herself dashed out from behind the water barrel. She came up behind the two men who stood at the rear, both of whom had their backs to her. Pivoting, she unleashed a kick at the neck of the first man.

Clever Evie. She had remembered to undo her coat this time, and the luckless sentry was smashed forward into the cart, nose and mouth crunching a second before he left a bloody streak on the crates as he slid to the dirt.

Evie had already swung to her left, bringing her gauntlet hand round and punching the second guard in the side of the head. This man had approximately half a second to live and he spent it feeling dazed and off balance, before Evie pulled her elbow back, engaged her blade and thrust it into his temple. By now the third sentry had made his escape, and the gunman on the rooftop lay dead. But it was too late. The alarm had been raised, and just as she pulled herself up to the wagon and used her blade to lever the nailed lid of the crate open, Jacob had jumped from the roof of the warehouse opposite and come sprinting across the apron toward the wagon.

"I think it's best we leave," he said, and never were truer words spoken. The docks were in an uproar. Doors of warehouses flew open to decant men in bowler hats, snarling dogs in tweed suits, all of them bearing guns or steel. Ever since Jacob and Evie's activities in the city had attracted the attention of the Templars, they'd hired the most mercenary, ruthless and bloodthirsty underlings they could lay their hands on.

Men came piling out of the meeting room, with Lucy Thorne screaming directions at them. She had picked up her skirts and with a great and righteous anger came barreling out of her meeting, only to find that her precious cargo was on the move. There were twin spots of emotion at her cheeks and her voice was a screech. "Get after them. Get after them."

Evie had a brief impression of that face. A lingering glimpse of fury to match. And the chase was on.

With Jacob at the reins their carriage flew out of the dockyard and onto the waste area that was its hinterland. On the top of the wagon, Evie hung on tight. Her cowl billowed with the onrushing wind as the horses gained speed. She wanted to scream at Jacob to go more slowly, but out of the dockyards emerged a second carriage, a porcupine of Templar men.

On the board was Lucy Thorne, resembling a raven with crinoline wings. Though she hadn't quite lost her black composure, it had certainly been rattled knowing she had let the precious crate out of her grasp, and she was pointing and screaming, her exact words lost in the wind but her meaning very clear indeed: get the twins.

Now the carriages came bursting out of the docks and careered left onto Ratcliff Highway. Tall buildings, shops and flat-fronted tenements lined either side of the street, windows looking impassively down on a highway packed with wagons and dock traffic below. Ratcliffe Highway, a street notorious for its violence, was now witnessing more of it.

The rattle of the two wagons over the cobbles was almost deafening, Evie terrified the wheels would come loose. Meantime she was desperately trying to make sense of what she saw in the crate—a cache of documentation and a book inscribed with the Assassin crest—as well as trying to cling on. A shot rang out and she heard a bullet whistle past her cheek, eyes reflexively going to Jacob to check he was all right.

And, yes, he was all right. His cowl flapped in the wind, his arms spread wide as he handled the reins, intermittently yelling insults over his shoulder at their pursuers and urging the horses on.

Ahead of them pedestrians scattered, traders flung themselves on their barrows to stop produce taking flight; coachmen steadied their horses and shook their fists angrily, and still the carts thundered on.

Another shot. Evie flinched but saw it take a lump out of brickwork nearby, even as they raced past. Now what came to her over the crash of cartwheels, the screaming of terrified pedestrians and spooked horses, was the increasingly panicked urgings of Lucy Thorne. Her head whipped around and once again the two women locked stares. Lucy Thorne seemed to simmer with hatred for the young Assassin. Whatever was in this packing box was important to her, important to the Templars—and therefore important to Evie.

If she could keep hold of it.

It was a big "if." Jacob was driving as fast as he could but their pursuers were gaining, the Templars pulling level now. Evie saw men hanging on, pulling pistols—and then remembered that thanks to Henry Green, she now had one of her own.

With one hand steadying herself on the crate, she pulled the Colt from within her coat, drew a bead on the man nearest who was aiming his own weapon, and fired.

Evie was not as good with a gun as she was with a

blade, but a good shot nevertheless, and her bullet would have made a new hole in the man's forehead were it not for the fact that his cart suddenly lurched as the wheels hit a pothole. As it was, he clapped his hand to his shoulder and screamed, dropping his own pistol, only just stopped from being flung off the wagon and to the cobbles below.

Meantime, the Templars' wagon had gone dangerously off course, the driver desperately trying to keep it from tipping over. Even Lucy Thorne had stopped her screaming and was hanging on to the boards for dear life, her hat a thing of the past, her hair tossed about by the wind.

The other cart tried to ram them. More shots rang out. Next Evie saw Templar thugs preparing to jump from one wagon to the next, Lucy Thorne's orders becoming increasingly more threatening as she pictured the two Assassins escaping with her documents.

"Look." Jacob was pointing, and sure enough there in the distance, rattling along the Blackwall railway line, was the train that the Assassins had made into their hideout.

Seeing it had given Jacob an idea. They could make a sharp right into Rosemary Lane, then, as long as they timed it right, they would be in the perfect position to leap from the cart onto the train.

The twins, with their preternatural link, seemed to decide on that course of action together without ever saying as much.

They reached the junction of Ratcliffe Highway and Rosemary Lane, and Jacob wrenched the horses to the right, already beginning to get to his feet, trying to control them at the same time as he prepared to make the jump.

They were level with the train now. Evie had no choice but to make the jump. With a cry of frustration she grabbed the notebook adorned with the Assassin crest—it was all she could take with her—thrust it into her coat and then, as her brother leapt from the wagon and into an open cargo door of the train, she did the same.

The two of them landed heavily on the boards: Jacob exuberant, flushed with excitement; Evie the opposite. All she had to show for the evening was one dog-eared notebook. And for her that wasn't good enough.

SEVENTY

Jacob and Evie continued to put their stamp on London, maneuvering the Assassins into what must have been the Brotherhood's strongest position for a century. They gave medicine to the sick of Whitechapel—like Henry they were winning hearts and minds.

The Templars were not happy. Their Grand Master Crawford Starrick was given updates of Assassin activity, receiving them from his position at the mahogany desk of his office.

"Frye intends to endanger all of London at the hands of the mob," his lieutenant, James Brudenell, told him.

"Or perhaps he doesn't intend much of anything at all," chimed in Philip Twopenny, as Starrick added a cube of sugar to his tea. "Perhaps he is simply content to dice with our lives."

Starrick lifted his teacup to breathe in its scent. His handlebar moustache quivered.

"Gentlemen," he said, "this tea was brought to me from India by ship, then up from the harbor to a factory, where it was packaged and ferried by carriage to my door, and packed in the larder and brought upstairs to me. All by men and women who work for me, who are indebted to me, Crawford Starrick, for their jobs, their time, the very lives they lead. They will work in my factories and so too shall their children. And you come to me with talk of this Jacob Frye? This insignificant blemish who calls himself an Assassin? You disrespect the very city that worked day and night so that we may drink this. This miracle. This tea."

Lucy Thorne had entered the room. She took a place by her master's side. The terrifying vision atop the wagon no longer, her hat was on her head, her composure repaired.

"I am nearing the end of my research," she said. "Our beloved London shall not suffer such a bothersome fool for much longer."

"And what of this sister I hear of? Miss Frye?" asked Starrick.

Lucy Thorne pursed her lips. "Miss Frye shall be gutted soon enough."

SEVENTY-ONE

Oblivious to the forces who plotted against them, Evie and Henry continued their research at his shop and in their hideout. "You may not have found a Piece of Eden," he told her, trying to console her, "but this material is invaluable."

She looked at him gratefully and the pair of them held each other's gaze for a moment until Evie gave an awkward little cough and looked away. Together they went back to looking at the notebook rescued from the crate until Henry hit on something. "Look. It says that the London Assassins had found a shroud."

A shroud.

Evie came close to read over Henry's shoulder. Closer than she needed to. Both knowing it. Both maintaining contact, tiny little shocks running through them.

"The Shroud of Eden is supposed to heal even the gravest injury," Evie read. "If the Assassins had found something like that, surely Father would have known."

No, he was obsessed with the Metropolitan artifact, thought Henry. The apple of his eye was the Apple. "There must be something we're missing," he said.

As if on cue Evie saw how documents inserted into the notebook came together as a map. She snatched them up, going to leave.

"Aren't you coming?" she said to Henry.

He looked awkward. "Fieldwork is not my specialty."

"We found a clue to a precursor object—don't you want to follow it?"

He did, of course. He wanted to stay with Evie too. "Put that way, one can hardly refuse."

The two of them followed the map, excited by the new discovery and thrilled to be in each other's company, as it took them to one of the more well-to-do areas of the city, where the streets were less crowded and the houses more grand. Something occurred to Henry. Could they be heading in the direction of Queen Square?

"Do you know, I think this map may be taking us to the Kenway mansion," he said.

"Kenway? The pirate?"

"Master Assassin and pirate, yes."

"It's surprising that you haven't already searched the house. Kenway was an Assassin, after all."

"Edward's son Haytham joined the Templars. They own the house now."

"So the Templars own a house with Assassin treasures stored in it—and never located them?"

Henry gave a short smile. "We must be better at hiding things than they are."

They came into the square, which even Henry knew had changed over the years. Once named Queen Anne's

Square it had been lined with mansions on all sides, the Kenways' among them, and though the statue of Queen Charlotte remained in place, and the alehouse on the corner, The Queens Larder, had stayed open for business since time immemorial, the mansions had since been occupied by hospitals and other charitable institutions, as well as booksellers and printers.

There were fewer buildings used as domiciles now, but the Kenways' mansion was among them. This was where Edward Kenway had lived on his return to these shores. His son, Haytham, had been inducted into the Templars, a long and ghastly story that had seen father pitted against son.

Jennifer Scott, Edward's daughter and Haytham's half sister had spent years living there, cursing Assassin and Templar equally though continuing to enjoy the benefits of her links to both, not least of them being that grand home on what had since been renamed Queen Square.

There Jennifer had remained, occasionally venturing forth to propose that Assassins and Templars should seek some accord, until her death of old age when the London Templars—and probably the Assassins as well—breathed a sigh of relief.

Evie and Henry came onto the square now, passing the Roman Catholic Aged Poor Society and the Society of St. Vincent De Paul, before Evie suddenly ground to a halt, dragging Henry toward the scant shelter of iron railings lining the square.

"Look," she said, breathing the word into his ear.

Sure enough, a carriage stood outside the Kenway mansion. Emerging from it was the unmistakable personage of Lucy Thorne.

"I'll be in the study," they heard her say to a male companion. "I don't want to be interrupted unless you have news of the lost notebook."

In the next second the two Templars were inside, and Evie and Henry were exchanging a look of concern. Getting in would be a challenge. Staying clear of Lucy Thorne would be another one.

But they had come too far now.

SEVENTY-TWO

Above them were open windows. No problem for an Assassin. The two of them scaled the wall quickly then dropped into what turned out to be a music room, complete with a vast grand piano and overlooked by a portrait of Edward Kenway standing with the young Haytham. Other paintings gave a clue to the mansion's seafaring history.

Henry brought his mouth close to Evie's cowl and she reached a finger to hook it back.

"What are we looking for?" he whispered.

Her eyes roved around the space. "I'm not quite sure." The pair of them set about conducting a search, finding that there were musical notes hidden around the room.

"What are the Templars not seeing?" said Henry, almost to himself.

"Something only we can."

"Edward Kenway was a pirate. Where would a pirate hide his treasure?"

"I'd hide mine in a library," said Evie, and Henry chuckled.

"Mine would *be* the library," he said and the pair of them shared another look. Kindred spirits.

"The piano is beautiful," he continued.

"Do you play?"

"No. I wish I could. I love the sound. You?"

"A little. Enough to pass as a genteel young lady if I need to."

"I would love to hear you play if the opportunity presents itself," he said, and noticed a blush come to her cheeks.

He went to the piano now. "Some of these keys are more raised than others," he said, and studied them, trying to find some rhyme or reason to the almost imperceptible way that certain keys sat more proudly than others.

He tried one, *tink*, that made Evie start, and she looked over, about to rebuke him for the noise, when suddenly the piano began playing itself. They forgot to panic when, at the same time, a section of the floor opened to reveal steps that led down into some unseen basement.

This, then, was the Kenway vault.

"Not enormously subtle, is it?" said Henry

Evie rolled her eyes. "Clearly Kenway had a strong sense of spectacle."

They went down and found themselves in the Kenway vault, their breath held as they began to make sense of a lifetime's worth of paraphernalia that was stored here.

"This is incredible. I think this is the Jackdaw," said Henry, his eyes alighting on a model of Edward Kenway's legendary pirate brig. "To think, this has been hidden for a century."

But Evie had moved to a high table in the center of the vault, where her eyes had gone to a document and an engraved disk. She scanned the document. "The history of the London Assassins . . . Bolt-holes . . . Vaults . . . A hidden key." Excited now. "This is it."

Henry moved across and again they enjoyed the sudden proximity, before the moment was broken by the sound of Lucy Thorne from the music room above them. "You say you heard music," she snapped at unseen guards." And then, "There was no opening there before."

Evie and Henry looked at one another. *Uh-oh.* Henry found a latch that he closed, exciting general dismay from those above.

"Help me block it," called Lucy Thorne, sensing that this newly opened door was crucial to their continued progress.

Down below, the door shut and Evie and Henry were left wondering what to do now.

A way out. There had to be one. Together they scoured the walls with a fingertip search until, with a small cry of triumph, Henry found it: a wall panel that opened to reveal stone steps spiraling down and beyond the reach of any lantern. Next they were making their way along a passageway beneath the great house, grateful to escape the clutches of Lucy Thorne but tinged with disappointment.

"An entire vault filled with Assassin history, left behind once again," bemoaned Evie.

"We'll just have to find an even better cache or reclaim this one later," Henry said.

She scoffed. "*We?* I thought you preferred to stay out of fieldwork."

"I . . . I was thinking more of you and your brother. I shall provide planning assistance. From the train."

"Jacob's off marauding," she said. "There is a vacancy, should you decide to broaden your horizons."

"I'll think on it," he said.

"You do that," she said with a gently mocking smile, "and let's get aboveground."

SEVENTY-THREE

"So, the hints you found in the Kenway house lead here . . ."

Jacob waved a somewhat disparaging hand at the huge column rising from the ground below them. They stood on a hillside overlooking it, yet were still dwarfed by it. The Great Fire Monument. Built near the spot in Pudding Lane where the eponymous Fire of London had started on September 2, 1666, and a suitably awe-inspiring tribute to that epochal event.

For some moments the twins simply gazed at it, eyes going from the sculpted plinth at the booth, up the fluted column and to the top, where a cage had been constructed to prevent people jumping. As the tallest tower in the world, it dwarfed surrounding buildings and on a clear day it was possible to see it from right across the city. At close quarters, it took their breath away.

Evie wished Henry were here. Then chided herself for the disloyal thought. After all, Jacob was her brother, her twin brother with whom she shared an almost supernatural communication. Things she'd save from a fire? Number one, her blade; number two, her brother. And on a good day, if Jacob were being especially pleasant company, well she might even rescue her brother first.

Today, however, was not one of those days. Jacob was not being pleasant company. Instead he was choosing to mock and lampoon her at every available opportunity, specifically, it seemed, the growing affection between her and Henry Green.

Henry, of course, wasn't here to defend himself. He was at the shop, reviewing the material, so Jacob was taking advantage of his absence.

"Oh yes, Mr. Green," he parroted his sister, "that's a fascinating idea. Oh please, Mr. Green, come and take a look at this book and stand oh-so-close to me, Mr. Green."

She fumed. "I do not . . ." then composed herself. "Well, perhaps you have nothing better to do, but *I* am busy protecting the Assassins."

"Are you really? What was it Father used to say . . . ?"

"'Don't allow personal feelings to compromise the mission'?" Evie rolled her eyes.

"Precisely," replied her brother. "Anyway, I'm off. If I find any more wild geese for you to chase, I'll be in touch."

To show his scorn, he lowered his cowl, retrieved his hat from inside his clothes, popped it out then rolled it along his arm to the top of his head.

And with that, he left.

She watched Jacob go, pleased to see the back of him almost as much as she mourned the tension between them, then made her way to the monument. On its base was a small and familiar-looking recess. Sure enough the disk she'd liberated from the Kenway mansion fitted perfectly. In response the stone seemed to crack, just enough to open, and she took a set of spiral steps up the inside of the monument. These were not the usual steps—not those taken by sightseers and suicides and James Boswell, who had apparently suffered a panic attack halfway up, before gathering himself, completing the journey then declaring the view an abomination. No, these steps were purely for he or she who was in possession of the disk.

Sure enough, when she reached the summit, sixty-two meters high, two things greeted her. Firstly, the view, and she stood buffeted by wind as she gasped at a panorama that bristled with chimneys and spires, a skyline of industry and worship. Secondly, she found another disk, this one larger, and with a slot. She compared the two disks in her hand and, on a whim, decided to try to fit the first one into the aperture of the second.

It fit. Perfectly. Still pummeled by the wind, she looked at it in blank amazement as a picture formed. If where she currently stood was London's best-known landmark, then this was pointing her to the second-best-known, another Sir-Christopher-Wren-designed building: St. Paul's Cathedral.

A short time later she had made her way there, wishing she'd stopped to collect either Jacob or, preferably, Henry on the way, but knowing they could be anywhere. She ascended to the roof of the grand cathedral. No problem for a woman of her skills.

There at the statue of St. Paul she inserted the two disk

pieces into a slot in the stine. Next—did she sense it or genuinely feel it?—a door deep below her opened, and shortly afterward she had gone down and was walking into a vault in the chapel.

It was a large room dominated by a table in the center. On one wall was an Assassin symbol. Ah, so it was a dedicated Assassin vault. Across the room was a stained-glass window, while in an alcove hung what Evie at first took for a beautiful item of jewelry. She moved closer, examining a chain that was decorated with links and small, intricate spheres, about the size of pearls but inscribed with odd, angular hieroglyphics, as well as a pendant that she lifted in her palm. Again there was something infinitely precious about it, as though it had been fashioned by a silversmith who was not of this earth or of this era. A thrill ran through her. The knowledge that in all likelihood she was holding something of the First Civilization.

A key of some kind. Inscribed on it was Latin meaning "the remedy is worse than the disease," and she picked it up, turning it over in her hands. It was nothing she recognized from any of her readings. Nothing she could make sense of there and then. Perhaps when she had the literature in front of her . . .

She hung it around her neck—just as the door opened to admit Lucy Thorne.

"Good day, Miss Frye. I'll take that," said the Templar. All in black, her features baked into a predatory stare, she crossed the chamber toward Evie. She came alone, supremely confident of her dominion.

Evie let the key drop to her chest. She raised her cowl

then let her hands drop to her sides, loose but ready. "You want the Shroud to cement your own power," she said, "but what if you cannot control it?"

Lucy pursed her lips. "And why do *you* want the Shroud? Merely to keep the Templars from having it? How like an Assassin—to hold the power of eternal life and yet be too afraid to use it."

Lucy had stopped a few feet away from Evie, just out of striking range. The two women sized each other up. Evie saw no obvious weapons, but then who could say what was concealed in the voluminous folds of her opponent's funereal garb. "Eternal life," she said, every muscle alert, "is that what you think the Shroud offers?"

"What I think is no longer your concern," said Lucy, whose eyes gave away her intentions a second before she made her move, and in one eye-wateringly fast motion she had snatched a blade from her boot and sprang, full-length, knife hand extended, in an action that almost took Evie by surprise.

Almost being the operative word. The young Assassin skipped back, triggered her blade at the same time and was pleased to see the expression on her opponent's face instantly transform. If Lucy Thorne saw easy pickings, she had made a dire mistake, for a Templar and a boot knife were no match for Evie Frye. A spirited attack it might have been, but it was predicated on surprise, and without that Lucy had nothing save a desire to win and an instinct for survival. And neither were enough to best Evie.

Their blades clashed. The ringing sound ricocheted around the stone walls. With bared teeth Lucy tried again but Evie fended her off easily, taking the measure of her opponent, biding her time, ready for the death blow.

But Lucy Thorne wasn't done. As Evie approached, her hand shot out. What bloomed from the center of her fist was a globe and for a strange, mad moment, Evie thought that Lucy Thorne was attacking her with a Piece of Eden, until it registered: a smoke bomb.

Blinded and temporarily disoriented, Evie staggered back, bringing her blade into a defensive position and restoring her balance, ready to meet a follow-up attack. Sure enough, it came. Lucy Thorne was an inferior combatant but she lacked for nothing when it came to commitment and she was brave. My God, thought Evie, she was brave. Through the smoke of the bomb, Lucy flew forward with her boot dagger slashing more in hope than confidence and thanks to the fog and ferocity of her attack very nearly succeeded.

Nearly being the operative word.

Smoke billowed as Evie turned smartly to one side, thrusting out her chest as she swept back her shoulders and brought her blade low, knocking Lucy Thorne's knife aside. In the next moment she swung about, bringing her right shoulder forward in a most unladylike but very Evie-Frye-like roundhouse punch that made hard and sickening contact with Lucy Thorne's jaw, sending the Templar's eyeballs spinning and her teeth rattling as she staggered back. Evie sheathed her blade then stepped forward and swung the gauntlet hand.

The move had been neat. It had won her the fight. But maybe Evie had a little too much of her father and brother in her. Perhaps she was overconfident. For the punch was too much and instead of flooring Lucy Thorne, it sent her flailing back, blade skittering off to one side, arms wildly pinwheeling, toward a plate-glass window behind.

Evie saw what was going to happen and realized her mistake. But too late. She sprang forward and in her haste lost her footing. Her grasping fingers failed to find Lucy Thorne, and for a split second the two women scrabbled at one another, trying to prevent the inevitable.

They could not. The glass shattered around Lucy Thorne and she seemed about to fall to her certain death when one desperate hand found the key around Evie's neck. Suddenly it was all that prevented her from falling and Evie was trapped too, crying out in pain as the chain dug into her flesh.

"Coming with me?" sneered Lucy Thorne and once again, Evie had to hand it to her opponent. She didn't lack for valor.

But . . .

"I have other plans," said Evie, and out came her blade and she sliced the chain, dismissing Lucy Thorne—but releasing the key into Lucy's grasp.

With a scream, the Templar fell and Evie was dumped back inside the room. She pulled herself up, coughing and panting as she dragged herself to check the broken window and the stone below.

Lucy Thorne was gone.

"Damn it," said Evie.

SEVENTY-FOUR

Evie sat and brooded. True, she had been pleased to hear of Jacob's progress. He had dispensed with the banker Twopenny, putting a crimp in the Templars' financial pipeline, for one thing. Other, smaller sorties had proved similarly effective.

Her own work had met with less success.

On the one hand, she had the opportunity to spend more time with Henry Green, and even Jacob's taunts could not take the edge off that particular pleasure. She and Henry were growing closer all the time.

But on the other, their investigations had yielded little of merit. The more they buried themselves in books and the more they pored over the material that Evie had taken from the crate, the less, it seemed, they learned.

She mulled over Lucy's words. How the Shroud offered eternal life. They already knew the Shroud of Eden was, quote, "supposed to heal even the gravest injury," but eternal life?

And now Lucy Thorne had Evie's key.

"What good is a key if you don't know what lock it

opens?" she said as she and Henry wasted another fruitless afternoon in the company of candlelight and mystifying literature.

"I daresay Miss Thorne is in the same predicament," Henry said drily, not even bothering to lift his head from the journal he was reading.

It was a good point. One that Evie acknowledged with a sigh and a heavy heart, her eyes going back to her own work. And then—just as she did so—she saw it. There in front of her was . . .

"Henry," she said quickly, put her hand to his arm then just as quickly, as she felt the same tingle of closeness as he did, dropping it once more, clearing her throat of the sudden embarrassment of contact. "Here. This is it."

Henry saw an image of the key beneath her finger. *So that was it.* Galvanized, he reached to a pile for another book, mind instantly making connections.

"This matches the collection owned by the Queen," said Henry, flicking through pages. He found it, looked at her, eyes shining with excitement. "It's kept in the Tower of London."

SEVENTY-FIVE

Hours later, with the city cowering beneath a curtain of darkness and fog, Evie Frye crouched in the crenellation of a wall overlooking the inner ward of the Tower of London. To her left were the darkened windows of Lanthorn Tower, which had been gutted by fire in the great blaze of 1774 and was still in urgent need of repair. For that reason it remained an uninhabited, badly lit and mostly unguarded corner of the Tower grounds. Perfect for Evie to take stock.

Squatting there, she was able to see into the central complex where the White Tower stood—"the keep," presiding over the smaller structures surrounding it. Dotted around were the familiar figures of the Yeoman Warders, the beefeaters who guarded the Tower day and night. Among them would be a man that Henry counted as an ally. Finding this man was her next task.

As she squatted there, watching, she stretched out her muscles. Four hours she had been waiting, and it had given her ample opportunity to study the movements of the Warders. What struck her was a sense of two distinct groups. Something was afoot, she thought, and she believed she knew what it was.

And then her attention was arrested by the arrival of Lucy Thorne.

Evie clung even more tightly to the shadows as her nemesis stepped from a carriage and crossed the courtyard to the lower steps of the great keep. The Templar woman's gaze swept around the walls surrounding the inner ward and Evie found herself holding her breath as it passed her hiding place. Then Lucy Thorne ascended the steps and stepped inside the keep.

Evie decided to bide her time some more. Below, the ceremony of the keys was taking place, but she was watching something else. Away from the ceremony two guards were dragging a constable away. The man was protesting in no uncertain terms, but his curses fell on deaf ears.

Except, not quite on deaf ears. Down below was another Yeoman Warder. Evie saw him looking on fretfully as the constable was frog-marched toward the Waterloo Barracks at the western end of the complex.

The look in his eyes. That was him. That was her man.

Spurred into action, she climbed down from her perch and into the ward close to where he stood, still a picture of indecision. From the shadows she attracted his attention with a low whistle, identified herself as a friend of Henry and watched a look of grateful trust overtake his features. "Thank heavens you've come," he said, and went on to tell his tale.

What emerged was a picture of the Templars extending their tendrils into the Tower hierarchy itself. Many of the Beefeaters were Templar imposters. Many were still loyal to the Crown, but gossip and suspicion reigned and the balance of power was being tipped.

"That Thorne woman has gone into St. John's Chapel." He jerked a thumb toward the keep, where the apse of the chapel was visible. "I could help get you in."

She nodded. *Do your worst.*

"All right, for this to work, you'll have to pretend to be my prisoner."

With that, he took hold of her arm and marched her across the apron of the ward toward Waterloo Barracks, maneuvering her over the threshold and into the main entrance hall.

Straightaway she could see the extent of the Templar infiltration. They mocked her with it as she was led through the barracks.

"Nice to see an Assassin in chains for once," called a guard.

Goading her. Taunting her.

"The Templars own London, Assassin. Don't forget it."

The ally led her into a passageway for the cellblock, closing the door on the men in the outer barracks.

Here, there were two sentries standing guard at a door in the far end. Like the others, the sentries were taunting and goading her. But now, Evie Fry made them eat their words. Pretending to slip free of her captor, she sprang forward in a fencing stance and triggered her blade in the same instant, thrusting it through the tunic of a startled guard. A second man never stood a chance. Still low, Evie punched forward with the blade, jabbing him quickly in the thigh then taking advantage of his doubling over in pain to thrust upward into the space between his collarbone and neck. He gurgled and slumped to the stone. Dead.

Her ally had watched, given her a sign of approval and, with the quiet assurance that he would organize the fight-back, slipped away. In moments she would hear the sound of battle from outside.

In the meantime, the short battle had been fought to the accompaniment of anguished cries from the other side of the locked cell door. The constable had been making his presence known for some time now, and sensing action a short distance away, called, "Is someone out there?" His voice was muffled by the thick wooden door.

She came to it, put fingertips to the wood, lips close to it. "Yes, a friend."

"Oh, that's good. Say, friend. Could you get me out?"

Evie was a good picklock. Her father had made sure of that, and she made short work of the door, finding herself in the grateful presence of a red-faced, excitable constable.

"Thank you," he told her. "It's treason, is what it is. And desecration of the chapel. Miss Thorne told me to be grateful they didn't kill me outright. The nerve."

"She's after an object of great power," Evie told him, "and she can't be allowed to steal it."

The constable's face fell. "Not the Crown Jewels?"

Evie shook her head. "Something much more important."

Henry's friend had seen to it that the barracks were made safe. Blood-soaked bodies were testament to that. The western section was theirs. Outside, the constable spoke to his men. "All right, gentlemen," he told them, "we are facing an enemy we never expected—traitors in our midst," before outlining a plan of action and a series of signals for when the men should strike back at the Templar stooges.

The men dispersed and, at a signal from Evie, launched their attack. In the ribbons of the inner and outer ward and in the courtyard outside the keep, the constable's men descended quickly upon the Templar guards. There were minor skirmishes but Evie could see the battle would be short and easily won. She was not even required to activate her blade as she made her way to the entrance of the White Tower.

There, she ran quickly and nimbly up the steps then knocked on the door, praying those inside were still unaware of the rebellion taking place in the wards.

She tensed, waiting, ready to dispatch whoever was unfortunate enough to answer her knock. However, no answer came. Steeling herself, she tried the great handle of the door and found that it turned. Next, she slipped inside.

Damn.

Straightaway she felt the point of a pike at her neck and realized she'd walked into a trap. At the same time, the razor-sharp edge of a Wilkinson Sword was placed to her forearm, just above the gauntlet, prohibiting any move-ment. She felt a warm droplet of blood make its way into the collar of her jacket, but the pain was nothing com-pared to her chagrin at being so easily caught.

"Looks like we've caught ourselves an Assassin," sneered one of the three men, "only for real this time.

There'll be no slipping your guard. No freeing the constable so that he can rally his men. We'll be taking you to Miss Lucy Thorne, see what she wants to do with you."

She wants to me kill me, thought Evie. But even so, they say that every cloud has a silver lining and here was hers. Lucy was in the chapel right now and she was searching for the Shroud. Certainly, thought Evie. Take me to Lucy Thorne. You're only taking me closer to it.

Any plans she had for escape were swiftly shelved. Instead she relaxed, allowing the blade of the pike to remain where it was, the sword to stay in place. The last thing she wanted to do was draw their attention to her gauntlet.

They did exactly as she wanted them to do. They brought her into the chapel.

Knocking and entering, they came upon Lucy Thorne, who was startled by their entrance and looking unusually flustered. Evidently she'd failed to find the Shroud of Eden, and her cheeks were flushed as she turned to Evie, who was flanked by her guards in the doorway of the darkened chapel.

"Welcome, Miss Frye," she hissed. "Would you care to tell me where the Shroud is?"

Evie said nothing. There was nothing she could say.

"As you wish," said Lucy. "I shall find it without your help. And then I'll strangle you with it." She stalked across the room, hands going to the paneling, pressing her ear close to the wood to listen for telltale hollowing, the sound of secret compartments within.

At the same time, Evie was readying herself for battle, sizing up her enemy. In the chapel were four opponents, but Lucy Thorne had already fought Evie once and lost. She was depending on the Yeoman Warders who for their part were off guard. They thought that having delivered Evie into the custody of Lucy Thorne their job was done.

Evie allowed her arm to drop a fraction, removing it from the immediate threat of the Wilkinson Sword, and then, all at once, dropped to one knee, engaged her own blade and buried it into the groin of the man standing nearest to her.

It was ugly but it produced a lot of noise and blood and, as she had often been taught, a lot of noise and blood is as helpful as surprise when it comes to a successful attack.

The guard fell screaming and his comrades shouted. But the pike had already been removed from her neck and with one gloved hand on the stone floor she was pivoting in order to face the second man. It was as though she punched him in the stomach, only with blade and gauntlet, and the blow drove him across the room, clutching at a stomach wound that would bleed out in a matter of seconds.

When it came to the third man, she wasn't so lucky. He had not been able to bring his pike to bear but instead used the pikestaff, swinging it around to clobber her on the side of the head. She staggered, knowing the lack of pain for what it was—a delayed agony—and slicing wildly with the blade.

She caught his clothes, opened a gash, but it wasn't nearly enough to finish him off. He darted to one side, more agile than he looked, and tried to hit her again with the pikestaff, aiming once more for the side of her head.

This time, however, he missed but she didn't. Her

strike was true, and she rammed it into his heart so that he fell, dead almost before he hit the floor. The other two men writhed and screamed, their final death throes noisy, but Evie was launching herself at Lucy Thorne, blade out, knocking aside the boot knife that had appeared, relishing the surprise and fear in her opponent's eyes, knowing the battle was won and allowing herself the grim satisfaction of feeling her blade strike home.

And now, at last, Lucy Thorne lay dying. Evie regarded her, almost surprised at her own lack of pity. "You sought a tool of healing in order to extend your own power," she said simply.

"Not mine, ours. You are so shortsighted. You'd hoard power and never use it, when we would better the condition of humanity. I hope you never find the Shroud. You have no idea what it truly can do."

Curious, Evie bent to her. "Tell me, then."

It was as if, in the last moment, Lucy Thorne decided against it. "No." She smiled and died.

Evie reached into her jacket for her handkerchief, which she carefully spotted with Lucy Thorne's blood, folding it and replacing it. Next she retrieved the key then stared dispassionately around St. John's Chapel. The Warders were dead in pools of their own blood; Lucy Thorne lay looking almost serene. Evie paid them a silent compliment then left and made her way back along the flickering passages of the keep until she reached the entrance. There she stood at the top of the steps and looked out over the courtyard, where the constable and Henry Green's Yeoman ally were rallying their men now that the battle was won.

The Shroud was not here, she thought. But the Tower

of London had been returned to the Crown, and that at least meant a job well done for Evie Frye.

During her journey back to base her thoughts went to Lucy's last words. It was true, Evie had thought of it as an instrument of healing. Naively, perhaps, given the Templars' interest. But then she had learned it gave eternal life—and now this. Was it possible that Lucy Thorne had known something about it that Evie didn't? Mulling it over, she remembered something she had read once, a long time ago. Later, as soon as she was able, Evie put pen to paper and wrote to George Westhouse.

SEVENTY-SIX

Crawford Starrick couldn't remember when he had last partaken of his beloved tea. His usually ordered life had taken on a distinctly chaotic tinge. The stress was beginning to show.

Not only had Lucy Thorne been stymied in her efforts to find the Shroud, largely because of the interruptions of Evie Frye, but the other Frye twin—it hurt Starrick to even think his name—*Jacob* had also been causing trouble. Templar agents were falling beneath his blade; plans the Order had spent years laying in place were being undone. Starrick had come to dread the knock on his office door, for every time one of his men arrived it was with more bad news. Another member of the Order dead. Another scheme confounded.

Now he raised his head from his hands and regarded the nervous scrivener who sat on the other side of his untidy desk, patiently awaiting his dictation. Starrick took a deep breath that was indistinguishable from a sigh, and said, "Take this down, then I want it sealed until you receive further orders."

He closed his eyes, composing himself, and began his dictation: "Miss Thorne. You supplied me with the means to secure London's future. The city thanks you. The Order thanks you. I thank you. But the Shroud can be worn by only one. Therefore, I hereby dissolve this partnership. I promise to endow you with an income into your old age, but that is the most I can do. May the Father of Understanding guide you."

There. It was done. Starrick sat listening to the scratch of the secretary's pen as his words were duly transcribed. Yes, he thought, the Shroud can be worn by only one, and he found himself relaxing almost sleepily into the knowledge that it was his destiny to be *the one*.

A knock at the door startled him from his absorption and straightaway he felt his jaw clench, reality intruding with the promise of more bad news, further havoc wreaked by the junior Frye club.

In that regard at least he was not disappointed. "What is it?" he snapped.

Entering, an assistant looked nervous. One hand fiddled at his collar, loosening it. "Miss Thorne, sir . . ." he said in a faltering voice.

"What of her?"

"I'm sorry, sir. She's dead."

One thing his associates had learned—or been forced to learn—was that you never knew with Starrick what he was going to do next. The two attendants held their breath as his shoulders rose and fell heavily and his hands went to his face as he absorbed the news.

All of a sudden he peeked through his fingers. "Where is the key?" he said.

The assistant cleared his throat. "There was no key found on her body, sir."

Starrick's fingers closed as he contemplated this new and even more unwelcome development. Next his attention went to a bowl on his desk that he began to turn over in his hands. His face was reddening. His men knew what was to come. One of his outbursts. And sure enough, the room was filled with his frustrated shriek, his hair, usually so neat with pomade, in disarray as the bowl was lifted high, about to be dashed to the tabletop, until . . .

The shriek died down. With exaggerated care, Starrick placed the bowl on the table. "The Shroud will be mine," he said, to himself more than his men. "Even if I have to raise hellfire to do it."

SEVENTY-SEVEN

"Please tell me again where we're going?" asked Evie, as she and Henry passed through iron gates and toward a set of benches at the opposite end of a leafy square.

In truth, she had been enjoying the walk. Time spent with Henry was a blissful antidote to the killing that had become so routine in her life. Her father had always warned her against becoming inured to it. "A killing machine is a machine, and we Assassins are not machines," he said, making her promise never to lose her empathy. Never to forget her humanity.

At the time she had wondered how that could ever happen. After all, she had been brought up to respect life. How on earth could she fail to be moved by the taking of it? But of course the inevitable had happened, and she had discovered that one way to cope with slaughter was to shut herself off from it, disallowing access to those parts of her brain that wanted to reflect upon it. More and more she found it a simple process to do that, so that sometimes she worried she'd lose all sense of her true self in her own survival mechanism.

Henry was a means of pulling back from all that. Her feelings for him helped Evie to center herself, and his reticence to take up arms served to remind her that there could be another way. He had told her about his life before he met her. She knew that he had once been where she was now and had returned from it. His was a tattered soul but nevertheless intact. He was an example of how it could be done.

Still, now came the next phase of their mission to retake London, and whatever her feelings for Henry, they would have to wait. Restoring the Brotherhood was her main priority.

They were close now. So close. Since events at the Tower the twins had struck again and again at the heart of the Templar organization. They had hit them where it hurt most. In the wallet. After neutralizing Twopenny, Jacob had closed down a counterfeit ring, helping to restore order to the city. Jacob had also put an end to the activities of Brudenell, who was working for the Order, trying to prevent the passage of legislation harmful to them.

Each successful operation had seen the Assassins' stature grow in the eyes of those in the East End and even beyond; Henry's gang grew exponentially. The Templars might have taken London by worming their way into its middle echelons but the Assassins were reclaiming it by working their way up from the bottom. The urchins who streamed through the streets saw the Assassins as champions and were eager to help in any way; their elders were more cautious and more frightened but offered their tacit approval. Henry would return to his shop and discover goodwill gifts left on the doorstep.

All of this was a benefit, of course. But in Evie's mind

(though not in Jacob's) it took second place to issues of
the Shroud. Now that they had recovered the key, they
still faced the problem of not knowing where the Shroud
was kept. They knew where it wasn't—it wasn't in the
Tower of London. But where could it be?

So she asked Henry again, "Where are we going?"

"I found a letter from the Prince Consort among Lucy
Thorne's research," he told her. "Dated 1847."

The Prince Consort. Prince Albert, for whom Queen
Victoria mourned still.

"From 1847?" she said.

"The year the Prince began renovations to Buckingham Palace," he explained.

"You think he added a vault for the Shroud?" said Evie
excitedly.

Henry nodded, smiling at the same time, pleased to
bask in Evie's approval. "And since no map of the Palace
has a room marked 'secret vault' . . ."

By now they were near the benches and there sat a very
singular-looking man. An Indian gentleman, he had a
rounded, well-fed face that made him look boyish. Nevertheless there was a handsomeness about him. A bearing.
He wore silks. Expensive silks.

He folded his paper, placed it down and rose to meet
them as they approached. "Your Highness," said Henry
with a short bow. A somewhat begrudging short bow, if
Evie wasn't very much mistaken. "May I present Miss Evie
Frye. Miss Frye, Maharajah Duleep Singh."

Evie and Mr. Singh greeted one another before Mr.
Singh's face became grave and he turned to Henry. "My
friend, the plans you asked for have been removed."

"Removed?" Henry's face clouded. "By whom?"

"Crawford Starrick's forces. Or someone employed by him."

Mr. Singh saw Evie's and Henry's faces fall. "Yes, I thought you might recognize that name. I know where they are, but it is heavily guarded."

Evie threw her shoulders back. "That part will not be a problem."

Mr. Singh looked her up and down. "I thought not."

It was a short while later that Evie and Henry were crouched on a rooftop, having raced each other to the top (winner: Evie) where they overlooked a fortress building they knew to be a Templar stronghold.

In there were the documents they sought, taken by Crawford Starrick, who had clearly reached the same conclusion they had.

However, *he* didn't have the key. They did. And now they wanted the documents.

Problem one was the guards, though Evie didn't think them too many. Henry counted guards at the windows of what might have been a small fortress but was well guarded. He saw men in the window, at the gate, guarding the grounds that surrounded it.

"We're going to need a plan," said Evie simply.

"I can provide a distraction for the guards while you discover a way inside," Henry told her, and she looked at him.

"Really?" she said with a mix of concern and surprise,

not sure if he was ready, and then—did she imagine it? Or did he blush?

"For you, Evie," he said, "certainly."

"Well," she said, "once I'm inside, I shall find someone who knows where the papers are stored."

"And we will meet later," he told her, and turned to leave.

"Be careful," she told his retreating back softly.

He provided just the distraction she needed. The guards on the near side began to disperse at the noise and she used the opportunity to scale the wall and let herself into a first-floor window. This was the administrative center where, if she wasn't very much mistaken, the plans would have been stored.

She was either very much mistaken or the plans were elsewhere. She had a brief look around the office into which she had climbed but there was nothing there. Right, she thought, now for Plan B. Find somebody and interrogate him.

She went to the office door and listened carefully for sounds from the passageway. Satisfied, she waited and then, as a lone guard made his way past, yanked open the door, punched him in the throat, crooked her right arm around his neck and dragged him into the office. Closed the door.

He sprawled to the floor gagging with the pain of the punch and scarcely able to believe the sight of his assailant. In a second, Evie was standing astride him and he stared up at her with terrified eyes, babbling, "I swear, miss, I do not know where they've taken him."

Her one hand held his collar, gauntlet fist drawn back, ready to threaten him with another, even more painful blow, but checked herself. *Taken him?*

"Taken who?" she snapped.

"The man dressed like you. The guards dragged him off . . ." the guard said.

Damn. "Henry." She gathered herself. "The plans you stole. Where are they?

He shook his head furiously. "I don't know anything about that."

She believed him, and with a quick jab of the gauntlet left him unconscious. Now she had a decision to make. Continue her search for the plans? Or rescue Henry?

Except, there really was no decision.

SEVENTY-EIGHT

Outside in the street, Evie got her first break when she ran into one of Henry's urchin informants.

"They've got him, miss," she was told. "They took Mr. Henry. We couldn't stop them. They dragged him off in a red carriage. They won't get far, though. One wheel looks like it was about ready to fall off. You can see the cart tracks. It looks all wobbly-like."

She thanked them and thanked her lucky stars that the Assassins could count on the support of the people. Let the Templars try to track a carriage through the streets of London without the eyes and ears of the populace to aid them. Just let them try.

She followed the tracks made by the carriage, weaving her way through the crowded streets, just a fast-moving face in the crowd until she came close to Covent Garden, where she found the carriage, abandoned.

She dashed onto the piazza, hoping to catch sight of Henry and his captors, but there was no sign of them. A trader nearby was looking her way with an admiring glance, so she hurried over—time to use her feminine wiles. "Did you see some men get out of that carriage?" she asked him, with the sweetest smile she could manage.

He simpered. "Yes, they pulled someone out of that carriage. Dead drunk, he was. They carried him into the churchyard. Maybe he wanted a quiet place to sleep it off?"

Next to him was a stall selling oils. "Yeah," called the trader, doffing his cap at Evie, "I saw them dragging someone out of the carriage after the wheel fell off. They said he'd hit his head. Not sure why they needed to take him into the church, but that's where they went."

Both were directing her attention across the piazza and to the familiar portico piers and columns of St. Paul's Lutheran Church at the west end. Despite the tall buildings on every other side, it still loomed over what was London's oldest square. On any other day, it would have been impressive, a sight to behold. Now, however, Evie looked at it and saw a mausoleum. She saw dread.

She thanked her two admirers, crossed the square and went to the churchyard at the back, glancing at the equally impressive portico at the church's rear as she threaded her way through the darkened churchyard, quickly at first, then with more caution when she heard voices in the near distance.

She was at the back of the churchyard now, where the undergrowth was thick and untended, when she came across what she could only describe as a Templar encampment. In the middle of it was Henry, trussed to a chair, guards standing over him. With a jolt of shock she thought they might have killed him. His head lolled on his chest. On second thought there was nothing about the way they were talking that suggested he might be dead.

"Why did you bring him here?" one of the men was saying.

"The man is an Assassin," replied his colleague. "We didn't want him getting away before you had a chance to question him, now, did we?"

The first guard was anxious and jumpy about something. "He was more secure where he was before. I told you not to come here."

"It can't be helped. Now, wake him up."

It was while the second guard was trying to shake Henry awake that Evie made her move, dashing out of the shadows with her blade drawn. She made short work of her opponents. She had no desire to prolong the fight even for the sake of her enemy's dignity or her own pride. She merely finished it, quickly and ruthlessly.

How different she was from the callow Assassin who had first embarked on this mission.

Only when they lay at her feet did she go to Henry, rushing to untie him.

"Did they hurt you?" she asked him.

He shook his head. "I'm fine. Listen, they sent someone back to move the architectural plans. Do you have them?"

Now it was her turn to shake her head.

"My capture has undone your plans," he said, as they made their escape. "I'm sorry."

Disconsolate, they made their way back to base.

SEVENTY-NINE

Crawford Starrick was preparing for a party. A very important party, one for which he had great plans.

A servant bustled and fussed around him, fixing his dinner jacket and waistcoat, flicking dust from the shoulders, adjusting his tie.

Starrick, meanwhile, admired himself in the mirror, listening to the sound of his own voice as he opined. "Order has bred disorder. The sea rises to flood the pubs and extinguish the streetlamps. Our city will die. Twopenny has failed, Lucy has failed, Brudenell, Elliotson, Pearl. All have gone into the night. It is up to me now. The Assassins have brought nature's fury into our homes. Men have become monsters, barreling toward us, teeth out. Our civilization must survive this onslaught."

His servant had finished his work. Crawford Starrick turned to go. "To prevent the return of the dark ages," he said, "I will start anew. London must be reborn."

EIGHTY

They were arguing again: Jacob and Evie. Watching them, Henry found his feelings conflicted. On the one hand, he hated to see the twins at each other's throats, and yet on the other, he could feel himself falling in love with Evie Frye and wanted her all to himself. Selfish, yes. But there it was. Hardly worth denying. He wanted Evie Frye to himself and if she was at loggerheads with her brother, well, then that day would arrive even more quickly.

Meanwhile the argument raged on.

"Starrick is making his move," Evie was saying. "The Piece of Eden is somewhere inside Buckingham Palace."

"Let him have it," Jacob retorted. He was still full of arrogance, noted Henry. In many ways, he had every right to be; so much of what he'd done had been so very successful. His latest triumph involved the assassination of Maxwell Roth. Henry could remember a time when he had leafed through documents full of Templar names given to him by Ethan. Thanks to Jacob, most if not all were out of action or incapacitated. Quite some feat.

And yet Evie, who was so fixated on finding the Shroud, couldn't see past the devastation he had caused.

"I have seen your handiwork across the city," she was telling her brother now. "'You suffer the penalty of too much haste, which is too little speed.'"

He rounded on her. "Don't you quote Father at me."

"That's Plato," she corrected him witheringly. "I am dreadfully sorry this doesn't involve anything you can destroy. Father was right. He never approved of your methods."

"Evie, Father is dead . . ."

Now it was time for Henry to step in. "Enough! I have just received word from my spies. At the Palace ball tonight, Starrick plans to steal the Piece of Eden, then eliminate the heads of church and state."

Which changed things.

Jacob and Evie looked at one another and knew that thanks to what was Starrick's last throw of the dice, a final, desperate attempt to win back what the twins had so far cost him, he had unwittingly synchronized her obsession with the Shroud and Jacob's need to wrest control via more traditional means.

What passed between them was that knowledge. A begrudging knowledge. But a knowledge all the same.

"Once more, for old times' sake?" he said with one raised eyebrow, and for a moment she remembered what it was they had between them and she mourned its passing. Who could ever have known that carrying out their father's wishes would end up tearing them apart?

"And then we're finished," she told him with a hard heart.

"Agreed with pleasure," he said, and added, "So what's the plan?"

The plan involved utilizing a relationship formed with Benjamin and Mary Anne Disraeli in order to steal invitations to the party—from none other than the Gladstones.

Evie set about arranging another meeting with Singh while Jacob was tasked with stealing the invitations—a job for which he was ideally suited. Being able to lift the invitation from a besotted Catherine Gladstone, Jacob also set about stealing the Gladstones' carriage. The fact that the invitation stated that "swords must be left at the door" was, they decided, a matter best left to Frederick Abberline, who promised to smuggle the weapons they needed inside the Palace grounds. It involved Jacob's having to steal a uniform. Meanwhile, Evie met with Duleep Singh, who told her the plans had been removed to the Queen's personal papers in the White Drawing Room.

Now she knew where the documents were kept. Now, thanks to Jacob, they had a carriage. They had the means of smuggling weapons into the Palace. They had invitations.

The game was afoot.

EIGHTY-ONE

Prior to setting out, Evie studied the available plans of the Palace: the eastern frontage where they would enter, the West Wing, where the terrace for the ball would soon host dancing, and inside, the five floors and over seven hundred rooms.

There was only one she was interested in, though. The White Drawing Room, and it was to there that she would go as soon as she was able. Go to the White Drawing Room, steal the blueprints, locate the vault, find the Shroud.

She and Jacob sat in the Gladstones' carriage, with the couple's invitations clutched tight as they joined a procession of carriages making their way toward the Palace at the western end of the Mall. Did Evie imagine it, or was there a certain excitement in the air? After all, the Queen had mostly shunned public appearances since the death of the Prince Consort, Albert. She had been the subject of some lampoonery as a result. However, it was reputed that she was to be making an appearance at her own ball tonight.

As they reached the main entrance, Evie saw immediately that the Queen's appearance was unlikely to be the night's only talking point. Their coach passed Mr. and Mrs. Gladstone arguing with Palace guards who wore bearskin hats and carried rifles with bayonets attached. Mr. and Mrs. Gladstone in full flight were not to be trifled with, but then again, neither were the Queen's guards, and the two parties seemed to have reached an impasse. Evie slipped down a little in her carriage seat as they passed, thankfully unnoticed by the Gladstones, still occupied in alternately threatening and pleading with the Queen's guards.

Out of sight now, their carriage clattered on cobbles through the columns of the entranceway and into the front courtyard of the Palace. At the top of the queue, immaculately attired footmen were either shouting angry orders at coach drivers, or opening carriage doors so that the distinguished personages within might step out and make their way into the main reception hall. In there, they would ascend the grand staircase and from there make their way either to the ballroom or the terrace. The party was already in full swing.

Meanwhile, as they sat in their carriage and awaited their turn to be decanted into high society, Jacob and Evie exchanged glances. An admission of nerves. Good luck. Take care. It was all in the look they shared.

"I shall go to find the Piece of Eden," she told him.

He pursed his lips. "As you wish. I am off to meet Freddie."

The door to their carriage was opened and they looked out upon a bowing, blank-faced footman then to the steps that led to the open doors of the Palace, again flanked by footmen, and a steady stream of immaculate guests making their way inside.

Well, at least they looked the part. Jacob in a formal suit for the occasion, Evie in satin trimmed with lace, a bodice, satin slippers, skirts and wire ruches. She felt trussed-up. A turkey ready for Christmas dinner. Still, she blended in, that was for certain, except for where most of the female guests wore diamond-encrusted necklaces, Evie had the vault key hanging on a chain at her throat. She had been through an awful lot to secure that key. She wasn't about to let it out of her sight.

Just as they stepped down from the carriage they heard a cry from some distance away. "That's my carriage!" The plaintive, indignant shout of Prime-minister-to-be Gladstone, a shout that thankfully went unacknowledged.

Now they split up. Jacob slipped off to meet Abberline, secure weapons then somehow prevent Starrick's plot to slaughter high society, while Evie had a White Drawing Room to find. Like other guests, she made her way to the Grand Staircase, deliberately joining crowds and keeping a low profile as she was carried along in a tide of silks and suits and polite conversation and hushed gossip. She smiled and nodded if spoken to, playing the part of a young debutante to perfection.

Leaving the stream of guests for a corridor to her left, she heard a well-meaning voice from behind her say, "My dear, the ballroom is this way," but pretended not to hear, slipping away, silently treading the luxurious Axminster in her satin slippers as she made her way deeper into the Palace.

She moved silently, like a wraith, every sense alert for

guards so she would hear them before they saw her. Sure enough, she picked up the sound of approaching footsteps and a murmur of voices, so let herself into an office. It was sparsely furnished, closed shutters letting in the only light, and she stayed by the door, open a crack in order to let the guards pass.

As they did she peeped through the crack and got a good look at them. They wore the uniform of the Queen's Guard but there was something about them. Something less ordered, less smart.

Imposters.

Of course. Starrick had infiltrated the Queen's Guard, posting his own men inside and outside the Palace. How else could they hope to pull off what was basically to be a massacre? She swallowed, hoping that at this very moment, Jacob would be learning the same from Mr. Abberline.

She let herself out of the office and back onto the Axminster carpet, hurrying along the corridor. She found her way to the White Drawing Room and let herself in. There she hunted for the plans she needed, keeping one ear on anything happening outside.

She found them. Spread them out on a desk and bit her lip with the excitement of her find. Unlike the plans of the Palace she had already studied, these included *everything*. Every room was accounted for, every corridor and passageway marked. These were the Prince Consort's personal plans.

And . . .

She caught her breath.

There was the vault.

She wished Henry were here to see this. She savored the thought of his reaction. In fact, she thought, she savored the thought of spending a lot more time with Henry Green when this was all over.

But that was for later. Right now she could only hope Jacob was neutralizing the threat from Starrick's men so she could concentrate on making her way down to the vault. She went to go, then caught sight of herself in a long mirror at one end of the drawing room, adjusted herself, smoothed her dress, then, with the blueprints hidden in her cleavage, let herself out of the drawing room and into the corridor beyond. She made one more stop to avoid sentries along the way and was quickly back into the throng of guests, anonymous and invisible once again. Now for the vault . . .

Just then came a voice that stopped her in her tracks. "There you are."

Damn. It was Mary Anne Disraeli, a friend and ally, and not someone to be easily palmed off.

"I have someone I am simply *dying* for you to meet," exclaimed Mrs. Disraeli, and brooking no argument, took Evie by the upper arm, leading her through the guests, skirting the ballroom and to the terrace outside. There stood a woman whom Evie Frye recognized. Such a recognizable woman, in fact, that the young Assassin had a moment of simply being unable to believe her own eyes.

"Your Majesty," said Mary Anne Disraeli, giving Evie a surreptitious squeeze to remind her to curtsy, "may I present Miss Evie Frye."

Her Royal Highness, wearing the dark garb that was now her custom and an expression to match, looked upon

Evie with a mixture of disinterest and distaste, then quite unexpectedly, said, "You are the one responsible for Mr. Gladstone's mishap?"

Evie blanched. The game was up. They had been discovered. "Your Majesty, I apologize—" she stammered.

And yet . . . the Queen was smiling. Apparently Gladstone's "mishap" had left her most amused. "The cake is particularly good," she told Evie. "Enjoy the ball."

With that she turned and left, a footman scurrying to her side. Dazed, Evie simply stood and gawped, too late realizing that she was all of a sudden the center of attention. She was in plain sight, and not hiding.

She moved to quickly go, but the damage was done and a hand grasped her upper arm, and not the friendly, assuring grip of Mary Anne Disraeli, who had drifted off in search of more socializing to do. No, this was the firm custodial grasp of Crawford Starrick.

"May I have this dance . . . Miss Frye?" he said.

It was a breach in protocol that drew gasps from those around them, but Crawford Starrick didn't seem to care about that as he led Evie to the middle of the terrace—just as the orchestra began to play a mazurka.

"Mr. Starrick," said Evie, joining him in the dance, hoping she sounded more in command of the situation than she felt, "you've had your fun, but the game is over."

But Starrick wasn't listening. Eyes half-closed, he seemed transported by the music. Evie took the opportunity to study his face. With satisfaction she noted the tiredness and anxiety written into the dark rings and wrinkles around his eyes. The Assassins' activities had truly taken their toll on the Templar Grand Master. Any other leader might have considered capitulation, but not Crawford Starrick.

She wondered about his state of mind. She wondered about a man so consumed with victory he wasn't able to admit defeat.

"One, two, three," he was saying, and she realized that he was gesturing around them at the rooftops overlooking the crowded terraces. Her eyes went to where he was looking. Yes. There they were. Men in the uniform of the Queen's Guard but evidently Templar marksmen, half a dozen or so. As she watched, they leveled their rifles, pointing them into the courtyard below, awaiting a signal.

The massacre was ready to begin.

"Time is a wonderful thing, Miss Frye," Starrick was saying. "It heals all wounds. We may make mistakes while dancing, but the mazurka ends and we begin again. The problem is that everyone forgets. They trip on the same mistakes over and over again."

Evie tracked her eyes from the men on the rooftops, expecting the shooting to begin at any second. What was he waiting for?

And then he told her. "This dance is nearly over. Soon the people will forget the generation on this terrace, the ruin you nearly wrought on London. When the music ceases, Miss Frye, your time is up and mine begins once more."

So that was the signal the men were waiting for.

The orchestra played on.

EIGHTY-TWO

When the mazurka ended . . .

Evie's gaze went to the rooftops again and her heart leapt to see the familiar figure of Jacob, now in his Assassin's clothes, hiding and very much in plain sight as he moved in on one of the marksmen and slit his throat.

She knew her brother. She knew that if there was one thing she could depend on him for, it was to get this particular job done.

And he did. By the time the dance was ended, the rooftops were empty and Starrick was suddenly roused from his reverie. Furious then frantic, his eyes went to the rooftops, saw them empty, then found the smiling face of his dance partner as she said, "I have a feeling someone is about to cut in . . ."

He bared his teeth. "Then with regret I will relinquish you."

He was fast. His hand had reached to snatch the key from her neck before she had a chance to stop him. Then he turned and was hurrying away, leaving Evie gasping, with her hand at her throat. Around her came outraged cries. "Did you see that? Did you see what he did?"

She moved quickly away in the wake of Starrick but had lost him in the crowd. Behind her scandal raged but she put her head down and made her way to the edge of the terrace, grateful for the sight of Jacob, who took advantage of the sudden tumult to emerge.

She pulled the papers from her décolletage, thrust them into Jacob's hands. "Here," she said quickly, breathlessly, "the location of the vault. Go."

He looked at the plans. Eyebrows knitted. "Just like that? No plan?"

"No time for plans. I'll catch up as soon as I'm rid of this." She gestured at the hated dress, took her gauntlet from Jacob's outstretched hand and scooped up a satchel containing her Assassin's garb, then made off in search of a suitable spot for her transformation.

Jacob ran. The vault marked on the blueprint was located close to the wine vaults, and presumably had been constructed at the same time before being struck from the plans and disappearing into secrecy. Its door was hidden, ordinarily just another part of the ornate paneling in that section of the Palace. But as Jacob arrived, he saw it ajar, no doubt opened with the key that Crawford Starrick had stolen from Evie.

The party was a long way behind him now. Probably the women were still clutching their pearls after what happened between Starrick and Evie. This part of the Palace was deserted, silent.

Except not that silent. As Jacob made his way along a narrow tunnel toward the vault he heard the dull thump of an explosion from ahead. Starrick had unsealed the vault.

Jacob tensed. He heard his knuckles crack. His blade made less noise as he flexed his forearm to engage it.

Even more cautiously now, he made his way toward the blown-out vault door. Stepping through he found himself in a room with medieval architecture. So, it was older than the wine vaults, which dated back to the building of the Palace in the 1760s. In fact, it looked very much to Jacob as though the Palace had been built on top of the vault.

Despite himself, he suppressed a smile. How Evie would have loved to have made this discovery for herself.

At the center of the vault stood the Templar Grand Master, having opened a box he'd found there. The trunk was a receptacle the like of which Jacob had never seen before. A dark gray, futuristic rectangle inset with strange, angular indentations, inscriptions and carry handles. And for a second all he could do was stare at it, as transfixed as Starrick by it. Just to lay eyes on the crate was enough to convince him that there was something otherworldly and unknowable about it. Perhaps Evie was right to place such store in these artifacts.

Crawford Starrick still wore his suit, but draped over it was a shimmering piece of linen that appeared to exude the same sense of suppressed energy and menace as the box. Even as Jacob watched, patterns seemed to form and disassemble on the golden cloth, and different colors glowed. Inside the box was a series of what looked like decorative baubles, and either they too hummed with power, or were reflecting it from the crate. Still Jacob was hypnotized, falling into deep belief, feeling the call of the artifacts—until, with an effort, he shook his head to free himself of it, stitched the smile back on his face and stepped forward to greet the Grand Master.

"Aren't we a little too old to put faith in magic?" he said.

Starrick looked up at him with a puzzled expression that Evie Fry might have recognized from the dance. Only now he was so transported that it was almost beatific.

"Come now," he said, with a smile, "allow an old man his indulgences."

"I will allow you nothing," said Jacob, bemused, stepping forward.

Starrick took no steps to defend himself, merely smiled indulgently. The smile of the truly wise. "The young think they can make their mark on this world, a world entirely built to exploit them."

Jacob shook his head and drew himself up to gang-leader stature. "I don't think I can make my mark, old man, I know."

Starrick's face hardened. He was back in the here and now, drawing ancient power from his find.

Jacob attacked.

EIGHTY-THREE

Henry had decided. He would leave the life. Leave the Assassins to whom he had become a burden, and leave Evie to whom he was a liability. He had spent his entire life running away from the knowledge that he was an unfit Assassin. Held prisoner on the grounds of St. Paul's Lutheran Church, Covent Garden, Henry understood that it had caught up with him.

Awash with memories, he had closed up shop and extinguished the lights at the front, retiring behind the curtain to his workroom. Clocks ticked and he wondered what Evie was doing now. No doubt she and Jacob were arriving at the Queen's ball. When they returned it would be the end of the line. Either way, win or lose, this battle would have been fought to its conclusion: the Assassins would be once more in the ascendant, with the rule of London by the Templars at an end, or they would be having to retreat, regroup, think again.

And Henry? He sat at the central table, with documents and inscriptions laid out around him, maps and plans over which he and Evie had pored, and put his face in his hands, thinking back to his life as a child and the years he had spent as The Ghost. A lifetime of delusion and shattered dreams and failure.

It felt like a lifetime ago he'd thought of leaving the Brotherhood. *You can't turn your back on a belief,* he'd thought at the time.

Yes, he decided now. Yes you could.

He drew a blank piece of paper toward him, reached for his stylus and inkwell.

"Dear Evie," he wrote.

And then was stopped by a sound from the front of the shop. It came again. Knocking.

Henry stood, reached for his blade and began to strap it on as he moved through the curtain, bare feet noiseless on the floorboards as he traversed the clutter of the shop to the door. He shook his sleeve, obscuring the blade, studied the glass of the door where he could see a figure, an outline he recognized at once.

"Come in," he said, opening the door, throwing glances up and down the busy Whitechapel street outside and stepping back to allow his guest entry.

Over the threshold, stepping from the balmy evening outside into the darkened, oppressive atmosphere of Henry's shop, came George Westhouse. "You're armed," he said, by way of a greeting. Trained eyes.

"We have the Templars cornered," replied Henry, "and you know what a cornered rat does?"

"It attacks shopkeepers?" said George.

Henry tried to force a smile but smiles never came easily to him and sure enough the muscles refused to obey. Instead he closed the bolts, turned and led George through tottering shelves to his workroom. There he brushed aside the letter he had begun and directed George to a chair, previous occupant Evie Frye.

George carried a small leather satchel that he placed on the tabletop as he sat down. "Perhaps you'd like to fill me in on events in the city?" he said.

Henry told how, with the help of his information network, Jacob had organized the gangs in the East End, then successfully carried out a series of operations against the Templars, severely weakening their position; how he and Evie had discovered the likely location of the latest Piece of Eden; how Jacob and Evie were at this very moment at the Queen's ball, Evie seeking the vault where the Shroud was kept . . .

At mention of the artifact, George's eyebrows rose.

Yes, thought Henry, more accursed artifacts. More death in the name of baubles.

"And you've had a willing cohort in the person of Evie Frye, no doubt?"

"We had different reasons for seeking the Piece of Eden," agreed Henry. "She wanted to witness it. She wanted to look upon the powers of the First Civilization. I already had done so. I wanted to make sure that power never fell into the hands of the Templars."

"*Had*, you say . . ."

"I beg your pardon."

"You said you *had* very different reasons for seeking out the Piece of Eden. What makes you think these events belong in the past tense?"

"I have every faith in the twins. Even if Evie should fail to recover the Shroud, then I am confident Jacob will neutralize Crawford Starrick. Either way, the Piece of Eden will be safe for the time being."

"And that's it, is it?" George pointed across the table to where Henry's "Dear Evie" letter lay. "Nothing else?"

Henry looked at him. "No," he said. "Nothing else."

George nodded sagely. "Well, then good. That's very good. Because, you know, as Ethan told you, and as your mother told you, the Assassins need their analytical minds as much as they need their warriors."

Henry avoided George's eye. "A true Assassin would be both."

"No, no." George shook his head. "What you're describing isn't a person, it's an automaton. Our organization—*any* organization—needs a conscience, Henry. It's an important function. We may be slow to recognize it on occasion, but the fact remains, it's a vital function. Whatever you do, I'd like you to remember that."

Henry nodded.

"Right, now that's clear, perhaps I should come to my next order of business . . ."

George opened the satchel, removed a leather-bound book and slid it across the table to Henry. "Evie contacted me about this. A book she dimly remembered seeing in her father's library, that may or may not contain some information about the artifact you seek."

Henry frowned at him and George shrugged. "Yes, all right, I knew about the Shroud. I merely wanted to hear it from the horse's mouth. Well, *another* horse's mouth."

Curious, Henry drew the book toward him, slipped open the cover and straightaway felt a tickle of the old excitement. Contained within was what looked to be a series of testimonies handed down throughout the ages, details of battles fought, assassinations carried out, treasures won and lost, all of it referring back to the very earliest years of the English Brotherhood.

Had Evie come across something about the Shroud, perhaps? Something that made no sense to her at the time but resonated now?

George watched Henry's face with a smile. "It took some finding, I can tell you," he said. "Hopefully it will be of use." He stood to go. "No doubt you will want to read it at once. I shall leave you in peace. You've done well, Henry. Your mother and father will be proud. Ethan would be proud."

When Henry had locked up after George he returned to the book. They knew that the Shroud was reputed to offer eternal life, and from that Evie assumed the artifact had healing abilities.

However, she had since become convinced that it also contained some greater, perhaps darker power. Her curiosity had sparked a memory; the memory had brought her to this book.

Henry leafed through quickly now, anticipating what he might find, until he came to a particular entry, one that told of—yes—a shroud. It was written in the most elliptical terms but nevertheless confirmed that it did indeed confer eternal life upon its wearer.

However, the account mentioned something else besides. A negative to its positive. The drawback—or maybe, for some, the advantage—of wearing the Shroud was that it would draw energy from whomsoever he or she touched.

The report concluded that nothing else was known of the Shroud; that what appeared here might be mere gossip or conjecture. Even so, it was enough for Henry to think of Evie—Evie going to the vault without knowing the Shroud's true power.

EIGHTY-FOUR

At last Evie was back in her usual clothes. She tossed the hated dress to one side, adjusted the clips on her gauntlet and shook her shoulders into her coat at the same time. Once more she caught her own reflection in a window of the small antechamber she had chosen for the quick change but was altogether happier with the results this time.

Forget that imposter's finery. This was her real self. Her father's daughter.

And now to the vault. Like Jacob she left the ongoing uproar of the party behind and rushed in the direction where she knew it to be, and like him she arrived to find the door open, rushing down the slope and into the tunnel, checking herself as she came closer to the open vault door.

From inside came the sounds of a struggle. The unmistakable sound of Jacob in pain, and her blade was already deploying as she rushed toward the portal, crashing through in time to see Starrick, wearing the Shroud and pinning Jacob with one hand.

She stood and gawped for a second. It wasn't possible, a man of Starrick's age and build managing to restrain Jacob. Yet there it was. Sourcing power from the Shroud it was as though Starrick was leeching it from Jacob at the same time. "You do not listen," she caught him saying as her gaze traveled to an ornately decorated chest. Inside were what looked like jewels that had begun to rise as if of their own accord, glowing malevolently in the murky gloom of the vault. Drones, they began to revolve as if setting up a protective perimeter around the Grand Master and his helpless victim.

She was about to find out how powerful they were, for having taken several steps into the vault she whirled at a noise from behind her. A guard had rushed into the vault, already breathlessly trying to address Starrick. "Sir, there's . . ."

But he never finished his words. The sudden movement from the doorway seemed to excite the drones and a bolt shot from one of them, catching the guard in the face and propelling him backward, dead before he hit the floor.

As his singed and blackened face lolled, she realized it was the sudden movement that had set them off. She remained still, one eye on the deadly hovering insects, but also monitoring the center of the room, where Starrick held her brother captive, sucking the life from him.

The situation was desperate now, Jacob holding on but only just.

"London will soon be rid of your chaos," Starrick roared. His eyes were wide and wild and saliva flecked his lips. "This city was a safe harbor. A light for all humanity.

You would rather destroy the fabric of society. What alternatives do you propose? Bedlam?"

Freedom, thought Evie, but stayed silent. Instead she directed her efforts toward her brother, feeling his pain as if it were her own. "Jacob, resist," she called, and heard her own voice crack with helplessness and frustration. Her brother's eyes bulged; the tendons in his neck were pulsing so hard she feared they might actually burst.

"Evie," he managed, "stay back."

"You do not know how to use the artifact," Evie called to Starrick. "The Shroud was never meant for you."

But Starrick wasn't listening. He was applying more pressure to Jacob's neck, the power surging through him as he did so. He snarled as he went to complete the death grip.

At the same time, as though they sensed events drawing to a close, the drones had withdrawn, their pulsing light fading as they receded. Evie took the chance to dash forward with a shout of defiance. Her blade rose and fell but Starrick was enjoying the assistance of the artifacts and seemed to easily dodge the blow. At least she'd done enough to knock him off balance, though, and in the next instant, Jacob was rolling on the stone, gasping and spluttering with his hands at his neck, released at last from the grip of Crawford Starrick.

Suddenly caught by the combined aura of the Shroud, the trunk and drone artifacts, Evie found herself disoriented and in the next moment was taken by Starrick, who held her in the same grip he'd used on Jacob.

"Another Frye to feed on," he shouted triumphantly.

His manic gaze bore into Evie. When they'd danced she wondered about his state of mind. Now she was in no doubt. Whatever was left of Crawford Starrick was in there somewhere but it was buried too deep. He was in some other place. "I admire your pluck," he was saying, showering her with spittle, "but there is little you can accomplish now. Like Jesus himself, I am immortal. Behold the power of the Shroud."

"Jesus wore it better," she managed, but if Starrick heard her, he made no sign, ranting on.

"I will begin again and this new London shall be even more magnificent. First you will fall, then the Queen."

Around her the drones had begun orbiting with greater urgency. It was as if they responded to Starrick's increased emotional intensity. Or perhaps—more likely—they were somehow inextricably linked to the impulses shooting through the Shroud he wore, drawing off his excitement.

Either way, Jacob had pulled himself to his feet but the drones prevented him from coming any closer. Now it was he who urged her to stay strong and resist the darkness of Starrick's death grip. Bolts shot from the drones, keeping him away.

"No amount of planning or might shall beat me," Starrick was raving. "I have history on my side. London deserves a ruler who will remain vigilant, who will prevent the city from devolving into chaos."

"Chaos that you are about to cause," Jacob shouted, and came in close, hoping to dodge the drones and strike at Starrick.

He was too slow. A bolt of energy slammed into him, knocking him into the wall. Starrick capitalized and with an almost unimaginable burst of strength pounced on him, his hand at Jacob's neck.

Now the Templar Grand Master held both Evie and Jacob. The power of the Shroud's energy seemed to flow through the linen, through his arms and to the hands he made his claws, gripping the twins harder, lifting them like trophies. Squeezing. They hung, helpless, shoulders thrown back, chins jutting, jaws working with an agony so intense it refused to allow them even to scream.

Evie felt that the very life force was being drawn from her. Short of breath, her vision clouding, her muscles refusing to respond to any of the weak signals of resistance sent by her brain. Starrick's clawlike hands gripped her throat but it was as if he was driving the point of a pike into her neck.

"Get. Out. Of. My. City," he snarled and these, she realized, would be the last words she ever heard because his grip was increasing, and her consciousness was receding. Thoughts passed through her dying mind. Regrets that she would never have the opportunity to tell Henry how she felt about him. Visit Amritsar with him. How she would never make her peace with Jacob. Tell her brother she loved him. Tell him she was sorry things had turned out this way.

EIGHTY-FIVE

At first she believed she was hallucinating. Surely the figure in the doorway was an image projected to her in death, an out-of-focus product of wishful thinking? She'd take it with her, she decided. Rather than the grinning, sweating insanity of Starrick, it would be this that she carried with her from this world to the next.

It would be Henry.

She saw his hand rise and fall. Light flashing on silver. Something spinning across the vault toward them.

And then from Starrick came a shout of pain, and his hand relaxed enough on her throat for her to see a knife handle protruding from his chest, a flower of blood already spreading across his shirt.

A familiar voice. Henry. He had come. It really was him in the doorway, resplendent in his robes, activating his blade, moving toward where Starrick was trying but now failing to maintain his grip on the twins.

The drones, she thought, but couldn't say. *Henry, beware the drones.*

She saw one of the probes seem to shudder with fury

then shoot a bolt of energy that snagged Henry's shoulder hard enough to knock him off his feet and unconscious to the stone. At the same time both twins pulled themselves free, sprawling to the floor and gasping for air even as they pulled themselves into defensive positions, blades at the ready.

They needn't have worried. Starrick looked beaten. Perhaps the drones were still responding to him but not for much longer.

"You're weakening," shouted Jacob in triumph. He dodged a shot from a drone. "You cannot maintain this."

He was right. Blood was spreading across Starrick's front and the Grand Master was already deathly pale. The probes glowed more faintly, their respective flight paths less certain.

"The Shroud will not protect you," called Evie.

Starrick bared bloodstained teeth. "You are wrong," he said. "The people of this city, my people, shall supply its energy." Whatever power the Shroud gave him was fading now.

"This city is bigger than you will ever be," Evie told him.

She and Jacob made to attack, and when Starrick pulled away, the Shroud fluttered off him and to the floor of the vault, releasing its host.

Simultaneously, the drones seemed to lose their energy, as though they, too, knew the battle was done, and they returned to the ornate First Civilization crate, theatergoers settling down to enjoy the show from the comfort of their box.

Starrick sank to his knees. His shoulders slumped, his head hung, regarding his scarlet shirt.

With Jacob covering Starrick, Evie ran to Henry, drop-ping to her knees and skidding across the stone toward him. She took his head in her lap and felt for a pulse. It was strong. He was alive; his eyelids were already begin-ning to flutter.

"Henry," she said, to let him know she was near. She cradled his head for a precious moment, allowing herself a kiss. There would be plenty more of those, she promised herself. A trip home for him, too—Amritsar.

But first . . .

Evie straightened, turned and crossed to where Jacob stood over Starrick, the Templar Grand Master, slowly bleeding to death before them.

The twins looked gravely at one another. There was no honor to be had in slaying a mortally wounded man. But there was even less in letting him bleed slowly to death on the stone.

To finish him quickly and humanely was the right way. Their father's way. The Assassin way.

They came forward.

"Together," said Evie to Jacob and they ran him through.

"London will perish without me," gasped Crawford Starrick as he died.

"You flatter yourself," Jacob told him.

"I would have made it into a paradise," said Starrick.

Evie shook her head. "The city belongs to the people. You are but one man."

"I am at the very top of the order," said Starrick with what would be his very last breath.

"The very top should be barricading their doors," stated Jacob. "We are the Assassins."

Yes, thought Evie. She cast her gaze at the carnage in the vault and knew that, for the time being at least, the death was done. Soon, Evie and Jacob would dab their handkerchiefs in Starrick's blood then the twins and Henry would leave this vault and knowing the Shroud's true power, they would leave it behind, to be sealed up and left in the care of the Crown. And tomorrow London would awaken as a city renewed and together the three Assassins would continue to bring it hope. There would be more battles to fight, she knew. But for now . . .

"We are the Assassins."

Epilogue

Henry was trembling a little, he noticed. But that was to be expected. After all, it wasn't every day that . . .

He composed himself and moved into the room where Evie sat studying the bouquet he had sent her, a perplexed look on her face, and he wondered if he were making a huge error of judgment. And if he was, how he would ever recover.

Because there was no doubting his feelings for her, none at all. He had fallen a little in love with her the second he first saw her. Their time together since had seen that feeling intensify into something so strong it almost felt like sweet pain, like a precious burden—the need to see her each day, just to be with her, breathe the same air as her; what interested her he found just as absorbing, what made her laugh tickled him too. Just to share a working day with her brought him more happiness than he could remember since childhood. She wiped his soul clean of his years as The Ghost; she scrubbed the slaughter from him. She made him feel whole and new again. His love for her was something he marveled at, like a rare butterfly find, such was its color and intensity.

And yet, like a butterfly, it could so easily take flight and escape.

Certainly, Henry *thought* she felt the same way about him, but aye, like Hamlet said, there's the rub, he couldn't be absolutely sure. All that time they had spent together researching the artifact had brought them closer, and for him feelings of friendship and attraction had swiftly blossomed into the love he felt now, this glorious renewal. But for her? Almost exactly a month ago she'd rewarded him with a kiss for saving her life. Was he reading too much into what might simply have been a hurried thank-you?

It was not long after those epochal events at the Palace that he had found her in her study one day. She sat with one leg pulled beneath herself, leaning forward, arms on the tabletop, a pose he knew well, and he was sure that she blushed a little at the sight of him as he entered the room.

(But then again. On the other hand. Maybe she didn't.)

He'd placed his still-empty herbarium down on the tabletop before her and watched her eyes go from her own reading to its cover.

"An herbarium?" she said. "Are you collecting flowers for someone?"

"Only myself," he replied. "I'm told it's something of a British pastime. Did you know they all have symbolic meanings?"

"I had heard something of the sort," she said.

"Of course you have. Unfortunately, I've had no time to fill the book."

"I'm sure I can find some samples if you'd accept my help."

"I would appreciate that. Thank you, Miss Frye."

So they had, building up an impressive collection together over the weeks, searching for the meaning of their own relationship just as surely as they deciphered messages in flora.

"Mignonette: your qualities surpass your charms," she said one day, as they pored over the now-bulging herbarium.

"I'm not entirely sure if that's meant as a compliment. Love in a mist, that's a pretty name."

"Alternately called 'Devil in a bush.'"

They looked at each other and laughed.

"Narcissus: self-love," she pointed out. "I should buy a bouquet for Jacob."

"Unkind, Miss Frye." Henry laughed, but he was pleased—pleased the twins were reconciled—and pleased that she was able to see Jacob with a little more perspective.

"Amusing as this all is, I really should get back to work. If you need me . . ."

"I'll send a bouquet," he said.

". . . of irises."

"'A message.' Indeed."

And so he had. He had assembled a delightful nosegay of iris, snowdrop, strawberry flower, and red tulip, each of them well chosen, selected to say something he himself was finding it so hard to express. The man in the mirror scoffed at his indecision and uncertainty. *Of course she feels the same way. She kissed you at the vault.* The man who stood before it couldn't be so sure.

"A message . . ." he watched her say, as her fingertips went to the snowdrop and strawberry, "of hope. Perfection?"

Next she went to the red tulip. She was more perplexed still, unable to decipher the meaning behind this one.

In the doorway, Henry took a deep breath, cleared his throat and said, ". . . a declaration of love."

She turned to see him there and stood from her seat, crossing to where he stood, falling over his words. "I . . . Miss Frye, you must know that I hold you in the highest esteem . . . and regard. And I wonder if you would do me the honor of . . . if you would give me your hand . . . in matrimony."

Evie Frye took Henry's hands, looked up into a face she loved with eyes that were misty with tears.

And, yes, he knew, she felt the same.

LIST OF CHARACTERS

Abberline, Police Constable Frederick: police officer

Ajay: Indian Assassin

Attaway, Pearl: proprietor of Attaway Transport, cousin to Starrick

Boot: lackey

Brewster, Sir David: scientist, linked to the Templars

Brudenell, James Thomas: Templar, Starrick's lieutenant

Brydon, Dr. William: officer

Cavanagh: director of the Metropolitan Railway

Charlie: young street urchin

Dani, Tjinder: Indian Templar

Disraeli, Benjamin: politician

Disraeli, Mary Anne: wife of Benjamin

Elliotson, Dr. John: inventor

Elphinstone, Major-General William, aka Elphy Bey: British officer

Ferris, Rupert: head of Ferris Ironworks, linked to the Templars

Fowler, John: railway engineer

Frye, Cecily: wife of Ethan, mother of Evie and Jacob

Frye, Ethan: Assassin and mentor to Jayadeep Mir, father to Evie and Jacob

Frye, Evie: Assassin and twin to Jacob

Frye, Jacob: Assassin and twin to Evie, head of the Rooks

Gladstone, Catherine: wife to William

Gladstone, Mr. William Ewert: Chancellor of the Exchequer

Hamid: mentor

Hardy: one of Cavanagh's fighters

Hazlewood, Leonard: private detective

Jake: vagrant

Kaur, Pyara: granddaughter to Ranjit Singh, wife to Arbaaz Mir, mother to Jayadeep

Kaylock, Rexford: gang leader

Khan, Akbar: Afghan leader

Kulpreet: Indian Assassin

Lavelle, Colonel Walter: Templar

Maggie: associate of The Ghost

Marchant: site manager at the Metropolitan Railway

Mir, Arbaaz: Indian Assassin, father to Jayadeep

Mir, Jayadeep, aka The Ghost, Bharat Singh and Henry Green: Assassin undercover agent

Other Mr. Hardy: one of Cavanagh's fighters

Pearson, Charles: Solicitor of London

Pearson, Mary: wife to Charles

Roth, Maxwell: Templar

Sale, Lady Florentia: wife to Major General Robert Henry Sale

Sale, Major General Robert Henry: British officer

Shaw, Aubrey: police officer

Singh, Maharajah Duleep: maharajah and Assassin
contact

Smith: one of Cavanagh's fighters

Starrick, Crawford: Templar Grand Master

Thorne, Lucy: Templar, expert in the occult

Twopenny, Philip "Plutus": governor of the Bank of
England, linked to the Templars

Waugh, Mrs.: wife to Robert Waugh

Waugh, Robert: pornographer with links to the Templars

Westhouse, George: Assassin

Acknowledgments

Special thanks to
Yves Guillemot
Aymar Azaizia
Anouk Bachman
Richard Farrese
Andrew Holmes

And also

Alain Corre	Thierry Dansereau
Laurent Detoc	James Nadiger
Geoffroy Sardin	Ceri Young
Xavier Guilbert	Jeffrey Yohalem
Tommy François	Clément Prevosto
Cecile Russeil	Romain Orsat
Joshua Meyer	Sarah Moison
The Ubisoft Legal	Alex Clarke
Department	Hana Osman
Chris Marcus	Viola Hayden
Antoine Ceszynski	Virginie Sergent
Marie Cauchon	Clémence Deleuze

Cover Art:
Hugo Puzzuoli & Grant Hillier

FROM
OLIVER BOWDEN

THE
ASSASSIN'S
C R E E D ®
SERIES

**Original novels based on the
multiplatinum video games from Ubisoft®**

RENAISSANCE
BROTHERHOOD
THE SECRET CRUSADE
REVELATIONS
FORSAKEN
BLACK FLAG
UNITY
UNDERWORLD

penguin.com